A Year
in the
Company of Freaks

Teresa Neumann

A Year
in the
Company of Freaks

All's Well House
Lebanon, Oregon

OTHER BOOKS BY TERESA NEUMANN

Domenico's Table
Bianca's Vineyard

All's Well House
PO Box 2489
Lebanon, Oregon 97355
www.teresaneumann.com

© 2015 by Teresa Neumann
All rights reserved. Published 2016.
Printed in the United States of America

ISBN: 978-0-9831210-4-6
Library of Congress Control Number: 2015958045

Cover Design by Luke and Marika Neumann, Neumann Films
Text Design by Jennifer Omner, ALL Publications

For Dave
my funny, freakishly smart, generous, insanely talented,
mold-breaking Italian-American soul mate
who has always believed in me,
stood by me, and endured my many quirks.
Thank you for loving me through all of them.
Mille baci!

"In the 1970s, the first wave of counter-culture types swarmed to portions of Mendocino, Humboldt, and Trinity counties in Northern California, an area called the Emerald Triangle. They grew their own vegetables—and a little pot."
—Maggie Tarnawa, *Real Change News*

Hippies, Loggers, Legends
and Bones

MY NAME DOESN'T MATTER. I'M JUST A legend. A whispering myth, if you will—one of thousands, maybe millions, roaming the wilds of northern California. Right now, you can find me floating around the crest of a rugged hill overlooking the town of Trinity Springs, in a place called Calvary Cemetery.

A crazy place, this is—Trinity Springs. *Crazy.*

And believe me, I've seen them all.

That's why I've decided to settle here awhile. Hang out with the bones.

You see, people don't realize that before hippies and wine enthusiasts took over this region, there were loggers and gold-diggers and fishermen and dirt farmers—and I'm not talking the marijuana kind. No sir. I'm talking the normal kind. The kind of farms that grow crops you can eat. Sustenance food they call it.

Don't get me wrong. There's a few similarities in the before and after make-up of Trinity County folks. Hucksters and charlatans, liars and thieves, for example. They've always been around—no matter how long the hair. Or short, whichever the case may be. Criminals and idiots are just a plain fact of life whatever generation you belong to.

Being as graveyards are the ultimate equalizer, I fit right in here. See, me and the bones share a lot in common. Because we've lost our flesh, we've had to lay aside our differences which, in turn, frees us up to share our stories without worrying about *them*. You know—the world's critics. The naysayers. The wet blankets. The know-it-alls who love nothing more than to divide and judge and condemn. What do they understand about life after death anyway?

Little do they know the departed don't truck with prophets of doom.

Problem is, folks have to travel a ways to get here in order to hear our stories. Not many do. Probably because this old pioneer cemetery is so remote. Or maybe it just freaks people out that it's haunted by hoot owls and crawling with ant colonies and alligator lizards.

Well, all I can say for those who don't take the time is: how much you miss!

Take a fellow legend of mine, a poet of the Old North—a sybil some say, a prophetess say others. She once wrote in her journal after stumbling across this graveyard on a full-mooned night:

> *Fat bones, lean bones, long bones, short;*
> *Old bones, baby bones, bones of every sort.*
> *Loosened from flesh; marrow-less, white*
> *Broken, brittle, hidden from sight*
> *Buried deep 'neath earth's dark clay*
> *Midst the rumor of a Brand New Day*
> *I hear them cry*
> *"Hope springs eternal.*
> *Here we lie.*
> *Come set us free!"*

So, come find us if you dare, and take the time to listen. Listen hard, 'cause besides everything else you'll hear, there's a story unfolding right now in Trinity Springs that'll make you laugh and cry and scratch your head with wonderment.

With that, let me introduce you to the sheriff and his wife . . .

The Sheriff and His Wife

———————

W E OFTEN SPEAK AS ONE, MY HUSBAND Otis and I. In fact, we've been known to finish each other's sentences. When that happens, people look at us like we're freaks of nature, biological twins instead of husband and wife. I suppose it's a good thing that we're more like-minded than not.

Did I say Otis is the sheriff of Trinity County, California? Has been for nigh on twenty-five years.

Most folks around here know we were both born and raised in the Texas Panhandle. As soon as Otis came back from the war—that's WWII—he got his degree in law enforcement. Right after that, we married and moved out West, trading gritty rural living for small town life. It was hard at first, what with leaving our families behind and us being newlyweds and all, but we made trips back and forth to stay in touch, and after a few years, we ended up feeling like we'd found a little slice of Paradise. Heck, we feel so connected to this place, we even bought the last burial plots available in Calvary Cemetery.

Nothing against Texas, but here in California the weather is as perfect as you can get. We're greeted every morning by rugged mountains and forests instead of flying sagebrush, scrawny mesquites, and heaving oilrigs. Best of all, there aren't any demon tornadoes or mind-rattling Chinook winds to contend with. The social life in Trinity Springs can be as randy and rip-roaring rowdy as Texas at times, granted, but our time-honored American traditions are respected here. Plus, we fit in with all the loggers and outdoorsmen in town—mostly because nobody puts on airs or assumes their way of life is better than another's. Well, until lately, that is. You see, this part of California is changing right before our eyes.

Otis and I aren't too happy about it. At all.

"Otis," I said, several days ago, after reading an article in the *Redding Record Searchlight* about the migration of "Flower Children" flocking north in search of land to build communes on. "I just don't see what those hippies from San Francisco think they're doing moving up this way, trying to change how folks around here have lived all their lives."

"Change happens, Pearlie," he replied. "I guess getting 'back to nature' is the new thing."

"Since when have people wanting to be close to God's green earth become a *new* thing? We've been doing it for years and we never needed to live in any commune to do it."

"Don't ask me what drives kids to do what they do, baby. I'm not a father. It's beyond me."

Otis said this so I would drop the subject. We don't have kids. Couldn't have them. It used to be a sore point for both of us, especially me, though it's gotten less painful as we've gotten older. So I won't go into it any further other than to say that when Otis resorts to using not being a father as an excuse to bow out of a conversation, I know something has him mighty rattled.

"Well, if it was just about getting back to nature, that would be fine," I continued. "But it's all that free love and wild music and drugs those hippies bring with them that bothers me."

"I admit I don't like it either." Otis cradled his jaw with one hand, placed the other at the base of his skull and cracked his neck—another sure sign he was trying to avoid the topic.

Being as I'm stubborn, I couldn't let it drop. "Hippies are bound to cause friction wherever they go. I would think that spells trouble when it comes to law enforcement, wouldn't you?"

Shrugging, he said nothing, so I used my last ploy. "Well, no matter. Being in the mountains this far north, we won't have to deal with them here in Trinity Springs like some other towns along the coast and down closer to Frisco."

"Not yet," he muttered under his breath.

"What do you mean, 'not yet'?"

"I mean, lately we've got our own share of homegrown hippies here. We don't have to wait for them to migrate up from the city."

"Are you talking about Max Quinn?"

"And his sister. And a few of their friends."

"Well," I blustered, "Kate Quinn doesn't live here anymore, and I thought Max was keeping his nose clean after serving that little jail sentence last year for disturbing the peace. Are you saying he and his friends are still smoking pot? That's news to me."

He cracked his neck again.

"Otis Ray Skinner, what are you hiding from me?"

"It's Sid." My husband gummed the name "Sid" as though it would break on his tongue if he wasn't careful.

"Our Sid? Sid Jackson?"

"One and the same."

"Well? Don't keep me in suspense."

"He's back home." Now Otis was twisting his wedding ring around his finger like he was prying a lid off a jar. "Appears he's a hippie now."

Typically, such a bombshell piece of news would have left me speechless. But my gut reaction was relief. I had thought he was going to say Sid was hurt, or in trouble, or in dire need of some kind. "Why is this the first I've heard of it?"

"I didn't find out myself until yesterday. The fact is, Pearlie, he doesn't want to see us just yet." I suppose he's worried I'd be hurt because he rushed to add, "We just need to give him a little more time, that's all."

"More time for what?"

Otis heaved himself out of his La-Z-Boy and steered me toward the couch where he instructed me to sit down next to him. Now I *was* scared.

"Someone told me two days ago," he began, "that they thought they'd seen Max Quinn hitchhiking out on Highway 3 toward Redding with someone that looked like Sid. Said they slowed way down to get a good look, but the car in front of them stopped and picked the hitchhikers up before they were close enough to tell for sure. They said if it was Sid, he's really changed, because he had long hair and a beard and was wearing torn-up jeans and all."

"Why, that's impossible. Sid wouldn't dress like that. He's always been neat as a pin. Besides, he would have let us know if he was coming home."

"We don't know that. After all, we haven't heard from him in nearly two years."

"But Sid would never become a hippie. They're so . . ."

"Hippies are people, Pearlie, not formulas. You can't

assume just because someone has long hair and dresses a certain way it means they're not . . ."

"Normal?"

"Well, I guess that depends on what the definition of 'normal' is these days."

"True enough. What did Max Quinn look like?"

"Same as always, though I've noticed his hair's a bit longer than it used to be. At least he doesn't look like a complete hippie . . . yet."

"I thought it was just a fad with those city kids in Frisco. Never thought it would take hold up here. Especially not with Sid."

My husband eyed me warily, and in that moment, I knew my blind love for Sid had set me up for disappointment.

"The reason I was home late last night," said Otis, "was because I parked near Max's place to see if what I'd heard was true. Sure enough, about ten o'clock, Sid stepped out of the house. In the light of the street lamps, I could tell it was him by his size and the way he walked. You remember how he walks, Pearlie."

You bet I do. Sid is nearly 6'1" and has always walked with purpose. Even when he was little, he marched around like he owned the world.

"Anyway, I pulled up alongside him, rolled down my window, and asked, 'Is that you, Sid?' He looked at me real funny-like and said, 'Yeah, it's me. What do you want, Otis?' I don't recall everything we talked about word-for-word, but the gist of it is that he'd come back to visit Max for a few days."

"Hmm. Maybe he wants to settle down and take over the farm now that he's graduated from college."

"Somehow, I don't think so."

"But he's going to be twenty-four soon and stands to inherit it next year. Why wouldn't he want to start fixing the place up?"

"Who's to say he even wants it? The fact is, Sid's changed."

We sat together on the couch for a long time, Otis probably thinking the same thing I was: recalling our long history with Sid and his folks and wondering how it had all come to this—to Sid returning unannounced to Trinity Springs as a hippie and not even letting us know he was back home.

Suddenly, I was seized with such a strong vision of Sid behind prison bars, I began to shake. "Lord, help us."

Sid

At eleven o'clock a.m. on Tuesday, August 15, 1972, less than two weeks from the day he and Max Quinn had been seen hitchhiking together, Sid Jackson found himself in the Trinity County courthouse in Weaverville, arraigned on charges of possession of, and growing, an illegal substance with the intent to sell.

Sid had told his court-appointed attorney that he'd known planting pot on his parent's unoccupied farm was against the law, but he hadn't planted all that many and, besides, it had just been a one-time deal. At the time, he'd thought it was a perfectly logical way of making enough money to fund a trip to Europe, where he could escape his troubled past and find himself. Now, sitting in a court of law, awaiting sentencing, faced with the real possibility of spending multiple years in prison, panic set in.

How could I have been so naïve? Sid held his breath as his lawyer consulted with the DA and made his way back to the dock.

"We've been working on a plea bargain," said the lawyer, scooting his chair close to Sid. "It's our only hope of keeping you out of prison. If you plead guilty to the charge of possession, but not to intent to sell, you might qualify for a deferral program." Straightening his tie, he added, "All I can say is, you're lucky you don't have a criminal record behind you. Let's just hope the judge approves the deferral recommendation. Now, here's the deal: because Trinity County can't afford a probation officer, everyone in Sheriff Skinner's office takes turns serving as POs when needed. Skinner was just notified that you might be green-lighted for the deferral and has already said he'd take you on."

Sid frowned. "You mean Otis would be my probation officer?"

"Yes, and it's a good thing, too. Judge Cooley trusts Sheriff Skinner and knows he'll be committed to seeing you complete your probation to the letter of the law. Hang in there, okay? I'm doing my best." Grabbing his file, the public defender stood and retraced his steps back across the well to consult again with the DA.

Sid tapped his fingers impatiently on the worn defense table, his mind traveling back in time to three months ago when he had first snuck onto the farm with his friend Max to transplant the marijuana seedlings he'd started in his apartment in Berkeley. *I should have found another place closer to Berkeley to plant the pot. What was I thinking? And I should have never come back up here to prune and water the crop. I could have just let Max do it. Why did I think I could hide out at his house in town and no one would see me?*

The fluorescent light above him flickered. Glancing up at it, he experienced a déjà vu moment. His father had given him a tour of this very courtroom when he was a little boy. The same lights had spluttered off-and-on back then, too. He shook off the memory and reflected on his last two weeks in Trinity Springs. He'd kept a low profile, staying in

Max's house when they weren't at the farm. But still, he'd seen enough on the sly to know that little in his hometown, located less than ten miles from the county seat of Weaverville, had changed since he was a kid.

The burg's premier diner, The Pearl Café, was still run by Pearlie Skinner, the sheriff's wife. Renowned for her cooking, intuition, forthright opinions, and ability to completely disarm her fiercest critics, she was also Sid's godmother. Her café dominated the corner of Fifth and Main, its daily specials still advertised via a duct-taped sandwich board perched on the sidewalk outside its entrance. A block away, Ralston Park yawned just as idly across from City Hall as it had when he was in high school—its neglected flower garden, peeling Victorian gazebo, and unfertilized lawn a sad testament to the town's insignificance. And the same hayseeds peopled the streets and governed the city, though they were noticeably older, grayer, and thicker around the middle than he remembered.

Compared to Berkeley, Trinity Springs might as well be on another planet.

What was the word he'd heard someone once use for hicks? *Chawbacon.* That was it. Sid raised his hand to his throat. This place was full of it. The monotony of his surroundings, the tedium and predictability of small-town life, suddenly had a suffocating effect on him. Granted, spending time in prison was a terrifying thought. But to think that he might have to live for an extended period in a place he no longer identified with on any level, a town sterilized with tradition, was just as inconceivable.

The urgent *thwacking* of Judge Cooley's gavel snapped him back to attention. "The court is re-convened," intoned the bailiff. "Siderno Porter Jackson, please stand and approach the bench."

As he rose to his feet, his knees went weak. What he wouldn't give to be stoned out of his mind right now, anesthetized from his moment of reckoning. But determined not to let his trepidation show, he stepped away from the table and, accompanied by a county deputy, sauntered toward the judge to join his lawyer awaiting his verdict.

With his head tilted down and his eyes fixed on Sid, Judge Cooley announced that the charge of intent to sell an illegal substance had been put on hold. He then explained that a deferral agreement had been reached between the DA and public defender on the lesser charge of possession. The fact that it couldn't be proven that Sid had planted the marijuana —only that he had been seen on the property during the time the crop was discovered—had caused him to dismiss the last charge.

Pounding his gavel again, the judge barked, "Sid Jackson, I hereby defer final sentencing for one year, subject to the terms and conditions of your probation which will be signed by you before your release. If, at the end of said year, which begins September 1 and ends September 1 of next year, you have failed to meet the probationary conditions imposed on you, or if you break any federal, state, county or city laws at any point during your probation, you will be transferred immediately to the Folsom State Correctional Facility where you will serve out an eight-year sentence for possession of an illegal substance. Your counsel will answer any questions you may have."

Thwack! "Next case."

MOMENTS LATER, SID found himself seated next to Otis's desk in the sheriff's cluttered office.

Pulling a pressed handkerchief from his pocket, Otis swiped his forehead. "Thank God, Judge Cooley was willing to accept a plea deal in your case, Sid. I was getting pretty worried there for a while. But now that's over, we can get down to the business of getting your life back together."

"We? My life is my business."

"It was your business up until a few minutes ago when you entered into our deferral program. Like it or not, you're stuck here for a year with me as your probation officer. Better get used to it." Otis stuffed the handkerchief back into his pocket and began rifling through a desk drawer in search of something.

While he waited, Sid swiveled his head around to take in his surroundings. Shoved into a corner of the office was a freestanding coat rack with a palmetto cowboy hat balanced over one of its hooks. Propped against its base was a pair of snakeskin boots. *What a redneck.* No sooner did the thought cross his mind, but he felt a pang of guilt; and yet it was the truth. Old family friend or not, the sheriff represented everything he'd learned to question in Berkeley: authority, tradition, the establishment . . .

A rap on the door signaled the arrival of Otis's secretary. "Here are the release papers," she chirped, holding a pen and clipboard toward Otis. "Sign your name by the X."

"Just a minute." With a grunt, the sheriff pulled a thick file from the drawer and slapped it on his desk before accepting the proffered documents. After reviewing them, he scratched his name on the dotted line and handed the clipboard back to her. "Do you remember Lynn Walker, Sid? I think you two were in the same grade in school."

Sid nodded. "Hey, Lynn."

"The name's Keating now. I married Paul Keating. Remember him? He was a few years ahead of us—in Kate Quinn's class."

"Sorry, I don't."

"If you thought hard enough, I'm sure you'd remember. You've only been gone from Trinity Springs for what—four, almost five, years? All that pot you've been smoking must have destroyed your memory." She shoved the paperwork into Sid's hands and ordered him to sign his name beneath Otis's.

Are you kidding? Four years is a lifetime ago. Sid rolled the pen between his thumb and index finger, as though stalling would give him a choice in the matter. He could feel Lynn staring at him—at his hair, no doubt, hanging over his shoulder in a loose ponytail, as well as his torn jeans, scuffed up sandals, and the oversized polyester suit coat his lawyer had lent him for his court appearance.

Chafing beneath her gaze, he finally scrawled his name on the appropriate line without bothering to read what he was signing. *What difference does it make anyway? I'm damned if I do and damned if I don't.*

"Hmm." Lynn sniffed. "You never dressed like that before you went to Berkeley."

"What's wrong with how I dress?"

"Everything. You used to be every girl's dream back in the day—Trinity Spring's Italian stallion. You'd still be downright handsome if you'd cut your hair, shave off that goatee, and wear something decent."

While Sid bit his lip to refrain from telling Lynn he thought she looked like an outdated throwback to the '50s, she retrieved the documents from him with a flick of her wrist. "You hippies love to set yourself apart from everyone else," she added. "You think you're above the law."

"At least I'm not a narrow-minded hypocrite."

"At least I'm not the one pretending to be someone they're not."

"That's enough, you two," growled Otis. "You can go now, Lynn."

Lynn started for the door, turning at the last minute to get a final word in. "Go ahead and look down on us in Trinity Springs all you want, Sid, but we've known you a lot longer than any of those freaks in Berkeley you hung out with. And speaking of freaks, I have some personal advice for you. You'd better stay away from Max Quinn from now on. If you can do that, maybe this time next year there's a chance you'll be seeing the light again. Besides, everyone knows the only reason you hung out with Max was because of his sister Kate."

"That won't be a problem." Otis coughed into his hand. "Sid isn't allowed to have any contact with Max during his probation anyway."

"What?" Turning back to the sheriff, Sid gasped.

"Guess you didn't read the fine print." Lynn flashed a self-satisfied smile at Sid and sailed out of the office.

"Actually, she's right." Otis poked his thumb at Lynn's disappearing form. "Having no contact with Max Quinn is one of the requirements of your probation. It was right there in the document you signed."

"But . . . why?"

"Because, even though it couldn't be proved that Max helped you plant and cultivate all that marijuana, apparently he was your only contact in Trinity Springs these last two weeks." Otis leaned back in his chair and crossed his hands over his belly. "I wasn't born yesterday. Had there been a jury, or had more time been taken to build the case against you, Max Quinn would surely . . ."

"It's over, Otis. You can forget about Max."

"Well, your relationship with Max *is* over, at least for the next year, so I'm afraid you'll be the one forgetting about him."

Max was the only person in Trinity Springs Sid had kept in touch with after moving to Berkeley. If he couldn't have anything to do with him, he'd basically be friendless for a year. "So it comes down to guilt by association then."

"If you want to call it that." Otis lowered his chin and stared at Sid beneath arched eyebrows. "Not to change the subject, but my deputy informed me that farming doesn't appear to be your forté. All those plants they dug up on the farm were half-dead. It played a major factor in the judge's decision to dismiss the charge of planting an illegal substance. Had they been healthy and anywhere near harvesting, we might not be sitting here discussing your probation. You'd still be in chains, Sid, on your way down to Folsom."

The reminder sent a chill down Sid's spine. "Okay, so I'm a lousy farmer."

"And that's about to change." Otis sat up straight in his chair and opened the file he had retrieved earlier from his desk. "Your parents' last will and testament indicates you'll need to hone your farming skills this next year."

"Why is that? I already know I'll inherit the farm when I turn twenty-five."

"Yes, but it's a bit more complicated than that. Let's see here." Removing the Jacksons' will from the file, Otis held it stiffly before him, mumbling as his eyes followed his index finger scrolling down the document: "*In the event we, Thomas Kingsley Jackson and Sofia Allegra Jackson, both die before our child/children, etc., etc. . . . and if our child/children's maternal grandparents, Agostino and Antonia Gianelli, are still alive and of sound minds, etc., etc. . . . we desire them to raise our child/ children and also appoint them trustees of, etc., etc. . . .*

Ah, here it is! *In the event Agostino and Antonia Gianelli are no longer alive, or found not to be of sound minds at the time of transfer and execution of this Will, we—Thomas Kingsley Jackson and Sofia Allegra Jackson—do appoint Otis Ray Skinner as secondary trustee and executor of our estate . . .*"

"Wait a minute." Sid's hands shot into the air. "My grandparents are both still alive. I don't see where you're going with this."

"Judge Cooley ordered an update of your grandparents' current health status before giving his verdict today. A phone call was made and—"

"You mean, my grandparents know I was busted?"

"Not yet, they don't. You're an adult, so it'll be up to you to tell them what happened. By the way, I sure am sorry about your grandfather, Sid."

"My grandfather's fine."

Otis swatted at his ear as though he hadn't heard correctly. "I'm bringing their health status up," he continued, "because for the next twelve months, you're restricted from leaving my jurisdiction without good cause. Since your grandfather's medical condition prevents him from travelling here, I'll have to see what I can do about arranging an exemption for you to go down to Sonoma in the event he worsens. I'm only warning you so that you're aware of the situation from the get go."

"His condition won't worsen."

"It's . . . cancer, Sid. Untreatable."

"The doctors don't know what they're talking about. My grandfather's a fighter. He'll make it."

"But Antonia. I don't see how—"

"What about her?"

"You really don't know?"

"Know what?"

"Your grandmother's been diagnosed with early stage dementia."

"That's impossible. I saw her not that long ago. She was no different than she's always been."

"And when was it that you last saw her?"

"At my graduation. The first week of June."

"At your grandparents' age, Sid, changes can happen quickly."

"Sorry, Otis, but I can't believe my grandmother told you she has dementia. If it were true, I would be the first to know. Not you."

"She didn't tell me. Judge Cooley had someone check with your grandparents' physician in Sonoma."

The fact was, Sid had yet to come to terms with his parents' deaths over a decade ago, let alone his grandfather's recent diagnosis of terminal cancer. And now, this? "I'll believe my grandmother has dementia when I see it for myself."

Otis set the will down. "Unfortunately, I felt the state of your grandparents' health needed to be addressed, because I wanted you to understand why I might be required to act as the executor of your parents' estate in the event they both pass away before . . . well, it's how your folks set up their wishes. I don't want any misconceptions or hard feelings to come between us if worse comes to worst. Not now. Not when you're at such a big crossroads in your life."

"How could there be any 'misconceptions'? It sounds like my parents thought of everything."

"No need to be sarcastic, Sid. Your pa was mighty far-sighted and generous when he crafted his will. His estate was large enough to pay for your education and keep the farm solvent up until your twenty-fifth birthday. If you choose not to take ownership of the farm within a month of turning twenty-five—that is, roughly a year from this coming Octo-ber—it'll have to be sold."

"How much is it worth?"

"You'd have to talk to a realtor. Why?"

"At this point, I have no interest in keeping the farm."

"But it's part of your heritage. Part of who you are. Not to mention, it's some of the best land this side of Redding. You'd be a fool to sell it."

"I might be a greater fool not to take the money and run." *Anyway, why would I want to live in a house full of memories I'm trying to avoid?*

Sid recalled that when he had first returned to the vacant property in June to plant the marijuana, he'd been completely unprepared for seeing the place again. Sure, he'd continued living on his parents' farm for a few years after the accident. His grandparents had sold their little house in Sonoma and moved up to Trinity Springs so Sid wouldn't have to endure any more adjustments than necessary. From the age of twelve until he graduated from high school, he immersed himself in life away from home. Between school, the library, sports, and friends, he was rarely at the farm. And the little time he did spend on the farm, his grandparents were there to soften his parents' absence.

But that first day back in June—realizing the farmhouse was still full of his parents' furniture, photographs, correspondence, and all the other personal items his grandparents hadn't had the heart to remove—Sid found he couldn't bear to go anywhere near it. It wasn't until the following day, during a break from planting, while Max took a dip in the creek, that he'd dared to venture closer—so close, he was able to peek into the windows on the lower level. In the dense silence of the countryside, with only a thin pane of glass separating him from the images of his past, he broke down and wept.

With the pain of that experience still fresh in his mind, Sid finally replied to Otis's comment about the family value of the farm. "As far as my heritage goes, it died with my parents."

"Now don't say that, son. As long as you're alive, you've got your heritage—and it matters what you do with it. Your parents still live in you. They always will. Why, just looking at you right now, I see your mama's sweet eyes and your pa's—"

"I really doubt my parents would care if I kept the farm or sold it, Otis. They'd want what was best for me, and they'd let me make that choice without trying to influence me one way or another."

"Can I be brutally honest with you?"

"Haven't you been already?"

"Your daddy would roll over in his grave if he could see you here today. And your mama? Let's just say she'd be sorely hurt and leave it at that."

Sid looked away. *Don't you think I already know that? If you had any inkling of how much I'm beating myself up right now over that very thing, you wouldn't have brought it up.* A muscle above his left eyebrow began to spasm uncontrollably.

"The fact is," continued Otis, "the terms of your deferral program are meant to get you back on the road to being a productive, upstanding citizen. I'm committed to seeing that accomplished. So is Pearlie. We owe it to your parents, and so do you. It means, among other things, that you're going to have to work hard and make the most of your current resources. I'm convinced you're going to do your parents proud yet."

"How am I going to make use of a college degree in this Podunk town?"

"Seems to me like you didn't have your degree in mind when you came up here to plant all that marijuana, now did you?" Otis leaned forward, his elbows set squarely on his desk. "It's true there's not much in the way of jobs right now in Trinity Springs—or Weaverville for that matter— which brings us back to farming. Since you have to have a residential address to be on probation, I figured we could kill two birds with one stone by having you move onto the farm where you can live for free while making an income by renting out rooms to boarders."

"What?"

"Boarders." Otis spelled out the word, "B-o-a-r-d-e-r-s. Now in addition, part of your rehabilitation will involve fixing the place up, managing it, and getting the land ready for *lawful* production. You'll also be assigned to community service on a regular basis with our regional Farm Bureau and Co-op. I'm still sorting out the details, but I'm convinced if you give it your best shot, you have it in you to be a decent farmer yet. But it's up to you."

"A farmer," mumbled Sid. "Just what I've always wanted to be."

"What *do* you want to be, if I might ask?"

Sid hedged. "I'm still working on it."

"I see. Well, hopefully, by this time next year, you'll have it figured out. Like I said, you're going to be inheriting some of the best property in the county, though you wouldn't know it by the looks of it now. The barn's in shambles, the fields are all overgrown with weeds, the fences need mending . . ."

A dull ache reawakened in Sid as he thought, *My life's in shambles. I'm broken. I need mending, weeding, pruning.*

"I remember when your pa bought that old place before you were born. He had all sorts of ideas for it. So did your ma, with her dream of having a vineyard of their own. But, what with working so much, your dad just never had time to get done everything he wanted to before the acci—" Otis raised his hands, his outstretched palms fanning the air as though he were swiping the years away. "But, that was then. For now, like I said, you're going to get the old place back in shape. This afternoon, I'm going to have Sally Jane at Lake Head Realty place an ad in the Redding and San Francisco newspapers. Hopefully we'll find enough boarders to be ready to roll by September 1."

Sid shuddered as he envisioned who his roommates might be.

Otis must have noticed Sid's reaction. "What's the matter? I thought setting up a boarding house on the farm was a perfect solution to where you would live and what you would do for income during your probation. Would you rather I place *you* as a boarder with someone I trust, and work for pennies stocking shelves at the Five and Dime—if there were an opening, which there's not?"

Sid understood the implication. "Someone I trust," meant living with some old local couple who needed an extra hand around the house. Maybe Otis was grasping at straws, but put that way, no; he'd much rather live on the farm. "Your idea's okay," he replied. "It's just . . . who's going to want to live way out here in the middle of nowhere?"

"Haven't you heard?" With a chortle, Otis tore through another pile of papers on his desk until he found what he was looking for. Holding up a copy of the *Redding Record Searchlight,* he pointed at the headline: "Hippies Flock North Looking for Nirvana."

"Don't get me wrong," he said. "The last thing folks around here want to see are hippies living out at the farm, but Pearlie brought this to my attention awhile back. I realize we might be forced to take whoever we can get, but I can place a waiver in the rental lease that forbids any drugs on the farm."

Sid shook his head at the paradox. Hippies and drugs went hand-in-hand. "Do you seriously think someone my age would agree to that?"

Otis jabbed his thumb at the newspaper headline again. "Hippies are looking for nirvana, aren't they? In my mind, nirvana means paradise, and Trinity Springs is as close to heaven on earth as anywhere I've ever seen."

"First of all, nirvana *doesn't* mean paradise. It means enlightenment. I can see finding nirvana in Point Reyes, maybe. Or Mendocino. There's already an artists' community established there. But here? No way."

"I beg to differ." Otis stood up and made his way around

the desk toward Sid. "The mayor of Willits told me some hippie communes have been popping up there in the last few months. I hear tell there's one in Rio Dell, too, which is pretty darn close. All that to say, I guarantee, in the end, it'll all come down to money. Give people a good enough deal on housing, and they'll sign the waiver on the lease." Placing his hand on Sid's shoulder, he added, "I think we're done here for now. It's time for lunch. Let's head back to Trinity Springs to the café and I'll buy you a burger. Pearlie's dying to see you. We can talk over the rest of the details there."

Sid rose from his chair. "How is Pearlie?"

"Full of love and feisty as ever." Motioning for Sid to step out into the hallway with him, he locked his office. "Nearly broke her heart when we got the call from your neighbor about what was going on up at the farm. But, I told her getting busted was probably the best thing that could have happened to you."

"Which neighbor called?"

"Never you mind. Making enemies in Trinity Springs is the last thing you need right now. So just leave it be."

Recalling Lynn Walker's greeting earlier, Sid said, "I have a feeling I may already have plenty of enemies here as it is."

"It goes without saying, I'm not one of them, and neither is Pearlie. We just want the best for you, Sid."

Sid lumbered alongside Sheriff Skinner through the corridor, into the foyer, and out onto the sidewalk in front of City Hall. A blast of heat radiating off the sidewalk nearly sucked the air out of him. Wincing in the bright sunlight, he donned a pair of sunglasses before sliding into the sheriff's car.

His earlier relief of having been ordered into a deferral program in lieu of a prison sentence had waned with the awareness that his trials were far from over. One misstep during his probation, and he'd be sharing a cement cell with who knows what kind of criminal, wasting the best years of his life behind bars. He'd reached a crossroads all right: Folsom Prison or Trinity Springs. Those were his choices—his only ones. Either eight years in prison or one year in a house he dreaded living in again, with total strangers hand-selected by Otis to be his roommates. That is, *if* he could make it through the temptations he knew the next year would bring.

If. With a gulp, Sid cast a sidelong glance at Otis, whistling lightheartedly as he maneuvered his squad car onto the highway.

The word "if" held his entire future between its two tiny letters.

The Arrivals

ABOUT EIGHT O'CLOCK A.M. ON FRIDAY, September 1—the day his probation officially began, as well as the day his new roommates were to arrive on the farm—a loud, persistent rapping at the kitchen door woke Sid from a deep sleep.

"Sid, honey! It's Pearlie. Open up!"

Dragging himself out of bed, Sid pulled on his jeans and glanced in the cracked mirror over his nightstand. The anguish he'd experienced the last two weeks while living in the house as he prepared it for the boarders' arrival was still etched on his face. Revisiting the nooks and crannies of his past had proved emotionally exhausting and there was still one room he didn't have the heart to enter: the library, once his favorite spot in the house. Another round of banging propelled him out through the kitchen where he opened the back door wide enough for the ample Mrs. Skinner, balancing three overstuffed grocery bags in her arms, to enter.

"Help me with this stuff," she ordered. Glancing down the hallway, she added, "I see you're sleeping in your folks' old bedroom. That sure does my heart good, Sid, knowing you're close to them that way. Real healing, I would imagine."

Healing? Morbid is more like it. What else am I going to do— let a stranger sleep in their bed? Sid shoved aside some clutter on his parents' old red Formica table to make room for Pearlie's sacks. Opening a cupboard next to the sink, he said, "We can put the groceries up here."

"Lord, have mercy." Pearlie took note of the empty shelves. "What have you been eating these last two weeks?"

"Whatever. I've had plenty."

"Plenty of nothing! No wonder you look like a scarecrow." Pearlie handed Sid a pound of butter from one of the bags and instructed him to put it in the refrigerator. "No food in the house and you with boarders arriving today! Back where Otis and I come from, folks keep their pantries stocked."

"This isn't Texas."

"Well, there's no state line around good common sense, now, is there? Speaking of boarders, it's a miracle you got some so quickly. Did Otis tell you what Sally Jane at Lake Head Realty said?"

Sid shook his head.

"Within three days of posting the ad, she had a dozen calls. A dozen! 'Course, you only have room for four to board here, so she and Otis had to do a little screening. It all happened so fast, but still . . ."

"I can't wait to meet them."

Clearly unfazed by Sid's sarcasm, Pearlie exclaimed, "Oh, I almost forgot!" Picking up her purse, she retrieved a checkbook from it and waved it in front of him. "Otis wanted me to give this to you. He got the first and last months' rent checks from everyone in the mail and deposited them in the bank yesterday. Said you know all about the joint account he opened with you so that he can keep track of your deposits and withdrawals. He assumes you'll be handling the money wisely, of course."

Sid took the checkbook from her. "You know what they say about assuming."

"It's a test, Sid, considering what would happen if you ran off with the rent."

"Nothing would happen if I could make it to Mexico."

"It's not a joke. Besides, you wouldn't do that anyway."

"How do you know I wouldn't?"

"Because I know you, that's why." Her eyes glistening, Pearlie added, "Seeing you in prison would just kill me."

Blindsided by the sight of Pearlie tearing up, Sid said nothing. She was so much like his mother and grandmother— fussing, teasing, touching, hugging, and expecting a hug in return, always speaking bluntly and offering unsolicited advice. He had once mentioned to his mother before she died how similar he thought she and Pearlie were to each other.

"Mama," he had said, "is Mrs. Skinner Italian? She doesn't look like she is, but she acts a lot like you."

His mother had kissed him profusely and laughed. "She's from Texas, *carissimo*. I suppose in many ways, Texans are like Italians. Pearlie is dear to me, so perhaps we rub off on each other. Friends often do, you know."

Pearlie, meanwhile, was still talking about the joint bank account. "Now remember, your boarders are paying room *and* board, so you'll need to use some of that deposit money to buy food for everyone. And don't forget to write a check for every purchase. Otis has to keep track of all your expenditures. These here groceries I brought over today are just something we wanted to do to help you get started." Resetting her purse on the table, she reached into one of the sacks and pulled out a 34-oz. Folgers coffee can. "I made you some of your favorite cookies."

Sid accepted the can from her. Without even opening the lid, he knew it contained at least two-dozen mouthwatering chocolate chip cookies. "Thanks, Pearlie. I . . . appreciate it."

Pearlie leaned close and stroked his unshaven cheek. "It seems like yesterday I was standing on this very spot in your kitchen talking to you and your mama. Was it really twelve years ago? Oh Sid, you were the sweetest boy—so confident and smart. Such attention to detail you had back then! You're going to make this farm sing again. I'm sure of it."

Sid turned and set the cookies on the counter, not wanting to discourage Pearlie or argue with her about her expectations.

"Well, gotta run. Today's going to be a busy one at the café." Pointing to the cupboards, she said, "Make sure you wipe those shelves down with warm soapy water before you go stocking them. I'll swing by later this week to see if you need any help."

"The phone gets hooked up tomorrow. Just call before you come."

Pearlie looked at Sid as though he were crazy. "Call? Family don't need calling for invites. And put some shoes and a shirt on before the boarders get here. You don't want to look like a naked vagabond when they meet you for the first time, do you?"

"Bye, Pearlie." Sid nodded. "And thanks again."

As Mrs. Skinner clomped down the porch steps and shimmied into her bronze Chrysler Imperial, Sid went to work wiping down the shelves and then carefully arranging all the boxes and canned goods on them. When he was finished, he folded the grocery bags into thirds and placed them on top of a stack of old newspapers piled in the laundry room adjacent to the kitchen.

Stepping back into the hallway, Sid caught a reflection of himself in the mirror through the open bathroom door. He recalled Pearlie's description of him as a scarecrow. Flexing his biceps, he thought, *She doesn't know what she's talking about.* As for his appearance? His boarders, whoever they were, would have to accept him for who he was—longhaired, bare-chested, shoeless and all.

And if they didn't like it?

Well, they could shove it. That's what they could do.

AROUND NOON THAT day, the first boarder arrived. He tore into the gravel turnaround on a custom Harley Springer Hardtail Sportster, his Kevlar gloved hands resting atop its towering ape-hangers. Despite the heat, he wore a fringed black leather jacket, chaps, and a pair of beat up Yamaha motocross boots. A sheathed knife hung from his belt. His hair, at least what showed beneath a faded navy bandana, reached nearly to his waist. Tied back at the nape of his neck with a narrow strip of leather, it was so white, Sid couldn't guess the man's age at first.

As the rider killed the engine, Sid held his hand up in greeting. "Hey, man."

"Hey," the man drawled in return. Lowering the kickstand, he eased off his bike. Next, he removed his gloves, shoving them into the already bulging pockets of his jacket. "Sid Jackson?"

"That's me."

"Will Ketchum. Call me Ketch."

"Cool chopper," said Sid, admiring the detail work on the Harley.

"Cool farm." Ketch removed his sunglasses and scanned the farmhouse and surrounding property.

Sid tried not to stare at Ketch's strange eyes—their color a cross between dark pink and lavender, like the deep recesses of a rabbit's ear.

Shifting his army issue canvas backpack to his other shoulder, Ketch asked, "So, where do I hang my stuff?"

"You're a boarder then?"

"Who else would I be? The Roto-Rooter Man?"

"Right," muttered Sid. "Follow me."

The two entered the house, turned right in the foyer, and climbed the stairway to the second floor. At the top of the stairs, Sid turned left and opened the south bedroom door.

Ketch stepped around him, tossed his backpack on the bed, and unzipped his jacket. "I'm wiped, man. Rode from San Francisco to Texas a week ago to get my stuff in order, then rode all night from Vegas to get here today. Think I'll crash."

Sid motioned down the hall. "The bathroom's right there."

"Far out. Later, man."

"Later."

No sooner had Sid gone back downstairs, than he heard another vehicle pull into the driveway. Heading into the kitchen, he looked out the window to see Otis help a blond girl out of his police car and retrieve her luggage from the trunk. Racing to his room, he returned a moment later, frantically buttoning up a wrinkled work shirt.

"Thanks, Sheriff," the new arrival said to Otis as they entered the kitchen. "You've been such a help!" Her smile revealed a wide set of straight teeth, perfectly formed and white as sugar cubes.

"No problem at all, Miss Larson," replied Otis. "Like I said, you just call me or Pearlie anytime you need something. That's what we're here for."

"Mornin', Sid," said Otis, suddenly acknowledging Sid's presence. "This here's Miss Larson, all the way from Iowa. I picked her up at the bus station in Redding this morning."

"Marishka," she corrected him. "I know. It's a weird name." Turning to Sid, she said, "My friends call me Mika. Or Meeks."

"Iowa, huh?"

"Chester, Iowa. It's on the border of Minnesota—not far from Rochester. Actually, most of my aunts and uncles and cousins live in Minnesota."

"Her folks are dairy farmers," grinned Otis. "Imagine that."

While Otis droned on about how Mika's parents were of industrious and prosperous Midwest stock, Sid sized up his new roommate: her bib-overalls, smoky blue eyes, sun-kissed complexion, straight narrow nose, and long hair plaited into two thick braids. She exuded a wholesomeness of spirit at odds with her delicate features, and he was stumped by way she looked straight into his eyes despite not knowing him from Adam because, by the same token, she also appeared incredibly naïve.

He snapped back to attention when he heard Otis say, " . . . and she'll be going to a school down Hayfork way."

Sid thought a moment. "There's no school in Hayfork."

"Is now," replied Otis. "Just started up."

"It's not really a *school* school," explained Mika, addressing both Otis and Sid. "Someday it could be, but right now, it's more of a ministry that prepares people like me for overseas missions."

"Prepare you for *what?*" asked Sid.

"The mission field. You know, where you go to feed and clothe the poor and minister the love of Christ to others."

Sid's mouth fell open. Staring dumbly at Otis, he aimed his thumb at Mika. "She's a Jesus Freak?"

"Now Sid, I'm warning you: there won't be any disrespect shown to Miss Larson. She's no freak. She's a God-fearing woman is what she is."

Mika's eye's widened. "Sheriff, I thought you said . . ."

Otis shushed her. "Now, now, everything will be fine. Don't you worry, Missy." Turning to Sid, he whispered, "Show your boarder to her room so she can unpack and freshen up. Give her the one on the ground floor next to your room. We don't know enough about the other boarders yet to trust where she'll be the safest."

Picking up her suitcases, Sid wordlessly led Mika down the hall. A moment later, he returned to the kitchen to find Otis snooping through some drawers. "Need something?"

"No. Just looking. I'm your probation officer, remember?"

Sid tilted his head toward Mika's bedroom. "Just what are you trying to pull on me?"

"I don't know what you're talking about."

"She's a narc."

"A what?"

"You know what I mean. An informer, a snitch, a spy."

"Doubt that would be legal for me to do, Sid. At least not under the present circumstances." Shaking his head, Otis added, "Mika is who she says she is. If anything, I'd say you're . . . what do you hippies call it? Paranoid?"

"Yeah, well, maybe I have good reason to be. What did you tell her about me, anyway?"

"I told her you're a hard worker and a deep thinker. A good decent boy who did something stupid, got in trouble with the law, and now you're working hard to make things right again."

"Wow. So you lied to her."

"You're not a hard worker or a deep thinker? Could have fooled me."

"You know what I mean."

"I only left out the part about the marijuana. That's not lying."

"Anything else you left out that I should know about?"

Otis shifted his weight to his other foot. "I told her she'd be a perfect fit on the farm because you're open to . . . change." Before Sid could respond, he turned and rushed out the back door.

Sid stepped onto the porch as the sheriff was turning out of the driveway. "Bring another Jesus Freak into my house, Otis," he growled, "and you'll wish you'd never cut a deal with Judge Cooley."

Then, turning to go back to the kitchen, he froze. Less than two feet away stood Mika, a wounded expression on her face. Or was it anger? It was impossible to tell on someone whose lips, even in a passive position, curved elfishly upward. All he knew was that Mika's doleful eyes sparked with disappointment.

She had heard every word he'd said.

BY TEN O'CLOCK that night, the other two boarders had arrived and settled into their respective rooms, all of them too tired to do much but unpack, shower, and go to bed. The occupants of the Jackson Farm now numbered five—three males, including Sid, and two females. Because there had been little, if any, time to learn about the boarders or figure out how to operate a house full of strangers, Sid found himself dreading what the next day might bring. He wandered about the ground floor for a while, listening intently to the nocturnal rumblings of his new roommates.

The sound of rattling pipes indicated someone was still using the shower in the upstairs bathroom. Sid paused briefly by Mika's door as he passed on the way to his bedroom. Her lights were off, but it sounded like she was talking to someone. Shrugging, he entered his room, stripped off his clothes and climbed between the sheets. But through the thin wall that separated their rooms, he continued to hear her monotone voice. Then it dawned on him. She was praying.

No way. He shoved a pillow over his head. Thirty minutes later, his blood pressure spiking, Sid crawled out of bed and put a box fan in his window, turning the setting to high in order to drown out her voice.

The First Day

THE NEXT MORNING, MIKA—CLAD IN A sleeveless t-shirt and bell-bottom jeans— stood at the kitchen sink humming a song to herself as she filled a teakettle with water. The distinct smell of smoke and the sound of boots thumping into the room caused her to glance over her shoulder. Behind her stood a leather-clad stranger with long white hair, a cigarette dangling from his lips.

Eyeing her intently, the man removed the cigarette long enough to let out a whistle. *"Buenos Dias,* baby."

"Good morning to you, too." Mika turned to place the kettle on the stove. "You must be one of the boarders. I need some matches. Wonder where they are . . ."

"Here, let me."

She watched as the boarder stepped next to her, pulled a book of matches from his pocket and lit the burner on the stove. "My name's Mika," she said, "but you can call me Meeks. What's yours?"

"Will Ketchum. But you, pretty lady, can call me Ketch."

"Well, Ketch, mind helping me find some coffee or tea?"

Ketch found a Folgers coffee can on the top shelf of the first cupboard he looked in. Within seconds, he'd opened it and devoured a cookie. "Want one?" he asked.

"No thanks." Mika spied a canister and opened it. It was full of tea bags. "We don't know who the cookies belong to."

"Who cares? We're in a commune, right? Share and share alike."

"This isn't a commune."

Leaning close to Mika, Ketch stuffed another cookie into his mouth. "You say po-*tay*-to, I say po-*tah*-to."

"You have a southern accent."

"You have a weird accent."

"I'm from Iowa."

"Texas—yours truly."

"I guessed as much. And not just by your drawl either."

Ketch replaced the cookie tin on the shelf where he'd found it and grinned. "Me being such a stud is what gave it away, right?"

Holding the kettle of now boiling water toward Ketch, Mika said, "Tea?"

"Texans don't drink tea."

"Of course. What was I thinking?" She handed Ketch an empty cup. "Here then. Make yourself some coffee. There's some instant in that jar there."

Ketch stared at her as she seated herself at the table. "You know, you're the spitting image of a girl I used to date back home."

"Dare I ask if that's good or bad?"

"It's *real* good, darlin'." Ketch, coffee in hand, sat down across from her.

"Sheriff Skinner's from Texas, too," said Mika. "I suppose that's how you found out about this farm."

"Nope. Texas is a mighty big state. I'm from the Hill

Country. Otis is from the Panhandle, up near Amarillo. He moved away from there before I was ever born."

"How do you know that?"

"He told me when I called him about the ad."

"So, where did you see the ad?"

"In *The San Francisco Chronicle*."

Mika removed the tea bag from her cup and set it in an ashtray in the center of the table. "What made you want to come out to California?"

"After my old man died and left me his motorcycle repair shop, I sold it and headed west to see about opening my own shop somewhere between here and Frisco, depending on . . . well, that's another story for another time." Flicking ash from his cigarette into the tray next to Mika's tea bag, he said, curtly, "Your turn to dish."

"Well," began Mika, eagerly, "before I got saved, I really wanted to go to San Francisco because, you know, it was such a happening place, but then—"

"Don't tell me you're one of them Holy Rollers!" Ketch slapped his thigh and howled.

"You asked me why I came here. Do you want to know or not?" When Ketch held up his hands in surrender, she took a deep breath and continued. "Anyway, once I got saved, I knew I had to do something important with my life. Something big. I want to—"

"Change the world."

"Yes—exactly! Anyway, I found out from a friend about this year-long discipleship training school on a ranch owned by the Rowes, an awesome Christian family who live in Hayford, not far from here. But when I—"

"*What* kind of school?"

"Well, it's like a program that combines Bible study, training for the mission field, and an outreach ministry to the lost and needy."

"Out here in the middle of nowhere, where the buses don't run? Who are you going to 'reach out' to? Hoot owls and coyotes? Hell, Mika, Jesus Freaks are a dime a dozen in Texas right now. That's where you should've gone."

"But that's the point." Mika waved her hand, taking in their surroundings. "Going on a mission trip overseas sometimes requires living in remote areas with unwelcoming people groups, so this set up is perfect."

"Unwelcoming, as in heathen, you mean."

"Well . . . yes."

"And if it doesn't work out?"

"What do you mean?"

"You know, if you change your mind about the whole thing, or don't make the grade."

"I won't change my mind, and I can't afford to fail. It's not an option. I'm pouring everything I have into this."

"Now or never, eh? Strike while the iron's hot?"

"Something like that." Mika rushed ahead before Ketch could interrupt her again. "Now, back to the school started by the Rowes. Their barn, which they've converted into living quarters, was already filled to capacity, which meant I had to find other accommodations. My aunt told her son—my cousin—that I was looking for a place out here. He asked a friend of his who lives in Redding if he knew of anything, and . . . "

"Whoa!" Ketch whirled his hand around in a wrap-it-up gesture. "Long story short?"

"Long story short, I got in touch with the realtor who happened to be listing Sid's farm, and it ended up being the most affordable place to rent close to Hayford. So, here I am. This house is beautiful, right? And the location is really peaceful and quiet—like where I'm from back in Iowa. As I said, it's perfect."

Ketch snorted. "Sweetheart, I hate to bust your bubble, but do you know what you've gotten yourself into? This place is about to turn into party central. Trust me, you're going to be a big square peg in a little round hole around here."

"You're wrong." Mika's eyes bulged. "My parents talked to Sheriff Skinner, and he personally assured them this place would be a good fit for me. Why, the lease he had everyone sign even stipulates that no drugs are allowed on the premises . . ."

"What Skinner doesn't know won't hurt him."

"But you signed your name to the lease, Ketch. You gave your word. It would be dishonest to—"

"Oh, don't get your britches so bunched up, Meeks." Ketch took a final drag off his cigarette and ground the butt into the ashtray. "I've just got me a ten-gallon mouth this morning. That's all. Forget I said anything."

Just then, Sid stumbled into the kitchen. Bleary-eyed, he nodded toward Ketch and Mika. "Why don't you two take it in the other room? I'll make breakfast this morning."

"Are you sure you don't want some help?" Mika rose from her chair.

Taking his cue from Sid, Ketch stood up and took Mika by the elbow. "Let's go, Sunshine. Looks like the boss is in charge."

WHEN THEY WERE done eating, the girls set off to shower, unpack their rest of their belongings, and rearrange their rooms. From the kitchen, where he was finishing up washing the dishes, Sid could hear their grunts and groans as they scraped beds and dressers back and forth across the aged hardwood floors. Later, after the two male boarders went into town to scope out the scene, Sid settled into a rocking chair on the front porch to recoup.

The morning had been a bust. In addition to ruining their meal—in all his life he couldn't recall botching eggs so badly—breakfast had been full of awkward moments. No surprise there. They were five absolute strangers thrown together for a year in his farm, each of them as different from the other as chess pieces on a chessboard, or suits in a deck of cards. At least on the surface it appeared that way. How the game would play out between them over the next twelve months was anyone's guess, but if today was any indication, it didn't bode well.

Their conversations around the table had been strained, too, with Ketch, the lone raconteur who never stopped talking, being the exception. The cocky Texan seemed to love the sound of his own voice. Either that, or he was in the habit of mistaking audacity for charm. Whatever the reason, it wasn't until they were done eating that the other boarders finally spoke up. Their comments, unlike Ketch's, unfortunately fell under the category of "constructive criticism" centering around the food Pearlie had provided for the meal.

One boarder, for example, complained his eggs were overcooked, his bacon undercooked, and his toast cold and hard as sandpaper. "Had enough of that crap in Nam," he'd groused, slamming his plate on the counter and storming out of the kitchen.

Another boarder hadn't touched her eggs because she apparently preferred oatmeal. "It's not that I'm a strict vegetarian," she explained, "but eggs gross me out, and besides, the less foods I consume that are animal-based, the better. And don't you know that freshly squeezed juices are superior to this stuff?" She poured her unconsumed orange juice down the drain, adding, "I mean, who drinks bottled, processed juices anymore? Not anyone I know."

Even Mika, whom he'd assumed would be the most passive of his roommates, had offered an unsolicited opinion. "You know, Sid, I love to cook, too," she'd said, resting her hand on his arm as though the gesture would mitigate what she was going to say next. "I've done it for years on our farm back home, so if you ever want some tips on how to scramble eggs so that they—"

They think I'm lying when I say I can cook. It's this house. This kitchen. These memories that are throwing me off my game. Sid kicked at several fallen oak leaves stuck between the floorboards of the porch near his feet. *What do they all expect from me anyway? I'm not going to be their personal servant, catering to their every need and desire. No—I'm going to settle this ASAP.* But how? The only way was for him to lay down some house rules and assert some authority—the very things he'd learned to hate at Berkeley. He recoiled at the hypocrisy of Sid Jackson suddenly turning into "the man."

Leaning back, he placed his hands behind his head. Otis was right—he was a deep thinker. Too deep, and too often, an over-thinker. He couldn't help it. Since his parents had died, it was the only way he knew how to tackle life's challenges. *How can I bond with four strangers well enough that we can get along as equals but still exert my right to do things the way I want in my own house? Especially when I'm basically their landlord. Is it even possible to find that balance? And then, there's always the risk—*

At the sound of Mika's voice calling out for help, Sid stood. Opening the screen door, he stepped into the foyer, that last word echoing in his mind: *Risk.* With risks, he knew from experience, came the likelihood of rejection. And with rejection, the certainty of loss. Loss always brought pain, and if there was one thing he'd already had enough of to last a lifetime, it was pain. It would be far easier to let things slide—let his roommates run the roost however they wanted, leaving him out of it.

"Sid, is that you?" Mika called out from her bedroom. "Would you mind helping me move a piece of furniture?"

"Sure. Just a minute." Pausing a few feet from her door, Sid took a deep breath. He'd think about it some more before making a decision. No rush risking rejection from his roommates even though he wasn't sure why he should care. If he really wanted to pursue living communally, it would be with those of his own choosing. People he could relate to; people who shared his interests and worldview. Not with Jesus Freaks, bikers or Vietnam vets.

For now, he just had to worry about not having a repeat of this morning. He'd take advantage of dinner tonight. Find out a little bit more about each person, and then work out some sort of arrangement for cooking and cleaning, so that everyone knew what was expected of them. From there, it should go easy.

He hoped.

The First Supper

T
HAT NIGHT, SID AND HIS FOUR NEW roommates gathered around his parents' 1950s Duncan-Fife dining table for supper. Toying with the food on his plate, Sid blushed with embarrassment. Dinner was yet another disaster. *This house is cursed!* How else could he explain it? He'd butchered the meatloaf and burned the store-bought rolls Pearlie had brought over the day before. The rice was gooey, and the green beans, straight out of a can, tasted like . . . well, canned beans. Even the wine Ketch had provided for the meal could not compensate for the pitiful fare.

Ketch raised his glass. "Seeing as we're all gonna be tighter than bark on a tree for the next few months, I'll start with the introductions. I'm Ketch from Texas, and I came here to party and have a good time. But if California is all it's cracked up to be, I might just end up staying—maybe even buy me some land of my own." Winking at the girl sitting across from him, next to Sid, he added, "And find me a woman to work it."

The bespectacled, bushy-browed boarder leaned close to Sid, her thumb angled toward Ketch. "I have to live with this moron for a year?"

"Excuse me, Four-Eyes?" asked Ketch.

"I said, get over yourself, Cowboy." Acting as though Ketch was invisible, she added, "I'm Eliza Drabek. I was born in North Dakota, but I've lived in Alaska ever since I was ten years old. I spent most of my early childhood wandering around the globe."

"You're from a military family, then?" asked Mika.

Eliza nodded. "My dad's stationed at Fort Wainwright outside Fairbanks."

"Army brat," muttered Ketch. "That explains it."

"Explains what?" snapped Eliza.

"Everything. How about we call you Liz? Having a sour-puss for a face is bad enough without having a name like Eliza hitched to it. Know what I mean? Or how about, Alaska Liz? Better yet, how about the initials AL, as in the name Big Al . . . "

Liz stiffened. "How about you shut up, albino freak."

Mika gasped. "Don't you think that's enough name calling, you guys? I would think we'd all want to get along."

Raising his voice over Mika's protestations, Sid intervened, asking Liz why she had chosen to come to Trinity Springs.

"I graduated from UAF in June with a BS in chemistry," she explained, "but I've always leaned toward the arts, too, so I wanted to take a year off before deciding whether I should continue and get a masters, or find a job in my field, or take off in a new direction." Liz paused, her eyes darting around the table. "I've always wanted to check out California. I mean, doesn't everyone?"

"What about work?" asked Mika. "Will you need to get a job here?"

"Maybe a part-time job at some point, but for now, since the rent here is so cheap, I have enough money left over from my loans and summer jobs to get by for a while. Anyway, the important thing is, I've really asserted myself, and here I am, blazing my own destiny."

"Surprise, surprise," muttered Ketch. "A women's libber."

Rushing to sidetrack the conversation before it got out of hand again, Sid nodded toward the brooding, chain-smoking character at the end of the table. A gray melamine ashtray next to his plate was overflowing with cigarette butts.

"Woolf?" asked Sid, when it became apparent the lodger wasn't paying attention.

Lowering his eyes, Woolf made a "V" with his index and middle fingers, removed the Camel stub from his lips, and crossed his heavily tattooed arms. "Yeah?"

Sid swept his hand around the table. "We're listening."

"Pablo Woolf's the name."

"Interesting name," said Liz.

"It's Puerto Rican. Just call me Woolf."

"You don't look like a foreigner," said Ketch. "Just saying."

"I have a mother, you know." Woolf took another hit off his cigarette. "And for your information, Puerto Ricans are Americans." Before anyone could ask another question, he added, "There's not much anyone needs to know about me other than I served in Nam."

"Have you found any work out here?" asked Mika.

"I'm on disability." Woolf didn't bear any obvious physical wounds, other than a thin scar that ran from his right eyebrow up along his temple and into his scalp.

"Oh." Mika turned to Liz. "Well, at least you two have something in common."

"Say what?"

"You know, your dad's in the military, and Woolf is a vet."

Liz looked incredulous, as though Mika was speaking another language. "My dad's stateside. He never served in Nam. There's a big difference. Right, Woolf?"

Woolf went pale.

Haltingly, Mika went next. "Okay, well, my name's Mika Larson as some of you already know. I'm a born-again Christian from Iowa. My parents are corn farmers. They raise livestock, too."

Liz groaned.

"Last summer, I was saved in a tent revival just after finishing my second year of college at MSU in Mankato. I decided to take time off my education to pursue God." Seeming to note the blank expressions all around, she forged ahead, albeit with less enthusiasm. "Anyway, a relative of mine had a friend who knew someone who started a school on some property about twelve miles south of here. Well, not really a school; it's still kind of in the developmental stages and pretty unconventional. The Rowe family in Hayford owns it. Their son David actually runs it. They call it the Ranch."

"So, Mika . . ." Liz pushed her glasses higher up the bridge of her nose. "What do your parents think of you living in the wilds of California while you do your . . . ?"

"Ministry. They were as disappointed as I was that I couldn't board at the Ranch. But my pastor and his wife helped me contact some realtors in the area, which is how we found Sid's farm. When I told Sheriff Skinner I was concerned about living with people who might not be Christian, he assured me there wouldn't be any drugs allowed on the premises and that everyone would be signing a contract agreeing to a strict code of conduct."

Until the end of Mika's explanation, the boarders had

worn expressions ranging from amusement to boredom to incredulity, but at the mention of a code of conduct, their faces imploded.

Grabbing his glass and a bottle of wine, Sid stood up. "I guess it's my turn to tell you about me. Let's move into the living room. This is going to take some time."

SID SETTLED INTO a wingback chair next to the fireplace in the enormous living room while the rest of the cabal sprawled about nearby. Through west-facing windows extending the length of the room, bands of saffron and magenta smudged the dusking September sky. A gleaming ebony grand piano separated the sitting area from the windows. Candles flickered on top of it, and on a low, round coffee table in the center of the room, curling tendrils of aromatic smoke rose from several sticks of Tibetan incense burning on a copper plate.

Nervously, Sid cracked his knuckles. He wished there was a common denominator they all shared—something that would allow him to say: *Look, this may be my house, but don't think of me as your landlord. I'm one of you. So, there are a few things we need to talk about to make this year work for all of us.* But the only common denominator the boarders had with each other was their choice to live in northern California and their decision to board at his farm. That, and with the exception of perhaps Mika, they were somehow financially able to get by without working during their stay.

"I'm not sure how much you may already know about my situation, so I'll start at the beginning," he said, finally. "My parents moved here from Chicago before I was born. They bought this place, met the sheriff and his wife Pearlie, and became good friends with them. My dad was a judge in town. When I was about twelve, they both died in a car accident. Afterward, my grandparents moved up here from Sonoma to live on the farm with me. When I graduated from high school, they moved back while I went to Berkeley. I graduated in June. Otis Skinner is one of the trustees of my parents' estate. So, long story short, he's been keeping an eye on this place until I turn twenty-five, when I'm legally set to inherit it.

"This last April, during spring break," he continued, "I came up here and planted some pot behind the barn, near the creek, where I didn't think anyone would notice. In July, I returned to check it out while I stayed with an old friend of mine in Trinity Springs. He made sure no one saw me or knew I was here. My plan was to go back to Berkeley and sneak back up here again in the fall to harvest the crop. Apparently, one of the neighbors ended up turning me in. After I got busted, my lawyer was able to negotiate a deferred sentence, so that instead of going to prison, I'm on probation for a year. Unfortunately, Trinity County can't afford a paid probation officer, so Otis is my PO. I'm required to report to his office in Weaverville every Wednesday. Not only that, but you should know that he'll be making unannounced weekly visits here. He's the one who set up this whole arrangement."

"A-ha!" said Liz. "I thought it was weird that the sheriff was involved with the rental, but I assumed it was because of some legalities with the property, not because of you." Addressing everyone in the room, she added, "I mean, isn't that what you guys thought, too?"

Ketch shrugged. Mika was speechless. Woolf stared out the window.

"Anyway," continued Sid, "if I get busted again during my probation, I'll go to prison. For a long time."

"What's a long time?" asked Mika.

"Eight years. That's why Skinner had you sign a waiver about not having any drugs on the property."

Ketch, sitting on the floor next to the fireplace, stretched his legs out in front of him and yawned. "I'm not saying you didn't get your plow cleaned good, Sid. You did, and I get why you and the sheriff are uptight about having dope on the farm, but . . ."

"I'm not uptight about it," argued Sid.

"But it don't matter," said Ketch. "Landlords have renters sign crazy stuff all the time. It's par for the course."

"Of course it matters!" exclaimed Mika. "Sid could go to prison." Lowering her voice, she added, "I just can't believe Sheriff Skinner didn't tell me all this."

"Look, I'm not freaking out about my restrictions, okay?" Sid brushed away Mika's concern. "I know what's expected of me. But I'd like to know exactly what Otis had you all agree to."

Ketch drew a cigarette out of his pocket and lit it. "He gave me the Ten Commandments trip. You know, don't do this, don't do that. Normal stuff."

"He laid the same trip on me." Mimicking Otis, Liz intoned, "*It goes without saying there won't be any wild parties out there on the farm that'll get you in trouble with the neighbors* . . . ' But how's he going to enforce that? Other than the no drugs stipulation on the lease we signed, nothing else was in writing."

"Like it would make a difference anyway." Ketch snickered. "There's all kinds of ways to get around the sheriff and have a good time without implicating Sid. How many acres you got here, anyway?"

"A hundred and twenty," said Sid.

"And the boundaries of your land run from where to where?"

"The county road follows the property line along the east. The field behind the barn slopes down to Ransom Creek. It marks the western edge. Across the stream is a national forest."

"No one lives on the other side of the road?" asked Ketch.

"Some rich dude in LA bought it as a tax write-off about the same time my parents bought this place. He probably fantasizes that he can develop it someday and make millions."

"Who are the other neighbors?"

"An old guy named Hank Plummer lives north of here. On the downside of Prospect Hill."

Ketch blew a billowing smoke ring from his pale lips, "So, there's a national forest across the creek? Looks like we won't have to go far to find a place where we can do what we want. As long as we're not having a good time on your property, there shouldn't be a problem. Of course, you're welcome to join us, Sid, but it's up to you how safe you want to play it."

"Obviously, I'd be taking a big risk if I did." Sid's eyebrows knit together. "I mean, I don't want to go to prison, but if I thought I wouldn't get caught . . . "

Mika covered her ears. "I can't believe I'm listening to this."

I can't believe I'm already being baited like this. As Sid pondered Ketch's suggestion, he glanced at Woolf, who was still staring out the window. *I thought he was spacey because of*

Nam. It never occurred to me that he might just be high. If he is, where's his stash? The possibility that Woolf, or for that matter Liz and Ketch, might have drugs on their person, in violation of the waiver they signed, sparked panic in Sid even as it seduced him. And what about being ratted out? He felt he could trust Ketch and Liz to be discreet, but Mika—and maybe Woolf—were wildcards.

Stymied by his growing dilemma and eager to wrap up the evening, Sid said, "Look, just do me a favor and make sure whatever drugs you might have now, or in the future, you don't keep here, and I'll pretend I don't know about what goes on across the creek. The less I know, the better. There's one more issue we need to get out of the way. Your rent pays for your room and board here, but what it *doesn't* cover is me being your chef and personal maid. In other words, I'll be paying for food, but all of you are going to have to help buy it and cook it. Everybody takes turns cleaning, too. Questions, anybody?"

"Yeah." Liz pointed her finger at Ketch. "No macho crap. *Everybody* pitches in."

Ketch slammed his forehead in a two-fingered salute. "Yes, ma'am."

"That means you, too," added Liz, turning to Sid. "Just because you're using *our* money to buy food, doesn't mean you don't have to do your share of work."

"Of course. I'm just saying, don't expect me to do everything."

"All right then." Liz leapt to her feet. "We need to take an inventory and get a schedule together. Mika, help me, would you?"

"Try to keep the groceries within the budget I give you,"

Sid called out, as the two girls headed for the kitchen. "And maybe make a calendar or something and post a schedule where everyone can see it."

Little did any of his boarders know, this was the first time Sid Jackson had delegated something to be done for him. Proud and highly self-sufficient, he rarely asked for help, which was why he'd been so galled at the deputy sheriff's insinuation that he'd make a lousy farmer. He'd never been lousy at anything, which also explained why Sid worried he might not live down getting busted for something as ill-conceived and poorly executed as growing pot on his parents' farm.

He should have known better. He shouldn't have listened to Kate Quinn. Now here he was, forced into being a supervisor in his own home. He hated it. But what else could he do—play lackey to his four roommates just because they were paying rent?

Not in a million years.

It took mika and Liz the better part of an hour to finish their inventory and organize a work schedule. Most of their time was spent haggling over how best to divide the five housemates into two rotating groups. Mika thought Liz should be in one group, and herself in the other—reason being that the men needed a woman to help do a decent job of meal planning and cooking. But Liz was adamant that the three men be on one team, and she and Mika on the other.

"Having one of us on their team would only enable the guys' natural sexist tendencies," explained Liz. "Trust me, Mika, they would take advantage of us, and then we'd end up doing all the work for them."

"But we'll have to eat the meals they plan," moaned Mika.

"Yeah, and put up with the toilets and showers they'll call clean. So? It's either that, or they do nothing, and we do everything. I swear, that's how it will work out."

Mika debated Liz's rationale, thinking it cynical and unchristian. Besides, it simply wasn't in her Midwest nature to withhold help when she felt it was needed. "If Sid is as good a cook as he claims to be, despite his dinner tonight, it might work okay. But I still don't see the harm in one of us being on each team. It seems more fair to me."

"Fair?" laughed Liz. "Do you think it's fair that any job I get, I won't get paid as much as a man with the same degree?"

"Of course not."

"Do you think it's fair that less than a hundred years ago, fathers had complete right to the custody, and control of, their children while, by law, mothers were subject to their husband's identity and authority? A father could abuse his children, force them into child labor, and deny them an education, and there was nothing the mother could legally do about it. Do you think that was fair?"

Mika rolled her eyes. "This is the 20th century, Liz. Besides, what does any of that have to do with us drawing up teams?"

"Joseph Conrad said, and I quote: 'Being a woman is a terribly difficult task, since it consists principally in dealing with men.'"

"And your point is?"

"We have to be vigilant, because men will always try and get out of us what they can. Besides, doing the schedule my way will give us leverage."

Mika raised an inquiring eyebrow.

"Basically, it will force each team to match the other's level. In other words, if the guys get lazy and cook crappy meals, we can tell them we're not going to put ourselves out cooking for them either." Liz snapped her fingers. "It'll make them rise to the occasion so fast, you'll forget you ever worried about their culinary abilities."

"But that's an—"

"An eye for an eye? Yes, Mika, it is. When it comes to men, it's the only thing that works."

In the end, because she valued compromise over conflict, Mika finally agreed. Men versus women it would be. While Liz added a final flourish to the schedule, she dug some masking tape out of a drawer. Then, after securing the schedule to the front of the kitchen's Frigidaire, they stepped back and analyzed the fruit of their labor once more, ticking off the most important rules they had written down:

- *Each team will be responsible for planning, buying, and cooking meals every other week.*
- *Said teams are also expected to keep all the rooms in the house, except for individual bedrooms, clean during the same period.*
- *Each team must keep track of food and household items running low on their shifts and let the other team know.*

"This is definitely going to work," said Liz. "It's not perfect yet, but we can tweak it as we go."

"We have the first shift, so I guess we'll see."

"Well, I'm going to head up to my room. See you tomorrow, Meeks."

Mika waited until she was sure Liz was in her room before sitting down to regroup. Fingering the chrome edge of the kitchen table, almost identical to the one her grandmother had owned, she took in the rest of the room, studying every detail: the square red-and-white porcelain wall clock above the sink, the glass-front cabinet doors on either side of the stove, and the green Hoosier-style hutch on the short wall separating the laundry room and porch from the kitchen. The farmhouse reminded her of her life in Iowa. Its remoteness was so calming, its beauty so simple, its layout so classic, she said out loud, "I think I'm in love with this place."

A footstep behind her made her jump.

"Liz said you guys finished the schedule." Sid pointed to the paper taped to the refrigerator. "Is that it?"

"Yeah. Go ahead and check it out."

"So you like this place, huh?"

Oh God, he heard me. "Don't you?"

"I'm not sure yet."

So MIKA LOVES *this place.* To Sid, it was simply home—a past habitation—a place he once loved, now haunted with unwelcome memories. But after overhearing what Mika said, he thought long and hard about it, wondering what had drawn his parents to it in the first place. There was so much more about them he wished he knew. If only he could travel back in time and see, firsthand, how they'd met. Ask them why they had moved to California. Why they'd decided to buy a farm in Trinity Springs. Why . . .

A Trip Back in Time

Tom and sofia jackson had fallen in love with their Trinity County farm at first sight. They were so instantly passionate about the property, they often likened it to the feelings they'd had for each other when they'd first met. Sid's father, if he had written about his life during this period, might have put it this way:

I met Sofia in 1946, just as I was finishing my last year of law school at the University of Chicago. Enduring four years of undergraduate school was hard enough; the last three years were grueling beyond belief. I use the word "enduring," because law wasn't the profession I would have chosen for myself. You see, after Japan bombed Pearl Harbor, my father, Thomas, Sr.—a wealthy scion of one of Chicago's long-established investment banks—claimed he had already sacrificed my older brother to the war effort and in his words, he "wasn't about to give the damn government his other son."

A wink and a promise here, a few well-placed phone calls there, and behind my back, Dad succeeded in subverting my deep desire to serve my country. Of course, I can't put all the blame on him; I could have rebelled and joined the army anyway. But right or wrong, at eighteen, I was still too intimidated by my father's larger-than-life, bullying persona to defy him. He cajoled me into believing I could serve my country just as well by becoming a lawyer. It was, I later discovered, a lie. All my father really wanted was a son who would serve him above all else—particularly his financial interests.

But it was the death of my older brother Eddie, in the Battle of Anzio in 1944, that ultimately destroyed my relationship with my parents. Where once Mom and Dad had considered Eddie a rebel, the black sheep of the family, they now idolized his memory to the point that—for all practical purposes—I became non-existent. On the rare occasion they did happen to notice me, it was to rip me to shreds or hold me to impossible standards so that I would fail.

Most children have one parent they can bank on to have their back in a family disagreement. Not me. My mother was every bit as stubborn, self-serving, and narrow-minded as my dad. Maybe it was the money. I used to tell myself Mom wasn't the only woman who had to count the cost of crossing her husband—even in the smallest things.

As for my brother Eddie, he and I were close. Don't get me wrong. I missed him terribly, too, and struggled to come to terms with my own loss while grieving his death. But my parents' grief took a sick twist—perhaps because they felt guilty for how they had hindered and hounded and harassed poor Eddie when he was alive. Or maybe by belittling me, they felt they were honoring my brother. All I know is, by 1946, our relationship was so strained, I considered dropping out of school and hopping a train west—chucking all my years of school to find a place to call my own and settle down, as far away from my mother and father as possible. But then, to do so would have admitted defeat, so I forged ahead—if for no other reason than to honor Eddie.

Then I met Sofia. Had I not met her when I did, who

knows what I would have done with my life. She was working as a live-in nanny for one of my law professors, Dr. Luca Manzetti. When I first laid eyes on her, shining before me like Venus on a dark night, I lost my mind. She was an impressionist painting—all light and bliss. Whatever I had been before, whatever insecurities, doubts, and regrets I may have entertained, vanished in her presence. I died to myself that moment and became the man I knew I was meant to be.

It sounds crazy, I know. My parents certainly thought so. But as I've always said, Sofia Gianelli saved me from a life of rejection, irrelevance, and urban monotony, and I owe what I am today to her. Of course, if you asked her, she'd deny it. She'd say that the man I claimed I was before we met never existed.

But he did.

Oh, he did.

AT THIS POINT, in a joint memoir, Sofia might have interjected:

I moved to Chicago the year before Tom's graduation from UC for the sole purpose of spreading my wings before settling down. Actually, it was my mother Antonia who pushed me into it. She feared I was too timid to ever find a man, that I was an overly unadventurous daughter who might easily settle for second-best in a husband unless I put myself out there to see what was available. Mama would always tell me how her marriage to my father had been arranged and that, although she had come to love him deeply over the years, she wanted more for me—her "American-born" daughter.

My mother's scheme came with one condition. I had to

promise to return home at the end of my year working as a nanny for Dr. Manzetti and not fall in love with a man from Chicago unless his intent was to marry me and bring our family up in California. It went without saying that he should be Italian.

I've often wondered if I hadn't met Tom that fateful day in Chicago, would I have settled for second-best as my mother feared I would? I doubt it. There are loves, and then there are Great Loves. Tom Jackson was, and is, my greatest love. He was the most persuasive person I'd ever met, and the fact was, I craved surety in a man like bankers crave money in their pocket. His self-confidence and charisma absolutely bowled me over the moment we met.

He claims I changed him, but really, it was him who changed me. Tom's boldness and drive propelled me places I would never have dreamed of otherwise. He encouraged me to be myself. He supported me in every way a woman possibly needs to be. Some may have misinterpreted his ardor for arrogance, but he wasn't vain in the least. In fact, my husband is the most balanced man I've ever known—humble in his convictions, modest with his means—always serving others regardless of the sacrifice.

So, no, I wouldn't have settled for second-best, because in any other man, their lack of what I valued most would have been obvious to me from the start. Tom Jackson was a blazingly brilliant, once-in-a-lifetime comet, and when he entered my atmosphere, I grabbed on and never let go.

WHEN TOM SAW Sofia herding the professor's three children into the house after dinner, his knees went weak. Beguiled, and driven mad with the certainty he would never again see such a ravishing creature, he went in search of her. He found her in the empty kitchen, preparing an evening snack for her charges, and though he was considerate, he was also shockingly bold.

"My name's Tom Jackson," he said in a husky voice, pulling Sofia toward him in one swift, adoring move. "And you are . . . ?"

"Sofia," whispered the future Mrs. Jackson.

He rolled her name on his tongue as though it were dessert. "*Sofia*." Then, nestling the palms of his hands into the hollow of her back, he whispered back to her, "If you'll have me, Sofia, I swear I'll make you the happiest woman who ever lived."

Stunned, she was unable, or unwilling, to disengage herself from his embrace. "But you don't even know me."

"They say eyes are the windows to the soul, and your eyes are telling me you have a heart of gold."

"That's impossible. You don't know anything about me."

"What's impossible, you gorgeous thing, is that you could have a mean bone in your body. What's impossible is that you could be anything but exquisite." He nodded toward the backyard. "I saw how you were out there with Dr. Manzetti's children. You're a natural."

"A natural what? Everyone loves children."

"Some people can't stand kids. I have a feeling you love animals, too."

"Well . . ."

"Aha! I'm right, then. Anyone who loves children and animals is pretty near perfect in my book."

"You probably say that to all the girls," she blushed.

Tucking two fingers beneath her chin, he lifted it up. "Look at me, and tell me you really believe that."

Hesitantly, she raised her eyes to his.

"The truth is, Sofia, no girl's ever fetched a reaction like this from me. Until today. Do you believe me?"

Sofia blinked.

"So, I'll say it again. I want you more than I've ever wanted anything in my life."

"But I'm moving back to California soon," she sputtered. "I have little time to pursue a courtship with anyone before I go."

"Who said anything about a courtship?"

She opened her mouth to reply, but nothing came out.

"When do you leave?" he asked.

"In . . . about . . . four . . . weeks."

"Will you give me half that time to convince you we were made for each other?"

"*Half* that time?"

"Yes. By June 1, if you decide I'm not the man for you, I'll drop it. I can't promise that I won't try to contact you to see how you're doing, but I do promise I won't try to convince you to marry me."

"*M-marry!*"

"But, of course." Tom threw his head back and laughed. "What do you think we're discussing here?"

"What is your last name again?" she blurted.

"Jackson. Tom Jackson. Ask Dr. Manzetti about me. Ask any of my teachers; any of my friends. Check with the police department. Do all the research you want, Sofia. Just don't talk yourself out of us yet."

"And . . . and you'll do likewise? You'd be wise to, you know."

Tom raised his hands, placed them at the base of her skull, leaned in and kissed her so emphatically she went completely limp in his arms.

Her head lolling back, her eyes half-closed, her lips parted, she panted, "This is just so sudden . . . Tom. I don't see how it can work."

"Nation's histories have been changed in less time than it will take for us to begin our life together, my beautiful Italian queen. You'll see."

AND "SEE" SOFIA did.

Six weeks later, Tom Jackson and Sofia Gianelli were married in a small, simple ceremony inside Sonoma's historic St. Francis Solano Church. In attendance were two of Tom's closest friends, the Manzetti family, and Sofia's parents, Antonia and Agostino—who tearfully braved their daughter's union with a man whom they knew absolutely nothing about.

Conspicuously absent that day were Tom's parents. How dare Sid marry a woman from the same country they viewed as being responsible for his brother's death? If he wanted to remain a part of the family, they told him before the wedding, he'd have to choose—them or Sophia.

"Just be aware," they warned him, "if you choose her over us, you'll never see us again. Not only that, but you'll be cut out of our will."

He didn't choose them.

He didn't see them again.

He was cut out of their will.

And he never looked back.

After the wedding, the newlyweds lived with Sofia's parents while Tom put the finishing touches on his career; studying for, and subsequently passing, the California bar exam. All the while, they assumed he would practice law in a local firm in Sonoma. But then, on a fluke, he was offered a vacant court seat in Trinity Springs. It was a once-in-a-lifetime opportunity for Tom, since a judicial bench, even on a municipal level, could lead to higher court appointments later on.

And so it was that Mr. and Mrs. Thomas Jackson, Jr. found their futures suddenly hanging in the balance of a welcoming, but rough, town in northern California—a small town intent on enticing a new young lawyer to gamble big on starting his career with them.

How the Jacksons Ended Up
in Trinity Springs

THE JACKSONS' FIRST VISIT TO TRINITY Springs had been solely for Tom to meet with the city council about the position they were offering him. During his meeting, Sofia strolled about town, finding it rustic and quaint in that manner common to old logging and gold-rush towns of northern California. She later told her parents that the air was pristine, the rivers were clear and sparkling, and the giant conifer forests flanking the area's mountains were like a warm, wild embrace.

Passing by The Pearl Café, she paused to smell the aroma of fresh-brewed coffee. She read the menu taped to the restaurant's window and thought that if she and Tom moved there, she might very well become a regular at the place.

The early drive from Sonoma had begun to catch up to her, as had the growing heat of the morning. So, seeing Ralston Park a block away, she decided to go rest in the cool shade of the gazebo. It was there, stapled to a community board next to the gazebo, that she saw the advertisement for the farm. Below a large photo of the Victorian farmhouse the flyer read:

BOONE REALTY EXCLUSIVE!

A DIAMOND IN THE ROUGH JUST WAITING FOR THE RIGHT OWNERS!!!

Historic house includes 4 bedrooms, 2 baths, kitchen, pantry, laundry, giant living room, huge attic, plus a massive stone turret housing a library/observatory that must be seen to be believed. Established gardens and flowerbeds.

Original barn is functional but in need of repair.

Borders Ransom Creek and Trinity National Forest.

Great farmland. Plenty of room to plant a vineyard or raise crops and/or livestock.

Perfect for a growing family—Every child's dream.

The mention of a vineyard piqued her interest, but it was the last sentence—the one about the farm being every child's dream—that set her heart racing. She was six months pregnant, and the house in the real estate photo was exactly the kind of place she'd always envisioned raising a child in. She'd struggled with the idea of living several hours away from her parents, even though she'd already spent a year away from them in Chicago. But she reasoned, with some mutual commitments to visit on a regular basis, it was doable. Excited, she jotted down the contact number, stepped into the nearest phone booth, and called the realtor to make an appointment to see the farm.

A few hours later, she and Tom were being led on a tour of the "Diamond in the Rough," by Sam Boone of Boone Realty. Sofia tried to follow her husband's advice and not let on that she liked the place, but she couldn't resist oohing and aahing at the turn-of-the-century house with its towering turret, brick sidewalks banked with screaming red geraniums, and its eight-foot wraparound porch encased in a gnarled wisteria vine. To her, it was heaven.

Tom took one look at the blooming meadow, the fruit-laden apple orchard, the trout-filled creek with its happy cataracts, the dense national forest beyond the stream, and the maple, madrone, and oak copses ringing the estate, and was immediately sold. After Mr. Boone—a gangly man with long sideburns and a lazy eye—escorted them through the redwood barn and stables, Tom said, "We'll take it."

"But what about the job?" whispered Sofia.

"I'm going to accept it."

"We haven't seen the inside of the house yet."

"Will it really make a difference at this point?"

"No." She smiled at this. "I told you so."

"You did, indeed, my little Italian siren."

The realtor, looking amused at their private conversation, motioned for them to follow him into the house.

Sidestepping a missing floorboard on the front porch as they entered, Sofia asked, "Who were the original owners?"

"Jedidiah and Ophelia Monroe. They made a fortune in real estate and railroads during the Gold Rush." Mr. Boone held the door open for Sofia and Tom, brushing aside several cobwebs blocking their way. The place smelled fusty, of wet newspapers and mothballs. "The Monroes were the talk of the town when they built this place," he added. "That's what old timers say anyway."

Once inside, they turned left into a lodge-style great room. The realtor threw open its heavy velvet curtains, loosing billows of dust into the air. The wide-planked oak floor, the high beamed ceiling, and the enormous stone fireplace were in stark contrast to the more delicate gingerbread detailing on the outside of the house. And yet, they complemented each other perfectly.

Brushing his hands together, Mr. Boone said, "The Monroes only had one child. Amos was his name. So it's always been a mystery why they designed the house the way they did. Except for this huge living room, which was only ever used by Mrs. Monroe, it's a bit like a rabbit warren. Guess her husband was an eccentric old coot."

"It's unique all right," agreed Sofia. She walked over to a large object in the corner of the room covered with a faded patchwork quilt. When the realtor removed the coverlet to reveal a Weber baby grand piano, she covered her mouth in surprise.

"Like it, Mrs. Jackson? No doubt it needs some fixing up. It comes with the house, along with the other few pieces of furniture, so it's yours to do with as you please."

While she studied the piano's intricate woodwork, Tom asked Mr. Boone to explain the history of the farm.

"Originally this was a 360-acre homestead," he replied. "When the Monroes got old and sick, they were forced into selling off some of the property and all of their livestock to pay their bills. The fences rotted. Weeds took over their fields.

The orchard fell into disuse. They were barely able to pay taxes on the place. Then the old man started selling off some of their furniture and tools. Just before he died, the story goes, he wanted to sell Mrs. Monroe's piano. 'Over my dead body,' she said. It was the one thing she wouldn't part with."

Hearing that, Sofia froze.

"Her husband got so mad at her," continued Mr. Boone, "he saddled up the only horse they had left and went out riding to blow off some steam. Problem was, it was wintertime, and being as he was in his eighties, he had no business playing the Lone Ranger. Fell off his horse while fording the creek out yonder, hit his head on a rock, and died on the spot. The old lady locked herself in the house after the funeral and wouldn't speak to a soul. Rumor was, she felt accountable for her husband's death. Their son found her dead a week later sitting at the piano. Right where you are now, Mrs. Jackson."

Backing away from the piano, Sofia edged close to her husband.

"Unless you're superstitious, Mrs. Jackson," the realtor grinned, "I wouldn't worry none about it. Now, let's look at the kitchen. I'm warning you, it's in a sorry state. You see, Monroe Jr. inherited the place." Making a circular motion near his temple with the tip of his index finger, he added, "He didn't quite have all his marbles."

"When was that?" asked Tom.

"Around the turn of the century. Amos was one hundred years old when he died. Just last year, as a matter of fact. He never married—no wife, no kids, nobody to inherit the place. I remember when we were kids, we used to come up here and tease old Amos. Did all kinds of stuff I'm ashamed of now. Ready to go upstairs?"

A moment later, the three were inspecting the second floor bedrooms. In passing, Tom mentioned that he had met the county sheriff during his meeting with the city council that morning.

"Oh, Mr. and Mrs. Skinner are fine, honest folk," said Mr. Boone. "We're lucky to have Otis as our sheriff."

"Yes," agreed Tom, "he struck me as an upstanding sort of guy. The kind of man you can trust—not one who might buy friendships or write people off for not agreeing with him."

"That's Otis, all right."

"He must be a good dad." Tom, no doubt, was thinking of his own lack of a caring father in his life.

"Oh, Pearlie and Otis can't have kids." Mr. Boone placed his thumb along his jaw, where a bushy sideburn threatened to overtake his untrimmed moustache. "Not sure which one of them has the problem, but suppose in the end it don't matter since most people in this town look up to them as Ma and Pa anyway."

Next on their tour of the house came the vast, light-filled attic. Then Mr. Boone led them back down the stairs. Stopping in front of a massive oak door situated off a landing halfway between the ground floor and second floor, he pulled a skeleton key out of his pocket, inserted it into the lock, and turned it. "Now for the icing on the cake."

The door groaned as he opened it, revealing an enormous octagonal room soaring upward as though it were the inside of a lighthouse. Sunlight flooded down from curved windows encircling the observatory high above them. A stone fireplace dominated the lower part of the room along the wall connecting the turret to the main building on the ground level. On either side of it, high bookshelves wrapped around in a semi-circled hug. A show-stopping wrought-iron staircase near the entrance to the study spiraled along the library's outer wall, leading up to the observatory.

Tom and Sofia were speechless as they descended the three steps into the heart of the room and gazed upward.

"This here is the town's best kept secret," said Mr. Boone. "Not many people have seen this room. They say Amos Monroe kept it locked from the day he inherited it. Probably thought it was haunted or something."

Sofia arched her back in a long stretch and planted her hands firmly on her hips. "No ghost could keep me out of here."

His eyes resting on Sofia's belly, the realtor blurted, "I can't resist asking, ma'am. When's the baby due?"

"October."

"Well, I hope you two can have this place livable by then. At least, according to your standards anyway."

Tom and Sofia turned and looked at each other with a smile that said it didn't matter what condition the house would be in by October.

They were home.

THE SPEED WITH which the Jacksons and the Skinners bonded and became close friends was extraordinary. The first day they moved onto the farm, Pearlie popped over unannounced, bearing a bouquet of wildflowers, a welcome card signed by themselves and a few neighbors, and a fried chicken dinner with all the fixings. "Just wanted to welcome you properly to Trinity Springs," she said. "I'm Pearlie Skinner, the sheriff's wife. Otis said you've already met."

"Yes, my husband Tom has met your husband." Sofia helped Pearlie unpack the basket. "I can't say that I've had the pleasure yet though. Tom's out back. Shall I call him in so you can meet him?"

"No need," replied Pearlie, excusing herself to head back into town. "This week you two are coming to my diner for supper. It's called The Pearl, and it'll be on me. Any night you like. Otis is usually there at suppertime, so you can meet him then." Waving over her shoulder as she made her way back to her car, she added, "If you need anything, you just call me or Otis."

That night, as they were lying in bed, bone-weary but fed to the gills, Sofia said, "It's the strangest thing, Tom."

"What's that?"

"I felt an instant connection with Pearlie Skinner when she dropped by today."

"Is that so?"

"She was just so . . . I don't know."

"Friendly?"

"More than that. She's—like a mother hen. Not in a nosy or condescending way, but in a straightforward way. Kind of like my mom. Do you know what I mean?"

"Uh-huh." At this, Tom rolled onto his side and kissed his wife. Then he bent his head and kissed her pregnant belly.

"I like women like Pearlie. I feel I can be myself with them. I think we're going to be good friends."

"Speaking of the Skinners," said Tom, "I saw Otis in town today. He told me he wants to come by tomorrow afternoon after church to help us finish unpacking."

"They don't even know us. And on a Sunday, too. That's so thoughtful of them, don't you think?"

"Yes, they're thoughtful—just like you." Tom placed his hand on the side of Sofia's head and stroked her hair. "Just like your parents. What do you think attracted me to you in the first place—your beauty?"

Her lips in a pout, she replied that he had better have seen more in her that day in the kitchen of Dr. Manzetti's house than what met his eye.

They teased each other awhile longer—Tom pretending he would turn Sofia out if she wasn't the perfect wife, and she threatening to poison him if he dared try—and before they knew it, they were making love as if it were the first night of their honeymoon.

As if she wasn't pregnant.

As if, despite being the town's new judge and owner of a fixer-upper, he had nothing else to do.

As if the entire universe revolved around them in their shabby bedroom on an old farm in the little town of Trinity Springs, California.

And Then There Were Three

THREE MONTHS LATER, ON OCTOBER 30, IN the middle of a crisp afternoon while Tom was presiding over a court case in town—the day before her mother was expected to arrive from Sonoma to witness the birth of her first grandchild—Sofia called Pearlie in a panic. "It's time!" she cried. "My water just broke."

"Your contractions?"

"Every five minutes—about. What do I do?"

"Stay right where you are," ordered Pearlie. "Doc Simpson and I will be there before you know it."

Within fifteen minutes, Pearlie—who had left her customers on their own, with instructions for the last one leaving to lock up the café—squealed into the Jacksons' driveway with the local doctor in tow. It was 4:15.

Just past midnight, at approximately 12:04 a.m., Siderno Porter Jackson—ruddy-cheeked, long-limbed, and with hair the color of lava rock—declared his independence with a lusty howl.

THE JACKSON FARM'S transformation became the talk of Trinity Springs in the months that followed. Despite being raised a city-dweller in a family of white-collar executives, Tom

Jackson proved himself a man imbued with a farmer's work ethic. He got up at the crack of dawn every morning to feed their sheep, chickens, and two cows, put in a full day on the judicial bench, and then returned home to finish his chores. Newly energized as only a first-time parent could be, Tom immersed himself even more in renovating the farmhouse. With the help of several townspeople Otis had recruited, he repaired the foundation, installed insulation, new siding, and a central heating system, replaced windows, updated the ground floor bathroom, and re-wired the entire house.

Sid was nearly four when his parents completed the initial stage of reconstruction, and although enlarging and modernizing the kitchen was next on their list, Sofia and Tom had decided that with their son getting older, they needed to spend more quality time together as a family. So, while work didn't exactly come to a standstill, it slowed considerably. Instead of spending most evenings and weekends building and repairing, Mr. and Mrs. Jackson lived their lives through the lens of their son's increasing wonderment with the world around them.

At the age of five, Sid was gathering eggs for his mother and helping his father feed and milk the cows. When he was seven, Otis taught him to fish for trout in Ransom Creek. In the summer of his ninth year, Sid and his father built a tree house in a giant oak overlooking the back porch. His father also showed him how to operate some of the farm machinery, letting Sid ride with him on the John Deere front loader as he moved hay into the barn.

"Sid's so eager, so precise and sure of himself in all he does," Tom would later boast to his wife. "If he keeps on that way, he'll have no problem finding success in life."

Sofia agreed wholeheartedly, with one modification. "As long as our son is happy and healthy, Tom, everything else will fall into place. Haven't you always told me you didn't find success until you found happiness?"

"My exact words were, 'I didn't recognize success until I discovered you.' And as usual, you're right. Sid wouldn't be who he is without our love and influence in his life. So if I keep training him to reach his goals and you continue teaching him what happiness is, he'll have all the tools needed to succeed in life."

And so it continued.

During the long rainy months of winter, Sid's mother would nourish her son's love of music, coaxing him to sit next to her on the piano bench so she could teach him to play by ear, her strong fingers guiding his smooth young hands over the ivory keys. His father, during those same months, nurtured Sid's sharp, inquiring mind and love of books. After building a fire in the library fireplace, Tom would settle into his leather Chesterfield and light a cherry cigar before asking Sid to read aloud from any of the hundreds of books in their collection. Later, if the evening clouds parted, they would climb the spiral staircase and gaze at the stars.

On such nights, huddled together in the turret with celestial glories unfurling before them like diamonds tossed onto black velvet, Sid thought he could touch Heaven.

The Library: A Return to the Present

T HOUGH ONLY A WEEK HAD PASSED SINCE the boarders' arrival, they were beginning to pester Sid about seeing the inside of the turret.

"What's in there, anyway?" asked Liz, as she helped Mika clear the table after dinner one night. "From the outside, it looks amazing."

"Nothing," said Sid. "It's just a library."

"Wait, there's a library in the house?" Mika spun around. "I'd like to see it."

Woolf, pulling out an after-dinner cigarette, grunted. "The room's haunted. Must be, if even Sid doesn't go in there."

"Far out," drawled Ketch. "When's the tour?"

"The library's off-limits." Sid was resolute. He wasn't about to tell them he hadn't been in the library himself since his parents died. They'd think it was weird, or feel sorry for him, and the last thing he needed, or wanted, was anyone's pity. He excused himself from the table, thankful he wasn't on the schedule to do chores this week. His arms and back already ached from cutting down several scrub oak trees that day in a copse that needed thinning. "I've got a cord of wood to finish splitting tomorrow," he said. "I'm going to crash early."

On his way to his room, he overhead Woolf say, "See? What did I tell you? This house is definitely haunted."

About three in the morning, Sid was awakened by an odd mewling sound echoing eerily throughout the house.

What is it about nighttime here in the country? It's so quiet I hear every little thing. Am I never going to get a decent night's sleep?

Throwing on a pair of jeans, he grabbed a flashlight and his keys. Stealthily, he made his way down the hall. The mournful wailing led him into the entryway, up the stairs, and to the landing just outside the library door. He held his breath, beads of sweat pooling along his brow and neck.

Before he knew it, he found himself placing the old skeleton key in the lock and turning it. The hinges on the thick door creaked and moaned as he pushed it open. *Am I really ready for this?* His hand poised over the light switch, he took a deep breath before flipping it on. There before him, in the soft light of half a dozen strategically placed wall sconces, was the soaring three-story library, exactly as he remembered it.

The flagstone fireplace loomed directly opposite him. Turning off his flashlight, he traversed the room, stopping next to a tufted leather chair positioned next to the hearth— his father's Chesterfield. Immediately, his attention was drawn to his dad's pipe, tipped into a marble ashtray on the little side table next to the chair. With a jolt, he imagined he could still detect the aroma of cherry tobacco in the stale air.

He took a step backward, not having bargained on the wave of nausea that came with entering the room. Harnessing his emotions, Sid listened intently for the strange noises to resume. He shivered in the cold, wishing he had taken the time to put a shirt on.

There! He heard it again. The sharp, intermittent cater-wauling seemed to be coming from the other side of the wall, midway up the tower. Since the turret loomed over the rest of the house, he guessed an animal was in the attic. As he was wondering what kind of animal it could be, a brilliant moon-beam escaped through a parting in the clouds. It pierced the room's upper windows and shot all the way down to where he stood. Like a long silver finger, it drew his attention to a bookshelf on which two framed photographs rested behind a neatly arranged pile of seashells and fossilized stones.

Picking up the first picture, he examined it closely. It was a snapshot of his mother in her early twenties, taken from behind as she knelt on a beach. She wore a white, one-piece bathing suit, her glossy truffle-black hair pinned in a loose French twist. In her hands, held close to her face, she cradled a fluffy Persian kitten. Sid recalled his father showing him the photograph years ago and remembered him explaining that it was taken on Lake Michigan shortly before they were married. At the time, Sid was just a kid, half-listening to his dad. Now, he squeezed his eyes closed and tried to recollect what else his dad had told him that day.

We'd only known each other two weeks when I took this pic-ture of her, he'd said. *Look at her, Sid. She still takes my breath away. She loves cats—especially kittens. If I wasn't allergic to them, our house would be running wild with them. She gave up having her precious cats inside the house just for me. What a woman.*

Sid returned the photo to the shelf. Apprehensive, he picked up the second photograph. It was a snapshot of him and his parents when he was about five years old, sitting together on the front porch swing, their arms interlocked, their heads resting on each other's shoulders. This time, Sid's throat constricted; his heart knotted in his chest. His intestines twisted as though someone were wringing them out. *God, I'm going to be sick.*

"Sid, can I come in?"

Wheeling around, he saw Mika's silhouette darkening the doorway.

Hesitant, she added, "I noticed the door was open."

"Stay right there." He set the photo back down next to the picture of his mother and hurried toward the door.

"A stray cat showed up today," said Mika. "Sorry, I forgot to tell you about it."

Sid stared up toward the garret where the sound of another high-pitched shriek seemed to originate.

"I named her Greta," continued Mika. "I made a little bed for her in my room, but she must have slipped out during the night. My door doesn't close all the way sometimes." Pointing in the direction of the attic, she added, "Sounds like she's up there somewhere."

Sid placed his hand under Mika's elbow and steered her back out onto the landing. Handing his flashlight to her, he said, "You can use this to find her. When you do, do me a favor and take her outside."

"But—"

"I'm allergic to cats." Without saying another word, Sid closed the door.

After the shock of being in the library again for the first time in nearly a decade, he hardly cared if he'd been rude to Mika. By the same token, he was also too energized and overwhelmed with memories to even think about returning to his bedroom. So, grabbing a plaid throw from the arm of the Chesterfield, he climbed the stairway to the observation deck on the uppermost level of the library. When he reached the crow's nest, he wrapped himself in the blanket.

Lying down on the hard oak floor, he began to imagine what his life would be like if his parents were still alive. He pictured the farmhouse filled with their voices and all their comings and goings and envisioned himself whole and complete in their midst. He was certain they wouldn't mind his long hair or grungy jeans. As a matter of fact, he was sure if they could speak to him now, they'd encourage him to be true to himself. That's the way they were. That's the way they would have always been.

But their reaction to him getting busted would have been a different story. No doubt about it. His father would have been angry, ashamed. His mother, too. Still, they would have been there for him, no matter what. *If they were alive,* he thought, his stomach knotting again, *I probably wouldn't have this bottomless distrust of life, this hunger to escape, to be anywhere but inside my own flesh.*

The next thing Sid knew, the morning sun was streaming into the observatory. His back was stiffer than it had been the night before, so he stretched out as best he could and stood up. Gazing out the window, he continued stretching. From his vantage point in the turret, the farm looked as if it had been lifted from the set of a movie; a patchwork of meadows and hills and forests lacquered gold in dawn's first light. Seconds later, the tranquility was shattered by a piercing keen. Glancing down, Sid saw Mika's cat, scratching at the back door of the house to be let in. What did she say her name was? Greta? *A hardy name. Old-fashioned.*

Old-fashioned. That reminded him: Otis had been hounding Sid for weeks about calling his grandparents to tell them what had happened, but he'd put it off because he dreaded hurting them.

Fine. I'll call them this morning.

Still peering out the window, he saw the back door swing open and a shirtless Woolf step out onto the porch. At a distance, his tattoos looked like a riot of scarlet and indigo bruises. He watched as the vet bent down and scooped Greta up in his arms, rubbing his nose with hers. Gently, Woolf carried her over to the barn and turned on the outdoor spigot. Cupping his palm beneath the flow, he filled his hand and offered her some water. Then, as though he could feel someone studying him, he turned and looked up at the turret, directly at the window where Sid stood.

Their eyes met for only a moment. Just long enough for Sid to catch a glimpse of a little boy trapped inside the body of a very wounded, very confused, old soldier.

SID WAITED UNTIL everyone had cleared out of the kitchen after breakfast before picking up the phone and dialing his grandparents' number. "Nonna? It's me."

"Siderno! Where are you? We haven't heard from you in ages! How's my *bambino?*"

Hearing his grandmother's voice for the first time in three weeks, he realized how much he missed her. "I'm calling to see how you and Nonno are doing."

"We are both alive. That's all that matters, no? *Un minuto.*"

Sid waited while his grandmother set the phone receiver down and called out, "Agostino! It's our Siderno calling!

Come in here!" At least three minutes passed before she picked up the phone again. "Hello?"

"Yes?"

"So, how are you?"

"*Bene*, Nonna. *Bene*."

"Not *molto bene*? Something is wrong, Siderno. You are not doing well in school, is that it?"

"I'm not in school. I graduated, remember?"

"*Si, si!* My memory isn't what it was. I'm old, you know."

"You're not old, Nonna.'"

"I am, but we Italians endure our winters well."

"Winters?"

"I'm talking about our aging bodies. What do you think? We age well—with the help of a little wine, of course. Which reminds me, when are you going to plant that vineyard your mama always wanted?"

"Uh, vineyard?"

"Si, vineyard." Antonia *tsked* loudly. "You sound like the one who is getting old, Siderno. Don't you remember your mama's dream to have a vineyard on the farm one day?"

"Actually, that's kind of why I'm calling. I'm living on the farm again."

"*Che cosa?* What!"

"Well, I . . ." Sid listened as his grandmother employed rapid fire Italian to relay what he had just said to his grandfather.

"We don't understand," came Antonia's voice a moment later. "Why are you in Trinity Springs?"

"It's a long story." Sid stalled, not sure how to explain his situation. "You haven't told me how you and Nonno are doing."

"We were doing fine until you called. Now we are worried."

"I'm the one who should be worried—about you two."

"Ha! I am the picture of health," said Antonia. "You should see me."

"And Nonno?"

"What about him?"

"Is he . . ."

Antonia's voice lowered to a whisper. "I think your Nonno might be getting worse. He's been having trouble breathing lately. The doctor says it's to be expected, but I'm worried about him. *Non è buono.*"

"He'll be fine, I'm sure." *I hope.*

"Do you really think so?"

"Sure," lied Sid.

"I'm not ready to lose him."

"We're not going to lose him—not yet. So, back to the farm. A month or so, before I graduated in June, I came up to . . ."

"You graduated?"

Sid froze. "Nonna, you don't remember?"

"I would have remembered such important news."

"Anyway," continued Sid, his heart sinking, "I came up here to Trinity Springs and did something really stupid and got arrested for it."

"What is stupid? Arrested for what?"

"For growing some marijuana on the farm."

"I do not like these funny jokes of yours!"

"It's not a joke."

Sid held the phone away from his ear, as Antonia shouted, "*Caro Dio!* Are you in jail? Do not tell me you are in jail!"

"No, no, no." Sid raised his hand above the telephone and pressed it against the wall. "I was put on probation for a year, Nonna. I have to stay on the farm until next September and fix it up while renting out rooms to some boarders. Until my probation is over, I've been told I can't leave Trinity Springs—unless there's an emergency."

His confession was met with a flood of unintelligible Italian.

"So," he continued, breaking through his grandmother's tirade, "I want to make sure you have my phone number just in case you and Nonno need me for some reason. It's the same one we used to have."

Sid waited again while Antonia searched her address book. "I can't find it," she said finally, sounding out of breath. "I have a pen and paper here though. Now what is it that you want me to write down?"

"I want to be sure you have my phone number—and make sure you write my name next to it." After Sid recited his number to his grandmother, a brief silence followed. Not sure if she had stepped away from the phone, he said, "Nonna? Are you still there?"

"*Si.*"

"Are you all right?"

"I wish your mama were here. Papa and I miss her."

"I miss her, too. More than you can imagine." His voice cracking, Sid rushed ahead. "Listen, I'd better let you go. I'll call again soon."

"You promise?"

"*Si*, Nonna. *Ti amo.* And give Nonno a hug for me. Tell him I love him, too."

"But of course. You be a good boy in school, now. *Capisco?*

Sid burrowed his forehead into the crook of his arm. "I'll try, Nonna," he whispered. "*Ciao.*" He hung up slowly, his hand lingering on the telephone receiver.

Why does life have to be this way—the people and things I love most ripped away from me before I have a chance to really appreciate them?

It's not fair.

It's not supposed to be this way.

The Jesus Freak

A FEW DAYS LATER, WHILE FOLDING CLOTHES in the laundry room adjacent to the kitchen, Sid overheard Liz and Mika talking as they washed breakfast dishes.

"Thank God this is the last day we're on schedule," groused Liz.

Sid peeked through the curtain on the glass door separating the two rooms. He caught Liz glaring out the window above the sink as Ketch peeled out of the driveway on his Harley.

"I'm sick of cleaning up after everyone," she continued. "Sid isn't bad, but . . ."

"Woolf isn't bad either," said Mika. "I mean, he's not a slob."

"Other than leaving a trail of filthy cigarette butts everywhere he goes, I guess he's neat enough. And fairly helpful. Not as much as Sid, but he keeps to himself, which is more than I can say for Ketch."

"I think there's more to Woolf than meets the eye," replied Mika. "Have you noticed how attached Greta's gotten to him? She follows him around like a . . ."

"Whatever. Woolf isn't the problem. It's Ketch. He's a pig. Do you know what he did the other night? He had the audacity to ask me if he could throw his dirty clothes in with my laundry. *Unbelievable.* I swear, he's one of the most self-ish, arrogant, abrasive men I've ever met."

"That's a little harsh, don't you think?"

"I take it you're the kind who only wants to see the best in everyone?"

"I try to."

"Maybe beneath all his sarcasm and stupid innuendos, you think Ketch is really just a nice guy. But I'm a realist, and trust me, not only is Ketch shallow, I'll bet you anything he's scheming to have you as one of his conquests."

"That's ridiculous, Liz. You don't know him well enough to make those kind of assumptions about him."

"And you do?"

"Granted, a few weeks ago, we were all strangers, but I feel like I know him well enough now to believe he's harmless."

"Oh, *really?* He's so tight-lipped about himself, how could you, or anyone else for that matter, know the real Ketch?"

"He's hardly what I'd call tight-lipped."

"When it comes to being real, he is."

"I'm sure he's just one of those guys who loves to tease people and get a rise out of them. That's all." Mika shook her head. "You shouldn't take it personally. Anyway, he's actually a very responsible person."

Sid, back to folding his clothes, heard Liz roar with laughter.

"But he *is,*" argued Mika. "He inherited a motorcycle shop in Texas and then sold it. He hopes to start one out here."

"No way!"

"Yes way. He told me. Our first day on the farm."

"And you believed him?"

"Why wouldn't I?"

"What exactly did he say?"

"Just what I told you."

Sid paused when he heard about Ketch having been a business owner. This was news to him, too. Cautiously, he peered through the curtains again, hoping he wouldn't be detected. He saw Mika open a drawer and toss some silverware into it.

Liz raised her voice above the metallic racket. "If that's true, and if Ketch is the opportunist I'm guessing he is, I'll bet he's planning on hitting Sid up for some help."

"Sid's not rich."

"Are you kidding? Look at this place. He's sitting on a gold mine, and Ketch knows it."

"Ketch doesn't need Sid's money. And even if he did, I could almost guarantee Sid wouldn't have it to give. Land rich doesn't equate to cash in the bank. I know because my dad's a farmer."

"Okay, but how many people our age do you know who own a piece of property like this?"

"Well . . . no one."

"I rest my case. Ketch may have had his own business, but who knows what he's done, or what he's doing now, with his money? For all you know, he could be up to his neck in debt." Liz flailed her hands in the air, pointing out their surroundings. "Now Sid—he's hit the jackpot. This is guaranteed security."

"Sid's on probation, Liz. What good does any of this do him if he ends up in prison? And anyway, who cares about security if you end up lonely and isolated and unloved in a jail cell? I'd take love over security any day."

Love versus security? Sid had never seriously weighed the

two against each other. For as much as he'd tossed around the word "love" in the last few years, he hadn't really parsed it in practical terms. Considering it now, in light of the fact that he could very well be in prison in the near future, Mika's response about love trumping everything sounded almost childish. There were thousands of convicts serving time who might be "loved" but would give anything for the guarantee of freedom in the outside world. No, it was Liz's comment about the importance of security—coming, surprisingly, from someone who seemed to be a feminist—that resonated with him.

What a radical switch. Him. Sid Jackson. The Berkeley grad. The counter-culture hippie. The rebel who'd spent the last few years of college railing against the privileged and protesting the establishment. For him to be in the same league as someone who was financially successful was, well, the ultimate taboo.

The girls, meanwhile, were still arguing about which attribute had the most value.

"Regardless," said Liz, "Ketch will end up squandering everything. But if Sid makes it through his probation, he'll definitely be a catch for someone. Not only does he have this farm—and hey, that dinner he cooked the other night was great, wasn't it?—but just look at him. If I was the type of girl who didn't want a career and needed financial stability in her life, I'd be after him in a heartbeat. I mean, have you been in town when he's there and seen how women stare at him as though he's the next Brando?"

"Brando? Uh, no."

"Just check it out sometime. Sid won't be single long. As soon as his probation's over . . . " Liz snapped her fingers. "*Bam.* I'll bet you anything."

"Maybe, but Sid's smart enough to know a gold-digger if he met one. Besides, I can't believe he'd be that easily seduced. He doesn't seem like the kind who would."

"He's a guy, Meeks."

"Well, for his sake, I hope he's smarter than that."

"Like I said, he's a guy."

A moment later, when it sounded like the girls were wrapping up their conversation, Sid spied on them one more time through the curtained door. He saw Liz turn back to the sink, wring out her dishcloth and hang it over the faucet to dry while Mika put the last of the pots and pans away. Then, grabbing a feather duster and some furniture polish and buffing cloths, they filed out of the kitchen and down the hallway toward the living room.

Sid let the curtain drop. He was flattered. Embarrassingly so. But another part of him was disturbed. Maybe he was naïve, but were there really women so calculating as to manipulate him for their own gain?

Money. Land. Ownership—Restrictions.

Leisure. Liberty. Escape—Freedom.

His mind continued to race as he stacked his clothes into the laundry basket. The last six weeks had been so crazy, what with his arrest and getting the farm ready for boarders, he hadn't had an opportunity to really consider the full impact of assuming ownership of his parent's property. Like a broken dam, it all came flooding toward him—the responsibilities and opportunities. The limitations, too. He'd always assumed he'd sell the farm and cash in on his inheritance when it was time.

But now he wasn't so sure.

It would be entirely different if he lived closer to a town

that was more hip than Trinity Springs. Or if he had inherited undeveloped property on which he could at least custom-build a house more to his tastes—something more simple, rustic, and aligned with nature. His transition from student rebel to privileged landowner would seem less conformist if that were the case. But his parents' house was anything but modest. It was big. It was grand. It was showy. The historic embellishments and unique architectural details of it were unequalled in Trinity county. Sid couldn't help but feel proud, yet embarrassed of it at the same time.

Lugging the laundry basket through the empty kitchen, Sid made his way to his bedroom. At his core, he found himself still conflicted about the concept of love versus security that the girls had spoken about.

Was love at the heart of human desire, he wondered, or was it an innate need for security that drove people toward love? But if the desire to have some sort of tangible foothold in the world—to be attached to something larger than oneself or be a part of something solid and sure—was a prime motivator for love, rather than love itself, he'd have to rethink his assumption about selling off the farm. He might not love the property now, but his attachment to it might grow if he held on to it for no other reason than that it could give him a level of security he'd been longing for since his parents' deaths.

Sid dropped his laundry on his bed and flung himself down next to it. Reconciling his ideology with his current circumstances, he realized, was mentally exhausting.

In Berkeley, he hadn't had time for truly deep reflection. There, he'd simply been a face. A number. One of thousands longing to be different and yet unable, or unwilling, to break from the crowd long enough to discover who he really was. He and his peers had been too busy attending classes, getting high, and clamoring for attention to do anything else. But here, immersed in this great rural expanse, with no one but his roommates and the hick town of Trinity Springs as a diversion, he could see himself as a ship launched far out to sea, slowly maneuvering his way back home.

Home. He breathed in the peppery scents around him; the maple floors, cherry cabinetry, cedar siding, and a century of life lived within the rich confines of the historic Monroe house. It smelled like the promise of—home.

Of purpose.

Security.

And love.

LATER THAT MORNING, while Sid was tinkering inside the barn, he stumbled across the ladder his father had used to harvest apples in the orchard. It sparked in him a reminder that autumn was just around the corner. Although the dog days of summer were still entrenched over Trinity County, the shortening days, cooler evenings, increasing clicking and buzzing and whining of crickets and katydids, and the rouging of deciduous trees were telltale signs a new season was nearly upon them.

Every year, by the end of September, Sid's father would change focus, devoting more time to getting the fields, orchard, and flower and vegetable gardens ready for winter. Energized by the prospect, Sid inspected the tractor near the entrance to the barn to make sure it had enough oil and that the blades on the tiller were sharpened and free of rust.

He wasn't quite finished when he glanced out and saw Mika standing on the back porch shaking out a large rug. To his surprise, he caught himself staring at her as she placed the rug over the porch railing and went back inside the house. A moment later, she reappeared with a broom in her hand and began beating the carpet until stubborn clouds of dust burst free from it.

Analyzing her with a critical eye, Sid reasoned that if Mika were to switch out her jeans for a plain dark dress, remove her earrings and bracelet, and put her hair in a bun, she could easily pass for being Amish—a simple beauty. An understated one. He turned away. *And far from my type.* She was nothing at all, in looks, like other women he'd been attracted to in the past. Not to mention, they had nothing in common.

Yet something about her intrigued him; caused him to do a double take every time he was around her. Then it hit him. Guileless—that's what she was. She reminded him of his mother.

Sofia Jackson, by all accounts, was a woman known for shunning gossip, and so was Meeks. If there wasn't something kind to say about someone, his mother said nothing at all. She was quick to forgive. Some thought too quick. And she defended people who didn't necessarily deserve or need defending.

Sid shook his head. Well, that's where the similarities ended.

Mika Larson might be nice enough, but she's a Jesus Freak. A killjoy. Nothing at all like you, Mom. Hoisting himself up onto the tractor, he pulled the clutch out. *And nothing at all like me.*

About seven o'clock that night, Mika made her weekly telephone call to her parents in Iowa. She'd been talking to her mother for about fifteen minutes and was waiting as the phone was being passed off to her father, when she heard someone go into the living room.

As she wondered who it might be, her dad's eager voice came on the line. "Mika, my girl! How's that car doing ya?"

Mika glanced out the window at her red 1958 Oldsmobile Fiesta, illuminated by the outdoor lights on the house. She'd found it during her first week in California, after her father had sent her the money for a deposit. Otis had taken her down immediately to Paul Keating's car dealership where she'd bought it on the spot.

"It's runs great, Dad, no problems at all. Thanks again for helping me get it. I'll pay you back as soon as I can."

Suddenly the stereo in the living room came alive, the music blaring so loudly the wall in the kitchen began to vibrate.

"What's that, Dad?" Placing a hand over her ear, Mika asked her father to repeat himself.

"How's your school going?"

"Oh, I've started leading worship at a Bible Study on Wednesday nights with David."

"Who?"

"You know, David Rowe, the guy I told you about. He runs the Ranch."

"Oh yeah. The basketball player. You said he's 6'6" or something?"

"6'7". He played at Humboldt State. I really like him. I think you'd like him, too, Dad. He's . . . solid."

Stretching the telephone cord as far as it would go, Mika

crouched down between the refrigerator and the garbage can in an attempt to find a quiet spot. A few minutes later, she stood to her feet and said, "Dad, I'd better let you go. I don't want to spend all your money on phone calls and . . . I can hardly hear you anymore."

"Can you hear me now?" yelled Mr. Larson.

"Not really. Look, I'll call again next Saturday, okay? Love you!"

Mika sighed in frustration. What would her parents think if they met the people she was living with? True, no one was openly taking drugs . . . yet. Otis's weekly checks and everyone's concern that Sid make it through his probation gave her that assurance for now. But she wasn't stupid. Her roommates were getting loaded on the sly all the time. They might not be doing it in the farmhouse or on the property itself, but with the exception of Sid, rarely did a day go by that most of them weren't high on something.

Without question, if her parents were to come out for a visit, as they had mentioned they might, they'd be, at best, concerned. Oh, Sid could be counted on to be respectful. And Ketch, though he couldn't help but be himself, would no doubt employ the phrases "yes, sir" and "yes, ma'am" liberally enough to give her parents the impression he might not be the hellion he appeared. But Liz and her in-your-face opinions? Woolf, the social misfit?

Wait. Mika recoiled. *I'm just as flawed as any of them. At least they're being true to who they are. I'm a hypocrite, acting one way here on the farm and another at the Ranch. If I'm as zealous for God as I think I am, then why am I so afraid to invite my roommates to church—like David's always encouraging me to do? And to think I want to be a missionary! Maybe I don't have a calling after all. What if everything I'm doing is for the wrong reason? What if . . .*

The possibility that she might only be attending the Ranch because it's what she thought she should be doing, not necessarily what she wanted to do, terrified her into taking action. Squaring her shoulders, Mika marched out of the kitchen and advanced toward the living room, determined that whoever was in there, she would invite to church with her tomorrow. Rounding the corner, she saw Ketch stretched out on the sofa, his hands pumping the air in time with James Gang's "Funk 49." Since he was completely oblivious to her presence, she waited until the song was over before walking over to the turntable and lifting the needle off the vinyl.

"Hey there, Princess!" Ketch leaped to his feet. Grabbing her hands, he said, "Come on, let's boogie!"

"I . . ." Mika's invitation caught in her throat.

Ketch grinned. "I know. It's hard to tell someone as good-looking as me that you're dying to dance with them."

In spite of herself, Mika laughed, and as she did, Ketch snatched her in his arms and spun her around. "See? You just can't resist me, can you?"

"It's true," she teased. "You're actually *so* captivating Ketch, I can't resist asking you to go to church with me tomorrow."

Ketch pulled her close. "What will you give me if I say, 'yes'?"

"I thought we were friends. Friends do favors for each other. They don't cut deals."

"I only meant that I'll expect something like a home-cooked dinner, or a little walk in the park together afterward, if I agree to go with you." Ketch shook his head and clucked his tongue. "My, my, Sunshine. What did you think I meant?"

A furious blush raced across Mika's cheeks.

"It's a date then." Softly, Ketch pushed some loose strands of hair back from her face. "We'll ride my chopper and have a picnic after." And when she leapt into his arms to thank him, he muttered, "Just don't expect me to get all gussied up or sing any of those hymns y'all sing. Been there and done that more times than I care to admit."

"No one dresses up at the Ranch. Wear whatever you want. You could wear pajamas, and I wouldn't care."

Ketch's eyes glinted. "I don't wear pajamas."

Noticing a quick movement in the foyer, Mika turned to catch a glimpse of Sid walking down the hall. *How long has he been standing there, and how much did he hear?*

From the sour expression on his face, he'd heard plenty.

The Cowboy and His Girl

M IKA WAITED UNTIL AFTER CHURCH, WHEN she and Ketch were digging into the picnic lunch she'd prepared, to ask what he had thought of the service. Somehow, she knew what he would say before he opened his mouth.

"Can I plead the Fifth, Meeks?"

"No."

"All right then, it was more'n a few bubbles off plumb." Diving into a cold, fried chicken leg, Ketch chewed on it awhile before adding, "What was all that hand waving, mumbo-jumbo about, anyway?"

"People were just excited about the Lord, that's all."

"I couldn't understand a single word they said."

"That's because they were speaking in tongues."

"In what?"

"You know—at Pentecost? The disciples were filled with the Holy Spirit and spoke in tongues."

"Tongues, lungs—it don't matter. This dude is beyond redemption."

"Don't say that! No one is beyond redemption."

Done eating, Ketch wiped his mouth with a napkin before lowering himself back onto his elbows. Peering closely at Mika, he asked, "You're not crying are you?"

"No. It's just that . . ." Mika swiped at her eyes, "I want you to go to Heaven. Don't you want to go there when you die?"

Ketch threw his white head back and hollered. "I'll be damned. She really is a saint! You sound just like my little girl . . . " Suddenly, he turned paler than he already was—if that were possible. His eyes glazed over. His pallid lips twitched.

Trying not to let her shock show, Mika reached into the picnic basket and offered him a buttered roll. "I'd like to hear about her."

Ketch took the bread and set it on his plate, his jaw muscles working. "Her name's Annabelle. She just turned seven. Reminds me of you, Meeks—real sweet."

"Is she back in Texas?"

"She moved with her mother to San Francisco a couple years back."

Mika gazed at Ketch's profile, his fine straight nose, high cheekbones and strong chin, and was struck by his stark beauty. If he would have been born with color, she thought, he might actually have been a less handsome man. Odd that she hadn't noticed before that he was so attractive.

As though he'd guessed what Mika was thinking, Ketch said, "Annabelle's not albino like me."

"I'm sure she'd be mistaken for an angel if she was."

"She's *my* angel. That's for sure." Turning to face Mika, he muttered, "I can't believe I'm telling you about her."

"You don't have to if you don't want to. Really."

"No, it feels right. As long as you don't . . . "

Mika placed her hand on her heart. "I promise I won't tell a soul."

"Yeah, I figured my secret would be safe with you. It's just that I don't want people bugging me about it, and I sure as hell don't want anyone's pity." Motioning for Mika to hand him a beer from the cooler, he opened it and took a swig. "Can you guess how old I am, Sunshine?"

"I was going to say twenty-two or twenty-three, but with a seven-year-old daughter you must be . . ."

"I'm almost twenty-eight. I wasn't quite twenty when Emma, Annabelle's mother, got pregnant with her. She wanted to get married and do the whole family trip, but back then, Will Ketchum was all about 'me, myself, and I.'" Shrugging, he added, "Emma and me weren't exactly what you'd call childhood sweethearts, but we'd known each other a long time. Started dating after she graduated. She'd only just turned eighteen, but she was so much more together than I could ever have hoped to be. At least, back then she was."

Ketch took a long draught from his beer before continuing. "Anyway, I accused Emma of trying to rope me into marriage. Even denied being the dad—told her she'd have to prove it to me. She was so pissed, she dumped me and moved back in with her parents. Her daddy warned me that if I ever set foot on their property, he'd call the sheriff to come pick up the leftover pieces of my body after he was done carving me up. I told myself I didn't care and did everything I could to forget about Emma and the baby. But, after years of partying and sowing my oats, out of the blue, it just hit me how bad I was screwing my life up." Ketch heaved himself up from his reclining position. Bringing his knees to his chest, he leaned forward. "Now why am I telling you all this again, Meeks?"

"Because I asked you to. Does anyone else know?"

"No, ma'am. It's not something I'm real proud of. Besides, if things don't work out with me and Annabelle, I'd rather the whole world isn't asking me about it."

"I can understand that." Mika thought of the times she'd made premature announcements that didn't pan out. It was always easier to reveal results after the fact than predict them before they happened and run the risk of looking like a fool. "There must be a reason you've already told me this much."

"You're probably right." sighed Ketch. "I suppose having you as a—what do you call it . . . ?"

"Confidante."

Ketch repeated the word, exaggerating the pronunciation. *"Con-fee-dahnt*—confessor, whatever. I suppose it's good to be accountable to someone."

Mika grinned. "Did I tell you I almost majored in Psych in college?"

"Explains why you're such a good listener."

"I am that, so you might as well keep going. What exactly happened to change your mind?"

"Well, I was standing outside of a bar one night, watching an old biker buddy of mine named Sam Bodeen—he was about twelve years older than me—beat the crap out of some poor long-haired stoner. I looked at Sam bashing in that hippie's head like there was no tomorrow and knew if someone didn't stop him, he'd kill the kid. So, I got in between them and broke it up, and I swear I saw myself in Sam's face when he looked at me and said, 'You miserable bastard. Since when do you think you're someone special?' Right then and there, I determined I wasn't going to end up ugly, mean, and lonely like Sam. I needed better influences in my life than him and Bud, Jack Daniels, and Mary Jane—not that I still don't keep 'em close. Know what I mean?"

"But it was too late." Ketch flicked a crumb off his jeans. "Some drug dealer by the name of Red Hollis had apparently swept Emma off her feet, taking her and Annabelle with him to San Francisco to live in a commune. By then, there was nothing her parents could do. They told her the only way they'd forgive her was if she dumped the dude and came back home."

"But that's punishing their granddaughter for something totally out of her control," said Mika. "And besides, I'd imagine giving Emma an ultimatum only made her more determined not to go back to Texas."

"Got that right. 'Tough love' is what her folks called it. More like 'bogus love' if you ask me. Comes back to bite you in the end. Anyway, her pa told me even if he knew where Emma and Annabelle were, he wouldn't tell me."

"But you're Annabelle's father."

"Well, can't say as I blame them, being as I'd denied paternity for so long. If I'd been done wrong by a snake like me, I'd probably do the same thing."

"No you wouldn't."

"You didn't know me then, Mika. I was a no good son-of-a-bitch, and I mean that literally."

"Literally . . . as in?"

"As in *literally*. My ma left my pa when I was still in diapers. Ran off with a married neighbor who owned the local strip bar at the edge of town. Then she hooked up with a cop in Abilene who got busted for illegal gun running. After he was sent to the pen in Beaumont, she snagged herself a traveling encyclopedia salesman and ended up in Houston. Rumor has it she's now living it up with a dead-beat country singer in Memphis."

After a lengthy pause, Ketch said, "Some folks said she left us because she couldn't stand looking at me, being albino and all." Whisking his hand in front of his face, he added, "I ask you—what kind of woman could reject this?"

"Your mother had to have been crazy, Ketch."

"She was a kid is what she was. Only 16 when she had me. My pa said that's why she left. Her heels just had too much kickin' left in them to waste on a greasy mechanic twice her age in a small town dump with a freak baby boy weighing her down. 'Course, there were always the rumors, too. That I wasn't hers to begin with. That I'd shown up on their door-step the day I was born like a feral cat, and my pa took pity on me."

Mika gasped. "I can't believe the stupidity of some people!"

"Anyway . . ." Ketch shrugged. "My old man made a vow to be successful—probably just to get back at my ma and all them gossips in town—and that's exactly what he did. He turned from being a laid-back, good ol' boy into a workaholic too busy to find a new wife. The only thing about him that stayed the same was his love of chewing tobacco. Within five years, he'd quadrupled business at his motorcycle shop, *Rev & Ride*. Long story short, I became his right-hand man up until the day the tobacco killed him."

"You don't have any other family?" Mika leaned back to rest on her elbows next to Ketch.

"I have some shirttail cousins somewhere but none worth calling family. After that episode with Sam beating up that hippie, I started wondering, 'What if something happened to

Emma out in Frisco, and Annabelle was left without a ma?' My name wasn't on the birth certificate so I figured she'd go to Emma's parents. My girl could end up never knowing me."

"That's when you decided to find her."

"It took a long time, but when I found out she was in Frisco, I hired someone to manage the business and drove my Harley out west to hunt her down. I found her, all right," said Ketch, his voice husky. "It wasn't good. In fact, it was a damn mess. Emma had shacked up with Red in a rat hole in Haight-Ashbury and was so strung out on smack that Children's Services came and put Annabelle in foster care. I spent a small fortune on lawyers trying to get access to her."

"Oh, Ketch, thank God."

"I'm not thanking Him yet."

"What do you mean?"

He gave her a sardonic smile. "You haven't had any experience with lawyers, have you?"

"Can't say that I have."

"Let's just say lawyers exist to torture suckers like me." Lowering himself on to his back, Ketch placed both hands under his head and stared at the clouds. "During the entire three months I spent in Frisco, I was only able to spend four days with Annabelle. Always in the presence of her foster parents, of course. They're good enough folk. Churchgoing like you. Annabelle is . . ." Ketch's voice caught. Quickly, he turned his head away from Mika.

Several moments passed before he looked back up at the clouds. "Annabelle is, without question, the most beautiful creature I've ever seen. Emma said she must look like my ma because she's dark and doesn't take after anyone in her family. I swear, my little girl's the sweetest thing this side of the

Alamo. And you know, after all my screw-ups, she doesn't even seem to hold a grudge against me. She warmed right up to me the first day I saw her." His eyes narrowing, he added, "When I found out from Children's Services all the crap Emma and her boyfriend had put Annabelle through, I wanted to kill them. I mean, really, seriously, kill them both."

"I take it Emma's trying to get her act together so she can get Annabelle back?"

"She is, but at this point, the case workers aren't sure she can do what they expect of her. One thing's for sure; Emma doesn't want Annabelle to go back to Texas with her folks. I'll do anything to get custody of my daughter, Mika, but I might have waited too long. With all the hoops I still have to go through now, it sure ain't going to be easy."

Mika flipped over onto her stomach. "Can I ask why you're up here in Trinity Springs instead of San Francisco?"

"Things got messy. Once the legal work was set in motion, my lawyer warned me not to entertain any expectations for at least a year. 'Don't get your hopes up,' he said. According to him, not only is it going to take that long to get my case ready to present to the judge, but I'm in competition with Annabelle's foster parents, too. Evidently, a few weeks before I showed up in Frisco, they started pre-adoption proceedings in the event Emma decided she didn't want to, or couldn't get Annabelle back because the court decides she isn't a fit mother."

Ketch turned toward Mika. "I was advised to stay close enough in case something breaks, so that I can prove my intent is genuine, but not so close that Emma and the foster parents can turn around and accuse me of trying to interfere or influence Annabelle. I started looking for a perfect place to wait it out—somewhere within a couple hours driving distance of Frisco. Eventually, someone turned me on to an ad they saw for the farm last month and, *bingo*, here I am."

Mika plucked a long piece of grass from beyond the edge of their blanket. Then, reaching over, she tapped Ketch's bare arm with it. "Well, it does seem to be an ideal location. I agree. Have you heard anything from your lawyer yet?"

"Nada. I didn't give him the phone number at the farm. Didn't want him checking out the premises in case I, or someone we live with, does something stupid. I'm not a saint like you, you know. Anyway, got myself a PO box in town, and I call his office twice a week from the phone booth outside City Hall."

Mika bit her lip. It dawned on her that in agreeing to keep Ketch's secret in confidence, she had put herself in a moral dilemma. He wasn't just confiding in her about his daughter. He was also, in so many words, admitting to her that he was still getting high. If anything were to happen, if anyone were to inquire . . .

"What's wrong, Meeks? Looks like your sunshine up and disappeared behind a cloud."

"Aren't you afraid of blowing it?"

"I don't catch your drift."

"You're smoking pot. Not at the farm, I know," she rushed to add. "Where are you getting it?"

"That's for me to know and you to find out." Ketch's upper lip curled back in a half-smile. "On second thought, scratch that. You don't need to know."

"Did you bring it up here with you, or are you buying it from someone in Trinity Springs?"

"The less you know, the better."

"But, if you're buying it here, and you're caught . . ."

"Buying grass isn't the same as dealing it."

"It doesn't matter. Even if you were busted for possession . . ."

"You can't let me have just one little vice, can you?" Ketch sounded flippant, but a sharp edge in his tone warned her to tread carefully.

"Your vices aren't any of my business," agreed Mika. "But the illegal ones could ruin everything for you."

Ketch reached out, and holding her chin in his hand, he said, "Look, I can't expect you to understand why I do some of the things I do. You've probably never been high. But honestly, it's the only thing keeping me sane right now."

Caught off-guard by his closeness, Mika recalled Liz's suspicion that Ketch liked her. But staring intently into his eyes, she knew it wasn't true—not in the way Liz imagined. He was looking at her with the faith of someone who had just sacrificed a part of himself in a demonstration of friendship. Pure and simple.

She reciprocated by taking his hand from her chin and squeezing it hard. "You might be surprised to know I was stoned throughout my entire senior year of high school and most of college. I just have no desire to do it anymore."

"Well, what do you know? The saint has secrets, too." Ketch kissed the back of Mika's hand, winked at her, and jumped to his feet. "What say we take a little Sunday spin before heading back to the farm?"

"Sure." Mika repacked the picnic basket while Ketch strolled over to his Harley. When she was done, she handed him the basket and mounted the bike behind him. Leaning back against the sissy bar, she wrapped her arms securely around his waist.

For a good hour, they cruised the back roads around Trinity Springs, the sun on their backs, the wind in their hair, exulting in the freedom of the open road. But inside Mika's heart, a cinching was taking place. With shared secrets and promises, and the risks that came with them, she and Ketch were no longer strangers or simply roommates.

They were brother and sister.

The Pearl

AD THE PEARL CAFÉ BEEN SITUATED directly along Highway 299, it might have been voted the best truck stop in Trinity County. Pearlie was often told her fresh peach-blackberry fritters, served hot out of the oven with a slathering of butter and a shot of cream, could put most upscale bakeries in San Francisco out of business. In fact, her cooking had gained such acclaim throughout the county that for the first time in the café's history, she sometimes found herself having to take reservations. But Trinity Springs wasn't on a main highway. For all intents and purposes, it was in the middle of nowhere. And with a population of just over a thousand, it had long ago surrendered any claim of importance to its close neighbor, and county seat, Weaverville.

So it was, on the morning of Friday, October 10, Mrs. Skinner asked her husband to relay a message to Sid she doubted he could refuse. If he and the other boarders wanted to stop by The Pearl, she'd give them all a complementary cup of spiced cider and a slice of her famous pumpkin pecan pie. And because Mika had been looking for some part-time work in town, she told Otis to ask her if she would be available to wait tables and help in the kitchen that night.

Mika showed up ready for work at five, but all the other lodgers, including Sid, declined the invitation. The hours flew by uneventfully until nine o'clock, when Pearlie locked the door and turned the window sign around to read, "Closed." Only two couples remained in the diner.

Pearlie plopped onto a stool at the counter with two cups of decaf coffee and two plates of pie. Motioning for Mika to come sit next to her, she said, "I was hoping Sid and some of your roommates might have shown up tonight."

"They had other plans, Mrs. Skinner. Otherwise I'm sure they would have come."

"Call me Pearlie, honey. Maybe my diner's just not their kind of place. I heard there's someone new in town who wants to open up one of them stores that sells natural foods, maybe a café along with it, too. I suspect that'll be right down the young folks' alley." The vertical lines between Pearlie's eyebrows deepened. "Oh, well. How do you think Sid's doing?"

"Okay."

"Do you talk to him much?"

"Once in a while."

"Is he getting along with the other boarders?"

"He seems to be. Why?"

"When I ask folks in town about Sid, they tell me he pretty much keeps to himself. Comes in to stores, buys what he needs, and leaves. Walter Jenks down at the Five and Dime said he's tried to strike up a conversation with him several times, but . . . " Pearlie shrugged. "I realize there are two sides to every story. Sid's long hair isn't making him any friends, that's for sure. But then, that's what they call prejudice, right? Not that I'm the biggest fan of hippies either, but I know Sid, and he's a jewel if ever there was one. You know, maybe it's just still awkward for him, what with being gone so long and having to face everyone in town who knows about the, you know, the dang pot he grew at the farm. That and—oh, mercy. I shouldn't talk so much. I'll just say what happened to Sid's mama and daddy is a wound that hasn't healed. Don't know that it ever will."

"Maybe with time, he'll warm up to the townspeople again."

"And vice versa."

"Yes. I mean, you're right, Pearlie. It must be hard for him with everyone in town aware he's on probation. That, on top of everything else."

Lowering her voice, Pearlie turned sideways and said, "Don't stare, but see those two over there in the back booth? The gal with the long, dark, kind of wavy hair, sitting opposite that boy?"

Mika glanced at the girl.

"Pretty thing, ain't she?"

"She's . . . gorgeous. Very exotic looking."

"Katherine Quinn's her name, and that's her little brother Max she's sitting with. Black Irish is what they call them. Max used to be one of Sid's best friends. Otis is sure he helped Sid plant all that pot on the farm this spring, though he can't prove it. That's why Sid can't be in contact with him for a year. Anyway, Kate's four years, nearly five years, older than Sid. She used to babysit him every once in a while until his folks died. You'd have thought she was Helen of Troy the way Sid would moon over her when she wasn't looking. 'Course, what young boy hasn't been smitten with an older woman in his youth? We thought it was cute at the time, but then some old crushes take a long time to die, don't they?"

Mika stole another glance at Kate.

"That girl was the sweetest thing when she was young. But then she grew up—grew up too fast, if you ask me. And ever since she left here, there's been rumors of . . . well, let's just say that it's suspicious that she's back home again, out of nowhere, just when Sid is here for a year."

Mika dove into her pie.

Pearlie scraped the last crumbs from her plate. "Now I don't like to gossip, but Max and Kate had lousy parents. You know the kind—a dad who womanizes and gambles his weekends away, and a ma who retreats into herself while he takes his orneriness out on her. In the end, Eamon just up and left them. Katie was fifteen. The only decent thing you can say about old man Quinn is he didn't gamble away their house."

"Mrs. Quinn's another story," continued Pearlie. "They say she took one too many smacks on the head during her husband's rages and isn't quite all there anymore. Max fixed up the basement in their house for his ma to live in—gotta give him credit for that much. Now that Kate's back, she'll be a help, no doubt. Oh, here I am talking up a storm about other people again. But then, I suppose you know folks back in Iowa who've had problems similar."

"Oh, yes." Taking a last swig of coffee, Mika rose, gathered her and Pearlie's empty cups and plates and stacked them in the sink. Then, untying her apron, she hung it on the back of the kitchen door. "I'd better get back to the farm, Pearlie. Thanks for the work. I can always use the extra money."

"Well, you're a good little waitress, Mika. We've got some busy weekends coming up this month, and after that there's the holidays, so I'm sure I'll be needing you again." Shooing her away from the counter, she added, "Now get along, sweetheart, and be careful driving. There's lots of deer out on those country roads this time of night."

As she opened the door, Mika caught a glimpse of Kate staring at her in the reflection of the glass. Stepping onto the sidewalk, she turned to wave good-bye to Pearlie and noticed Kate whispering intently into her brother's ear, her head bobbing up and down animatedly.

Is she talking about me, or am I just imagining it?

Chin up, Mika rounded the corner of Fifth and Main, determined not to entertain small town gossip about Sid Jackson.

Dust Up at Digger's

NO ONE REALIZED IT WAS SID'S BIRTHDAY until Otis and Pearlie showed up at the farm shortly after supper on Monday, October 30, with a four-layer chocolate-coconut cake studded with twenty-four striped candles. The boarders, ribbing Sid about not letting them know it was his birthday, gathered together in the dining room to sing "Happy Birthday" while Pearlie cut the cake. After serving up the last piece, she dabbed her eyes with the sleeve of her sweater and handed Sid a card.

"Thanks." Sid slid the card into his pocket. "Mind if I open it later?"

"That's fine," replied Pearlie.

Leaning down close to Sid, Otis lowered his voice. "Don't want to embarrass you, son, but we're sure glad you're back in Trinity Springs. Even if, well, you know . . . the circumstances and all." Straightening back up, Otis took his leave, Pearlie at his elbow.

After the Skinners were gone, Sid could feel everyone's eyes on him in expectation of what to do next. They had another thing coming if they thought he wanted to party. After having spent all day fixing a broken pipe in the barn, all he wanted to do was get away by himself and relax.

Pushing himself away from the table, he said, "Think I'll go up to the library and unwind. Thanks, everyone."

"C'mon, birthday boy." Ketch, shoveling down another piece of cake, garbled, "Let's celebrate."

"I'm burned out. Maybe another day."

"Hey!" Liz lit up. "The Sons of Champlain are playing tomorrow night at Digger's. It's Halloween. We could all go there and celebrate your birthday."

"Can we go somewhere else?" asked Mika. "I don't drink."

Ignoring her, Liz said, "Everyone in favor of going to Digger's tomorrow night, raise your hand—and Sid, you don't count. This is on us. We'll buy the drinks."

Ketch and Woolf raised their hands.

"Majority rules," said Liz. "Digger's tomorrow night, it is. Let's all be there at eight o'clock—in costume."

Mika frowned. "I don't celebrate Halloween either."

Rolling her eyes, Liz groaned. "Then I guess Sid will find out who his real friends are, won't he?"

"But that's not fair," protested Mika. "Just because . . ."

"Come on, everyone." Sid stood to his feet. "It's *my* birthday, right? I'm fine not doing anything, but if you guys insist, I'll meet you at Digger's tomorrow night. Don't expect me to be in costume, though. Not that I don't celebrate Halloween. It's just not my thing."

Shortly later, safely sequestered in the library, Sid lit a fire in the hearth and settled into his father's easy chair. Although his muscles ached, his mind was so wired, he couldn't relax.

What I wouldn't give for a joint right now. Just one toke. It was such a natural, simple pleasure to get ripped. That pot was illegal made absolutely no sense to him. If only he could snap his fingers and experience the sedative effects of being high. He spent at least ten minutes brooding over the injustice of it all before remembering the birthday card Pearlie had given him. Pulling it out of his pocket, he opened it. A crisp new $50 bill fell onto his lap.

Have a great birthday, Siddie, the card read. *We have faith in you. You're becoming the man your ma and pa knew you would be someday. Love, Pearlie and Otis. P.S. There's always free coffee for you at the diner if you ever come by.*

Sid slid the money into his pocket and toyed with the card, trying to decide what he should do with it. A twinge of nostalgia got the best of him. Rising from his chair, he opened the top drawer of his father's desk and looked for a suitable spot to store it. As he flipped through an assortment of papers, Mika's cat Greta, apparently locked out on the front porch, wailed for someone to let her in.

That cat. He was almost jealous of the stupid needy thing. There were times he felt so trapped by his circumstances, so hog-tied by the pain of his past, he wished he, too, could just sit on the porch and yowl his lungs out. As he finally slid the card into a pile of letters and pictures in the back of the drawer, one photo in particular caught his attention.

It was a picture of him and Max Quinn when they were boys. Having just climbed out of the water, they stood, wet and shivering—barely any fat on their bodies to keep them warm—on the edge of Ransom Creek.

Sid's eyes zeroed in on Kate, posing in cut-offs and a swim top in the background, off to Max's side. He remembered the day clearly because his mother, who was getting ready to spend a few days in Sonoma with her parents, had taken the picture just before she'd left. Kate had graduated from high school a week earlier and had brought Max out to the farm to hang out with him while his father was at work.

It was the very day he had fallen in love with Katherine Quinn—or what he'd thought, at the time, was love.

SID ARRIVED AT Digger's Saloon the next night at the appointed time. After paying the five-dollar cover charge to a bald, burly bouncer who eyed him with the kind of contempt rednecks often reserved for hippies, he elbowed his way through knots of boisterous revelers. Not seeing his roommates anywhere, he selected an empty table near the dance floor and sat down to wait for them.

A leathery-skinned, middle-aged waitress approached him. "Need to see your ID," she barked.

Sid flashed his stamped hand at her. "They already checked it at the door."

"Don't care. I'm double carding you tonight."

Leaning forward, Sid pulled his wallet out of his pocket and handed her his driver's license.

The waitress peered closely at the laminated card for a long time, all the while smacking a wad of gum between her front teeth. Finally, she returned it to him. "So, you just had a birthday. First drink is on the house. What'll it be?"

"A beer on tap." Sid slid his billfold back into his pocket. "Coors if you have it."

"You don't know who I am, do you?"

Sid studied her face a second. Her raccoon-like eyes triggered a distant memory. "You look . . . kind of familiar."

"The name's Peg Hopkins. My son, Frank, was about three years older than you."

"Oh, yeah—Frank. I remember him. What's he up to these days?"

Peg's expression imploded, deep creases in her forehead and cheeks collapsing into each other until her face was as creviced as a walnut shell. "He's asleep up in Calvary Cemetery," she snapped. "Go give him your regards sometime. He deserves it."

It took a few seconds for Sid to realize that she was telling him her son was dead. "I'm so sorry," he stuttered. "Really . . . I didn't know."

"Frank died serving his country. Not that you or your kind would care. Treated our boys like scum, you all did, when they came back home from Vietnam—instead of the heroes they were."

"The last time I saw Frank was in high school," stuttered Sid, stunned by the accusation. "I haven't been back here in years."

"Yeah, well look at you now—alive and well, with your long hippie hair and anti-American ideas while my son, God rest his soul, is wrapped in his country's flag, six foot under."

"Like I said, I'm really sorry."

"Sorry doesn't quite cut it." Peg turned her back on Sid and marched off, condemnation wafting off her like noxious fumes from a tailpipe.

Sid's defenses flared. Sure, he was against the war, but lumping him in with guys who supposedly spit on Frank when he came back home wasn't fair. He would never have done that to someone he knew. *Well, forget her. She's probably just one of those close-minded bigots who refuses to see the world through any lens other than her own; a typical reactionary. Doesn't she know it's attitudes like hers that push people like me into the counter culture?*

But then, replaying her comments in his mind, Sid's conscience was pricked. He recalled a particular anti-war demonstration he'd taken part in during his junior year at Berkeley that had gotten completely out of hand. He hadn't spit on anyone, *per se*, but in light of Peg's perspective, it suddenly occurred to him that the buckets of red paint he'd hurled at some ROTC recruits, accompanied by a barrage of curses and obscenities, had more to do with his own fired-up emotions than with the real issue of ending the war.

Yes, he was proud of being a pacifist. He believed peace to be one of the noblest goals of mankind. He idolized Gandhi. He'd mourned deeply the assassination of Martin Luther King Jr. But this new self-revelation, courtesy of Peg the Waitress, had nothing to do with overarching philosophies, or international politics, or enmity and bloodshed; rather, it was his own hypocrisy that dogged him. Peg's distrust of hippies was no different than his own preconceived notions of rednecks. Though he touted love and peace, he had thought nothing of attacking people who disagreed with him—like the ROTC soldiers at Berkeley—flesh-and-blood human beings with mothers who loved them.

Like Frank Hopkins. Dead-before-his-time Frank Hopkins. *This damn war. How many more deaths before it ends?*

A moment later, Peg reappeared with his beer, slamming it down on the table in front of him. "By the way, did you see that notice over there?" She pointed across the room to a tin sign nailed up near the entrance. It read: *Hippies Use the Back Door; No Exceptions.* "That's for all you long-hairs invading Trinity Springs. You might want to do what it says. No telling who might be waiting for you out in the parking lot when you leave tonight."

Swallowing down a belligerent response, Sid said, "I'll leave the same way I came in, thanks."

As Peg skulked off to take orders at another table, he made up his mind that as soon as he was finished with his drink, he would head home. But just as he swigged the last of his beer, he heard his name called. Turning, he saw Ketch jitterbugging toward him, his arms extended wide to display thin strips of fringe cascading down the sleeves of his leather jacket. The sight instantly lifted his spirits.

"Dig my costume?" crooned the Texan.

"Dig mine?" Sid pointed to his everyday denim work shirt.

Woolf, appearing in Ketch's wake, was decked out in army-issue fatigues, combat boots, a tie-dyed t-shirt, and a black fedora. Protruding from his mouth was a fat Cuban cigar. Sid tried, but couldn't imagine what kind of statement the vet was trying to make.

Seconds later, Liz materialized, shimmying past Ketch and Woolf. She tripped and nearly landed in Sid's lap before catching herself on the arms of his chair. Clumsily, she righted herself, a tipsy greeting clattering around her tongue and along her teeth like pool balls on a billiard table: *"Happy birthday, Sid, you handsome, handsome boy you!"*

Sid's jaw hit the floor. Liz was dressed totally out of character as Carmen Miranda with strappy metallic heels and a frilly, flowery wrap-around skirt exposing one of her thin thighs. Her glasses dangled crazily off the tip of her nose. She wore a bright silk turban, a clump of cheap plastic fruit glued to the top of it. Meeting his gaze, Liz raised one arm above her head and, with a dramatic flair, gave her hips an exaggerated swivel. "In case you're wondering, Carmen was my alter ego when I was a kid."

Just then, Mika appeared. Like Ketch and Sid, she wasn't in costume either. "Sorry I can't stay long, Sid," she explained. "I just wanted to swing by and wish you a happy birthday."

Ketch pulled her down into an empty chair next to him. "Relax, Meeks. You can stay for one drink."

"But I . . ."

A look of feigned helplessness spread across Ketch's face. "But I need you to help keep me in line tonight. Remember my angel? I can't afford to get in trouble."

"Well, all right . . . I guess I could stay just a little while."

"That's my girl." Ketch snapped his fingers at Peg and ordered a round of drinks for their table.

After they were served, Liz grabbed her margarita, read-justed her glasses, and pointed to a cluster of men lounging against the bar. "I've decided I need to be more assertive in *all* aspects of life. Catch you guys later."

Mika stared as Liz made a beeline to the bar and threw herself at a man masquerading as a pirate.

Ketch waved away her obvious concern. "Stop worrying, Meeks. She's a big girl."

A few moments passed. Suddenly Liz reappeared at their table, complaining that her mission to snag a man had failed. Then, she begged Sid to dance with her.

He looked over his shoulder. "You couldn't find any takers at the bar?"

"See that big pirate over there with the eye patch?" asked Liz.

"Yeah."

"I almost bagged him. Said his name was Jake. Jake Claw-something."

"Jake Clausen?"

"Um—sounds right."

Sid went cold. Jake Clausen, who'd always had a thing for Kate Quinn, had been the class bully in high school with a special, inexplicable hatred reserved for Sid. He couldn't count the times Clausen had made his life hell—threatening him in the hallways and after school, spreading lies about him, making him the butt of vulgar jokes. He'd even ambushed him after a football game once. If it weren't for Otis Skinner patrolling the streets that night, hearing the shouts and rushing to the scene, Sid was sure he would have ended up in the hospital.

"See the chick he's talking to?" continued Liz. "The one dressed like Pocahontas? She told me to get lost." Jabbing her thumb into her chest, she added, "Otherwise, he would have been *mine*."

Sid studied the woman, who appeared to be in a deep conversation with Jake.

As though she had just felt his presence in the room, Kate Quinn turned and locked eyes with Sid. Before he knew what was happening, she was at their table, Jake at her side. "Sid! Imagine seeing you here."

Sid stood to his feet. "It's been a while, Kate."

Reaching out, she playfully tucked his hair behind his ear. "Too long, don't you think?"

"Not if you consider what happened the last time we were together."

"Oh? Refresh my memory."

"That's the problem, Kate. I shouldn't have to."

The tension between the two flamed up so quickly and with such intensity, that Jake Clausen—built like a Mack truck with a temperament to match—lowered his arm protectively in front of her. "Is he hassling you, Kate?"

"Actually, yes," she smiled. "He is."

Without warning, Jake charged Sid, knocking him off his feet into a throng of unsuspecting patrons. Drinks spiraled into the air, glasses shattered, girls shrieked and cheers erupted as Jake began pummeling Sid.

Ketch whisked Mika to safety and rushed back to the scene. Strong-arming Jake from behind, he held onto him as Sid retaliated with a vengeance. Outnumbered two to one, it took Jake a while to break free. When he finally did, he tossed the Texan headlong into the jukebox. Then he charged after Sid again.

The band stopped playing. Under Jake's fresh assault, Sid's head began to snap back-and-forth so violently, he felt his brain rattle and go light, as though it were a light bulb flickering off-and-on in a thunder storm. Nearly at the end of his rope, he staggered backward, tripped over a chair, and crashed to the floor. Jake was over him in a flash. Renewing his salvo, he began kicking Sid with such force, he had to curl up in a fetal position and cover his head to protect himself. In the background, Sid thought he heard Mika screaming for Jake to stop.

He definitely heard Kate shout, "No, Max. Stay out of it!"

Seconds later, Jake's drubbing ceased. Sid waited a moment before lowering his arms. Then, lifting his head, he saw Max Quinn pulverizing Jake into submission. Those who had merely been bystanders before, now leaped into the fray, tossing chairs, bottles, and glasses at each other. The band dove behind the stage for cover. Some girls cowered under tables while others clung to their boyfriends, desperately trying to hold them back from joining the brawl. When the bouncer was unable to bust up the melee, he shouted to the bartender to call the sheriff. Within five minutes, Otis was at Digger's, blocking the entrance to the club so no one could leave.

A DISGUSTED SHERIFF Skinner herded the alleged perpetrators of the fight, along with some witnesses, into one of the bar's back rooms and closed the door. Accusations flew between the Clausen and Jackson camps, but when Otis finally deduced that Sid and Jake alone were at the bottom of the bust-up, he was furious.

"Sid was the one who started it," said Kate.

"That's right, sheriff," rasped Jake, clutching a bar towel to his still-bleeding nose. "I was just defending myself."

"I'll bet." Flipping his ledger open with a snap of his wrist, Otis began taking notes. He turned to Sid, whose face was already swollen and bruised. "What do you have to say for yourself?"

Before Sid could answer, Ketch said, "Sheriff, Sid didn't . . ."

"Did I ask you?" Otis's threatening tone silenced Ketch and anyone else thinking of defending Sid. Noticing Mika standing behind Ketch, he barked, "What in the world are you doing here? What happened?"

She pointed to Jake. "He started the fight."

"That's a lie," said Kate, jabbing her thumb at Sid. "He started it."

"That's not true," insisted Mika. "Jake hit Sid first. I saw it."

The sheriff turned to Jake. "Did you?"

"He was bothering Kate, Otis. What was I supposed to do?"

"Sid didn't touch her," said Mika. "They were just talking, and suddenly Jake freaked out."

Otis glanced at Kate's brother Max. Like most of the other patrons, he, too, was in costume—disguised, ironically, as a cop. "What about you, Quinn. How do you fit into all this?"

"I was an innocent bystander, Sheriff."

"Yeah? Why is your mouth bleeding?"

Max swiped his face with the back of his hand. "Guess that's what happens when you try to be a good cop and break up a little disagreement."

"Get out," growled Otis, sweeping his pen around the room to include Max and most of the other witnesses. "Sid and Mika, you stay. I'm not done with you yet."

Jake shot Sid a look that said they would meet at another time in a different place to settle their score and stormed off, Kate following close behind.

"And there'd better not be any more trouble coming from you, Clausen," Otis called out after him, "or you'll be spending time in my jail. Hear me?"

Over his shoulder, Jake yelled, "Loud and clear, Sheriff."

MEANWHILE, THE BAND picked up where they'd left off. Ketch, who had hung back from the others, nodded at Otis before exiting the room and signed to Sid that he would wait for him outside. Digger's thin walls and cheap ceiling fixtures began vibrating wildly in sync with the music. Through the half-open door where Ketch loitered, curious patrons peeked in to see what was going on.

His thumbs tucked into his belt, Otis said, "Sid, you can thank your lucky stars I didn't find you drunk, or Jake injured worse than he is. Otherwise, I'd have to include it in my report. All I can say is, you'd better hope Digger's insurance policy covers the damage you boys did tonight. What the hell were you doing here, anyway?"

"We were just celebrating his birthday," explained Mika, lamely, when no answer was forthcoming from Sid. "I mean, yesterday was his birthday, but . . ."

"Well, I would *know* yesterday was his birthday, wouldn't I?" Exasperation laced Otis's reply. Turning back to Sid he said, "Even though it's not against the rules of your probation, don't you know that being here is a flat out invitation for trouble? It's not even November yet. You've still got ten more months to go before you're free and clear. Not to mention Jake Clausen is a brainless bully who picks fights at the drop of a dime. What did you do or say to tick him off?"

"Nothing," muttered Sid.

"Come again?"

"Kate accused me of hassling her for something I said to her. That's all."

"What did you say to her?"

"I don't think that's any of your business."

Otis rocked back on his heels. "You're right. It's not. I was just hoping that with your cooperation we might avoid another blowup in the future . . . since who knows how long Kate is back in town for."

Rubbing his jaw, Sid winced in pain.

Mika stepped closer to inspect his face. "Are you all right?"

"I'm fine." Turning away, he asked Otis if he was finished.

"I guess we're done for tonight, but Digger's is going to be off-limits to you from now on. At least, until your probation is over. My orders." Snapping his ledger shut, Otis added,

"I'll take you over to Doc Simpson so he can get a look at your injuries, and then I'll take you home. You can come back here tomorrow to pick up your truck."

"I said I'm *fine!*" growled Sid, limping toward the front door. "I can drive myself home."

As Mika made a move to follow Sid out into the hallway, Otis stopped her. "Leave him be."

"Look at him, Otis. He can barely walk."

"There's no forcing someone to do what they don't want to do. Maybe you can talk some sense into him when you get back to the farm. My hands are tied on this one."

"But someone needs to be an advocate for him."

"And you don't think I am?"

Mika swung around. "Well, you didn't take his side. I'm telling you, Jake started the whole thing. Can't you arrest him for assault and battery or something?"

"I have no proof who started the fight. It's Sid's word against Jake's. Without more witnesses speaking up, or someone willing to press charges, there's nothing more I can do about it." Otis lowered his voice. "Besides, how do you think an incident like this would reflect on Sid's probation record?"

"I . . . never thought of that."

Otis lowered his voice. "It was the first thing I thought of."

"Oh." Chastened, but still ruffled by the injustice she felt on Sid's behalf, Mika turned to leave.

"One more thing," said Otis, blocking her exit again. "I want to apologize for my shock at seeing you here tonight. I just never imagined you being in Digger's of all places, caught up in a mess like this."

"Well, I'm sorry if I disappointed you, but maybe if you

would have told me about Sid's probation in the very beginning, before I signed the lease and moved here, I would never have been here tonight in the first place."

Although her disappointment with how Otis had orchestrated the farm rental agreements had been festering for weeks, it was the first time Mika had openly confronted him with it. It felt good to get it off her chest; that is, until she saw the sheriff's shoulders slump. Looking suddenly tired beyond his years, Otis gave her a fatherly pat on her shoulder, guided her out of the room, and then hurried past her to speak to the owner of Digger's, who was angrily assessing the damage done to his establishment.

Mika watched Ketch and Sid exit Digger's through the front entrance. Ketch had his arm draped protectively over Sid's shoulder, while Sid held what appeared to be a bag of ice over one cheek. Then, she spied Liz and Woolf standing together at the end of the long narrow corridor leading into the main room. To get to them, she had to brave a gauntlet of oglers lining the way like a hog line of fishermen glutting a salmon run. Taking a deep breath, she dodged their groping hands and slobbery propositions until she finally reached her roommates.

"How did you get here, Liz?" she asked.

"I didn't want to drive, so I hitched a ride to town."

"Well, I'm leaving now, so I can take you back home. I don't like the idea of you hitchhiking at night."

"C'mon, Meeks. For God's sake, it's 1972."

"I'm going to hang out here some more," said Woolf. "I'll give you a lift later if you want."

"Sure," said Liz. "Thanks."

Mika studied the vet. He seemed sober enough. Turning

back to Liz, she made a silent gesture that said, *"Are you okay with that?"*

Liz leaned close to Mika. "Woolf's cool," she whispered. "Stop worrying."

Mika dreaded having to retrace her steps back down the corridor to get to her car. Woolf must have picked up on her trepidation because he chugged his beer, set the mug down on the floor, seized Mika and Liz each by one arm, and escorted them down the hallway.

As they sailed outside, he said, "Liz and I'll make sure you get to the farm okay, and then we'll come back."

"You don't have to do that, Woolf. Really. I'm fine now."

"I insist."

Amazing the difference it makes having a guy like Woolf at our side in a place like this. After two months of living with the vet as her roommate, it dawned on Mika that she had never once allowed herself to be in a vulnerable situation with him. Even though she'd noticed his tenderness with animals, at least with Greta, she'd let his brooding silences and guarded behavior intimidate her. Now she realized how ungrounded her fears perhaps were. *Perhaps.*

Mika buckled herself into her car, started the engine, and slowly pulled out of Digger's parking lot, keeping Woolf's taillights in front of her. At least Woolf was making sure she and Liz got home all right. That was more than she could say for Ketch and Sid.

But then, Sid was so banged up he probably couldn't think straight.

And Ketch, well—she supposed she should be thankful he was tending to Sid. Someone needed to.

Calvary

THE NEXT DAY, SID FOUND HIMSELF WISHING he had heeded Otis's advice and seen Doc Simpson. At the very least, the town's doctor might have prescribed some pills to alleviate the screaming pain radiating from his left shoulder to his wrist every time he raised his arm above his head. He ran his tongue along the inside of his cheek. *Great.* Several of his back teeth seemed loose. His nose was swollen, as was his right eye, and his lower back spasmed whenever he tried to stand up straight.

Just great.

Although it wasn't too late to get checked out at the clinic, Sid's pride prevented him from giving anyone the satisfaction of seeing his battered body. In fact, it was pride that had prompted him to get up before dawn that morning to avoid contact with the boarders—Ketch being the exception. He owed him big time for coming to his rescue at Digger's last night.

Yes, sympathy from his roommates was the last thing he wanted. Which was why he now found himself driving aimlessly along a network of remote county roads, reliving the previous evening, trying to understand just how he'd gotten himself roped into a confrontation with Jake Clausen in the first place. Part of it was the look on Kate's face when she had told Jake he was harassing her.

She'd smiled.

That's Kate for you. I should have known better. She never smiles when she's happy.

When Kate was happy, he remembered, she'd get bedroom-eyed, slack-jawed, dopey looking—as though she was stoned out of her mind. It was when she had ulterior motives, or was stirring up trouble or inflicting revenge that she smiled. Like last year, when she'd first begun trying to convince him to plant pot on the farm. She was all smiles then.

Not that Sid could really blame her for him getting busted. After all, he'd been stupid enough to listen to her in the first place. But if Kate was anything, she was shrewd. In fact, he suspected that her idea that he plant marijuana was because she'd heard him talk so often of wanting to go to Europe someday. She'd told him that lots of people she knew were making a fortune growing pot, using the money to fund overseas trips.

He recalled her exact words. "I know more dealers than you do, Sid. A lot more. The minute you harvest your crop, I'll make sure the money's in your hands." Then came the clincher: "Like you, I've always wanted to go to Europe. Just think, we could go together if you pull this off."

Trekking through Europe with Kate at his side? Staying in grand hotels? Dining in great restaurants whenever it suited them? Seeing things he'd only dreamed of? The prospect of spending several intimate, adventuresome months with Katherine Quinn had been too much for him to resist, and she knew it. It simply had never occurred to him that if he were caught red-handed growing weed before it was harvested—which he had been—she'd walk away smelling like a rose while he, alone, paid the price.

As Sid maneuvered his truck back toward Trinity Springs, he berated himself for being blind to Kate's connivances, susceptible to her dark beauty. He had thought he was over her. Why, then, had he found himself still wanting her when he'd seen her at Digger's last night? Why had he cared that she was with Jake Clausen—or anyone else for that matter? Would he ever be able to look at her and not feel his heart race? He hated that when he was around her, he was like a junkie needing a fix. Yet, invariably, when she was gone he felt nothing but relief.

Cresting a hill, Sid snapped out of his reverie just in time to see the sign for Calvary Cemetery emerging from a break in the fog. Immediately, he pulled onto the gravel shoulder and killed the engine. He sat for a moment, stunned, not knowing what had come over him. Stopping at the graveyard had been an involuntary reflex, a knee-jerk reaction, and he was at a loss as to what to do next. Part of him wanted to run; restart his truck, peel out, and not look in the rear view mirror. But the other part of him couldn't budge.

The wind picked up. He shook his head. Tapped his ears. If he didn't know better, he'd swear he was hearing voices. Old legends and myths he'd heard as a child tugged at his memory; stories of people who'd seen, heard, and felt things—supernatural things—while visiting Calvary. He wasn't about to be cowed by local superstitions, but neither could he deny an unexplainable force pulling him toward the graveyard.

Inside the cab, it was so cold, he could see his breath.

Having left the house without a jacket, he reached into the backseat and grabbed an old Pendleton wool blanket. Throwing it over his shoulders, he stepped down from the truck and let himself be drawn, like a magnet to iron, through the gate and toward the center of the cemetery. There, a decaying wooden bench, positioned beneath the only tree in the enclosure, beckoned him. He shuddered, realizing that the last time he'd stepped foot in the graveyard was the day his parents had been buried there.

He took a seat and closed his eyes. A death-like stillness made it possible for him to hear the pounding of his own heart inside his chest. Three, maybe four, minutes passed before he reopened his eyes. As he did, he lifted his gaze and saw, no more than eight feet in front of him, his parents' black granite headstones. Ice crystals had accumulated in the lower corners of the carved lettering making their names—*Thomas Kingsley Jackson* and *Sofia Allegra Jackson & Unnamed Loved One*—appear larger, more gothic, than they were. The stark contrast of white on black, the remote location, the overwhelming sense of isolation, the exposed bark of the leafless tree he sat beneath, the biting frost, and the creeping fog—the otherworldly eeriness of it all shook him to his core.

A primal scream escaped from his throat. "*Why?*"

At his cry, a red-tail hawk perched in a giant hemlock near the edge of the graveyard shot from its roost. A brush rabbit feasting on frozen blades of grass between the burial plots dove into its nearby burrow.

"Why was I the only one to survive?" howled Sid again, his hands clenched into fists. "Why can't you be here now when I need you most—when Nonna and Nonno need you?"

In the midst of his grief, a blurry image of his parents' mangled remains flashed in his mind. Undone, he stumbled to the foot of their graves and collapsed, remorse overtaking his rage.

"Dad," he cried, his words mushed with pain, "I'm sorry for all the stupid grief I gave you before you died. And Mom—I'm sorry for not appreciating you more, for resenting you wanting another baby so badly. For fearing you'd love me less. I was so selfish. God, I'm sorry!"

He had no idea how long he lay there, his body spread-eagle over their graves, but glancing up at the bluing sky, he guessed he'd been in that position for the better part of an hour. With all emotion drained out of him, he struggled to his feet. Feeling curiously lightheaded, almost giddy, he tugged his ponytail over his shoulder. Holding it out toward the headstones, he smiled.

"What do you think of this?" he quipped. "Otis hates long hair, but I'm guessing you wouldn't mind so much. I'm still me, right? Besides, if you think I look different, you should see some of my roommates."

Just then, he noticed a small spray of end-of-season cabbage roses nested against his mother's headstone. Bending down, he examined them. Although frost had burned the blossoms, he wagered the wilted flowers had recently come from Pearlie Skinner's garden.

"So . . . " He sighed, straightening. "It looks like the Skinners have been better about keeping your memory alive than I have. Guess I owe them an apology, too. Maybe someday. I've had enough remorse today to last me a lifetime. I'll be back, Mom and Dad. I promise."

Lifting his hand to his heart, he bid farewell to his parents.

Then, turning from their graves, he retraced his steps back to the graveyard entrance. As he did, the wind died down and shifted directions, taking its gnawing whispers with it. Buoyed with new expectancy, he climbed into his pickup, the aches in his body noticeably diminished.

A purging had begun.

Catharsis was in the making.

He'd found a lifeline in the graveyard . . . of all places.

The Grotto

IN EARLY NOVEMBER, SHORTLY AFTER Richard Nixon overwhelmingly defeated George McGovern in the presidential election, some of the boarders found their own sort of lifeline—a perfect place to do drugs clandestinely. It started when Woolf, in one of his wandering moods, stumbled across a glade in the woods roughly a quarter mile from the west side of Ransom Creek. After he reported his find, Ketch and Liz returned with him to check it out.

They christened the place the "Grotto" and debated who they should let in on their secret discovery. It went without saying that Mika would never go there, and Sid couldn't— or at least he shouldn't. In the end, they told Sid about it in vague terms without giving him the precise location. They needn't have worried. Having grown up there, Sid knew exactly where the Grotto was. Mika, on the other hand, was left in the dark. The less she knew, they all figured, the better.

Within a week, Ketch, Liz, and Woolf had lugged river rocks up from the creek bed and built a fire pit in the center of the Grotto. The more time they spent there, the more they realized it was, indeed, an ideal place to party as it was only a ten-minute hike from the farmhouse. A narrow, easy path meandered from the opposite bank of the creek to a hollowed out limestone rock formation at the base of a steep hill. It provided a protective backside to the glen, which in turn, was surrounded by a semi-circular swath of old-growth fir trees interspersed with wild rhododendrons, each the size of a small elephant.

They also rigged a giant green canvas tarp between four sturdy trees, creating a canopy over the area to protect themselves from the elements. Their drug stashes, along with a supply of matches, lighters, bongs, and other paraphernalia, were stored in airtight boxes and wedged into a hollow in the trunk of a rotted-out cedar. Complete with a cooler they kept stocked with beer, a few woven plastic lawn chairs, some sleeping bags, and a folding aluminum camp table, the Grotto quickly became the preferred locale for their private bashes. It was rugged, yet comfortable, and safe from prying eyes. Most importantly, it wasn't on the farm, so any illegal activity that took place there technically had no bearing on Sid.

With Otis appearing unannounced for his weekly probation checks, they had all been on tenterhooks—paranoid that someone might slip up, and say or do something that would cause him to search the house more thoroughly. Now they could rest, knowing anything incriminating was stored safely, far removed from the premises.

Days after the Grotto's grooming was completed, the dry season ended, ushering in northern California's annual parade of storms that turned Trinity County into a mythical wonderland of glistening forests, steaming rivers, misty mountains, and swirling fogs. Ketch, surprisingly, wasn't in the least deterred by the cold rains, but the others were less appreciative. Liz whined that she had left Alaska to get away from such weather, never imagining that California was ever anything but sunshine and balmy temperatures. Woolf complained of feeling walled in, suffocated by the cloudy skies.

It was also about this time that Sid began to hear a voice in his head. Subtly, it said things like: *"Since you're never going to make it through the year anyway, you might as well go with Ketch and the others when they go across the creek to get high."* And, *"Is prison really the worst that could happen to you? You're already practically under house arrest on the farm."* Or, *"Surely, you could figure out a way to meet up with Max without Otis finding out. Max always came through with some pot when you needed it before."*

Then one night, shortly before Thanksgiving, after all the boarders except for Mika had escaped to the Grotto, the voice intensified. *"What could one joint hurt? Skinner will never know."*

Sid glanced in the direction of Mika's bedroom. The light escaping from beneath her closed door indicated she must be studying. *"She'll be in there all night,"* said the voice. *"She won't even notice you're gone. Go ahead. Join the others across the creek. Have some fun."*

Listening to the steady rain lash against the house, he gave in. *I'm sick of being inside all the time. I'm going to the Grotto.* Stepping into the mudroom adjacent to the kitchen, he pulled on his boots, grabbed a hooded, insulated jacket and flashlight, and started off for Ransom Creek. Just as he was passing near the barn, however, a car turned into the driveway.

It was Otis.

Switching off the headlights, the sheriff cracked his door open. "I was in the area and thought I'd stop by," he called out. "Heading into the barn to do some chores? I'll go with you."

"Sure." Sid glanced nervously across the creek.

Otis pulled the hood of his rain parka up over his officer's cap and eased out of his car.

"*Play it cool*," said the voice inside Sid's head. Taking the lead, he hurried to the barn and switched on the lights. Otis followed, peering around the dimly lit interior. Sid moved toward a mooing sound coming from one of the stalls while Mika's exiled cat, Greta, fat on barn mice, eyed them from a nearby rafter.

Otis, shadowing Sid to the stall, said, "How's that new heifer doing?"

Sid grabbed a handful of hay and began to feed the calf. "Fine. Thanks again for finding her for me, Otis."

"No problem. I figured Old Man Norton would sell her for a good price. He felt confident enough with your progress to trust you'd take good care of her. See? You getting involved with the Farm Bureau and connecting with local farmers as part of your probation is working in your favor, just like I knew it would."

Sid shrugged. "I guess. But I won't be getting any cows, in case you're wondering. This isn't a working dairy farm, Otis. It may never be."

"Well, neither was your daddy's, but he always said that when he retired he'd like to make the farm work for him as many ways as possible." Otis, apparently sensing Sid's discomfort, hurried to add, "So, what do you think of the heifer's name?"

"Hester? It's weird."

"Pearlie said Mrs. Norton named her after Hester in *The Scarlet Letter.* Hester Prynne, or something like that. It's supposed to mean 'second chances.' I guess the cow that birthed her miscarried its first calf. Pretty fitting, don't you think?"

"I suppose so. How old is she?"

"About a year, I take it. You'll have to find a bull to breed her."

"Why? I just told you not to count on me making this a long-term working farm . . . of any kind."

"What I count on is you working this farm as though it'll last a hundred years, regardless of who ends up owning it. That's the way we do business around here. That's how your pa would do it. Now, Bud Aikens has a prize bull he might lend you." Otis glanced at his watch. "Let's give him a call now and talk to him. I'll let you do the honor."

Sid stiffened. He imagined he could hear bouts of laughter echoing from across the creek. *Good thing it's raining hard. Hopefully, it'll drown out their voices.* Pulling his hood back over his head, he excused himself, telling Otis he'd be right back.

"I'll go with you," said the sheriff, taking up the rear.

Inside the house, Sid dug out the phone directory, opened it, and ran his finger down the column of A's until he found the number he was looking for. While he made the call, Otis wandered into the living room. Sid stretched out the extra-long cord on the phone as far as it would reach and watched as the sheriff lifted curtains, looked underneath pillows, opened and closed the lid to the grand piano, ran his hand along the top of doors and windows, and checked beneath the cap on the newel post at the bottom of the stairs. Then he walked back down the hallway and peeked into Sid's bedroom.

Returning to Sid, he said, "Get a hold of Bud yet?"

"No one answered," said Sid. "I let it ring a long time."

"How long?"

"I don't know. Really long."

"Well, knowing Bud, he's probably out doing chores. Try him again tomorrow." Otis paused, a puzzled look on his face. "Where is everyone, anyway? It's awfully quiet in here."

"Mika's in her room studying, and . . ."

Before he could finish his sentence, Liz burst into the house. Seeing the sheriff, she froze. Rivulets of water streamed down her parka onto the faded linoleum, creating a puddle at her feet.

Otis sized her up. "Something the matter?"

"I saw car lights pull up to the farm, and we wondered—I mean, *I* wondered . . ."

"Where were you in this weather?"

"Just . . . out . . . for . . . a . . . walk."

Sid stared at Liz's bloodshot eyes, a dead giveaway that she was wasted. How could Otis not notice?

"Now listen to me, Miss . . . uh . . . " said Otis.

"E-Eliza," she stuttered. "Eliza Drabek."

"A bit tipsy, Miss Drabek?"

"Well . . . "

"Let me remind you: what you do anywhere else is your business, but what you do here on this farm is *my* business. Remember, if you break your lease agreement, you'll have to find another place to live. Is that understood?"

"Yes, Sheriff."

"Well now, go about whatever it was you were doing. And

don't forget Sid here can't afford to have you boarders messing up his probation." Shaking his head, Otis said, "I've gotta run, Sid. Maybe next time I can stay longer, and we can do some catching up. What do you say?"

"Sure," said Sid, still shocked that Otis had thought Liz was drunk, rather than stoned.

Taking one last look around the kitchen, Otis tipped his cap to Liz, smiled, and ambled out the door. Both Sid and Liz watched as the sheriff neared his car, then hesitated and stopped. A second later, they saw Otis head toward the barn.

"Everyone's in the barn." Liz's voice cracked with dread. "We're busted for sure."

A few moments later, Otis re-emerged. Sliding into his car, he revved the engine and pulled out onto the rain-slick road. As soon as his taillights vanished over the hill, Sid and Liz raced outside. When they threw the barn doors open, no one was in sight, but music from a radio and a chorus of laughter floated down to them from the loft.

"Hey!" shouted Sid.

Ketch leaned over the edge of the railing above them. "Is Skinner gone?" he asked.

"He just left."

Hustling down the ladder, Ketch howled, "Man, that was a rush."

"What happened?"

"Well . . . " Ketch leapt off the bottom rung. "We were having a good time at the Grotto, and then Liz started bellyaching that she was cold, so we—"

"I did not!" snapped Liz. "It was dry enough underneath the tarp. I was just ready to come back."

"Anyway," continued Ketch, "we were almost back to the house when we saw Skinner's car and hightailed it into the barn."

Liz nodded. "I thought I'd better go in the house and find out was going on with you and then come back and let everyone know."

Sid shook his head. "Did it never occur to you that Otis might be able to tell you were high?"

"Did it never occur to you," said Liz, "that Otis is too much of a redneck to know what being stoned even looks like?"

"Trust me, Liz. He's a sheriff. He knows way more than he lets on."

Woolf's head appeared over the hayloft, Greta draped across his shoulders. "Relax, you guys. It was no big deal. We were all up here playing poker when Otis walked in."

"My idea, by the way." Ketch paused to pick some straw out of his hair. "Lucky thing I was carrying a deck of cards on me. I figured if the sheriff started nosing around, it'd look a whole lot better if we were doing something legit than just hanging out in here looking guilty as hell."

"I hate to admit it," muttered Liz, "but it *was* a brilliant idea."

"You bet it was brilliant," said Ketch. "Skinner moseyed on in here, heard us talking and asked what we were up to. I yelled back, nice and friendly-like, 'Woolf and I are up here in the loft playing poker, Sheriff. Wanna join us?' Of course, he didn't. Said he had work to do. Thanked me though, just the same." Looking over Sid's shoulder, Ketch paused. "Hey there, Meeks. What brings you out here in this weather?"

Looking small and pale in the glow of the barn's interior lighting, a dripping wet umbrella held up over her head,

Mika stood facing them, her face a mask of suspicion. "I could ask you guys the same question."

Ketch lifted the deck of cards he was still holding and snap-shuffled them with his thumb. "Poker. Wanna play?"

Disregarding his offer, Mika pointed to Sid. "Kate Quinn just called. I thought you were in the house, but when I couldn't find you, she asked me to have you call her back."

Woolf let out a whistle. "Is that the chick you and Clausen fought over in Digger's, back on Halloween?"

"Appears to be," drawled Ketch.

Sid shot Ketch a look that said "shut up" and hurried to usher Mika out of the barn. Huddled together beneath her umbrella, they raced toward the house. As they spoke, translucent puffs of condensation from their warm breath mingled in the frosty air between them.

"What did Kate say?" huffed Sid.

"She said it was important she talk to you."

"Did she give you her number?"

"She's at her brother's house. She said you know the number."

"You're sure she didn't say what she wanted?"

Reaching the mudroom, Mika lowered her umbrella. "Yes. Why do you ask?"

"Well, unless it's something really important, I don't think it's necessary to call her back."

"But I told her I'd have you return her call. I don't want her to think I didn't tell you."

"Fine." Sid didn't bother to remove his parka or pull off his boots. Tramping into the kitchen, he dialed Max's number and let it ring at least a dozen times.

Mika, emerging from the mudroom in her stocking feet,

looked at Sid's footprints on the linoleum and shook her head.

"There," said Sid, holding the phone receiver out to her before hanging it up on the cradle. "I called Kate, and no one answered. Are you satisfied?"

"I am. Thank you." Mika nodded toward the dirty floor. "It's a good thing you're on the schedule this week, because Liz would have a fit if she saw what you tracked in here." Leveling her gaze at Sid, she added, "And by the way, what were you guys doing out there in the barn? I felt like I walked in on a crime scene."

Sid gulped. He had agreed with his roommates that Mika should be kept in the dark about the Grotto. They all assumed she would eventually put two and two together and figure it out on her own. No fuss, no bother. No guilt-trips. Now he wondered if that was such a good idea. Seeing how perplexed she looked, and empathizing with how left out she might feel, it suddenly seemed cruel. Still, he didn't want to be the one to confess the ruse. "They were playing cards," he replied, lamely. "It must have been your imagination."

"I don't think so. I wasn't born yesterday, you know."

"If it makes you feel better, they don't tell me everything they do either." It was partially true. Ketch and Woolf and Liz had divulged few details about the Grotto, basically only telling him the general location of their hang out. He had simply deduced the rest.

"Whatever you say." Mika threw her hands up in surrender. Nonchalantly, she added, "Someone else must have been here earlier. I heard a car pull out of the driveway when I was on the phone with Kate."

"Otis stopped by. Anything else you want to know?" All

of a sudden, Sid felt completely drained, tired of everyone and everything, including himself. "Sorry," he said, squeezing past Mika. "I didn't mean to bite your head off."

Mika seemed stunned by his apology. "No, I'm the one who should be sorry. I don't know what got into me tonight. Maybe it's the rain, or—I don't know. Your life is none of my business. In fact, I've been thinking I should probably spend less time on the farm and more time at the school than I have been. I'm so different from everyone else here—the odd man out—and, well, I can't expect that all of you should feel like you have to walk on eggshells around me."

Surprised, Sid thought, *That's big of her.* But he was too relieved that she understood the situation to argue with her. "Good night, Meeks," he said, using her nickname as a peace offering. "And don't worry. I'm sure Kate will call back."

As Mika turned and made her way out of the kitchen, Sid was struck by the significance of their mutual separation from the other boarders. He and Mika were in the house, in different rooms, while the others were out together in the barn. And though Mika might feel like a square peg in a round hole, he was even more so. But, whereas Ketch, Liz, and Woolf were free to have a good time together—and Mika could hang out with people from her school—he was stuck in no man's land. He didn't know where he belonged anymore. He couldn't be in contact with Max; he couldn't even be with the only family he had left because he couldn't leave Trinity County while on probation.

A picture of Kate burst into his mind, and with it, an unwelcome urge to try calling her again, to ask her to come over and discuss in person whatever it was that was so important. Hanging his parka on the coat rack, Sid returned to the kitchen and picked up the phone. He started to dial her number, hesitated, and hung up, his heart racing.

No. I'd only be using her to fill a void in me. I've got to be firm. Then again, hadn't she used him plenty of times?

Resolutely, he turned off the light in the kitchen and stepped into the hallway. Maybe she had used him in the past, but he could still remember the real Kate—the Kate before she realized she could get anything she wanted with her looks. Before she'd decided that life owed her big time for a crappy upbringing; owed her for having a loser for a dad and a victim for a mother; owed her for sticking her in a dead-end town like Trinity Springs.

She might not have had any great talent and she was certainly no academic. But Kate Quinn used to be funny and carefree and full of life, with a heart as big as the sea—always the first to take a risk, first to apologize, and the first to lend a hand to those who stumbled while taking risks along with her. On the surface, at least, he recalled Katie as being a normal teen-age girl simply trying to find her way in the world.

That's the Kate Quinn I should remember when, and if, I see her again.

But until then—as though he were sitting at a table looking at a map of his life with a much older version of himself pointing out the dangers and pitfalls of what lay ahead—he understood that he'd be wise to discern the old from the new and leave well enough alone.

Thanksgiving

———————————

KATE NEVER CALLED BACK AND SID MADE no attempt to contact her. A new kind of discouragement settled over him in the days following the close call with Otis. It had been a long time since he had felt this aimless, this lackluster, this defeated. On the surface, he went through the daily motions of life, avoiding his roommates whenever possible, but internally, he found himself agonizing over his identity and his relationships.

What is it that prevents me from fitting in here—from fitting in anywhere? Sure, in Berkeley there were some who treated him like he wasn't hip enough because he didn't join the Weather Underground or shoot smack, but here in Trinity Springs, people treated him like a freak from another planet. *So, who am I, really?*

Perhaps the reason he felt like an imposter in his own skin, the reason he struggled so much to fit in wherever he was, was because he'd been forced to grow up faster than his peers. That's what his Nonna had told him shortly before his high school graduation. Before they had moved from Trinity Springs back to Sonoma to be closer to him while he attended Berkeley.

"Siderno," she had said, "you seem much older and wiser than your friends. You know why, don't you?"

"Yes, Nonna. You've told me many times."

"In Italy, my generation married young. We had children while we were yet girls and boys ourselves. We worked hard so we could eat. There weren't hospitals and department stores and movie theaters in every town like there are here. We expected nothing, but we were happy. Our lack made us appreciate what little we had. In America, you can't understand this because you really have no need. Not like we did. Without loss or hardship, your generation will never grow up. But you, Siderno, you have already lost what was most precious to you. It has made you into a man before your time. It is the only good thing that will ever come from my Sofia's death, God rest her soul."

At the recollection, doubt crept into him. Would he ever again be the boy who loved and trusted others and believed in himself 100 percent? He could barely remember what that was like, it was so long ago.

THE NIGHT BEFORE Thanksgiving, Sid found himself reminiscing over past Thanksgivings and lamenting the fact that his probation and his grandfather's ill health prevented him from spending the holiday with his grandparents. It would be only the second time in his life he wasn't with family on Turkey Day.

The first time was four years ago, during his first term in college. He had declined his grandparents' invitation to spend the holiday with them in Sonoma, deciding instead to return to Trinity Springs. Having been only recently turned on to drugs at Berkeley, and guessing that Max and Kate smoked pot, he'd looked forward to staying with them. That is, if they didn't have other plans. But when he phoned Max a few weeks before the holiday to tell him of his decision, he discovered Kate no longer lived with him.

"Yeah, you can spend Thanksgiving at our house," Max had told him. "We'll figure something out. I'll be here, but you know Kate. Not enough action here, so she split."

Sid recalled his disappointment. It was the first time he had admitted to himself that he had come to view Max as more of a connection to Kate than as a friend, though certainly, they were that. "Where did she go?" he asked.

"Last I heard, she's living down by you—somewhere in Berkeley."

"Do you know where?"

"No idea," said Max. "She's shacking up with some guy."

"Who?"

"How would I know? She comes and goes as she pleases. I'm not high on her list of confidantes. I suppose if our mom had it together . . . but . . . "

"Yeah, sorry about your mom, Max. Pearlie told me about her . . . problems. Look, I'll get back to you about Thanksgiving."

"Whatever. I'll be here."

A week later, the Saturday before Thanksgiving to be exact, Kate showed up at Sid's apartment—a funky, ant infested, two-bedroom duplex he shared off-campus with a political science major named Bryan.

"Max gave me your address," she told him, tossing her backpack on their secondhand Naugahyde couch and making herself at home. "I need a place to crash. Do you mind?"

"Not at all. But I thought—well, Max said you were living with someone."

"It didn't work out." The way Kate had looked at him when she said those words had made his heart skip a beat. He told himself it was stupid to think someone as beautiful and experienced as Kate would ever view him as anything other than the snotty-nosed kid she used to babysit.

It just so happened that Bryan had recently scored some acid and was at that moment in the process of getting ready to drop it. "Hey, I've got plenty," he said, holding up a pint-size plastic baggie of fine white powder to show Kate and Sid. "I'd rather not trip alone."

Kate jumped at the offer, but Sid, who had never dropped acid before, hesitated. "Come on, Sid," she coaxed. "You don't know what you're missing until you try it."

"Yeah, just run your fingers along the bottom of the bag when we're done and give it a taste," said Bryan. He passed the bag to him after he and Kate took some for themselves.

Sid scooped some up and hesitated, not sure what to expect.

"Go ahead, lick it," laughed Kate.

Sid ran his powdery fingers across his tongue.

"That wasn't enough to do squat," protested Bryan. "Here, take some more."

Sid did. Quite a bit more.

Experiencing no effects at first, Sid told Kate he was going to his room to change the sheets for her. When she told him it wouldn't be necessary, he insisted, saying he'd be fine sleeping on the couch until she could find somewhere else to live. The gesture made him feel noble, as though after all these years, the tables had turned, and he was now the mature one.

Meanwhile, Bryan had dimmed the lights and stacked

some records on the turntable. "Just wait, Sid. You'll be flying high soon. It's going to blow your mind."

The first rush came half an hour later, so hard and strong, it knocked Sid off his feet. He and Bryan and Kate laughed until their jaw muscles ached and their skulls prickled with ecstasy. But then Sid's rushes began accelerating until he found himself swimming in a vortex of crazy fantasies. Bryan, immersed in his own hallucinations, came down from his high around dawn the next day. But Sid didn't crash until much later.

When he finally awoke, he found himself in bed with Kate. Sprawled out naked next to him, she was asleep, her dark hair fanned away from her face in sea-like waves. She looked for all the world like a mermaid sculpted on a ship's bow. Bending down to kiss her, he noticed a trail of chartreuse bruises spiraling down both of her arms.

With a start, Sid forced himself out of the memory—mainly because he had discovered, at a graduation party three years later, that he wasn't the only one who had shared his bed with Kate that night. He'd spent weeks recuperating from the acid trip, skipping classes and avoiding people as much as possible. Then, another memory rushed in to take its place—this time of a conversation he had overheard between his father and mother shortly before the car accident that had killed them. They were discussing whether they should continue trying to have another child.

As clearly as if they were there in the room with him, he heard his father say, "Sofia, don't lose heart yet. If we don't give up, we win."

To which his mother replied, "I'm not giving up, Tom. I'm letting go. It's not the same thing."

"How is it not the same?"

"Giving up is turning your back on a problem and living with the regret of not seeing the breakthrough that might have happened had you stayed the course. Letting go doesn't lose sight of the problem. It just frees you to live without any expectations."

Letting go.

Those were the last words reverberating in Sid's mind when he finally fell asleep that night. The next thing he knew, he awoke to the smell of turkey roasting in the oven, a vision of flickering shadows swirling outside his sunlit bedroom window, and the sound of Ketch teasing the cooks in the kitchen.

"Sid!" called Mika. "We're waiting on that famous Italian turkey dressing you've talked so much about."

"Yeah!" shouted Liz. "We didn't stuff the bird 'cause you promised you'd make it. Get on down here!"

"Take your turkey farts outside, Ketch."

Everyone around the table howled at Liz's mock outrage.

Sid couldn't resist laughing with them. And that simple act of letting go—of joining in lighthearted banter rather than focusing on himself as he'd been doing the last few days—was so liberating, it felt like a dam bursting in his brain.

"So, what do you think?" asked Liz, passing the bowl of mashed potatoes around the table a second time.

Ketch heaped a double portion on his plate. "Best spuds I've ever had—bar none."

"Seriously?"

"Would I lie? But I have to hand it to Sid. The dressing was off the charts, buddy."

"No kidding," said Woolf. "What's in it anyway?"

Sid recounted the ingredients he'd learned from his mother. "Italian sausage, sourdough bread, pancetta—"

"Pan what?" muttered Ketch.

"Pancetta. It's Italian bacon, but there's not much of it around here, so I actually just used regular bacon. I also added garlic—a lot of it—fresh sage, rosemary, basil, some parmesan and, uh, chicken broth and white wine."

"It's amazing." Mika rose from the table. "I want the recipe so I can make it next year. How were you able to keep it so moist?"

"Easy." Sid shrugged. Clearly, his kitchen, at least, was no longer cursed. "Just covered it really well and slow-cooked it."

Mika went into the kitchen and returned moments later balancing two pies in her hands; deep-dish pumpkin and caramel pecan. Pearlie, she explained, had sent them home with her from the café the night before. Her announcement was met with a round of moans. Sid couldn't imagine eating one more bite, but then he wasn't going to decline one of Pearlie's famous desserts either.

Setting the pies on the sideboard, Mika sliced them up and placed them on individual plates. "Oh, by the way, Sid," she said, "Pearlie wanted me to tell you that she would have had all of us over to their house for dinner today, but Otis is on call, and their dining room isn't big enough for everyone. Plus, the café's closed tomorrow for a minor repair. Most people will be eating leftovers anyway." Scraping some gooey pecan filling from the pie server back into the dish, she added, "I sure feel sorry for them spending the day alone."

"I do, too." Sid took the plate Mika offered him. "Maybe some of us should go over and visit them after dinner."

"Yeah, after you guys do the dishes," said Liz.

"Excuse me?" Ketch howled with laughter. "It's your shift this week."

Liz's untamed eyebrows shot up over the frames of her glasses. "Back me up, Mika. The guys are cleaning up, right?"

Mika shoveled the last bite of pie into her mouth and set her fork down. "Sounds fair to me."

A moment later, after the girls had vacated the dining room, Sid rose from his seat and started stacking dirty dishes. "Go on, Ketch. I'll take care of it."

"Nah," said Ketch, his voice low. "I need to talk to you about something anyway. It's private, and it'll take a while."

"Oh yeah? What's it about?"

"A little girl named Annabelle and her messed up daddy who could use some advice."

Perplexed, but also intrigued, Sid said, "I'm no expert on kids. Sounds like you need to talk to someone who is."

"What I need," said Ketch, soberly, "is a friend and an ally—someone I can trust."

Several hours later, Mika stood knocking on the Skinners' front door.

"What are you doing here?" exclaimed Pearlie, pulling her into her arms. "We just finished dinner. Would you like something to eat?"

"We just had a big meal at the farm. Thanks anyway."

Otis, dressed down in stonewashed Levis and a San Francisco 49ers sweatshirt, lumbered into the entryway, his eyes nap-swollen. "What brings you here tonight, Mika?" he asked, taking her coat and hat from her, while Pearlie slipped into the kitchen to get her something to drink. "Everything okay?"

"I just felt like getting out of the house and paying a visit. I . . . we all . . . felt bad you two were alone on Thanksgiving."

"Well, that's real thoughtful of you." Otis hung Mika's things in the hall closet and led her into the living room.

Taking a seat on the sofa, she said, "Sid said to tell you he'll come by soon. He had some chores to do first."

Otis called out to the kitchen, "Did you hear that, Pearlie?"

Pearlie appeared with a mug of steaming-hot coffee and handed it to Mika. "Sid might come over?"

"Actually, it was Sid who suggested it." Mika blew into her drink a moment before taking a sip.

"I'm surprised." Pearlie plopped down next to Mika.

"Me, too. Although, I have to say, I've seen some changes in him lately."

"Oh? Tell me about it."

"Maybe I'm imagining it, but even though he's been kind of withdrawn lately, he seems to be . . . softening. Like he has less of a chip on his shoulder or something. I don't know how to explain it."

Otis leaned forward and fixed his eyes out the window toward the street. "When do you think he'll be here?"

"He got into a long conversation with Ketch before I left, and then he still had some chores to do, so I don't know. Maybe an hour?"

Otis fell back into his chair. "Well, you're here now. We appreciate it, don't we, Pearlie?"

Pearlie patted Mika's hand. "We sure do."

"The truth is," said Mika, "the holidays are making me homesick. This is the first year I haven't spent Thanksgiving in Iowa with my family."

"Don't you worry now," said Pearlie. "We're here for you this year."

"We sure are." Otis leaned sideways to remove a pipe from a rack on the side table next to him. It was a Billiard imported Briar pipe, he noted proudly, pointing to his initials carved on the stem. He opened a small tin with the words *Samuel Gawith—Curly Cut Tobacco* inscribed on the front, filled the bowl to the brim, tamped it down, and placed the stem of the pipe loosely between his teeth. Reaching for a match, he lit it. "Sid's daddy gave me this pipe for my birthday, just before he died. Tom Jackson was one of the best friends I've ever had."

"And Sid's ma was one of the best friends *I* ever had," said Pearlie. "But then, Otis and I count a lot of folks in Trinity Springs as friends, don't we, Otis?"

He nodded. A pungent vanilla-spice aroma began to fill the room. "Though when you're the sheriff of a town, you're never quite sure if the feeling's mutual. We've got our church family, of course—good, decent folk. They'd give us the shirts off their backs if we asked. Still, it's a common fact that some people, God-fearing or not, will always place restrictions on your friendship. They'll say one thing to your face, then something else behind your back."

"That's why we usually spend our holidays alone," explained Pearlie. "People tend to get jealous and talk if you're partial to others. We can't afford to do that, what with Otis being sheriff and all."

"We learned our lesson with the Jacksons, didn't we, Pearlie?" Otis had tilted his head back and was now staring up at the ceiling, where the halo-shaped smoke rings he had exhaled were about to disintegrate.

"What lesson was that?" asked Mika.

Playing with the corner of her apron, Pearlie said, "We learned that true friendship's a sacrifice. If it comes easy, it probably ain't real. And we found out that real friendships can be a threat to people. Especially if the friendship is with someone who's not their kind. It doesn't make sense to them. You see," she added, "me and Otis were different from Sid's parents in a whole lot of ways. There were some who hated that we got along so well despite of it."

"How were you different?"

"For one thing, although neither of them ever put on airs, Sid's parents were a cut above most folks in Trinity Springs. Kind of like that show *Green Acres*, you know, except Sofia was nothing like Eva Gabor. Tom Jackson was an educated man. It showed in the way he walked and talked and ran the farm. Even in the thick of doing chores, you wouldn't guess he was farming by the looks of him—so cool and gentleman-like. And Sofia, well she was just plain smart and classy. The only place you'd ever see her in jeans was at home. Otherwise, she dressed like a movie star—make-up, hair styled just so, heels, nylons, the latest fashions." With a chuckle, she added, "Just like me. Right, Otis?"

Otis pointed his pipe at his wife, scolding her for her self-deprecation. "Now, Pearlie, like I've always said, you're beautiful just the way you are. But you're right as rain about Sofia. Women were jealous of her because she was such a beauty. Let me tell you, Mika, Pearlie was about the only one in town who didn't see her as a threat."

Mika studied Pearlie, who had closed her eyes as though

she were picturing Sofia Jackson in her mind. It didn't surprise her in the least that Pearlie would befriend someone other women avoided. In fact, for all she knew, the mindset in town still existed, and people were at this moment criticizing Pearlie behind her back for being friendly with the "hippies" living on the Jackson farm.

Otis gazed at the embers glowing in the bowl of his pipe. "Sounds strange," he muttered, "but I think it's why the Jacksons and us got along so well."

"You mean, because of your differences?" asked Mika.

"That's right. Like peanut butter gets along with jelly."

Pearlie opened her eyes. "More like bacon and eggs, I'd say."

Otis grunted. "No difference."

Mika glanced at the tawny brew in her cup. She couldn't imagine drinking coffee without cream.

"Sofia loved my cooking," continued Pearlie, "so I taught her how to cook American dishes, and she taught me her Italian ways. She made the best ravioli this side of the Sierras. I suppose you've tasted Sid's cooking by now."

"Yes, I have. Wow. And I thought I was a good cook!"

"Can you imagine what the three of us could do if we pooled our culinary talents together?" Laughing, Pearlie leaned back into the sofa and crossed her arms. "Many was the time Otis and I would go over to the Jacksons' for dinner, and little Sid would be right in the kitchen next to his mama, insisting she let him cut the vegetables, carve the meat, taste the soup, and serve the salads. It was the cutest thing to watch him follow Sofia around, hanging on her every word, asking her a million questions, begging her to let him take the bread out of the oven and slice it. Why, I even let him come down to The Pearl sometimes and work with me in the kitchen, thinking that someday he might have a restaurant of his own. If he would just . . . " Pearlie put her finger to her lips. "Whoops. Gossip's the devil's talk. I've said enough."

Otis rushed to fill the gap in his wife's monologue. He told Mika that the town's people had been intimidated by Tom Jackson because he was a judge. "They held him at arm's length," he said, "so I took him under my wing. Showed him secret fishing holes and told him where to find the healthiest livestock, hire good help, and get the best deals on construction materials for the farm. Tom was an honest, decent man with more drive and determination than all the residents of Trinity Springs put together."

"We learned a lot from them," said Pearlie, leaping back into the conversation. "Sofia taught me a few songs on the piano and how to grow perfect cabbage roses. Tom got Otis interested in reading again. See those books over there on that shelf? And that there family Bible? Tom and Sofia gave it to us when they asked us to be Sid's godparents." Tilting her head so that her face was close to Mika, Pearlie lowered her voice. "Sofia was raised Catholic, of course, and Tom called himself an agnostic, but that didn't stop them from making decisions based on what they thought was best for Siddie."

"You're Sid's godparents?" Mika gaped at Pearlie. "But you're . . . "

"Baptists. Yes. Don't even believe in infant baptism. Believe me, it was no small sacrifice on our part, but we did it out of love for Tom and Sofia."

Otis tapped his emptied pipe into a silver and plaid beanbag ashtray. "A few folks in our own church wouldn't talk to us after we agreed to be Sid's godparents. Oh, our pastor defended us," he hurried to add. "He reminded everyone that 'love covers a multitude of sin.' Not that we were necessarily sinning, mind you. Most agreed with him, but it didn't matter to the others who already had their minds made up. When we weren't kicked out of our congregation for our 'transgression,' the ones who still had a problem with it left the church."

It took a moment for Mika to absorb all she was hearing. "Tom Jackson must have believed *something* if they had Sid baptized."

"Maybe. Me and Pearlie thought so." Otis rolled his head around, as though trying to get a kink out of his neck. "Tom was never a man to shrink back from what he didn't understand. A mighty deep thinker, he was. Said it came from having to make some tough decisions about his family. The Jackson clan back East weren't what you'd call 'close.'"

"You can say that again." Pearlie shook her head. "The way Tom's parents treated him was downright shameful. His mother cared more about what her country club friends thought of her than her own children. His dad was no better. It's an absolute wonder Tom turned into the man he did considering what heartless parents he had. Why—"

"Pearlie . . ." warned Otis.

"Well, Otis, you know it's true."

"Just because it's true doesn't mean Mika needs to know about it."

But Pearlie's indignation had built up far too much steam to be diffused so quickly. "And as if having his own parents disown him wasn't bad enough," she continued, "Tom had to deal with his share of no-good backstabbers right here in Trinity Springs, too. I swear . . . "

"Pearlie, that's enough."

"Well, Otis, he did. And when Tom and Sofia died—Oh Lordy, what a day that was. You should have heard the talk."

"Pearlie!"

Pearlie's lips clamped shut in a pout. *Humphing* out of her chair, she took Mika's empty coffee cup and retreated to the kitchen, grumbling under her breath the entire way. Less than a minute later, the telephone rang.

Mika heard Pearlie say, "Hello?" and then gasp loudly, "Sweet Jesus! We'll be right there."

Without knowing what the call was about, Otis shot up from his chair and raced into the hallway. Grabbing his jacket and gun holster, he buckled up.

Pearlie rushed out of the kitchen. "That was Doc Simpson. Kate Quinn's been hurt. He wants us to come over right away." Opening the hall closet, she retrieved a wool jacket and muffler and slipped them on. "Mika, before you leave, give Sid a call," she cried as they tore out of the house. "Kate asked to see him. Tell him to go to Doc Simpson's. And don't bother locking the door."

Kate

KATE LAY ON DOC SIMPSON'S EXAMINATION table, her eyes scrunched shut, her lips pursed in pain. She shook violently beneath several thin, hospital-issue cotton blankets. A thin gash curved down her right temple and along her hairline to the bottom of her ear. Her entire right cheek was tinted the color of moldy bread. As Otis and Pearlie approached her, she turned her face to the wall. "Go away," she groaned.

Undeterred, Pearlie stationed herself next to the bed. "I'm not going anywhere until I see you up and at 'em, Kate Quinn."

From the sink where he stood washing his hands, Doc Simpson motioned for Otis to come near. "Max brought her in an hour ago," he said, in a hushed tone. "He couldn't, or wouldn't, tell me what drugs she's been doing, but I'm pretty sure they have something to do with her condition. Particularly, the uncontrollable shaking she had."

"Where's Max now?" asked Otis, moving back toward Pearlie.

"Well, with their dad passing away late last night, I told him he might as well go home." Drying his hands on a paper towel and tossing it into the trashcan, he added, "I told him I'd call when Kate's ready to leave."

"Eamon Quinn died! How did we not hear about it?"

"Being as it's Thanksgiving, the word hasn't spread far yet. I'm sure by tomorrow it'll be all over town."

Pearlie glanced at Doc Simpson and mouthed the word, "How?"

Dean pointed to his heart.

Leaning down over the patient, Pearlie whispered, "Oh, Katie, honey. I'm so sorry."

Kate growled incoherently.

The doctor drew closer to Pearlie and Otis, his voice low again. "All Max would say is that he found her in her bedroom like this. Her wounds, however, were dirty—consistent with injuries clearly suffered outdoors. I cleaned a good deal of mud and debris from her cuts, and her hands were scraped as though she'd been running through the woods. Her hair was full of leaves and bits of moss. I even found pine and fir needles between her toes, even though she was wearing shoes when Max brought her in."

"So either Kate made her way back to her house after being outdoors somewhere, or . . ."

Doc Simpson finished the sheriff's sentence. "Or Max is lying."

"If he's lying, what was he trying to hide? Whose tracks would he be covering?"

"That's your department, Otis. I'm just the physician."

"How did Max look to you?"

"Like he just crawled out of bed. But then, with his dad passing only last night . . ."

Otis's eyebrows squirrel-tailed together. With a nod toward Kate, he asked, "Will she be okay?"

"She's shaking less now than when she was first admitted,

so that's an improvement, but marks on her arms indicate she's used needles in the not too distant past, which opens up a can of worms . . ." Doc Simpson shook his head. "Nothing's broken, though. I patched her up as best I could. I'll keep her under observation a bit longer until I feel comfortable releasing her."

The door into the examination room opened and Ellie Simpson entered, carrying a tray filled with teacups and a pot of boiling water. "Oh, Pearlie and Otis—so glad you're here! Isn't this just awful? What a Thanksgiving! Would you like some tea?"

As Ellie prepared their drinks, the foursome stood around Kate's restless form, comfortable in silence as old friends are apt to be who enjoy a long, shared history. Doc Simpson and his wife had moved to Trinity Springs the same year as Tom and Sofia Jackson—over twenty years ago.

A no-nonsense sort of man, Dean Simpson was still the only doctor in town, his office taking up the back half of their sprawling stone and stucco Craftsman bungalow. With the nearest hospital over sixty miles away in Redding, the Simpson clinic was often the first and last stop for many of the townspeople suffering minor medical conditions and injuries.

Otis finished his tea and handed his cup back to Ellie. Bending down toward Kate, he said, "Katie girl, can you tell me what happened?"

"Nothing. Nothing . . . happened."

As weak as her reply was, it was a sign Kate could hear him and had the presence of mind to respond. "But something did happen to you, Kate," insisted Otis. "Something bad. What was it?"

When Kate refused to answer, Pearlie pushed a clump

of Kate's matted hair out of her eyes. "How about some tea, sweetheart?"

"Yes—please."

Doc Simpson took Kate's wrist and checked her pulse. "Back to normal. Okay ladies, help Miss Quinn sit up, but take it slow and easy and don't raise her too high. You may have to help her with her tea."

Pearlie and Ellie boosted Kate into a quasi-sitting position. When Katie's trembling hand failed to grasp the cup they offered her, Pearlie lifted the tea to her lips and coaxed her into drinking it all.

"Remember now, Katie," said Otis, sidling up next to his wife. "All of us here are old friends. Did any of this have to do with your dad's passing?"

"Thanks. I'm done." Katie shoved the teacup away, her hand suddenly appearing steadier. "My old man dying means nothing. I had a little fall is all."

"Doc Simpson seems to think drugs might have been involved with your . . . mishap."

Kate pushed herself into a fully upright position. "I want to go home now."

Dean objected, saying he'd have to check her vitals again.

He took her temperature: 98.6.

He listened to her heart. "Good."

He studied her hands and feet, fingers and toes. "Tremors —pretty much gone."

"Katie," he said, "your vitals are back to normal, but I'd like to keep you here awhile longer for observation. Just to be on the safe side."

"I need to go home," insisted Kate, attempting to stand up. "*Now.*"

"Steady now." Dean grasped Kate's elbow. "If that's what you really want to do, I can't stop you. At least let me call your brother to come pick you up."

Rushing to help the doctor, Otis said, "That won't be necessary. Pearlie and I can take her home."

As Ellie bustled about gathering gauze, tape, ointment, antibiotics, and aspirin for the patient to take home, Pearlie helped Kate put her coat on. Another anxious glance passed between the doctor and sheriff.

"Okay now," said Doc Simpson. "I'll need to see you tomorrow to check on that head wound of yours, Kate. Just call when you get up, and we'll make an appointment for you to come in. In the meantime, be sure to contact me if you begin to feel lightheaded or dizzy. I'll call Max in a bit and give him some instructions for your care."

The expression on Kate's face froze, as though she were digging for a thread of a thought she had lost and couldn't retrieve. "Max? No, no. I need Sid." Looking wildly at Otis, she said, "Did anyone call Sid?"

No sooner had Kate asked about Sid, but he entered the examination room. Taking one look at her bandaged head, he instinctively pulled her into his arms. "What happened?"

She clung wordlessly to him for several moments before finally letting go. "Take me home."

"Pearlie and I were just getting ready to take her," said Otis. "Maybe you could stay here, Sid, and let the doctor fill you in." Dropping his voice to a near whisper, he added, "Her pa died last night. Heart attack."

Kate reached for Sid again. "I'd rather Sid took me home."

Otis hesitated. "All right, but remember, Sid: no interaction with Max. Just drop Kate off and leave." Then, turning toward Pearlie, he asked if she was ready to go.

Pearlie nodded. "Yep, but can you go out and start the car first, Otis? I'll be out in a minute." While Otis headed outside, and Ellie and Doc Simpson went over final post-care instructions with Kate, Pearlie led Sid into the waiting room. "Kate's all doped up. Any idea what she's on?"

"How would I know? What did Doc Simpson say?"

"He wasn't able to tell for sure. She was tight-lipped around us. Wouldn't say how she got so scratched up either. Maybe you could get to the bottom of it. For her sake, you know."

Sid tried, but he couldn't conceal his concern. "What do you mean, 'for her sake'?"

Pearlie hushed him. "Not so loud. Dean's got some red flags about some of the marks on her body. What if it wasn't an accident like she said? What if someone did this to her? What if she tried to kill herself?"

Kill herself? In a million years, Sid would have never pegged Kate Quinn as being suicidal—ever. "Other than our run-in at Digger's," he said, "I haven't had anything to do with Kate since she's come back to Trinity Springs. Honestly, I have no idea what she's been up to."

Jabbing her thumb in the direction of the examination room, Pearlie said, "Wouldn't have been able to tell it by the looks of that little display of affection between you two back there. What was that all about anyway?"

A quick honk from Otis's car signaled it was time for Pearlie to wrap it up. Pulling her gloves on, she said, "All I'm saying, is keep your eyes and ears open. Maybe you could ask Max a question or two real quick when you drop her off at the house." Glancing over her shoulder at Kate, who was being helped into the hallway by Ellie and Doc Simpson, she sighed. "I never thought I'd see the day when drugs would entice young folk in this town like flies to flypaper. What is the world coming to anyway?"

Turning back to Sid, she whispered, "Don't get me wrong. I love Katie Quinn. I really do. Lord knows there was many a time I wish I could have just scooped her up from her situation at home and adopted her. But watch yourself around her. It's obvious she's looking for love in all the wrong places. Even if she found it, I doubt she could keep it long."

"Why would you say that?"

"Because she doesn't feel like she deserves to be loved. It's plain as day."

Before Sid could reply, Kate was in the waiting room with them. He held his elbow out to her as Doc Simpson passed her off, while at the same time, Ellie gave him a small white paper bag containing Kate's medications. Pearlie pulled the collar of her coat up around her neck and, telling Kate she'd pray for her, she left.

Kate melted into Sid's side.

"I know I've said it a million times," said Ellie, her forehead furrowed with concern, "but please call Dean or me at any time if you have questions or need something, Kate."

"Thanks, Ellie. I appreciate everything you've done for me already."

Doc Simpson held the door open as Sid half-carried Kate over the threshold and onto the porch. Then he followed Sid to his truck. "Sorry Ellie and I haven't come up to visit you since you've been back, Sid. It's no excuse, but we really have been incredibly busy."

Sid eased Kate into his truck. "I understand."

"I thought, maybe, you were going to pay me a visit a few weeks ago after that brawl I heard you had at Digger's. I almost called you to see how you were doing. Your injuries must not have been too bad, I take it?"

Sid closed Kate's door and turned back to Dean. "I survived."

The doctor followed Sid as he made his way around the hood of the pickup. "I just want you to know that Ellie and I are here for you," he continued. "We loved your parents and cared about them—and we care about you, too."

Sid shot Dean a look of bewilderment. Then it hit him— the way the doctor's voice had softened, the concerned slant of his eyes, the downturned mouth, his slumped but tense bearing, the patronizing hand on his shoulder. Recollections of the moments and hours following his parents' deaths surfaced in his memory.

He shrank back from the doctor's touch. "I don't recall you caring about me after the accident," he blurted. "Nobody did."

"Why, what do you mean?"

"No one cared what I was going through the day my parents died. I might as well have been invisible. Everyone treated me as though I was just a dumb kid; a nuisance, an afterthought. No one bothered to ask me if I wanted to view my parents' bodies before they were buried. And after their funeral it was almost like they never existed. People assumed my grandparents would help me pick up the pieces, but they would break down at the mere mention of my parents' names and run off to their room. Either that, or pretend nothing had changed—probably because they didn't want to upset me. It was like I'd been exiled to this land of shadows, this fake reality, to deal with my grief on my own."

"Sid, believe me, I had no idea." Dean looked stunned. "Everyone meant well, I assure you. We all felt terrible for your loss. Tom's and Sofia's deaths were devastating for us as well. For the entire town."

"That's the problem. People felt sorry for me, so they avoided me. I not only lost my parents that day, I lost everyone else. Other than my grandparents and the Skinners, Max and Kate were the only people who stayed in close contact with me."

"I'm sorry, Sid. I truly am. I never knew you felt that way."

"How could you know? You never asked." Sid slid into the driver's seat of his truck. "I've got to go, Dean. Thanks for patching Kate up."

As he pulled away from the curb, Sid rolled down his window, stuck out his arm and waved goodbye to Dean. He assumed the doctor saw it for what it was—a conciliatory gesture meant to soften his harsh words. He hadn't meant to be so blunt, but then, he hadn't banked on any of this— Kate's injuries, his outburst about the aftermath of his parents' deaths, how it had all been handled . . .

And all of this happening on Thanksgiving night.

One of his favorite days of the year.

WHEN THEY ARRIVED at Max's house, Kate refused to get out. She told Sid that although she was beginning to feel better from the medication she'd taken before leaving the clinic, she needed a bit more time to pull herself together. Max, she also told him, had taken their father's death much harder than she had, and she simply wasn't ready to deal with it, or her brother, quite yet.

"Go figure," she said. "You know what a bastard my dad was. Why would Max care so much now that he's gone? You'd think he'd be happy."

"Maybe it's the finality of it that's bothering him." Sid lowered his head in an attempt to see into the Quinn house, but couldn't determine if Max was home or not. "Too bad I can't have any contact with Max while I'm on probation. Otherwise, I'd be at the funeral. I hate to think of you guys going through it alone."

"Nice thought, Sid, but I doubt anyone will show up anyway. After all, we weren't the only ones who hated our dad."

"That's not what I meant."

"I know what you meant." Kate reclined her head so that her neck rested along the top of the leather bench seat. "I haven't forgotten the day your folks were buried. So many people showed up for their funeral, it was crazy."

"It didn't matter. I might as well have been by myself."

"Yeah, well, I just want to get the whole thing over with and move on. Hey—maybe I can talk Max and my mom into forgetting about a funeral service altogether. It's not like we can afford a decent one anyway." As she lifted her head up, another moan escaped from her throat.

"Are you okay?"

Pointing to the square bandage taped to her forehead, she winced. "Except for this, yeah."

Sid had seen Kate out of it enough times to guess what her lingering grogginess and slurred speech were from, and it wasn't from the pain reliever Doc Simpson had given her.

Figuring he had nothing to lose, he dove in for the kill. "You still shooting up?"

She shrugged.

"Is that a *yes*?"

"It's a maybe."

"Where would you get it around here?"

Kate wagged her finger in Sid's face. "You're in enough trouble already. Let's just say, I found someone who's willing to do anything for me." Leaning in close to him, she reached out and stroked his chin. "Nice moustache and beard, by the way. Sexy. You were clean-shaven last time I saw you."

"'Last time' meaning in Berkeley, when you convinced me growing pot on my parents' farm would be a great venture?"

"You're not blaming *me* for what happened, are you?"

"No. But I've spent a lot of time wondering what my life would be like if I hadn't fallen for the idea."

"You wouldn't be on probation, for one thing."

"Obviously."

"And we'd be in Paris right now. Eating. Drinking wine. Dancing in a romantic jazz club." Snuggling close to Sid, she added, "What a downer it didn't turn out that way."

"That's putting it mildly." Sid gently nudged her away. "What did you do when you found out what happened?"

Though Sid's brush off was subtle, Kate stiffened. "I moved on. Like I always do."

"I didn't mean 'What did you *do*?' I meant what was your reaction to me getting busted when you heard about it?"

Kate's eyes glinted. "I didn't freak out, if that's what you mean."

Is it really that hard for her to be open with me about her feelings? Sid lifted the handle on the truck door to get out. "Forget it."

"Wait!" Kate seized his wrist. "Why are you so uptight? Don't you love me anymore?"

"Love!" Sid laughed. "Did we ever love each other?"

"We made love . . ."

"I hate to be the one to tell you, Kate, but it's not the same thing."

"Since when did you start caring about the fine details of love?"

"About six months ago. I admit it took a while for me to come to grips with what our relationship was really about. But after finding out you slept with Bryan the same night you slept with me, I don't feel anything for you other than the friendship we used to share."

"I slept with Bryan that night, too?"

"Come on, Kate."

"If I did, I don't remember."

"I suppose you don't remember your other nights with him, then?"

"How did you find out?"

"He asked about you before I left Berkeley and came up here to tend to my plants. We had a long talk."

"You're jealous."

"Hardly."

"You *are* jealous."

Grinning, Kate made a move to kiss Sid, but again, he pulled away. "What exactly is it that you want from me, Kate?" he asked, throwing his hands up in surrender. "Why did you come back, anyway? What is it you're looking for here?"

The last thing Sid expected to see was Kate dissolve into tears, but—as out-of-character as it was for her—that's exactly what she did. Dumbstruck, he realized he hadn't seen her cry since she was publicly bullied and humiliated by her father shortly before he had walked out on their family.

It seemed like yesterday that Eamon Quinn—in a blind rage because his fifteen-year-old daughter hadn't come straight home after school to help his wife fix dinner—had tracked Kate down, cornering her outside Ralph's Mini-Mart on the far end of Main Street. He had yanked his sobbing daughter behind him, parading her down the street like a bagged trophy as he shouted to everyone within earshot, "See this face? Get a good look at it because next time she tries to pull something over on me, she won't be worth looking at!" It had been the talk of the town for weeks.

Sid took her hands in his, and with a much softer voice, said, "Talk to me, Kate. Maybe I can help."

"That's just it," she choked. "I'm so desperately empty, I don't even know how to begin to tell you—let alone understand it myself."

"Try."

"You'll hate me. You already do. I can tell."

Sid squeezed her hands. "That's not true. I don't hate you."

"I bet you'll never forgive me for your getting busted, though, will you?"

"I already have. *Well, kind of.* Look, Kate, it was me who made the decision to plant the pot, so I have only myself to blame. But . . ."

"But what?"

"Why did you want me to do it so badly? Was it just so you could see the world?"

Removing one of her hands from Sid's grasp, she fanned it in front of herself. "Travelling, money, love—I want anything, anyone, that will take me away from *this*. From *me*. I know it sounds crazy, but I think it's why I'm never satisfied."

It doesn't sound crazy. As a matter of fact, Sid understood too well the escape she was looking for. His pain might come from loss rather than abuse, but the torment was the same.

"I want what I've never had," she continued. "I want what everyone else has. Is that so bad?"

Sid shook his head.

"Please don't tell me I'm the only one in the world who feels this way."

"Of course not." Sid was speaking to himself as much as to Kate. "The problem is, it's an impossible ambition."

"I know it's impossible, yet I keep thinking that my next move, my next relationship—my next whatever—will work out and make me happy, but . . . "

"But it never does."

"Exactly. There's this big hole inside of me I can't fill no matter what I do. God, what's wrong with me?"

Sid wished he had the answer. He wanted to tell Kate that nothing was wrong with her and that everything would be okay. But she wasn't fine, and he couldn't promise that her life would be okay. Besides, he had no answers for himself, let alone her. "I'm not a shrink," he said finally, "but if I was, I'd say you might be barking up the wrong tree."

"What do you mean?"

"I'm just saying I think the bigger issue is probably your fear of commitment and trust, not so much the emptiness you feel inside."

It seemed to take Kate a moment for his comment to

sink in. "I never thought of it that way," she said. "You could be right." Lifting her hand to his cheek, she added, "Of all the people I know, Sid, you're the only one who's not totally screwed up yet."

But I am screwed up. You have no idea how many fears I'm battling right now. "I'm on probation, remember? I'd say I messed up big time."

With a sniffle, Kate dropped her hand and mopped away her tears. "Well, regardless, no matter what happens, you're still going to inherit your parents' farm. You'll never have to worry about money. My dad just left us with a huge debt and terrible memories. Max and I are broke."

"Is that why you called awhile back saying you needed to talk to me about something important?"

Smiling weakly, Kate lifted her chin. "Thanks for returning my call by the way."

"I tried calling you back, but you didn't answer."

"Oh? But then, you kept on trying, right?"

"Well, no. I . . ."

"No, of course not. Why would you?" Kate's face crumpled.

"Kate . . ."

"Look, Sid, it doesn't matter. You asked why I came back home? The reason is, I need to recoup from a . . ." As though something had just come to her, she paused.

"Recoup from what?"

A porch light switched on, a sign that someone—probably Max—might materialize any minute to see what was going on. "Don't worry," she said. "I won't be here for long. Help me into the house, would you?"

Reluctantly, he got out of the truck, offered his elbow to Kate and guided her up the sidewalk. When they reached the front door, she let go of his arm. "You need to know something, Sid."

"What's that?"

"Jake Clausen has a thing for me."

"Obviously," he grunted. "I guessed as much at Digger's."

As though she needed to defend herself, Kate crossed her arms. "Yeah, well, he's the only guy in town right now willing to give me what I need."

"If it's money you need, I can help."

"How? By taking out a loan against your farm? I'm sure you can't have that much cash on hand. Although, if you hadn't gotten busted that wouldn't be the case, would it?"

"Well, that's true, but . . ."

"Besides, money isn't the only thing I need."

A vague picture, like a dim object advancing out of a dense fog, formed in his mind. As unlikely as it seemed, he said, "Let me guess. Jake's a dealer."

"Not really. He just has connections and knows what strings to pull for me."

"And what does he get in return?"

"Never mind." Kate recoiled. "I shouldn't have told you."

Not that Jake was ugly, or dumb, or broke, but he wasn't handsome or brilliant or rich by any means. He was, thought Sid, a humorless, volatile, bully with a twisted penchant for abusing and fleecing anyone weaker than himself . . . just like Kate's dad. The similarities between the two men made Sid's stomach turn and he told Kate as much.

"For your information, Jake and I have more in common than you think," she argued, backing away from Sid. "Unlike you, we both grew up struggling to make ends meet, with at least one weird parent who made our lives hell. He probably understands me better than you could ever hope to." A note of finality signaled she was finished talking. "So yeah, I'll be hanging out with Jake—for a while, anyway."

But Sid wasn't about to let Kate play yet another head-trip with him. Not after seeing her so broken at Doc Simpson's. Not after what she had just confessed to him. "Did Jake do this to you today?" he asked, pressing behind her as she stepped through the doorway into her house.

"I don't remember."

"Really? Just a few minutes ago, you admitted you let yourself get involved with people to escape the emptiness you feel. Jake can't give you what you need. He's going to end up hurting you, and besides . . . "

"Good-bye, Sid." Pushing him away, she slammed the door in his face.

A second later, the outdoor light switched off, leaving him standing on the Quinn's darkened, dilapidated porch, unable to speak with Max and unwilling to pursue Kate any further, as much as he wanted to pound on the door and insist she come back out and tell him the truth. Feeling as alone, frustrated, and confused as ever, he slowly made his way back to his pickup. He'd never bargained on any of this happening when he'd first come up north to plant weed last spring. It was as though by stepping back into Trinity County, he'd been enlisted, like the Tin Man in *The Wizard of Oz*, into a vortex of unwelcome encounters, confrontations, and responsibilities.

And right now, they seemed insurmountable.

Three months down and nine to go until August, he thought. *I don't even want to think about what's going to happen between now and then.*

The Storm

A MONTH LATER, DURING THE EARLY morning hours of Saturday, December 23, Sid scuttled out of bed, shivering in the pre-dawn darkness to the sound of ripping, snapping, and ground-shaking *thuds*. He flipped the light switch, only to discover the electricity was out. Stumbling toward the window, he pulled the curtains back. A fierce storm had swept through the mountains overnight, depositing tons of freezing rain.

Dumbfounded, he watched as nearby tree branches tore away from their trunks, some scraping against the house like giant cat claws. Long twisted icicles rimmed gutters, porch railings, and telephone lines. Illuminated by moonlight piercing through staccato breaks in the clouds, he could make out his roommates' cars parked out by the barn, encased in the stuff, giving them the appearance of jumbo ice-cubes. The parade of stooping cypresses bordering the road strained beneath the heavy weight—hulking Quasimodos frozen in their deformities.

Intermittent booms thundered from across the creek as thousands of board feet of uprooted timber surrendered to the ice, collapsing into each other like drunken dominos. Sid imagined that the sum total of the sounds being released at that moment—the riving, roaring, and splintering wails

—was what a wooden ship must sound like breaking apart in a storm at sea.

Letting the curtain drop, he threw on a pair of jeans, some wool socks, a thick sweater, and slipped his feet into some sandals. Then, getting down on all fours, he reached under his bed and fumbled about for a flashlight. Finding it, he made his way into the hallway, the floorboards creaking beneath him.

Mika cracked open her bedroom door as he passed by. "What's going on?"

"An ice storm."

Opening her door all the way, she tugged her pink chenille bathrobe up close about her throat. Her hair, a mass of wild curls, hung loose to her waist. "Where are you going?"

"To check on things."

"It's so cold—I can see your breath."

"The power's out."

"Do you mind if I come with you?"

"It'd probably be better if you stayed in your room."

"Why?"

Detecting a trace of panic in her voice, he aimed his flashlight at her bare feet and relented. "All right, but you'd better put some shoes on."

A moment later, she reappeared, her feet clad in a pair of leather moccasins. Sid resumed his inspection, Mika trailing close behind. First, he went into the kitchen where he checked the faucet in the sink to be sure the pipes hadn't frozen. Next, he went into the bathroom and performed the same ritual.

"Where I'm from, we wrap our pipes in the winter," said Mika.

"Yeah, well, this isn't Iowa." With barely enough room for one person in the bathroom, let alone two, he elbowed his way past her.

As he started up the stairway, Mika stopped him. "Do you know what the forecast is for today? What the road conditions are?

Sid waved his flashlight. "No power, no radio."

"There's no battery-powered radio anywhere?"

"Not that I know of."

"It's just that my flight home leaves tomorrow—the day before Christmas. If the roads are closed, I don't know how I'll get to the airport."

Sid tried not to let his irritation show. "Look, I can only do one thing at a time, so let me make sure everything's okay in the house first."

"Sure. Sorry."

Proceeding to the landing on the second floor, Sid heard Ketch snoring in his bedroom. He cracked the door open, did a quick visual once-over, and moved on to the next room, asking Mika to peek in on Liz.

"She's not here, remember? She left to go home for Christmas yesterday."

"Right. I forgot."

Silently, they continued together up the adjoining half-flight of stairs to the library.

Crack! Thump, thump, THUD.

Sid stopped dead in his tracks and listened intently. Mika huddled so close to him, he could feel her body heat warm him.

"That one sounded like it might have hit the house," she whispered.

"Only one way to find out." Sid placed his key in the door lock, turned it, and entered the library.

Shadowing him up the narrow spiral staircase to the turret, Mika let out a squeal when they emerged onto the top floor. She grasped the handrail running beneath the windows along the curvature of the room and paced back and forth excitedly. "It's like a lighthouse—you can see 360 degrees up here!"

They pressed their noses against the windows, studying the crystallized vistas stretching in every direction, aglow in the cloud-breaking moonshine. Sid scoured the landscape to see if any trees had fallen on the barn or outbuildings, and studied the utility poles running along the driveway and county road to make sure there were no power lines down.

"Thanks for letting me come up here with you." Mika's voice was so hushed, Sid could barely hear her.

"It's no big deal." *That is, as long as you don't expect me to invite you up here on a regular basis. This is my refuge, not yours.*

Nervously, she rushed ahead. "When I was six, our house burned down. It was July—a really hot night. My grandpa, who was living with us, wasn't allowed to smoke in the house, but his bed was next to a window, so he'd open it and sneak a cigar or cigarette sometimes. That night, he went to bed early, about the same time I did. A few hours later, after my parents went to bed, our dog started barking and woke me up. I looked out my window and thought it was the Fourth of July—even though the Fourth had already come and gone— because the sky was all lit up, and sounds like firecrackers were going off everywhere."

"I heard my dad yell and my mom scream," she continued, "and I could have sworn I heard my grandpa—his bedroom was on the second floor right above mine—crying for help. The next thing I knew, my mom was running outside with me in her arms, crying and screaming for my dad. We stood there, waiting for the fire trucks to come, watching for any signs of my grandpa and my dad. When my mom started praying, I got scared. I figured they were both dead, and I'd never see them again. I'll never forget that feeling. It was like I died myself."

Sid had been listening intently, but with a measure of reserve. Not sure why Mika was telling him all this, but curious to know the outcome, he asked, "Then what happened?"

"Just as the first fire truck pulled up, my dad stumbled out the front door. He was covered in ash. His skin looked like . . . like a baked potato, and he was coughing something fierce. He told the firemen that he'd tried to get my grandpa but couldn't because the door was locked. I guess grandpa would lock the door when he took to smoking. My mom was so beside herself, they had to take her by ambulance with my dad to the hospital."

Sid had expected her to say he'd been saved. "So, you mean your grandfather died in the fire? Wow, Mika. I'm . . . sorry."

"That's why I didn't want to be left alone downstairs. I still have nightmares about it. I'll get up at night in a cold sweat and can't go back to sleep because I'm afraid I'll wake up and be trapped in a burning house again. I mean, there's no fire of course, but when I heard all the noise tonight, it freaked me out."

"Trust me, there's nothing to worry about." Sid gave her a reassuring pat on the back. "We're going to be fine."

"Right. I don't know what came over me. Usually, when I pray, the fear goes away."

Recalling his anger at God after the car accident, Sid stepped back. "Yeah, well, praying didn't help me when my parents died." Not giving her a chance to reply, he turned around. "We need to keep checking things out."

Moving to the opposite end of the turret, they were able to get a good glimpse of the tree nearest the house—a giant Douglas fir, at least 100-feet tall. The top third of the tree, bent at a 30-degree angle, leaned dangerously over the roof. At least two of its limbs had split away from its monolithic trunk at the junction where it bowed. The tip of one of them protruded out of a crack in the eave of the attic.

Mika pointed to it. "It looks like a branch might have gone through the dormer there."

"Maybe." Sid started down the observatory stairs. "We'll have to go see."

Exiting the library a few seconds later, Sid locked the door behind them and ascended the last flight of steps to the top floor. They found Woolf's bedroom door wide-open, his room piled with debris. Stunned, Sid eyed a tear in the ceiling between the rafters. Stretching down through it, like a giant flexing its arm, was the broken tree branch they had seen from the turret's windows.

"It just missed Woolf's bed." Mika bent down to pick up an amber colored prescription container. "But where is he?"

A loud tapping caused them both to pause and listen. Sid cast the beam of his flashlight into the corner of the room where the sound was coming from, but all he could see was a sheared-off section of sheetrock covered with insulation and chunks of roofing material. Above them, through the gaping hole, a hint of moonlight and an abundance of ice-cold air flooded the room.

"Woolf?" Sid motioned for Mika to stay behind him. "Woolf, are you in here?"

Tap, tap—tap, tap, tap. Tap-a-tap, tap.

"It sounds like Morse Code, don't it?"

Sid and Mika swung around to see a bare-chested Ketch, clad only in his underwear and cowboy boots, standing in the doorway. He shined his flashlight in their eyes, causing them both to raise their arms over their faces.

"Either that," added Ketch, "or Wolfman's earning his chops with a set of drums he's been hiding from us. Lord, it looks like King Kong partied here."

Sid nodded toward Mika. "Give your flashlight to her, will you? And help me move some of this stuff."

Ketch obliged. Plowing through the rubble behind Sid, he helped lift the torn sheetrock away from the wall. There, crouched in a fetal position, was Woolf brandishing a Colt .45. Seeing Ketch and Sid, he began shouting crazily, "Cong! Cong! Cong!"

Ketch lowered himself down on his haunches. Resting his elbows on his knees, he said, softly, "Woolf, it's just us: Ketch and Sid and Meeks. We ain't no Cong. An ice storm brought a big honkin' tree branch down through the roof, that's all. You're safe now." Slowly, he reached one hand out, his palm upturned. "Give me your gun, Woolf—nice and easy like— and everything will be okay."

Woolf blinked several times before a semblance of recognition registered on his face. Then, like a little boy caught with his hand in the cookie jar, he handed his gun over to Ketch. Unfurling from his cramped position, he stretched his legs out in front of him and leaned back against the wall. Though shivering, he was drenched in sweat.

"He's probably in shock." Mika grabbed a blanket from Woolf's bed and rushed to his side to cover him with it.

Sid edged close to Ketch. "Can you give me the gun and help Mika take Woolf downstairs?"

"Sure. Let me check it first." Ketch opened the gun's chamber. It was unloaded. Handing it over to Sid, he asked, "What if he's got a stash of ammunition hidden somewhere?"

Sid glanced around the room.

"Or," added Ketch, "more guns."

"Exactly. Well, while you guys take him downstairs, I'll search his room to see what I can find. Then, I'm going to get rid of this thing."

"Whoa, wait a minute. Not sure you can do that, Sid. I mean, he's got his rights, you know."

"Are *you* comfortable with Woolf having a gun in the house?"

"No more than you are. But, look, if I had a gun here—and I'm not saying I do—and you took it from me, I might just take you to court to get it back."

Mika, helping Woolf to his feet, called out, "Ketch! Can you come over here?"

Sid tucked the nose of the gun into his jeans. "I don't want to take any chances, with me being on probation and all. Can you blame me?"

"Hide it then," hissed Ketch. "Somewhere Woolf won't find it. Just don't get rid of it. You can give it back to him if he gives you a hard time about it, or when he leaves next summer. After we get Woolf taken care of, I'll come back and help you clean up this mess."

"Thanks."

"And I've got a favor to ask."

"Yeah?"

"It's about what I talked to you about on Thanksgiving. Remember?"

Sid didn't dare tell Ketch he remembered only part of what he had divulged to him—the part about him being a dad who wanted to see his little girl again. All the drama with Kate that day at Doc Simpson's had eclipsed their conversation.

"Sure," he said. "I'll go get a ladder and chain saw from the barn and meet you back up here. Then you can refresh my memory and we'll talk. Oh, and . . . why don't you put some clothes on. All that whiteness is blinding me, man."

MIKA WAS ABLE to coax enough water out of the tap to fill half the teakettle. While Ketch got Woolf settled at the kitchen table, she put the pot on the gas stove to boil. Ten minutes later, she and the vet, sitting silently across from each other, were drinking honey-sweetened hot tea. Finally, she set her cup down, looked Woolf in the eye, and said, "So, what exactly happened with you this morning? Did you have some kind of relapse?"

"Is that what you call it?"

"You don't have to give me an explanation, Woolf. I just want to make sure it wasn't something else."

"Like?"

"I don't know."

"I'm not losing it, if that's what you think."

"I'm worried for you. I'm only trying to understand."

A faint smile tugged at Woolf's lips. "You're like my mom. And my sister. They get really paranoid when storms roll in because they know I could freak out. They're always trying to protect me from being around loud noises."

"You have a sister?"

"Her name's Jett. She's a year younger than me. A singer—musician."

"You know, we've been living together in this house for almost four months, and I don't even know where you're from."

"New Jersey."

"Wow. How did you end up all the way out here?"

"It wasn't working out, me living with my parents. Like I said, my mom was getting pretty uptight with me around, and my dad, who failed his WWII physical, was basically clueless about what I was going through. Anyway, I was drafted right after high school. Shipped out of San Francisco Bay the day after I turned nineteen. That's when I saw California for the first time. I really dug it here, so my sister asked her friend in Frisco to find me a place to rent somewhere out of the city where I could find some space to chill out. Other than being in the army, I've never really been on my own."

Mika had never heard so many words come out of Woolf's mouth before. "So what you're saying is, basically, this is your transition back into society."

Woolf nodded. "My sister calls it 'Baby Steps to Independence.' Maybe you'll meet her soon. She's talking about coming out to see me."

"Oh." Mika felt a sudden pang of loneliness. "I bet it's going to be hard not seeing your family at Christmas."

"I thought of flying back to Jersey to spend the holidays with them, but they live in the city, and with all the loud celebrations and fireworks on New Year's and stuff . . . I just thought I'd stay here and give them a break. I'd rather have them not feel like they have to walk on eggshells around me."

"I'm sure they'd rather that you were there with them. But it's thoughtful of you, anyway." Reaching out, Mika placed her hand over his. "You sound like a good son."

Woolf pulled away. "I'm sure they're relieved I'm *not* there. I'm their only son. There's a lot of things my parents would rather I was besides a tripped out recluse."

"I can't believe that. They're probably proud of your service to your country and just waiting for time to heal what needs to be healed in you. Like your sister said, it'll take a lot of baby steps, right?"

Out of nowhere, Woolf bared his teeth. Because it lasted only a second, it was hard to tell if it was deliberate or an involuntary reaction to something he adamantly disagreed with. Regardless, Mika feared the similarity between his surname and the beast causing Woolf's lips to curl back might not be coincidental.

Meanwhile, in the attic, Ketch and Sid had removed the branch and nailed a tarp over the hole in the ceiling until they could repair it permanently. Now they were busy shoveling debris aside in Woolf's bedroom to dispose of later.

"So, did you talk to Skinner about my idea, yet?" asked Ketch. "The one I mentioned on Thanksgiving?"

Ketch had wanted to know if he could use the side of the barn for an advertisement announcing the future opening of a *Rev & Ride* Harley shop in Trinity County. Nowhere in particular, Ketch had said, being as he'd have to wait to see what the outcome of the custody battle over Annabelle would be. But his lawyer had told him it might help his case if he appeared to be actively pursuing some kind of business venture while he was in California, to prove how serious he was about being a responsible dad to his daughter. Ketch believed having a giant advertisement on the side of Sid's barn might be just the ticket, since the area drew a fair number of back-road enthusiasts in the summertime. He just didn't know if Sid would need Otis's permission to have it done.

"Sorry Ketch, I haven't. It's been crazy around here, and the right time to talk to Otis hasn't come up yet. But I promise I'll talk to him the next time I see him."

"Swear?"

"I swear. I'm looking forward to seeing your daughter up here on the farm someday." As soon as Sid said it, he realized the commitment that was implied in his statement. "I mean . . ."

"You mean if you're still here. If you decide not to sell your farm."

"Right."

"Well, if you do keep it, and I get my girl, maybe I could open a shop on your place, eh?"

"Like I said, I don't know yet what I'm going to decide. There are a lot of factors that play into my decision." *Like making it through my probation, for one.*

"You may not realize it, Jackson, but I've got a good head for finances. My business could help pay your taxes, not to mention give you some extra income. I could help you figure out long term plans for the place. Ever thought of planting a vineyard?"

"I have. I've got a few other ideas, too, but more for investment purposes in case I lease the farm out to someone instead of selling it."

"Oh." Ketch spent a moment reflecting. "I don't blame you for being gun shy about my proposal. I've got a long record of puttin' the cart before the horse. Impulsivity, my pa used to call it. My teachers swore I would never amount to anything being as I couldn't sit still long enough to let a thought take root in my brain. But my pa also told me that it's the ones who don't move fast enough that get moss growing between their ears and never amount to a hill of beans."

Sid stopped shoveling. "Ketch, you have nothing to do with why I'm dragging my feet. I can't think of anything cooler than to have a repair shop on this property if I were to keep it. But the neighbors might not like it, and who knows if the county would go for it? Plus, there's no guarantee you'd be satisfied with your business being located out here in the middle of nowhere. All that to say, I'm not quite ready to make any long-term decisions yet. Not until I can figure out what I'm going to do with this place."

Ketch's grin lit up the room. "Until then, if Otis approves, I can advertise on the barn though, right?"

"Absolutely."

Ketch's smile disappeared.

"What's wrong?" asked Sid.

"It's a pretty desperate spot I've got myself into, my friend. What if I'm just chasing a jackrabbit down a hole with all this dreamin' of mine? What if I get my girl and turn out to be a lousy dad?"

"Why would you say that? You'd be a good dad."

"You think so?"

"You said you've changed."

"But have I changed enough? I guess there's only one way to find out, but . . . "

Yeah, thought Sid, as Ketch continued talking. *The only way to find out what you're made of is to go through a trial of fire, just like what I'm going through here on the farm.*

WHEN POWER TO the house still hadn't been restored by dusk, Sid ventured outside. He wasn't gone long. Mika was waiting for him in the living room when he returned.

"The roads are impassable," he said. "They're still a sheet of ice."

"But my flight's scheduled to leave tomorrow morning at 8:45. Do you think it'll thaw later tonight so I can make it to Frisco?"

"The thermometer on the barn read 18 degrees, so I doubt it. Might as well forget Christmas in Iowa, Meeks. I know how hard it must be for you. Otis gave me permission two days ago to drive down to Sonoma to spend Christmas Eve with my grandparents. I can't even call to let them know I might not make it. Even if I had a set of chains for my truck, which I don't, and we left now, it would take forever. There's no way we could get you to Frisco in time to catch your plane." Sid shook his head. "No one's going anywhere for a while. Not you. Not me. Nobody."

Mika flopped down on the sofa. She wished she would have booked her flight on a different date, like Liz, who had left two days earlier.

"I'm sure someone's been able to contact the power company." Sid's voice turned consoling. "They've probably got crews working around the clock to get electricity back up. That's a good thing, right?"

Half-heartedly, Mika nodded.

"Until then, I'm going out to help Ketch tinker with an old generator we found in the barn. He's going through a hard time and could use some company, though he'd never let on."

Mika had been so consumed with her own disappointment, she hadn't noticed Ketch was down in the dumps. "What's wrong?"

"He said you know about his daughter?"

"Oh . . . that. So, he told you, too."

"Yeah. He had his heart set on being able to see Annabelle over Christmas, but then he found out, just the day before yesterday, that he wasn't granted permission. I guess he's gone through the legal process of acknowledging he's the father, but Emma's still fighting it."

"Do you think she's doing it out of spite—to get back at him for denying paternity when she was pregnant with Annabelle?"

"That'd be my guess. Anyway, with a family already lined up and waiting to adopt Annabelle . . . "

"It's a mess."

"A big one. Ketch is kicking himself for waiting so long to get the ball rolling."

"Poor guy—he must be so disappointed. The only thing that might have been worse is if he would have gotten permission and then couldn't go because of the storm."

"That's one way of looking at it." Sid turned to leave. "Anyway, I'm heading out to the barn. There's a gas lantern hanging by the kitchen door that you can use while I'm gone.

Woolf's upstairs getting his room back in order. He's got a lantern, too. Just yell at him if you need anything."

"Thanks. I will."

Mika rose and followed Sid into the kitchen. Grabbing the lantern off the wall, she turned and made her way back down the hallway. Once in her bedroom, she placed the lamp on her nightstand, lit it, and began unpacking the suitcase she would no longer need. Out came her clothes, all the carefully wrapped Christmas gifts for her family, and the homemade fudge she had made the day before the storm. Lastly, she transferred her Bible, a journal, and some other reading material into her dresser drawer. Then, pulling on an extra sweater and another pair of wool socks, she turned off the light, crawled into bed under a mountain of blankets, and begged for a deep sleep to put her out of her misery.

California for the Holidays

T HE NEXT THING MIKA KNEW, HER ROOM was awash with sunlight, and the teakettle in the kitchen was whistling so loudly, she could hear the spout cap blow off and scuttle across the floor. Still dressed from the night before, she threw off her covers and ventured into the kitchen. She found Sid standing barefoot near the stove, his hair plaited in a low braid, hanging like a burnished rope down the middle of his back—as black as the feathers on the Jersey Giant chickens her parents raised on their farm. From behind, he looked like a Sioux warrior.

"You're up early," she said, bending over to retrieve the errant teakettle cap.

"I just called my grandparents to let them know I can't make it down for Christmas. By the way, the power's back on." Sid tilted his head toward a radio perched on top of the refrigerator, an announcer's monotone voice droning from it. "The weatherman says it's not supposed to warm up above freezing until tomorrow."

Normally, Mika would have been thrilled at the news. But since it was too late for her to catch her flight home, she found the timing almost cruel. It was so toasty in the kitchen, she slipped off her outer sweater and draped it over a chair. Then she opened the cupboard and retrieved a box of peppermint tea. Pouring some boiling water into an earth-toned pottery mug, she plunked a tea bag into it and watched as Sid made himself some coffee. She couldn't quite put her finger on what was different about him this morning. Wondering why he seemed preoccupied, she plugged the toaster in and reached into a bag of whole wheat bread. "Do you want me to put a slice down for you?"

"Sure. Thanks. So, it looks like we'll all be spending Christmas together."

"It appears that way." A moment later, the toast popped up. While Mika buttered the slices, Sid sidled up to her. She paused, her knife suspended in the air. "Yes?"

"Nothing."

"Do you want some jam on yours? It's strawberry. Pearlie made it."

"Maybe a little." Sid hovered over her, seemingly inspecting how evenly she was distributing the jam. "That's enough. Thanks."

Taking the toast from her, he set it on a plate and took a seat at the table. Motioning to the chair opposite him, he asked, "Can we talk a minute—before Ketch and Woolf wake up?"

"Sure." Mika sat down. "What about?"

"Do you plan on seeing Otis and Pearlie?"

"Today?"

"Anytime soon."

"Since I didn't expect to be here, I hadn't made any plans to, but I'll probably see them sometime over the holidays. Why?"

"Are you going to tell them what happened yesterday?"

"You mean about the hole in the attic roof?" She took a bite of toast.

"No, about Woolf."

"Why would I say anything to them about Woolf?"

"I just don't know what Otis would think about a gun being in the house."

"Oh." Mika thought a moment. "I don't recall the lease that we signed saying anything about firearms. I mean, my dad and brother own several guns between them. I doubt Otis would think it's an issue. Having a weapon comes with the territory when you live in the country."

"I know that. My dad had a few guns, too. Otis sold them after I went to Berkeley and my grandparents moved back to Sonoma. But you know what I mean, Mika. It wasn't like Woolf was out hunting deer. He had a meltdown. In the house. With a Colt .45 snub-nosed pistol."

"But it wasn't loaded."

"What if it would have been?"

He's got a point, she thought. But still, the fact was, it wasn't.

"Anyway, afterward, I noticed Woolf opened up to you," continued Sid. "Did he say anything about me taking his gun from him?"

"What are you getting at?"

"What if a gun on the farm compromises my probation? What if Woolf decides to—I don't know—sue me for taking his gun from him?"

"That's ridiculous."

"I'm not taking anything for granted." Sid paused, as though debating what he should say next. "Maybe I can do something to make up for your missed flight to Des Moines. Or was it Minneapolis?"

"Cedar Rapids." Mika froze. "Are you trying to . . . *bribe* me?"

"Shh! Not so loud. I'm only saying—"

"I know what you're trying to say. You're afraid I'll go blabbing to the Skinners about yesterday or that somewhere down the road I'll try to blackmail you or something, or . . ."

"Come on. Now *you're* the one being ridiculous."

"Oh, *really?*" Mika shot to her feet. "Then why did you bring this all up in the first place?"

"You're the one making a big deal out of nothing. I was simply stating the facts."

"Here's a fact for you, Sid. The only thing you can do to 'make up' for my missed flight—which, last I remember, was an act of God and nothing you had a hand in—is apologize to me for being . . ."

"Hey, what's all the ruckus about?" Ketch shuffled lazily into the kitchen, a towel flung over his shoulders, his damp hair tied into a knot on top of his head. "Y'all are noisier than a couple of cats makin' kittens."

Mika *grr*-ed, and then acting as though she were looking for something to eat, she marched over to the refrigerator and opened it.

Sid rose, went to the sink, and set his empty mug in it. "Mika and I were just talking about how it's a good idea that the Skinners don't find out about what happened here yesterday with Woolf."

"Right on." Ketch lifted his hands above his head in a long stretch. "Hey, what say we find ourselves a little tree to decorate today? This place could use some Christmas cheer."

"Fat chance of that," snapped Mika, rummaging through the fridge. She instantly felt guilty for her attitude, considering Ketch must be as disappointed about Christmas, if not more so, than her. Softening her voice, she added, "The roads aren't supposed to clear up until this afternoon."

Ketch laughed. "Look out the back door, Meeks, and take your pick. There're only a million trees out there."

Mika turned just in time to catch Sid gesture toward Ketch that they should leave her alone for a while. "I'll get some saws," he said.

Ketch hung back a moment while Sid lumbered out to the barn. "Come on, Meeks," he pleaded. "We need a woman to come with us and help pick out the tree."

"I'll meet you outside pretty soon." It was all she could manage to say, given her nose was running and tears were streaming unchecked down her cheeks.

Several moments of silence ensued. Finally, hearing the door to the mudroom shut behind Ketch, she closed the refrigerator. Pulling the bottom of her flannel shirt up to her face, she wiped her eyes. Then she took a deep breath, lifted the receiver on the wall-mounted phone, and dialed her parents' phone number.

"Dad?" she blurted, hearing the familiar voice on the other end of the line. "The roads are iced over here from a big storm that came through yesterday. It's not supposed to get above freezing until tomorrow, so I won't be able to make it home for Christmas. Can you tell Mom and Brad?"

"They're at the store. Are you sure you can't make it to the airport, Mika? The roads are that bad?"

"Yeah, they're that bad. When Mom and Brad get back, can you explain what happened and tell them I love them?"

"They're going to be so disappointed. I know I am."

"Trust me, I'm more disappointed."

"Well, I'd rather have you safe where you are than risk

your life on bad roads to get home. We're sure going to miss you though, sweetheart."

"Not as much as I'm going to miss you guys. I'd better go . . ."

"Sure. We'll call you tomorrow. Merry Christmas, honey. Love you."

"Merry Christmas, Dad. Love you, too."

Steeling herself against despair, Mika girded her emotions and set her gaze out the window toward the barn, where Ketch was brandishing a roaring chainsaw. Sid, armed with a handsaw and pruning shears, stood next to him. Heavy footsteps thudded down the stairs behind her.

Woolf called out, "What's Ketch doing with that chainsaw?"

"He's getting ready to celebrate Christmas. Looks like we all are."

AFTER SCOURING THE property for nearly an hour, Mika finally selected a stout six-foot Sitka spruce. Since it had been protected from the ice beneath a giant fir, she was able to tell it was the perfect size and shape. On her command, Ketch felled it and Sid trimmed it. Woolf and Ketch then dragged it into it into the mudroom to thaw out a bit while Sid tore through storage closets in the house looking for a tree stand.

By noon, they were all in the living room, Woolf holding the top of the tree upright as Ketch and Sid groveled at its base, trying to position it in the rusty metal stand.

"There!" said Mika, standing in the middle of the room. "Perfect!" But moving sideways a few steps, she changed her mind. "No, no. It's still leaning a little too far to the right."

Ketch and Sid groaned, made the minor adjustment, and then belly-crawled away from the tree to join Mika before she could change her mind again.

"I think that'll do," said Sid, rubbing his shoulder.

"It'll have to," said Woolf, eyeing the tree with his head tilted and his arms akimbo.

Ketch pulled a martyr's face. "I'm starving, Meeks. All that hard work you put us through this morning . . ."

"All right, I'll go make some popcorn while you guys finish in here. We can use some of it to decorate the tree."

"Decorate?" Ketch's voice sounded an octave higher than normal.

"Yes, decorate." Grinning widely, Mika made her exit.

She returned a short while later, bearing a tray of coffee mugs and a fresh pot of coffee. Passing it off to Woolf, she went back to the kitchen, returning the second time with two overflowing bowls of popcorn and a small canvas packet. Nestling herself on the floor in front of the fire Sid had built, she opened the envelope and handed her roommates each a needle and several long sections of thread. Excitedly, she showed them how to thread the popcorn to make a tree garland.

"It's actually starting to feel like Christmas," she said, her cheeks flushed.

"Now, if I had me some good Scotch and a rack of Texas prime rib," said Ketch, "*that* would feel like Christmas."

Woolf stared wistfully into the fire. "A big slab of Honey Ham and a Bloody Mary would do me just fine."

"Mashed potatoes and gravy," sighed Sid. "With turkey and dressing. It doesn't get much better than that."

Mika didn't want to think about the Christmas dinner

her mother was preparing back home, let alone what else she would be missing out on with her family. But as determined as she was to make lemonade out of the lemons she'd been served this holiday, she felt her throat ache, clear down into her chest. Covering her mouth, she coughed, fearing she might start crying again if she mentioned what her favorite Christmas meal was: Swedish meatballs with lingonberry sauce and boiled potatoes with butter.

"We'll just have to make do, you guys," she said, finally. "Remember, Liz and I weren't even going to be here, and since there's no one on kitchen duty this week, the cupboards are almost bare. Even if the roads were clear, there're no stores open, so we're stuck with what we have."

The glare from the sun pouring into the living room as it lowered in the sky caused Ketch to pull his ever-handy sunglasses down over his eyes. Mika studied him a moment. The black turtleneck he wore made his face look like chalk. In the harsh winter light, she could make out his bubble-gum pink scalp peeking up through the center part in his hair, as well as the stubbly beginnings of a blanched goatee spackled across his upper lip and chin line.

Unaware he was being inspected, Ketch pulled the sleeves up on his sweater, revealing a blanket of white fuzz on his forearms. Until now, Mika hadn't realized just how hairy Ketch was. Her laugh made him glance up.

"What's so funny?" he asked.

"You look like a yeti."

"A what?"

"You know, the Abominable Snowman."

Ketch lifted his sunglasses and winked at her. "I am a

mysterious dude if I say so myself." Pointing his needle at Sid, he said, "What about him?"

"Hmm. He looks like a . . . a famous horse."

"The Black Stallion?" asked Sid.

To Mika's surprise, Sid said it with feigned bravado, as though he might be aware of his good looks but didn't dare let on that he was. In truth, she really was going to say the Black Stallion. Instead, she said, "No. You remind me of Bree, Shasta's horse."

"Who the hell is Bree?" asked Ketch.

"Who the hell is Shasta?" asked Woolf.

"Bree," muttered Sid, "was a talking horse who thought he was better than every other horse."

"You've read *The Chronicles of Narnia?*" Mika was stunned.

"You sound surprised. The series is upstairs in the library."

"Your parents got them for you?"

"The Skinners did. A long time ago."

"I never pegged Otis and Pearlie as being C. S. Lewis types."

"Some clerk at a bookstore apparently told them I would like them."

Mika coughed again. Harder this time. She couldn't figure out why her chest still burned. This bout of homesickness was worse than she thought. "And did you like them?"

Something must have triggered a memory in Sid, because a cloud passed over his face. Handing his string of popcorn to Mika, he said, "I need to go out to the barn and check on Hester again—make sure she's warm and has plenty of hay in her stall."

No sooner was he gone, than Ketch gave her his string of

popcorn, too. "Sorry, Meeks. My eyes are bugging me. Think I'll head to my room for a nap. Much-deserved, if I say so myself."

"Me, too," said Woolf, rising from the couch and dropping his garland at Mika's feet.

Mika shrugged. "I have to say, you guys lasted longer than I thought you would . . . even though *I* helped get the tree and bring it in. Tonight when you're all hungry, don't come running to me to fix you something to eat."

Ketch, almost to the hallway, turned around and gasped. "You wouldn't."

"But, it's Christmas Eve," blustered Woolf.

Mika smiled. "Try me."

Ketch seemed to seriously consider the gamble. A second later, he strutted out of the parlor, calling over his shoulder, "Just yell when dinner's ready."

Woolf, who still lingered nearby, said, "Meeks, who do I remind you of?"

Typically, she would have considered Woolf, at least on the surface, an intimidating grizzly of a man. But then there were the odd times he seemed more like a puppy. Trying to respect his masculine ego, she struck a middle ground. "Baloo in *The Jungle Book.*"

"Never heard of him."

"Oh, he's a great brown bear with lots of charm. People love being around him."

"Really?"

Mika didn't want to lie, but bolstered by a desire to believe in things not yet seen, she said, adamantly, "Really."

A Mayflower Eve

THAT AFTERNOON, DESPITE FEELING OUT OF sorts, Mika ransacked the kitchen for food. There was no milk, no bread, and very little sugar or salt left. In the freezer, she discovered two pounds of hamburger, a whole chicken, two boxes of corn, a bag of frozen peas, and a half-eaten gallon of vanilla ice cream. The pantry yielded a few canned goods and two varieties of pasta, minute-rice, peanut butter, and a bag of chocolate chips. She decided the only dinner that could be put together on such short notice with so few ingredients on hand was spaghetti.

Onto a hot burner went the largest pot she could find, and into it, the frozen hamburger. Lowering the temperature, she covered the pan tightly and gathered ingredients to make bread. Fortunately, there was just enough yeast and flour to make one rustic loaf, with several dashes of salt left over to flavor the ragù. She tossed flour onto a large cutting board and mixed the dough, kneading the spongy mass with her hands.

Placing the dough into a greased bowl to rise, she covered it with a cloth and checked on the meat in the pot, now completely unfrozen and starting to sizzle. She broke it up with a long handled wooden spoon, then opened four large cans of tomato sauce and poured them in. Next came some healthy doses of dried oregano, rosemary, and thyme; three cloves of garlic; the last of the salt; and a diced red onion. Still not satisfied, she called for Sid, who had just returned from doing some outdoor chores and was taking off his boots in the mudroom.

Entering the kitchen, he sniffed the air. "You called?"

"The sauce needs something. You're the expert. What do you think?"

He took the spoon from her and dipped it into the simmering sauce. Sniffing it, he asked, "How much garlic did you use?"

"Three cloves."

"You might want to add one or two more."

"Anything else?" She handed him another spoon.

He took a tiny taste. Then another. "Hmm. It needs some wine."

"Red or white?"

"Red. A nice Cab would do."

"Cab?"

"Cabernet." Sid handed the spoon back to Mika. "I think I may have a bottle up in the library. I'll be right back." Several minutes later, he returned with a half-empty bottle of Merlot. Ketch and Woolf were with him, having been lured out of hibernation by the aromas emanating from the kitchen.

"This should do," said Sid, handing the wine to Mika. "Do you need anything else? I'd like to help."

Mika brushed her hair out of her face and pointed to the sink. "Dishes."

Rolling up his sleeves, Sid nodded at Ketch and Woolf to pick up some towels and help him. "I'll wash."

By the time the dishes were done, Mika had folded the

dough into a greased pan, covered it for the second rise, and tossed together some tomatoes, slices of onion, and black olives, with the rest of the olive oil and a bit of wine vinegar, for a salad.

Then, they all went their separate ways until suppertime. Sid retreated to the library while Ketch went out to the barn where he changed the oil and cleaned the sparkplugs on his Harley.

Disappearing into her bedroom for a while to read, she fell asleep, waking a half-hour later with a throbbing headache and an even worse sore throat. At about 5:30, she dragged herself out of bed and set herself to the task of making the dining room table look as festive as possible. An earlier raid on the laurel hedge near the road and a holly shrub in the back yard had yielded a bounty of glossy-leaved branches, which she arranged into a centerpiece framing the last of the candles remaining from the blackout. She tied white linen napkins with twine woven through springs of holly and laid them next to Sofia Jackson's Crown Ruby Wedgwood settings.

Were these the plates she used for her Christmas dinners on the farm?

Mika imagined Sid's mother as Pearlie had described her, elegant and sophisticated, yet humble and down-to-earth. She could see her cooking up a storm at Christmas, taking joy in gift giving and sharing in her son's wonder and excitement. She thought of her own mother back in Iowa, at this moment performing the same rituals herself. The pain of being two thousand miles away from home was softened a bit by the sense that Sid's mother, had she been there, might have put her arms around Mika and told her how grateful she was that someone was dusting off her china and silver, making sure her little boy, no longer a little boy, would have a decent, memorable Christmas.

Ketch poked his head into the dining room. "Soup yet?"

"Just about." Mika struck a match and began lighting the candles. "Do me a favor, and put some hot plates on the sideboard, would you? And can you ask Woolf or Sid to pour the drinks?"

Dutifully, Ketch obeyed as Mika made several trips back to the kitchen to get the bread, salad, and spaghetti. Woolf poured water into goblets while Sid opened another bottle of wine. Finally, Mika settled herself at the far end of the table and waited until everyone was seated. Placing her napkin on her lap, she bowed her head and said, "Let's pray."

Ketch, Woolf, and Sid bowed their heads and waited patiently for Mika to finish the blessing. The moment she was done, they dug in, attacking their food as though they hadn't eaten in months. Mika would have kept up with them, but tonight she could barely even eat the small portions she had served herself.

Soon they were toasting each other. To everyone's surprise, Ketch paid homage to Liz, admitting that he missed having her around to tease. "That girl's got snap in her garters," he said.

Woolf saluted Ketch. "Maybe you're not as shallow as I thought you were."

Sid, on his turn, lauded Mika for toughing out the holiday with three slobs like themselves. "I know this isn't easy for you, Meeks. It wasn't easy for me not being able to go to Sonoma." Nodding toward her, he added, "But I don't know what we'd do without you. You turned a day that started out less-than-ordinary into something really special."

Ketch and Woolf hollered, "Here, here!"

Mika made light of their praise, assuring them they would have done just fine without her. Thanking them all anyway, she raised her glass toward Ketch, ready to congratulate him for trying to be a good dad and do right by his daughter. Then she remembered only she and Sid knew about Annabelle. Instead, she said, "Ketch, may this Christmas mark the beginning of all the things your heart desires in the New Year. You're a good guy, my friend." Clinking her glass with Woolf, she added, "You, too."

Lastly—in a gesture she intended as an added olive branch over the confrontation they'd had earlier in the morning about Woolf and his gun—she tipped her glass toward Sid and said, "And you, too, of course."

While the boys dished themselves seconds, Mika unexpectedly found herself with a new appreciation of these odd comrades—men she might not have normally sought out companionship with—but who she now called friends. It was surreal, feeling comfortable, almost nostalgic, in their midst on Christmas Eve—a day she should have been celebrating in Iowa with her own flesh-and-blood.

Even so, she reminded herself that there were very real barriers dividing her from her roommates. Like the pilgrims and strangers confined together on the Mayflower, they were each living out the year cocooned within their own personal histories and life experiences. Distinctly different. Almost ridiculously so. She couldn't understand Sid's pacifism or his love/hate relationship with the farm, or Ketch's wild streak, or Woolf's dark broodings. Nor, she was sure, did they comprehend her passion for God and her longing to change the world—to pierce the supernatural, to taste true love.

But so what? Since when are friendships based on having identical likes and dislikes? These guys are my friends, regardless. Rising from the table, she excused herself. "I have to get something. I'll meet you all back in the living room."

Preoccupied with eating, Sid said, "Don't worry about the dishes. We'll do them. The meal was great, Mika."

"Yeah," garbled Woolf, intently buttering another piece of bread. "It really hit the spot."

"My hat's off to ya, Meeks." Ketch stuffed a fork-load of pasta into his mouth. "We owe you, big time."

But as she made her way toward her bedroom, Mika discovered her mental fortitude wasn't equal to her physical stamina. She stopped to catch her breath. *Who knew being homesick could feel like dying?*

Mika slipped back into the living room to find her roommates gathered silently around the fireplace, each one holding a glass of wine, staring into the flames as they listened to the soulful refrains of "Sweet Melissa" playing on the stereo. Startled out of their post-Christmas Eve dinner trance by her appearance, they stared in disbelief as she began handing out gifts.

"I gave Liz's to her before she left," said Mika. "Go ahead. Open them."

Ketch unwrapped his box first. Holding up a rainbow-colored, wool-knit cap, he said, "Don't tell me you made it?"

"Of course, I did," she wheezed.

In the midst of opening his present, Sid shot Mika a concerned look. "Are you all right? That cough doesn't sound very good."

Nodding, she motioned for him not to worry.

Seconds later, Sid held up an embossed, leather-bound journal. "This is perfect. Thanks, Mika. I'll keep it in the library."

Woolf opened his gift last. Staring dumbly at the navy wool scarf Mika had knit for him, he said, "I . . . I don't know what to say. No one's ever made anything like this for me before."

Another coughing fit struck Mika. Standing up, she swooned. "Anyone want some ice cream? There's a little left in the freezer."

"Forget the ice cream." Ketch jumped to his feet. "What's wrong, Meeks?"

Sid and Woolf rushed to her side.

Placing his palm on Mika's forehead, Sid said, "You feel warm. I'm calling Doc Simpson."

Insisting she only had a cold and didn't need to see a doctor, Mika apologized for crashing so early on Christmas Eve and went straight to bed. Woolf helped Ketch and Sid finish cleaning up. When they were done, he said, "I'm gonna crash, too. Man, I hope Meeks feels better in the morning."

Not long afterward, Ketch was in the living room, watching Sid put out the fire in the fireplace. "You think she's really okay?" he asked.

"She says she is, but that cough of hers sounds pretty bad."

"I feel like an ass not getting her anything for Christmas."

"Tell me about it."

Ketch wrestled a cigarette out of his pocket and lit it. "Guess that's women for you though. Thoughtful. At least, that's what they say . . ."

"Yeah, my mom was that way. Always thinking of everybody else before herself."

"Must have been nice. My old lady was all about me, myself, and I."

Sid shoveled the ash into a pile in the center of the hearth. Staring into the glowing embers, he said, "You mentioned it's been a long time since you've seen your mom. Maybe she's changed."

"Or not. Some people never change. I gave up waiting to find out. I've never been a sucker for manipulation. Besides, being a martyr's not my forté." Tossing his half-smoked cigarette onto the ash heap, Ketch added, "Not that you and me are perfect, right? And not that I necessarily care to change things about me that might drive other people crazy."

It suddenly occurred to Sid that, for all his joking and swagger, Ketch was a pretty deep thinker. "So, you believe personalities and our expectations of people are subjective?"

"That's a fancy way of putting it," said Ketch. "I'm just saying different strokes for different folks is fine and dandy, but no man's an island. I lived for myself for years and then— *whoop!* Something slaps me upside the head and wakes me up to the fact that I'm a daddy and I better start acting like one if I want to have my little girl back. Subjective, objective—it don't matter. Sooner or later we all get a chance to change. If we pass it up, we pay the price."

Sid placed the shovel back in its tray. *What's the price of passing up change, exactly? Alienation? Regret? Lost opportunities?*

He was about to ask Ketch, when the Texan lurched his lean body into motion and headed upstairs. "Merry Christmas, dude. Don't let the bed bugs bite."

That night, before falling asleep, Sid was still wondering about the cost of passing up change. He was already acutely aware that he was at a crossroads in his life. But what bothered him was, there were no road signs directing him which way to go. And with his horizons currently obscured from sight, whatever options he might have appeared as giant question marks. Without a doubt, the pressures of his circumstances were forcing him to examine himself, to question his decisions and motives for doing things. As Ketch had alluded to, he was discovering flaws he knew he should repair—knew could cripple him in the long run if they weren't dealt with.

But he was loath to change. It was too risky. Required too much sacrifice. Anyway, he already had his hands full with surviving the present. If he could only get through his probation. If he could just squeeze by the next few years of his life making as few decisions as possible, then maybe he'd have less a chance of screwing up. Maybe then, he could think about what needed to be changed.

Maybe then, he'd have the desire to transform himself.

Christmas Fever

THE FIRST THING SID DID THE NEXT morning was call his grandparents and wish them "Merry Christmas." After talking to them for about ten minutes, he hung up and started a pot of coffee.

Ketch entered the room, rubbing his belly. "What's to eat?"

Sid pulled a saran-wrapped bowl out of the refrigerator and plopped it on the counter. "Good thing Mika made lots of spaghetti."

"Speaking of Meeks, is she up?"

"I haven't heard her moving around yet."

"It's not like her to sleep in so late."

A look of concern passed between them. Forgetting the food, they made their way down the hall to Mika's bedroom and rapped on her door. When there was no reply, they knocked again.

A faint voice replied, "What?

"Are you okay?" asked Sid.

"No."

"We're coming in," said Ketch, opening her door. "Rise and shine, clementine! It's Christmas."

"Funny, the last time you were here it was Thanksgiving." Doc Simpson strode into the waiting room of his clinic. "What is it with you and the holidays, Sid?"

"Bad karma's my guess."

Chuckling, the doctor held out his hand to Ketch. "Who's this you have with you?"

Sid introduced Ketch. "He's one of the boarders at the farm."

"Well," said Doc Simpson, his voice more professional, "Miss Larson has pneumonia. Not a severe case—at least, not yet. I'm putting her on a round of antibiotics rather than admitting her to the hospital in Redding, but she needs someone to keep an eye on her. Can I count on you two to do that?"

They nodded in unison.

"Unfortunately, being that it's Christmas Day, the pharmacy's closed." He handed Sid a brown plastic cylinder. "There's enough penicillin in there to get her through tomorrow. Make sure you follow the instructions on the label exactly." Pulling a square white pad out of his pocket, he scribbled a prescription and gave it to Sid. "And get this filled as soon as you can."

The door to the examination room swung open. Ellie Simpson escorted Mika out to the reception desk, fussing over her as she went. "Now be sure to get plenty of rest," she was saying, "and let someone else do all the cooking." Noticing Sid and Ketch, she chirped, "Merry Christmas, boys."

"Same to you," said Sid.

Ketch touched his cap with the tip of his finger. "Merry Christmas, ma'am."

"You know," said Ellie, passing Mika off to them, "she could still end up in the hospital if she doesn't take it easy. Is she the only girl out there on the farm right now?"

"The one and only." Ketch held Mika's purse while Sid helped her put her coat on.

"That's too bad. Dean and I are going to our daughter's house in Eureka for Christmas dinner this evening, otherwise we'd bring supper over for you."

"Well, that's real nice of you, ma'am, but we'll be just fine." Ketch slapped Sid on the back. "Sid here's a five-star chef. Aren't you?"

"Hardly." Sid reddened. "We'll make do with what we have at the farm, which, to tell the truth, isn't much since the ice storm hit."

Ketch's face fell at the reminder.

"Actually—" Ellie's forefinger flew to her cheek. "Otis and his deputy have been working around the clock since that storm hit, so my guess is Pearlie's by herself. She'd probably love to bring Christmas dinner over for you. I'm sure she's got plenty. I'll telephone her."

Mika retrieved her purse from Ketch and crumbled into a nearby chair, her face almost as pale as his.

Ellie called to her husband, who was busy jotting notes down on Mika's chart. "Dean! Did you give Miss Larson some aspirin for her fever?"

"Yes, dear. Two." Peering over his glasses at Sid, Dean asked, "Do you have any analgesics out at the farm to give her later?"

Sid looked at Ketch, who looked at Mika.

Mika shrugged.

"Ellie," said the doctor, "in the examination room there should be several aspirin bottles in the cupboard over the sink. Can you bring one here?" Turning back to Sid, he added, "You should always have some out at your place. You never know when you might need it."

When Ellie returned, she handed the bottle to Sid, who stuffed it in his pocket along with Mika's antibiotics.

"Now remember," said Dean, "the directions for the penicillin are on the container I gave you. As for the aspirin, make sure she takes two pills every four hours as needed. Never more than eight a day though. If that doesn't keep her fever down, call me immediately." Grabbing a different writing pad, he scribbled something, tore off the page, and gave it to Sid. "Last of all, here's our daughter's number in case you need to reach me while we're gone. The roads are pretty clear now. As long as they stay that way, we should be home by midnight tonight."

"Thanks, Dean." Sid motioned to Ketch and together they helped Mika to her feet while Mrs. Simpson bounded ahead into the foyer.

"Now, you boys have a merry Christmas and take good care of Mika. She's going to need you," cautioned Ellie, holding the door open for them. Then, before closing it, while the three were still within ear shot, she called out to her husband, "Don't that beat all, Dean? Sid spending Christmas out at the farm without any family. It's heart-breaking is what it is. Just heart-breaking."

AROUND TWO O'CLOCK that afternoon, while Mika slept and Ketch journeyed cross the creek to assess any storm damage to the Grotto, Pearlie called to say she was bringing over a meal. She arrived a half-hour later, laden with sacks and boxes of food. Giving Sid a hug, she apologized for not being able to stay longer.

"Poor Otis has been burning the candle at both ends since the storm," she explained, "and once he gets home, it'll be all he can do to eat something and go straight to bed." Inclining her head toward Mika's room, she added, "Storms, sickness. Oh my, what a Christmas!"

Within minutes she was placing a potato casserole and cooked ham in the oven and a pot of beans on the stove to simmer. Next, she wrapped some homemade buttermilk rolls in foil, with instructions for Sid to warm them just before it was time to eat. Opening a large Tupperware container, she lifted out a coconut raspberry cream pie and put it in the refrigerator along with a bowl of fruit salad topped with sweetened sour cream. Lastly, out of a sack on the counter, she retrieved a round, red tin emblazoned with sleighs and reindeer and clamped it firmly under her arm.

"Now that everything's taken care of," she said, "I need to see Mika before I go."

"Sure," said Sid. "Just a minute."

Pearlie watched as Sid checked the time on the wall clock in the kitchen, filled a glass with water and grabbed some pills before leading her down the hall to Mika's bedroom. *Well now, isn't he being a good caregiver,* she thought. When they stepped inside, she saw Mika was awake, sitting up in bed.

Lifting her knees up beneath her comforter, Mika patted a spot on the mattress near her. "Come sit awhile, Pearlie." Then, she took the glass of water from Sid and the two pills he handed her. Dutifully, she swallowed them as he looked on.

"Here, missy." Pearlie opened the tin and held it out to her. "You need something solid in that stomach of yours. Choose any one your heart desires."

Mika picked out a frosted sugar cookie in the shape of a star. Round silver dragées adorned its edges. "What an angel you are, Pearlie." As she bit into the cookie, little grains of green, crystallized sugar fell onto her lap. "You can't imagine how good this tastes."

"Oh, I can imagine, all right. I had pneumonia myself once, a long time ago. Me and Otis had just moved out here. Can you believe it—my family back home in Texas, and us not knowing a soul in Trinity Springs yet!" Pearlie selected a nice fat Russian teacake out of the tin and popped it into her mouth before continuing. "It was about this time of year, too. A week before Christmas, and I was sick as a dog." Turning, she offered the tin to Sid, who was still standing silently behind her. But he declined a cookie and excused himself, saying he had to check on something upstairs.

When he was gone, Pearlie asked, "How's he treating you these days, Mika?"

"Sid? Oh, I think he feels sorry for me that I'm sick."

"Well, he should. We all do." She paused to place the lid back on the cookie tin. "Anyway, as I was saying—I was sick as dog. My chest felt like a ton of bricks was sitting on top of it, and I was burning up with fever. Otis was so scared, he rushed me over to Doc Simpson's in his police car with his sirens blaring. That was the first time we met Dean and Ellie."

"They're really nice—the doctor and his wife. I like them both." Mika closed her eyes and settled back into her pillow, her voice trailing away.

Pearlie waited several minutes, listening worriedly to Mika's labored breathing. When it appeared she had fallen asleep, she leaned over, brushed the sick girl's cheek with her lips and whispered, "Merry Christmas, sweetheart." Then, tucking the cookie tin under her arm, she tiptoed out of the room.

"Is she asleep?"

"Oh!" she exclaimed, bumping into Sid in the hallway. "I didn't see you. Yes, she's out like a log."

"You think she's going to be okay?"

Why, he actually looks worried about her. "Of course, she's going to be okay. Dean's her doctor, isn't he? Nothing will happen to her on his watch." Pearlie tapped Sid's forearm and smiled. "Or, I might add, on your watch. Appears you're taking good care of your sick boarder. Mighty admirable, Sid."

"I'm not taking any better care of her than I would any of my other roommates."

"No need to be embarrassed. I was just teasing is all."

"I'm not embarrassed."

"Well, then, your cheeks must just be red from the heat coming out of that oven." By now, they were standing in the warm kitchen. "Oh, I nearly forgot. Otis wanted me to tell you he hasn't forgotten Billie's request for—"

"Billie?"

"Whatever y'all call him. Will Ketchum. Bill. Your roommate!"

"We call him Ketch."

"Anyway, what with this storm and all, Otis hasn't had time to give his request much thought, but he said he'd let you know his answer by the first of the year."

"Okay. I'll let him know."

"I'm leaving these cookies here for you." Pearlie set the tin on the table and grabbed her coat off the back of a kitchen chair. "And by the way, Otis and I have a little something for you at the house. Maybe you can swing by in the next couple of days to open it."

"Pearlie, you didn't have to . . ."

"We wanted to."

Sid shifted his weight to his other foot. "Well, thanks. Be sure and tell Otis 'Merry Christmas' for me."

"Oh, I will."

"Here, let me help you with your coat."

"That's fine, I've got it." Focused on buttoning her coat, she said, "You know, if it hadn't been for that blasted storm, he could come here to the farmhouse tonight while I serve up the dinner and we could celebrate Christmas together. Wouldn't that be great? It's been way too many years since we've done that."

Fighting back tears, she looked up. "They were the best times, Sid. Really—they were. Don't you think?"

THE BEST OF *times. Yes, that they were.*

As he quietly escorted Pearlie out to her car, Sid found himself recalling past Christmases on the farm—days ribboned with laughter and joy, wrapped in the timelessness of youth. Idyllic. Perfect. Unsurpassable. Suddenly, he was blindsided by the stark contrast between those Christmases and this one. The gulf seemed so deep and wide, his chest contracted with a sense of overwhelming loneliness and loss. A sharp intake of breath whiffled loudly down the back of his throat.

When would this heartache end?

At his side, shambling down the slick sidewalk, Pearlie cast him a curious look. "Did I say something wrong?"

"No, no. I just . . . " Dare he say it? "I miss those Christmases, too." Immediately, he was glad he'd admitted it. He felt instantly lighter. "I know we can't relive the past, Pearlie, but you being here tonight's just brought back a lot of good memories. Maybe someday . . ."

Stopping, she reached up and cradled his chin in her hand. "Keep on dreaming, Sid. It'll keep you young. Dreaming keeps all of us young, no matter how old we are. I guarantee, the day you stop dreaming's the day you might as well hang up your hat. As long as that head of yours keeps looking ahead to the future, you'll be just fine."

"I'll try."

"Promise?"

Sid nodded and continued toward the car. "I feel bad I didn't get you and Otis something for Christmas. I meant to, but then the storm hit and, well, I never got around to it."

"Oh, stop! You're the only present Otis and I need this Christmas, honey. Just having you here in Trinity Springs is the best gift you could give us."

"Yeah, well the dinner you brought over tonight is the best gift you could have given me. Really. Thanks again. It means a lot."

Pearlie hesitated as Sid held her car door open for her.

"Now, don't forget to put the rolls in the oven fifteen minutes before you eat, and remember, everything else is already cooked."

"Got it."

"And make sure you save some for Mika. She needs to eat whether she feels like it or not."

"Will do."

Looking up as though she were thinking about something else to remind Sid, she suddenly grinned. Standing on her toes, she reached up, waved toward a window on the second floor of the house and shouted, "Merry Christmas, Billie!"

There, leaning out of his bedroom window, was Ketch waving back at them, his face looking whiter than ever in the bold winter sunshine. "Hey there, Miss Pearlie. Merry Christmas! Can't wait to eat your fine cookin'!"

Pearlie sighed. "That roommate of yours has really grown on me, Sid. How I love down-home Texas men! Even if they do have long hair."

Mika woke up at six o'clock that night to see Sid sitting on her bed holding a plate piled high with food. Her throat was parched, her lips cracked and dry. He helped her into an upright position, set the plate on her lap, handed her a glass of water and told her it was time to take two aspirin again.

"Could you get me a warm washcloth?" she asked.

"Sure. Be right back." Returning a moment later with the requested washcloth, he asked, "You have a headache?"

She nodded, pointing to her temples.

"Here, let me." Gently, he placed the warm, wet cloth on her forehead. "Why haven't you started eating?"

"I'm not really hungry."

"Doesn't matter. You've got to eat. Orders from headquarters."

"Pearlie?"

"And me."

"I suppose you're right." A few moments passed. "That feels better, already. Thanks, Sid." As he removed the cloth from her head, she asked where Ketch was.

"After we finished dinner and did up the dishes, he went into the living room and fell asleep on the couch."

"And Woolf?"

Sid smiled. "He's so worried about you, I think he's having sympathy pains."

"Sympathy pains?"

"He complained of a headache and sore throat and locked himself in his room after telling me, in no uncertain terms, to let him know as soon as you're better."

"Aww . . ."

"I think he's scared to death about you."

"You're the one who looks scared to death."

With a snort, Sid said, "What would I be scared of?"

Mika, wondering where his sudden defensiveness was coming from, took a bite of ham, winced at its saltiness, and then aimed her fork at the baked beans. "Poor Woolf. Can you tell him I'm doing much better?"

"I will, but I'll let him get a good night's sleep first."

"What a boring Christmas for you all."

"What a boring Christmas for you, is more like it. Do you want me to call your parents or anything, to let them know what's going on?"

"No, I'll call them tomorrow. I don't want to spoil their

Christmas worrying about me." Mika quit playing with her beans and set her fork down. From the corner of her eye, she noticed Sid lift a large sack off the floor near his feet and place it on the bed next to her. *Why is he being so secretive? So fidgety? It isn't like him.*

"Doc Simpson called about an hour ago to ask how you're doing. He's going to swing by tomorrow to check on you."

"That's sweet of him." Suddenly tired, she pushed her food away. "I think I'm done."

Sid took her plate and replaced it with the sack. "It's for you," he said, hurriedly. "Merry Christmas."

As he rose to leave, Mika asked him to wait. Reaching into the bag, she pulled out a 1950s first edition, hardback set of *The Chronicles of Narnia*. Overcome with emotion, she hugged them to her chest, her moist eyes telling Sid what her chapped lips couldn't. *Thank you.*

He dismissed her gratitude with a shrug. "They were just gathering dust in the library. You'll appreciate them more than me. I never finished . . ."

A series of sharp knocks on the back door took them both by surprise. "I'll see who it is," said Sid, standing up. "Be right back to check if there's anything else you need." Re-entering her room seconds later, he said, "There's a guy here who wants to see you."

Again, Mika was stumped by Sid's odd behavior. The way he weighed his words and kept his voice soft and low; his concerned looks, his unusual protectiveness. "Who is it?" she asked.

"He says he's a friend of yours—David Rowe."

"Oh, David!" Energized by the prospect of a visitor, Mika

couldn't contain her excitement as he hurdled into the room past Sid. "What are you doing here?"

"I came as soon as I heard what happened." Handing her a gift box wrapped in silver embossed paper, he leaned down to kiss her on the forehead. "Why didn't you call me and let me know you were sick?"

Sid, meanwhile, had elbowed David out of his way. Now he stood closest to her bed. "She was only just diagnosed with pneumonia this morning," he said, gruffly. "What? Were you supposed to be the first to know or something?"

What is going on? It obviously bothered Sid that David had heard about her illness and responded so quickly. But why? Did he think that he and the other boarders were the only people in the county who would care if she was sick? Well, whatever his problem was, Sid was being ridiculous. Ignoring him, she reached for David's hand and squeezed it. "I can't believe you came all this way on Christmas Day to see me. It's so thoughtful of you."

Sid cleared his throat.

"Would you mind if we had a few moments together?" asked David, turning around. "Alone."

Acting as though he hadn't heard him, Sid said, "Meeks, do you need anything else while I'm here?"

"No, I'm fine. If I need anything, I'm sure David can find it and bring it to me."

"That's right," said David, clearly annoyed. "I can handle whatever Mika needs from here on. Nice meeting you . . . was it Sam? Sal? Sid? I forgot."

Dead silence.

No Sid. Don't. Mika watched as Sid began to smirk, his

features soldering together, deviously, as though relishing a confrontation. She'd seen that expression one other time— at Digger's, the night Jake had threatened him. *Don't say a word, Sid. It's Christmas. I'm in no mood to deal with this and David gets offended easily. Please, just let it drop.*

But Sid apparently had no intention of backing down. "Siderno to you," he growled, in response to David's question. Then, taking a threatening step closer to her guest, he added, "And for your information, the name's Italian. My family's from Calabria. Not far from Sicily. You've seen *The Godfather*, right?"

David's eyebrows shot up. "I don't watch R-rated films."

"Of course you don't."

Stunned, Mika thought, *I knew Sid was Italian—but the Mafia? Really! Why would he say such a thing?* "Don't mind him, David. He's like a brother to me," she said, aiming a death glare at Sid. "Right?"

Sid didn't reply, but as he turned to go, he pointed his finger at David. "Just make your visit short. We're all tired around here, and I don't want to stay up all night waiting for you to leave."

The Miracle Makeover

MIKA SURVIVED HER BOUT WITH PNEUMONIA, albeit with a persistent cough, heaviness in her chest, and an overall fatigue that idled for days afterward. But by December 31, she was well enough to bake a batch of chocolate chip cookies to greet Liz, who was returning that day from her Christmas sojourn in Alaska.

When someone who claimed to be Eliza Drabek walked into the farmhouse shortly after three o'clock that afternoon, Mika took her suitcase from her and handed her a cookie. This could not, she thought—absolutely could *not*— be the drab boarder she had said good-bye to a little over a week ago. Yet, it was Liz—her mannerisms and her voice. Definitely her voice; the same sharp inflections, the same rapid-fire speech.

"This cookie is great," garbled Liz, between bites. "What's the matter, Meeks? You act like you're meeting a stranger."

"It's just that . . . your eyes, Liz. Are you wearing contacts?"

"You noticed, eh? I'm getting so used to wearing them, I forgot I had them in. Yeah, I actually got them last year." Liz devoured the last of her cookie before adding, "I didn't wear them before because I thought people wouldn't take me seriously without my glasses."

"Well, the difference is amazing. Your eyes almost look amber, or . . . " She leaned closer to get a better look. "Hazel?

Like there's a bit of yellow and green in them. I never noticed their color before."

She was astonished by the sum effect of Liz's freshly plucked and groomed eyebrows, the smoky shadow on her eyelids, and the subtle lashing of black mascara. Not only that, but her roommate's long graham-colored hair had been trimmed, layered, and lightened so that rather than hanging limply in indiscriminate waves as it had before, it now had body, shine, and swing, accenting her high cheekbones and straight nose. She found herself so distracted by Liz's transformation that it took her a moment to realize her right arm was in a splint. Pointing to it, she asked, "What happened?"

"It's a long story," said Liz. "Too long to go into now. Man, do I need a bath. I haven't been able to take one since they put this stupid thing on me."

"Here, I'll carry this upstairs for you." Mika shifted Liz's suitcase into her other hand and followed her down the hallway.

Ketch popped his head around the corner of the living room as they passed by. "Meeks, you shouldn't be carrying that." Reaching for the suitcase, he said, "Let me."

"It's fine. I've got it."

Glancing behind her he said, "Whoa, who's this?"

"One guess." She stepped back so Ketch could get a better look at Liz.

"No way," he whistled. "This can't be old four-eyes."

"I'm wearing contacts, stupid," snapped Liz.

Ketch's eyes traveled over Liz's thigh-hugging, bell-bottom jeans, silk blouse, and snug velour vest. "Well, I'll be damned. What brought this on?"

"None of your business. It's the same me on the inside. That's all you need to know."

"Who cares what's on the inside when the outside's looking so good?"

Rounding the stairway, Liz muttered, "You're so immature, Ketch."

But Mika, mounting the stairs behind Liz, noticed a smile overtake her profile. When she reached Liz's room, she deposited the suitcase on her bed while Liz ran water in the claw-foot tub in the second-floor bathroom. Knocking on the door a few moments later, she asked, "Are you going to be able to get in and out of your bath okay?"

"I think so, but if you want to hang around just in case . . ."

"Sure." Mika entered the bathroom, closed the door and sat down on the toilet seat. "I'll just wait here till you're done, in case you need me."

"Thanks. I really want to try this myself, but I'll let you know if I need help." Awkwardly, she lowered herself into the steaming tub. It was an antique, slipper-shaped affair whose enamel had long ago lost its luster. "You sound congested, Meeks. Are you sick?"

"I had a little bout of pneumonia over the holidays."

"What!"

"I'm fine now. It's no big deal."

"If you say so. I didn't see Sid when I came in the house. Is he here?"

"Last I saw, he was in the kitchen on the phone."

"Ah. I suppose that chick, Kate Quinn, is still bugging him."

"She calls here every once in a while, but he always finds an excuse not to talk to her. Sometimes when the phone rings, and he doesn't know who it is, he'll slip outside and yell for someone else to answer it. Unless it's his grandmother, he asks us to tell them he's not in the house and to take a message." Mika shrugged. "It's really none of my business, though. What about you, Liz? I'm dying to hear about your holiday and what brought about this big change in you."

"WHERE TO START? I guess with my mom." Liz blew a few bubbles in the bathwater before launching into a brief history of her family.

She explained that ever since she could remember, her mother—an attractive, chatty, opinionated beautician—had lamented the fact that her daughter had inherited her father's genes: his angular features, scrawny build, thin hair, swarthy skin, myopia, and slight, but definite, overbite. Her mother, noted Liz, had perfect teeth, 20/20 vision, womanly curves, and a flawless complexion.

"One day when I was in junior high, in the throes of full-blown puberty mind you, I overheard my mother tell one of her customers at the salon, 'You never know what the gene pool's going to cough up. Just look at the difference in my two daughters. Eliza will clearly never be the beauty her sister is. If only she'd let me enhance her looks a little bit, she'd be downright pretty. She could even attract a few boys if she'd play her cards right.'

"Of course, what's said in a salon rarely stays there, so it was only a matter of time before I was confronting her public campaign to change me. I asked her—I said, 'Mom, how could you be so heartless? Now everyone in town knows what you think of me. Thanks to you, I'm just a complete loser. Not to mention, my own mother thinks I'm ugly.' Do you know what she said, Meeks?"

Mika shook her head.

"She had the nerve to say, 'I never said you were a lost cause, Eliza. I'm only saying that if you would correct your more serious flaws, you'd have a shot at being decent looking enough to attract attention. And just because you take after your dad instead of me doesn't mean it's the end of the world—not if you do something about it. The truth is, if you refuse to enhance your looks, you're going to bear the consequences of being forever handicapped with homeliness. I'll tell you what though, if you promise to do something about it, I promise I won't talk about it at the shop anymore. What about we start with braces?'"

"She said all that?"

"Well, I paraphrased it a bit, but yeah . . ." Liz grimaced. "I mean, I know I'm not beautiful, but can you believe it?"

"Beauty's only . . ."

"Forget the 'beauty's only skin deep' trip, Meeks. I'm not fishing for compliments or pity. It was a rhetorical question."

"Ah, got it. No, I can't believe it."

"Anyway, I agreed to be fit with braces. My mom, of course, believed she'd won the battle of shaping her daughter into her image. But really, her threats only made things worse. I started deliberately bucking every fashion trend just to spite her. Meanwhile, my sister Claire, who's four years younger than me and a natural beauty from birth, grew more effortlessly beautiful each day, so by the time she was thirteen, she was keen on the latest fashions, hairstyles and makeup trends. I got so sick of her and my mom conspiring to mess with my looks," moaned Liz. "After a million blow-ups, they finally gave up and left me alone."

"So, if your sister's that beautiful and that into fashion," said Mika, "I suppose she's an aspiring model or something."

"When she was a kid, she was an aspiring cosmetologist, like my mom. I don't know what she'll actually end up being because she's been a hermit for years."

"A hermit—as in a recluse?"

"Exactly." Liz carefully repositioned her bad elbow on the rim of the tub. "You'd think that, given our differences, I'd be the wallflower and Claire would be the outgoing one. If the earthquake hadn't happened, I suppose that might have been the case. At least, as far as Claire goes."

"What earthquake?"

"The *big* one. You know, the Great Alaska Earthquake of '64." Liz tilted her head to gape at Mika. "Don't tell me you've never heard of it."

"Kind of."

"*Kind* of? Are you kidding me! It was only the second strongest earthquake in recorded history. I mean, 9.2 on the Richter scale—do you have any idea how enormous that is?"

"I was only about 12 then, so I can't really say . . ."

"Well, I can say. I was 14. Claire was 10. It changed our lives forever—and not just us. No one who lived through it was ever the same. I still have nightmares about it." Lifting her free hand out of the water, Liz made a swiping motion along her chin. "I survived like my dad did—stiff upper lip, seize the day, soldier on, and all that. For better or worse, I am my father's daughter. And, I have to admit, I'm a stronger person today because of what I went through. It's what made me want to really live life, experiment with it. Take risks.

It's partly why I ended up here in California. But it broke Claire. She was born fragile like my mom. After the quake, my mother got herself some happy pills to cope. Claire just shut down."

"What do you mean?"

"I mean she tuned out of society. She developed agoraphobia —an irrational fear of being around people."

"I don't understand. How does being around people have anything to do with the earthquake?"

"Only everything. For starters, imagine being on the scariest roller coaster ride of your life, multiply it by a million, set a timer for four-and-a-half minutes, and you might—I repeat, *might*—get the faintest idea of what we went through that day. On second thought: no. You could never in a million years possibly imagine the horror." Liz sunk deeper into the water, a faraway look in her eyes.

"It was Good Friday," she continued. "My dad was on duty. My mom and my sister and I were in Anchorage visiting my grandmother for Easter weekend. It was March. Cold. The days were still really short. We had just sat down for dinner in Gram's dining room when the quake hit. Actually, we heard the earth move several seconds before we felt it. It was so surreal, so *eerie*. It sounded like, I don't know, like the roar of some underground monster coming to life. Add to that the noise of furniture and lamps and appliances and every imaginable household item jangling and vibrating and crashing to the ground, and . . . " Liz winced. "You never get that hideous sound out of your head."

"Our house burned down when I was young," ventured Mika. "I still hear the sounds of the fire. It wakes me up from my sleep sometimes."

"Hmm—that's pretty heavy, Meeks. Well, there's no escaping an earthquake. You can't hide from it or outrun it. We were stuck—plain and simple. Suddenly, the floor gave way. It just flat out dropped from under our feet. First, the table where we'd been sitting lurched, sending our dishes and glasses and silverware flying everywhere. Then, our chairs toppled backward, throwing us against the walls. Before we knew it, the table tipped over on its side and skidded across the floor, trapping my sister between it and the back door, which kept flying open and closed on its hinges. Claire hung on to that table for dear life, screaming for help."

Mika's eyes widened.

"The thing is, the back door of my grandma's house was just a few feet from the edge of a twenty-foot cliff that dropped down to the river. Later, my sister told me that she looked out the door and saw a giant fissure burst open in the ground running parallel to the river. It was impossible for any of us to get to her. All we could do was try to keep our heads covered for protection and hang on to whatever we could so we wouldn't be thrown around like rag dolls."

"Wow."

"That's an understatement. What's crazy is, I remember my gram's cat Percy even flipped out. Somehow, he found his way up on to the dining room chandelier. You have to remember that the earthquake lasted almost five minutes— five freaking *minutes*. Anyway, I opened my eyes and saw Percy dangling by one paw from the light fixture, screeching his lungs out. I'm telling you, it was literally like all hell had broken loose. Then there were the aftershocks. Not as huge as the first one, but they were still plenty big—at least 6.0. Always without any warning. They lasted for days. It was terrifying—like being stuck in a haunted house with all the exits blocked."

"How did anyone survive?"

"My grandma didn't. At least, not in the long run. Poor Grams; her hip was fractured during the quake, and she never recovered from it. Died several weeks later."

"I'm so sorry."

"You always assume the ground beneath your feet is safe, solid, but when even that's taken from you . . . well, you can see why my sister became so paranoid. She was afraid another quake would hit when she was by herself, or away from home, or naked in the shower, or . . . I mean, I get it. I dealt with the same fear for a while. Everyone did. But Claire never snapped out of it. She eventually picked the place she felt safest, which was home, and parked her body there 24/7."

"But she had to go back to school, didn't she?"

"At first she did. Her phobia didn't begin overnight. But by the time she was in high school, she'd talked my parents into getting her a tutor and letting her finish her studies at home. In addition to her fear of being caught in an earthquake again, I think she was freaked out about developing new relationships with people, because she was afraid of losing them—especially losing them without any warning."

"Like Sid losing his parents."

"I suppose so. Like Sid—and probably Woolf, after being in Vietnam." As though in a daydream, Liz added, "You know, Meeks, it wasn't only the ground that liquefied during that earthquake. It liquefied my sister's heart. Sid's soul was probably demolished the day his parents died, too."

"Demolished." Mika repeated the word softly.

"Yep. Well, I'm not one to wallow in the past. This Christmas, Claire and I made a deal." Lifting her injured elbow toward Mika, she smiled. "Thus, *ta-da!*"

Mika raised an eyebrow expectantly.

"I basically saw that my sister was worse than ever and figured I had to do something about it. I mean, it won't be long before she's twenty-one, and she has zero friends and no life. My mom and dad are way too close to her to see what's happening; plus my mom is self-medicated to the point that everything's just a bed of roses to her. So, I made a bargain with my sister that if she'd let me take her skiing and out to dinner and a movie afterward, I'd let her do a complete makeover on me. It was the only incentive I could think of that might get her out of the house. I didn't think it would work, but it did. I had to promise her that I wouldn't leave her side for a moment."

"Ah, and while you were skiing . . . "

"I fell—backward, obviously, on my elbow. But really, I think it was my injury that might have put a dent in Claire's phobia. She came with me to the hospital and stayed with me the whole time I was there. It ended up just being a tiny fracture, but by the time they released me, she was so relieved that the restaurant and movie we went to later turned out to be not as terrifying as she had worried they would be. The next day, Claire picked up her scissors, hair color kit, and make up bag, and . . . *voila.* I lived up to my end of the bargain."

"And your new clothes?"

"I indulged her, let her take me shopping a couple of days before I left. Any excuse to get her out of the house again was well worth it."

"All I can say is, you look sensational, Liz. You remind me of Eliza Doolittle in . . . "

"Stop! Don't start with the *My Fair Lady* comparison. My mom tried pulling that one. I don't want to be a lady, and I certainly didn't do any of this to please a man. Least of all, I didn't let Claire make me over to placate my mother. This was totally between my sister and me."

Mika handed Liz a towel. "Well, I've got some things to do. I'll help you out."

Liz let Mika support her as she stepped out of the tub. "Whoo, that's awkward."

"Need any help getting dressed?"

"Nah, I've got to learn to do it myself sometime. It'll just take me a while. Thanks, anyway."

As Mika made a move to leave, Liz said, "Wait a minute."

"Yes?"

"What would you think if I kept all this up?"

"Your new look, you mean?"

"Yeah. Would it seem like I was copping out? Do you think people might take me less seriously with me looking more . . . ?"

"Feminine? No. You're just letting yourself be the best you can be on every level. There's nothing wrong with that. In fact, it's not the cards we're dealt that determine if we win the game, right? It's how we play them. So I say, go for it. Give yourself some time to get used to your new look. I bet soon you'll soon be so comfortable with it, you'll never want to go back."

"Thanks, Meeks. I know you wouldn't lie to me."

"By the way, tonight is New Year's Eve. Did you have plans?"

"Nope. Do you?"

"Well . . ." Ketch had cornered her earlier in the day about ringing in 1973 on the farm. Like Sid, he didn't want to celebrate in public in case he ended up doing something stupid he'd regret. Getting high in the Grotto was one thing, he told her; getting into another fight like he had with Sid on Halloween at Digger's was another. His lawyer had warned him to do everything he could to keep his nose clean.

"That's my New Year's resolution this year," he had told Mika. "I'm not going to let anything jeopardize getting my little girl back. Even if that means spending New Year's Eve at home instead of flat on my face in a bar like I've done too many times in the past."

"Earth to Mika." Liz snapped her fingers in her face. "Well, *what?*"

"Oh! Sorry, I just spaced out. Ketch and Sid and I are going to celebrate New Years here at the farm."

Sticking her lower lip out, Liz said, "Am I invited?"

"Of course!"

"Well, since there's nothing else going on, I suppose. But then . . ."

Nothing else? Oh, but for me there was. Mika didn't tell Liz that she'd turned down an offer from David Rowe to accompany him to a New Year's Eve party in his family's barn. Liz would want to know why, and she was in no mood to explain her decision. Part of it was physical. She wasn't sure her lungs could handle being out at night in the cold and wet quite yet. Ketch and Sid would certainly give her a hard time about it if she were to go to the Ranch. But she also was having very real worries about growing temptations in her life. She had to be careful. What if she slipped up? Considering

David's recent overtures toward her, spending New Year's Eve on the farm with her roommates had seemed the easiest solution and, perhaps, the safest.

All of these musings flashed through Mika's mind in an instant as she stood at the bathroom door, her fingers pressed down on the handle, ready to make her exit as soon as Liz gave her a definite answer.

Deftly, Liz finished drying off using her one good arm. "I'm tired from travelling so, yeah, celebrating News Year's Eve here will be perfect. Count me in."

"Cool." Noticing the new clothes Liz had hung on the hook over the bathroom door, Mika added, "I'd better change into something nicer for tonight. I don't want you showing me up, Miss Alaska."

KETCH INTERCEPTED MIKA after dinner that night as she was finishing dishes. "You'll be staying up to ring in the New Year, right?"

"I'm planning on it. Don't know if I'll make it to midnight, though."

"Still wiped out from the pneumonia, eh?

"Kind of. Why?"

"I want us to share a toast when the clock strikes twelve. I've got some special champagne, and with you being my lucky lady and all, it'd make me feel like 1973 will definitely be the year Will Ketchum gets his daughter back."

"Okay, if you put it that way—but only a little champagne. And you realize I don't believe in luck."

"Don't matter. You believe whatever you want, and I'll go on believing you're my guru angel."

"Oh stop it, Ketch. Guru angel—*really*."

"Oh stop it, Mika," teased Ketch, imitating her perfectly. "Tomorrow, you'll be thanking me for showing you the best time of your life."

"I doubt that."

"Wanna bet?"

"I don't gamble."

"Is there anything you *do* do?"

"I milk cows pretty well."

SEVERAL HOURS LATER, a quasi-drunk Ketch, an equally intoxicated Sid, a fairly inebriated Liz, and a teeny-weeny-bit tipsy Mika were in high spirits. As for Woolf, he had bowed out of the evening early, saying he was going to his room to crash. "Loud New Year's parties aren't my thing," he said, without further explanation.

No one questioned him. If sleep would prevent Woolf's evening from being spoiled by whatever memories lurked in his past, who were they to argue?

The boarders had begun their festivities in the fire-lit living room, taking turns playing each person's favorite game. Liz had chosen Scrabble; Mika, the German card game Euchre; and Sid, Briscola—an Italian card game his grandparents had taught him. They finished with Texas Charades, a version invented by Ketch in which the subject of every mime had to have some correlation to the Lone Star State.

By the time the games were over, it was 11:45.

With only fifteen minutes remaining in 1972, Ketch leaped from the couch and put a new album on the turntable. Manually guiding the arm so that the needle hit the groove on the vinyl at exactly the right spot, he turned up the volume. One-by-one, each of them began dancing separately to side one of Santana's *Caravanserai*. Swaying effortlessly to its Latin rhythms, they soon picked up the pace and formed a conga line, snaking around the living room, down the hall, and back into the living room again, shouting, *Who-hoo! Arriba! Arriba!*

Just before midnight, "Song of the Wind" began—a song so ethereal, it was as though a summer breeze whooshed into the room and swept them off their feet. Sid reached for Mika's hands. Ketch grabbed Liz. With smiles as wide as the state of California, the four revelers lost themselves in the music and each other's arms. It wasn't until the grandfather clock in the foyer struck midnight that they opened their eyes.

Ketch blazed a scorcher on Liz's lips. "Happy New Year, baby!"

Sid took in Mika's transparent smile, felt the warmth of her body close to his, and desperately wanted to follow suit. But afraid that an impulsive whopper would freak her out, he gave her a quick, friendly kiss instead. To his great surprise, though she blushed, she didn't seem to mind.

Ketch uncorked the champagne bottle. Filling everyone's glass, he raised his in a toast. "To 1973," he cheered, clinking it with the others. "A year of Jubilee for you, and you, and you, and me!"

Then, with a wink to Mika, he laughed. "I told you so. Was tonight fun, or was it fun?"

A New Year's Kiss of Death

ARLY THE NEXT MORNING, AROUND FIVE o'clock, Sid was awakened from a deep sleep by a phone call from his grandmother, telling him that his grandfather had died.

"I went into the bedroom to check on him at midnight to give him a New Year's kiss like I always do," sobbed Antonia. "When he wouldn't open his eyes, I shouted, 'Agostino, wake up!' But he never woke up."

Sid rubbed his eyes. He had to be dreaming. But Antonia's continued wailing soon confirmed that it must be true. "Where's Nonno now?" he asked.

"They took him away. I don't know where he is! I need you, Siddo. Come quickly!"

As the news sunk in, Sid pulled a kitchen chair close to the wall phone and sat down. "I'll be there as soon as I can, Nonna, but first I have to make arrangements. I'll call you right back, okay?" He comforted his grandmother a few more minutes, assuring her that he would do as he promised, and then—clearing his throat and wiping his eyes—he said good-bye, hung up, and called Otis.

"Get your bags ready," ordered Otis, his voice groggy from just being woken up. "I'll have to make an executive decision and waive the restriction on you travelling outside the county since it's New Year's Day. I'll have Lynn clear a three-day pass for you. I'm sure there won't be a problem, since I'll be with you. Pearlie and I will be out to the farm after lunch to pick you up."

"You guys don't need to go. I can drive myself to Sonoma."

"It's not that we *need* to go, Sid. We want to. We counted your mom's folks as good friends. It wouldn't be right to have Agostino's passing go by without paying our respects to him. He was a fine man. One of the finest."

"But . . ."

"No 'buts,' Sid. I don't want you to risk messing up your probation. We'll see you at one."

Click.

In the stillness of the cold kitchen, Sid dropped his chin to his chest and wept.

WITH EVERYONE IN the house still fast asleep, Sid showered, dressed, and packed his suitcase. When he was finished, he pulled on a wool muffler, his parka and gloves, and headed to Calvary Cemetery. Even though he had vowed to visit his parents' graves more regularly, he hadn't been back to the graveyard since his first visit after Halloween at Digger's. Now, crouching in front of their tombstones, he apologized for his absence and explained why he was there.

"Your papa's gone, Mom. Maybe he's with you now. I don't know. All I know is that Nonna and Nonno were the only real family I had left, and now . . ."

The wind picked up, whipping Sid's hair around his face. Reaching into his pocket, he brought out a stocking cap and stuck it on his head, pulling it down snugly over his numb ears.

"I'm heading down to be with Nonna this afternoon," he continued. "You know her—she'll be beside herself with grief, and I won't have a clue how to comfort her. If you were here, you'd know what to do. You were always good at saying and doing the right things to make people feel better. But then again, Nonno was your dad, so you'd probably be as torn up and useless as Nonna and me."

Sid fell back on his haunches, allowing a few meditative moments to pass before adding, "I think Nonna might have dementia. I'm worried about her. With Nonno gone, she could go downhill fast, and then what?"

As if in response to his hypothetical question, Sid noticed—like the last time he'd visited Calvary—that the faintest thread of a voice began to whirl in the air around him. It was as though the swirling clouds in the sky above channeled themselves into a funnel, descended upon him, and whispered this lament:

> *Sooner or later, death comes to all*
> *'Til then, stop worrying*
> *Quit running*
> *Live your day in the sun*
> *Lest our bones cry out for you*
> *To join us before your time*

Was he imagining it, or was he really hearing things? It was impossible, he realized with a jolt, to distinguish between the voices he thought he was hearing with the voices of despair and fear inside his own head. His grandfather's death was simply too fresh, too raw, too life changing, to allow him to separate what was real from what was not. Standing abruptly, he brushed off his jeans, said good-bye to his deceased parents and exited the way he came—beneath the cemetery's rusty iron gate.

He recalled Ketch's New Year's toast, given at roughly the same time his grandfather had died.

God, if this is how a Year of Jubilee begins, he groaned, *You can have it.*

TWO DAYS LATER, Agostino Gianelli was laid to rest in a burial plot behind St. Francis Solano, the church he and Antonia had attended ever since their arrival in Sonoma, notwithstanding their time in Trinity Springs. Sid and his grandmother sat in the front pew during the hour-long funeral Mass, where she clung to him, sobbing. Later, at the gravesite, when they lowered her husband's body into the earth, Antonia collapsed into her grandson's arms.

Pearlie and Otis did their best to help Sid comfort the grieving widow. "I wish we weren't so far away, Antonia," sniffled Pearlie. "I don't like the thought of you being down here all by yourself. Although I'm sure you have many friends . . ."

"I do have many friends." Antonia pressed herself deeper into Sid's side. "And I always have my Siddo."

Sid flinched. "Nonna, there's not a lot I can do to help you right now. Not until my probation is over."

"Unfortunately, that's true." Otis tugged nervously at his shirt collar.

"But Otis," argued Pearlie, "couldn't she move into an apartment or something in Trinity Springs until, you know . . ."

"The problem is," said Otis, "I don't know of any apartments or houses in town that are available for rent at the moment. And by the time one does become available, well . . ."

"You don't understand," said Antonia. "I do not need your help and I do not want to live in an apartment in Trinity Springs. I'm not ready to leave my home here. Not yet. This is where my Agostino's memories are. I need more time to say good-bye to him properly."

"Maybe we could work something out until my probation's over," said Sid. "I could find a nurse to look in on you for a while, Nonna. Maybe stay with you at night, until . . ."

"A *nurse!* I am not sick." Antonia let go of Sid's arm. "Where did you get such an idea?"

Sid cast Otis a look of desperation. *Help.*

"Sid only wants what's best for you, Antonia," blurted Otis.

"That's right," he agreed. "I'm just concerned for your welfare—now that Nonno's gone. That's all."

But instead of being pacified, Antonia bristled. "So, you think you know what I want, or need, better than I do?"

"Well . . . " Lobbing another panicked glance at Otis, Sid muttered, "I'm just saying I don't want you to be alone, Nonna. None of us do. That's all we're saying."

"I told you, I won't be alone."

Sid's mind raced. "Well, what if, instead of a nurse, I made arrangements for, say, a housekeeper to clean your house once a week? Or a handyman to take over some of the more difficult chores around the house? That way I'd know for sure you were having some regular visitors. Or maybe I could . . ."

"*Basta!* That is enough." Narrowing her eyes, Antonia looked fierce. "Siderno, I do not want to hear any more of these 'maybes' from you. My mind is made up. I promise you, I will not be alone. My friends will keep me company. That is the end of our discussion. *Finito.*"

"You do realize that I can be as tough as you, Nonna."

"I would expect nothing less from my grandson."

"All right, then—here's the deal," smiled Sid. "I'll agree to not bug you about being alone if you give me the names and numbers of three of your friends."

"Why?"

"Because if you insist on staying here by yourself, I need someone to contact in case I can't get a hold of you. Just like you can call Otis and Pearlie if you can't get in touch with me for some reason."

"I'm not a child."

"I know you're not. But we're all that each other has left." *Besides, you may not realize it, but you're losing your memory. I'm terrified for you.*

Lifting the hem of her cardigan to her eyes, his grandmother agreed. "You are right. It is only you and I now, Siddo. Don't worry—I will give you the information of my friends."

"And you promise to call me if you ever need help?"

"Of course I promise."

"*Bene.* And I promise, Nonna, that someday we'll be together again."

Letting herself fall back against him, his grandmother sighed like a contented child.

In that moment, as he soaked up the unspoken trust and approval of an old woman he owed so much to—a woman second only to his mother in terms of giving him love, support and acceptance—Sid realized that what he *wanted* to do with his future lined up perfectly with what he felt he *should* do with it. They weren't, as he had always assumed when it came to responsibilities, mutually exclusive. His probation, his return to Trinity Springs—they'd happened for a reason. How else could he explain this peculiar sense of suddenly being in the right place at the right time for the right reason, despite the circumstances that had brought him to this point?

A plan of action, though sketchy, took form in his mind. Visions of a thriving farm with him at the helm and his grandmother at his side began to paw at his imagination. A farm complete with cows and, maybe, chickens. Acres of vegetables and fruit trees. Even a vineyard . . .

"I hate to say this," said Otis, disrupting Sid's daydream, "but we need to head back to Trinity Springs."

Sid gulped. Giving his grandmother a final kiss and hug, he encouraged himself with the thought that, for the time being anyway, they would both get through the loss of his grandfather just like they'd survived his parents' deaths.

With a lot of perseverance.

And a little help from their friends.

Back to Eden

A FEW WEEKS LATER, ON THE AFTERNOON of January 22, one of the farm's friendships suffered a fracture. It started when Liz burst into the house, jubilant with the news of the Supreme Court's *Roe v. Wade* ruling making abortion legal in the US.

Mika, who was watering houseplants in the living room, collapsed into the nearest chair, in shock.

"What's wrong with you?" asked Liz. "This is a victory for women!"

"Killing children is a *victory?* How could you believe such a lie?"

The two girls began arguing so loudly, Ketch strolled into the room to intervene. "Hey, what's this cat fight all about?"

"For your information, it's not a *cat* fight," hissed Liz, storming off to her bedroom.

Mika followed suit. Before reaching her room, she heard Ketch call out to both of them, "Could have fooled me, girls. Guess it's just that time of the month then . . . "

For Mika, who spent the rest of the day mourning over the Supreme Court decision, her argument with Liz became a catalyst, forcing her to choose which living environment would take precedence in her life: the farm or the Ranch. Not that one was heaven and the other hell; she was too pragmatic not to realize each had its advantages and draw-backs. The Ranch was a refuge, a safe place where she could grow spiritually with those who shared similar passions and goals.

The farm, on the other hand, challenged her, kept her plugged into the real world—a world she was called to get her feet dirty in. There was also, she had to admit, the ele-ment of fun and, yes, even happiness on the Jackson farm. She couldn't count the number of times Ketch had made her laugh hysterically, or Sid had made her day with a subtle compliment or word of encouragement. Or that Liz had . . .

Well, maybe she should call David and get his advice. After all, he was the one who'd originally told her that board-ing at the farm would be good "training" for the mission field. But then, what if he asked for specifics?

In the event he did ask, she rehearsed what she might say:

"Well, David, sure my roommates get drunk once in a while. And many's the time I've seen them disappear and come back hours later stoned out of their minds. But hey, it's not like I didn't spend most of my high school and college years high myself. So I understand the cravings, the longing to escape, the power drugs have to fill a void. That's not really the issue though. I mean, what if I was working a nine-to-five job with people totally different from me? I'd be spending even more time with my co-workers than I do now with my roommates, right? The bottom line is, I'm not defined by who my roommates are any more than a boss defines his employee, or a parent defines their child."

Mika snapped out of imagining.

Her excuses for justifying her time on the farm might sound unbiased and reasonable to her now, but how would they sound to David? Would they hold up if he pressed her for more details? What if he asked her if she knew where her roommates got high? Who they bought their dope from, or what kind of people visited them on the farm?

Of course, she could always say it was none of his business, but still—it would be awkward. And what if she slipped and mentioned the episode during the ice storm with Woolf's gun? Ultimately, she knew she couldn't lie. Even if the truth compromised Sid's probation. She might beat around the bush, or respond to a question with another question. She could change the subject. Plead the Fifth. But she could never tell an outright lie. At least, she didn't think she would.

So in the end, she decided against calling David.

Yet, what to do? Her anger at Liz continued to fester. Liz—who had crowed her excitement at the news abortion was now legalized. Liz who had, in her mind, provoked the dispute to begin with. Unyielding Liz, with her condescending attitude and unfair accusation that Mika was a self-righteous fool.

Living under the same roof with someone whose belief system celebrated abortion, Mika concluded, was simply unacceptable. Really, it was just too much. Later that night, however, as she lay awake in bed, still fuming over their argument, she began to feel the faintest twinges of guilt.

I should have turned the other cheek when Liz called me a fool. Instead, I blew up and called her a liar . . . and an idiot. I'm the one who's an idiot! If only I'd kept quiet and said nothing. Yet that was exactly the problem in a nutshell. She couldn't remain silent when it came to issues of life and death. To her, it was all black-and-white. There was no middle ground. Not when it came to abortion.

Finally, she made a decision. First thing tomorrow—that is, if they were on speaking terms by then—she would apologize to Liz, but she'd also explain that it was impossible for her to compromise her conscience on the issue of abortion any more than she was sure Liz could.

Secondly, Mika vowed to be at the Ranch as much as possible, limiting her time on the farm to sleeping and being on schedule for chores. Period.

The bottom line is, Liz needs to realize there are some things I won't back down on. And I need to separate myself more from worldly people. That's all there is to it.

THE NEXT MORNING, after Mika left for school, Liz cornered Sid and Ketch in the kitchen as they were doing breakfast dishes.

"So what do you guys think?"

"Of what?" asked Sid.

"Of Meeks not agreeing with the *Roe v Wade* ruling?" Before either of them could reply, she added, "Who does she think she is anyway? Acting so sanctimonious, insisting she's right and I'm wrong? She's got a lot of apologizing to do if she ever wants to hang out with me again."

"Sounds to me like she was trying to apologize before she left for the Ranch this morning," said Ketch. "Why'd you brush her off?"

"Why shouldn't I? I don't owe her anything. Especially not my forgiveness. Besides, the only thing she apologized for was calling me an idiot."

Sid handed Ketch a plate to dry. "There's not many things worth ending a friendship over, Liz."

"He's right," agreed Ketch. "You sure this is one of them?"

"Of course, I'm sure. I can't be friends with someone completely opposed to something I believe so strongly in."

"Fair enough." Sid let the water out of the sink. Shaking out his wet hands, he asked, "But how do you intend to live in the same house with her until your lease is up if you refuse to talk to her?"

"Yeah," said Ketch, hanging up his towel. "It's not like you've made a million friends here. Meeks and you got along real good before all this happened. I mean, who else are you going to hang with if she's out of the picture?"

Liz pointed to Ketch. "You—that's who."

"Me!"

"Yes, you. Don't look so shocked. Sid can't do much because he's on probation, and Woolf's . . . well, you know."

"But—"

"God knows you're a pain in the ass, cowboy, but we both like to have a good time, so it could work." Liz leveled a challenging gaze at Ketch. "Right?"

Sid rolled his sleeves back down and buttoned his cuffs. He couldn't believe what he was hearing. Apparently, neither could Ketch, who was now belly-laughing at Liz's suggestion.

"What's so funny?" she asked. "We do have *some* things in common."

Still guffawing, Ketch brushed aside her question and headed out to his Harley, leaving Liz inside. Sid excused himself and made his way to the woodpile behind the house. As he split some kindling, it struck him that Liz could actually be right. She and Ketch might be worlds apart when it came to lifestyles and worldviews, but they did have a few things in common. They both had rough edges. They were both risk takers. They could both be brutally honest . . . to a fault. But were their commonalities enough to build a real friendship?

No way. Not in a million years.

As he began stacking the wood he had split, he caught sight of Liz marching out toward Ketch, who appeared to be happily waiting for her on his motorcycle. Her tinted hair shone in the sun. A fitted denim jacket accentuated her small waist. She walked with her head held high—bathed in a self-confidence he'd only seen displayed by her once: at Digger's, on Halloween, when she was in costume as her alter ego. Reminded of the drastic transformation she'd undergone since then, and remembering how she and Ketch had hit it off on New Year's Eve, Sid paused to reconsider.

Nope.

No way.

WHILE LIZ AND Mika went their separate ways, Sid continued to reel from his grandfather's death. Whatever had made him think that his sorrow could be mitigated with a little help from his friends? What real friends did he have available to him anymore? He was forbidden from fraternizing with Max, and now Meeks was spending most of her time at the Ranch. Woolf, in his own little world most of the time, was practically a non-entity on the farm. Add that to the fact that Liz was now monopolizing all Ketch's attention, and it left Sid alone with his never-ending farm work.

By late January, he was so lonely and fed up from the chill of Liz and Mika's stalemate, and so cognizant of his inability to grieve properly for his grandfather, that one day he almost picked up the phone to call Kate. But what would he say? *Sorry I don't answer your phone calls, Kate. It's just that I really don't want to hear about your problems right now—you've got too many and don't seem willing to do anything about them. Got a few hours to listen to mine, though? Oh, and by the way, are you still seeing that jackass Jake Clausen?* Therefore, he nixed the temptation, chastising himself for being weak and desperate and for having no empathy for Kate, who was probably as weak and desperate as himself.

Then, on February 1, the long rumored Back to Eden came to town. The organic food cooperative and café opened in the old Trinity Springs' depot, only two blocks from The Pearl. Because it was the very first store of its kind in the area, within days, it became the county's premier counter-culture hang out. From hidden communes scattered throughout the Trinity wilderness, to myriad little rustic towns dotting the nearby mountains and valleys, hordes of hippies flocked to town to shop and eat at Eden.

Having been turned on to healthy eating in Berkeley, Sid was eager to support a local health food business. He and Liz, also a natural food aficionado, immediately signed up as members. In exchange for volunteering one day a week at the store, they received a 20% discount off all of their purchases.

But not everyone in Trinity Springs was excited about the town's newest business. Not by a long shot.

A FEW DAYS after Eden's grand opening, Pearlie Skinner, fearing the store posed a threat to her establishment, embarked on a clandestine scouting expedition to the new store under the guise of being an interested customer. It was a frustrating venture for someone used to shopping in a traditional grocery, where all the merchandise is clearly marked and where one has been on a first-name basis with the clerks for thirty years. Once inside, she clumsily weighed and marked bulk products and openly gaped at the exorbitant price of fresh produce on display. Worse, she had to ask complete strangers what certain items were—like tofu, carob, yoghurt, kefir, and alfalfa sprouts.

An hour later, she returned from her shopping spree with a month's supply of whole-wheat flour, honey, carob chips, and organic unfiltered apple juice, feeling utterly clueless as to what to do with it all. But, she told Otis, she was at least satisfied she wouldn't be losing her customers anytime soon to the new store or café. The food they served was just "too weird."

Otis, when asked for his opinion, agreed that Eden probably was too weird for most of the people in town, but he also worried that it wouldn't be good for the community in the long run. His reservations, he explained, were due more to the influx of hippies into his jurisdiction than the business threat it presented to his wife's restaurant.

"I'm afraid this town is about to change," he said, recalling the article they had read a few months ago in the *Redding Record Searchlight* about the migration of Flower Children into northern California. "And I'm pretty sure I'm not going to like it."

Valentine's Day Bombshell

SPRING ARRIVED IN ALL ITS DIZZYING GLORY on Valentine's Day, much earlier than it had in years, claimed old-timers. Seemingly overnight, blossoms swelled in the fruit orchards on the valley floor and garden daffodils stretched out their slender green arms toward the sun. Daphne, camellias, heather, meadowfoam, Brodiaea, and primroses bloomed bold and sassy.

In the county's lower pastures and wetlands, wood ducks and snow geese spiraled and swooped in delight while sheep nursed their wobbly newborn lambs. Deep in the mountain's silent evergreen forests, herds of elk and deer bore the Bambi-tailed fruit of their past rutting season. And on the farm, everyone woke that morning in a sort of dulled frenzy—rummy, but as hungry for life as starving grizzly bears after months of hibernation.

Sid was scheduled to work at Eden that day. When he arrived, Lenny Tobin, the store's owner, had just finished unloading a special shipment of flowers and boxed chocolates.

Lenny, letting Sid take over, put his hands on his back and stretched. "Heard you own a cool farm, Sid. How's it going?"

"Fine."

"I don't mean to pry, but since I'm fairly new to the area,

it's just that I'd like to get to know all my employees and volunteers."

"Sure. It's cool."

"One of your roommates who volunteers here told me your grandfather died not long ago. Sorry about that. You doing okay?"

"You must be talking about Liz." A discomforting heat flushed up Sid's neck at the mention of his grandfather. "Yeah," he muttered. "I'm hanging in there."

"Good, good." Lenny moved closer, his voice confidential. "Uh, Liz said there's a chick living out at your farm from Iowa by the name of Tiki or something?"

"Her name's Mika." Sid recalled hearing that Lenny was a transplant to California. "Are you from the Midwest, too?"

"No, I'm from Jersey."

"So's one of my roommates."

But Lenny didn't seem interested in anyone other than Mika. "I heard she's a real looker. Blond, right?"

Sid nodded. *What's he getting at?*

"Liz told me they had a falling out."

"Oh yeah?" *Weird. Why would Liz be confiding in Lenny?*

"She didn't go into detail. Just said Mika was—naïve, I think that was the word she used."

Sid retrieved a box cutter from his apron pocket, bent over, and sliced through the seams of an unopened box. "Yeah, that pretty much describes Meeks."

"Kind of an odd combination, don't you think? Good looks and innocence?"

"Not really," lied Sid. *Of course it's an odd combination. It's not every day you meet a good-looking chick who's not been jaded by life.*

Lenny glanced at his watch. "Well, almost time to open the doors. I'm surprised she hasn't come in here yet."

"Who—Mika? She probably won't. She's pretty busy. Keeps to herself. Plus, she doesn't seem to be that into organic food."

"Someone needs to turn her on to it then, don't you think?"

Sid straightened. "Why?"

Ignoring the question, Lenny waved at a customer waiting outside for the store to open. "Sorry, Sid. Gotta run." Slapping him on the back, he added, "We'll talk later. I have a feeling sales are going to be crazy good today."

As soon as Eden's lunch crowd thinned, Sid meandered into the wing of the old train station where the café was located and grabbed a seat at a bistro table in front of a large window facing Main Street. He ordered an avocado, tomato, and alfalfa-sprout sandwich on rye bread and a cup of vegetarian chili from Charlotte, the only waitress on duty. While he waited for his food, he noticed David Rowe bolt by the window. He was carrying a bouquet of red roses. Stretching his neck, Sid watched as David stopped to run his fingers through his hair before entering The Pearl.

So Mika's got herself a Valentine. Ever since Christmas, when David had come to the house to visit Mika, he had nursed a suspicion that they were seeing each other. And now, with Mika spending so much more time at the Ranch, he was sure of it. *Not that I care, but you'd think she'd be more open about it.* Was she ashamed to have him out to the farm— was that why she was gone so much now?

A moment later, Charlotte brought him his meal. "Here

you go, Sid. Happy Valentine's Day. I'll bring you a treat when you're done with this."

"Thanks, but this is plenty."

"It's hard being single on Valentine's Day, isn't it?"

Sid glanced at Charlotte's hand and noticed she wasn't wearing a wedding ring, even though Lenny had initially introduced Charlotte as his wife. Or had he just said "old lady?" He couldn't remember.

"What would you know about being single?" he asked. Feeling stupid as soon as he said it, he rushed to add, "I mean, even if you weren't married, you wouldn't have a hard time finding—"

"I wasn't talking about me. I was talking about you." Charlotte rolled her eyes. "I was going to say that if you're ever lonely, I know a far-out chick you'd really dig. She lives over in—"

A voice behind them interrupted her. "Don't bother. He's too picky for his own good. It's why he's still single." Kate muscled her way past Charlotte. "Can you move, please. I'm in a hurry. You can set this table for two."

"Well, *excuse* me!" steamed Charlotte. She eyed Kate with contempt before turning back to Sid. "This okay with you?"

As Kate settled into the chair opposite him, he nodded. *Why not?*

"All right then," said Charlotte, addressing Kate. "What do you want?" The "t" at the end of her last word lingered hard and defiant on her tongue.

"One of those breakfast muffins in your display case, and a cup of coffee," she replied, as though she were talking to the wall instead of a person. "Black."

"No sugar. No cream. No surprise." Frowning, Charlotte stalked off, swishing her long gypsy-style skirt in a "good-riddance" flourish in Kate's direction.

"What's with her?" asked Kate.

"Your attitude. Discretion's never been your strong suit. You could try being polite sometimes."

"Funny. I'd say you're the one with a communication problem."

"I was doing just fine until you got here, Kate."

"Oh, I get it." Her eyes sparked as she glanced in Charlotte's direction. "I forgot it's Valentine's Day. Hope I didn't interrupt your little chat-up with her."

"How could you? I have a problem communicating, remember? Then again, you're alone today too, so maybe you're the one with the problem."

"I have to say, your sarcasm is still one of the sexiest things about you, Sid."

"Thanks. You always bring out the best in me."

"Wish I could say the same."

His molars grinding against each other, Sid made a deliberate attempt to slacken his jaw. "Okay, so enough with the preliminaries. What brings you here today?"

"You."

"Must be important if you have to track me down in public."

"How else can I expect to talk to you? You never return my phone calls. Don't tell me you're still mad at me because of Jake?"

"I was never *mad*."

"Jealous then."

Sid concealed his growing discomfort by glancing casually

around the room. "Like I told you a few months ago, Kate, I'm not mad, I'm not jealous—I'm not anything. We've gone over this already and agreed to be friends, remember?"

"Friends return phone calls."

"Look, I apologize, okay? I thought we'd said everything there was to say that night I took you home from Doc Simpson's. Besides, whatever we might have had together in the past is long gone. We both know that. So, if you feel you need what Jake Clausen can give you, then that's your business—not mine. Just spare me all the ups and downs and messy accounts of what that entails."

Charlotte returned with Kate's muffin and coffee, putting a temporary halt to their conversation. When she moved on to wait at another table, Kate hissed, "I don't like her. And I don't like the way she stares at you."

"You can't be serious."

"Don't look at me like I'm crazy, and don't act like you don't know she has a thing for you."

"That's ridiculous. Charlotte's married to Eden's owner."

"Really? She's not wearing a wedding ring."

"Lenny refers to her as his wife."

"Even if she was, so what? Since when did your conscience become so pure that you'd think a married woman was off-limits anyway? You don't think I know women like her—or men like you?"

Sid wasn't easily riled. Sure, David Rowe had provoked him at Christmas with his patronizing attitude. But that was rare. And he almost never blew up, as he had when Jake Clausen had attacked him at Digger's. That had been a purely knee-jerk, physical reaction to an equally physical confrontation.

No, when he was really, really enraged, he became internally calm. Either he'd say nothing or he would speak calmly and quietly, enunciating each word with great precision. He felt that steely composure, that cold peace, come over him now as he slowly he raised his index finger to signal Charlotte that he was ready for his bill. *Kate's problems, or insecurities, or delusions—or whatever it is that's causing her to lash out at me—be damned. I'm not taking her bait.*

Kate, clearly incensed by his brush off, exploded. "Why did you vandalize Jake's shop?"

"Say again?"

"Don't play stupid with me."

"I don't have a clue what you're talking about." As Charlotte slapped the bill down on their table, Sid dug his wallet out of his back pocket. In an even voice, he added, "I think we're done here, Kate."

Kate glared at Charlotte until the waitress moved beyond her range of hearing. "No, we're not done, Sid. Far from it. You went to Jake's last night, tore his shop up, and slashed the tires on his truck. One of his dogs is missing, too."

"They say the Clausens have lots of dogs and a lot that go missing. What's new?"

"Stop being such a cynic. I'm being serious."

"So am I. It sounds like it's Otis you should be talking to—not me."

"Jake already did. When Otis told him how involved an official investigation would be, he decided against going ahead with it."

"Tell him to go ahead anyway. I don't have anything to hide."

Kate dismissed Sid's sincerity with a wave of her hand. "Then tell me who else would want to vandalize his shop?"

"How many enemies does Jake have in Trinity Springs?"

"Jake's convinced it was you. That's why I came here today—to warn you to watch your back." Her eyes glinted. "After all, everyone knows you hate Jake because his dad killed your parents."

Sid froze.

With a gasp, she began to backpedal. "You didn't—oh, my God, Sid—you really didn't know it was Jake's dad driving the truck that day? I mean, everyone in town knows."

Sid felt the café lurch into a tailspin.

"If you don't believe me, ask Otis."

He heard himself say, "Why him?"

"Because he was there when the accident happened, right? But I get why you might not want to talk to him about it. If you don't believe me, check the newspaper—the archives in the library. I'm sure you'll find everything there." Kate touched a spot on her hairline near her right temple and flinched, as though the injury she'd received last Thanksgiving had reawakened. "I'm sorry I had to be the one to tell you—I really am—but it's the truth, and it's time you knew."

"That's why Jake thinks I have a vendetta against him."

"Of course."

Sid found himself going through the motions of opening his billfold and counting his cash, but his mind was reeling with memories. In particular, he recalled how emergency responders at the scene of the accident—once they had extricated him from the vehicle—had kept him away from the crash. He'd seen enough to know that it had been a large truck that had hit his parent's car. But was it a log truck? He couldn't remember. Or maybe he just didn't want to. It was all so blurry—so deeply buried in his brain. Come to think of it, he'd never read any news reports afterward either. Neither had his grandparents. They hadn't even read the obituaries. They'd handed off that responsibility to Otis and Pearlie. In fact, after the accident, no one ever spoke about it, nor was Sid allowed to ask questions. It was considered too painful, too pointless, to discuss.

Lost in thought, Sid placed several dollars on the table next to his bill. "You can tell Jake . . ."

But Kate was gone. Looking up, he caught a glimpse of her jolting out of the café.

"You can tell Jake I wish it *was* me who wrecked his shop," he muttered to himself.

Fifteen minutes later, Sid was back inside the co-op, ringing up purchases at the cash register. He was still so stupefied by Kate's slip-of-the-tongue that he didn't even notice the person stepping up to his counter with a large bag of bulk pecans. He simply grabbed the sack of nuts without looking at who handed it to him and weighed it. "That'll be $4.23."

Ketch tossed Sid a five-dollar bill. "Keep the change."

Recognizing his voice, Sid's head jerked up. "Oh, it's you. Sorry, man."

"What's got you so bothered, Jackson?"

"I just had a run-in with Kate Quinn."

"Ah, her." One of Ketch's eyebrows peeked up over the top of his sunglasses. "The chick you fought over at Digger's on Halloween."

"I didn't fight over *her*. I was defending myself from her

goon friend if you'll remember. But yeah—her. What brings you in here, anyway? I thought you said you didn't care about Back to Eden."

Ketch held up his purchase. "Pecans, dude—a taste of home. And I never said I didn't *care* about this place. My exact words were, 'I don't give a rat's ass whether the steak I eat is from a feedlot in Texas or some hippie's backyard.' Did you never think there were other things that might bring me in here?"

Sid looked in the direction Ketch was pointing and saw Charlotte and Liz deep in conversation. *He must have some business to do with one of them.*

Liz, who apparently sensed the two looking at her, turned and waved. She was beaming from ear to ear. Ketch waved back, his grin at least as wide as hers. Slapping another five-dollar bill on the counter, he ordered Sid to ring up a dozen of the prettiest flowers in the store.

Stepping around the checkout stand, Sid skimmed over the display of flower arrangements and came back a moment later with a bouquet of lavender rose buds wrapped in silvery tissue paper. "Who's the lucky girl?" he ventured, ringing up the purchase.

"Liz, of course. Who else would they be for?"

No matter how hard he tried, no matter how often he saw Ketch and Liz having fun together, he still couldn't wrap his brain around them being more than roommates. "I thought maybe your daughter, or . . ."

"Don't you worry about my Annabelle." Ketch laughed. "I had a whole barrel of flowers sent down to her in Frisco, along with a big box of chocolates and a Valentine's card the size of Texas. I'm limited in how often I can phone her, and someone has to be there with her while we talk, but I'm pretty sure our lawyers will let me call her tonight." Picking up the bouquet, he added, "No, like I said, this here's for Miss Lizzie. She's a real spitfire isn't she? That's how I like 'em."

Sid leaned forward and whispered, "You mean, you two are now a bona fide . . . couple?"

"As in?"

"As in, more than just friends having a good time?"

"She saw the light, dude! Fell hard for me. What can I say?" Gesturing to Liz that he'd be with her in a second, he winked at Sid. "I finally met my match."

Lenny

FINISHED WITH HER LUNCH SHIFT AT THE Pearl, Mika hung up her apron and said good-bye to Pearlie.

"Honey, I can't thank you enough for your help today. Even though it wasn't as busy as I thought it would be." Pearlie stood over the stove, stirring a lemon cream sauce, her head lopped sideways, her eyes focused out the small window over the sink, facing the bustling new health store just down the street. "In the past, my Valentine's Day lunch has always been nearly as popular as my Fourth of July brunch. I'd hate to think that you took off from school today for nothing."

"Of course it wasn't for nothing." Approaching her from behind, Mika placed her hands on Pearlie's shoulders and gave her a quick hug. "I only missed one class, and it wasn't an important one. Besides, I had to come into town this afternoon anyway."

"Oh—what for?"

Mika hesitated. She might as well tell her. From her perch at the window, Pearlie was bound to see where she was going after she left anyway. "I have to run into Back to Eden for a minute."

The circular motion of the whisk in Pearlie's hand slowed. Then it picked back up with even more gusto. "Well that's fine, sweetheart. Don't forget to take them pretty flowers that young man brought over for you today. Sure was thoughtful of him."

"Yes, David's very—considerate," agreed Mika. "I'm sure you have something just as nice waiting for you at your house tonight."

"That's a fact. Otis has something waiting for him, too. Now, go on you. You've got errands to run."

Scooping up her Valentine flowers, Mika ambled reluctantly toward the door, muttering under her breath, "And it's not an errand I'm running, Pearlie. It's more like a walk of shame."

FIVE MINUTES LATER, Mika sloughed through Eden's front door. To her left, she saw Sid behind the cash register waiting on a customer. Beyond him, at the front of the vitamin and herbal remedies aisle, she noticed a man with a sandy colored Afro and a Fu-Manchu moustache, studying her intently as though she were a shelf item for sale. When her eyes met his, he winked and nodded his head in a "come-on-over-here" motion.

Instead, Mika veered left and wandered down an avenue of fruit and vegetable bins. There, near a short corridor leading to Eden's café, she caught sight of Liz talking with Ketch. She was hugging a spray of red roses to her breast. To Mika's astonishment, their mutual joy was palpable, even at a distance.

Instantly losing her nerve, she ducked behind a tall display of kitchen utensils. *I can't believe what I'm seeing. Liz and Ketch an item? I mean, granted, I haven't been at the farm much, but in less than three weeks—this happens?*

The realization that she'd been so absent as to have missed such a monumental shift in her roommates' relationship left her feeling more disconnected than ever. Seconds later, she heard the distinct scuffle of Ketch's cowboy boots fade down the hallway. Stepping out from behind the screen, she made her way toward Liz. "Hey," she said.

"Hey," replied Liz, guardedly.

"Beautiful flowers you have there."

"Ketch gave them to me." Nodding to Mika's bouquet, Liz asked, "And yours?"

"They're from David—you know, at the Ranch."

"The big guy, yeah. I've seen him pick you up at the farm a few times."

Steadying herself, Mika pushed ahead, vaguely aware that she was holding her breath as she spoke, as though she were under water and had to get everything said before she passed out from the effort. "I just got off from helping Pearlie with her lunch crowd and thought I'd swing by and say Happy Valentine's Day and also say I'm sorry for yelling at you and for the attitude I had when, when—you know."

Without warning, Liz sprung across the distance separating them and buried Mika in a hug. "I'm sorry, too, Meeks."

The two girls clung to each other a moment, neck-to-neck, sniffling and bracing themselves for the inevitable explanations that always follow such thaws in relationships.

Liz was the first to pull away. Retrieving an envelope from her apron pocket, she handed it to Mika. "I was going to slip this under your bedroom door tonight while you were sleeping. I didn't have the guts to face you in person."

Mika lifted the flap on the envelope and saw it was a Valentine's Day card. The front featured a photograph of two old women laughing as they haggled over who was going to take the wheel of a sleek new red Corvette for a test drive. The caption below it read, *Friends May Not Always Agree on Everything, but Real Friends are Friends Forever.* Opening the card, she read Liz's inscription. "This reminds me of us, Meeks. Time to get over this stupid stalemate, don't you think? I'm not sorry about defending what I believe, but I *am* sorry about getting so mad and everything. Truce?"

Mika flashed a peace sign before leaning in one more time to give her roommate a bonus hug. "I actually got you a card, too, but I couldn't find the right words to write. That's why I came in person." Lifting her chin, she added, "I understand why you can't apologize for what you believe in, because the truth is, I can't either."

"Fair enough."

"So, for the sake of our friendship, how about we just table the topic of abortion for a while?"

"Fine by me—unless we both decide we want to go at it again."

"No thanks. Not anytime soon anyway."

"What about politics?" asked Liz, flicking Mika's shoulder teasingly.

"Sure. I'm game if you are—as long as we can agree to disagree." Mika returned the flick. "How about religion?"

"Nah, one firecracker at a time is enough for me." Lowering her eyes, Liz added, "About Ketch and me. I know it must seem crazy—us fighting like cats and dogs so much before—but all things considered, he was really the only available roommate that was left to hang out with. And you know, once I cut him some slack, I realized he's just all talk. Actually, he's pretty . . . cool."

And your bark is worse than your bite, Liz. "Yeah, Ketch can be a rascal, but he's a good one for sure."

"The only thing is . . . " Liz's voice trailed off. Toying with the petals of a rose, she blurted, "I get a vibe that I might be horning in on your friendship with him."

"You think Ketch and I . . . ?" The way Liz had said "friendship" made Mika laugh so loudly, several customers turned to stare. "No, Ketch and I are just good friends. I promise you, that's all. I'm sure he'd tell you the same thing."

Looking enormously relieved, Liz switched gears. "I suppose you'll be getting back to the farm late again tonight."

"Yes, I've kind of over-committed myself at the Ranch. Why do you ask? Don't tell me I spaced out on our schedule. Are we on this week?"

"No, no. We're on next week. I was just wondering if you and David were doing something for Valentine's Day."

"We're both too busy." Mika held out her bouquet. "This is the extent of our celebration. What are you doing?"

"Ketch and I are heading over to the coast on his Harley as soon as I get off work. He made dinner reservations at some fancy restaurant in Eureka."

"Sounds fun." Mika checked herself. "Wait, I thought you didn't like motorcycles. You said you hated the whole macho image thing and . . . "

"Enough with the reminders, okay? A smart, strong woman knows how to give and take when it's worth it. Let's just say I'm open to change—to a point. Dig what I'm saying?" With a nod of her head, Liz excused herself. "Got to get back to work. Thanks again for coming by, Meeks. I'm so glad all this is behind us now."

"I am, too. Believe me."

"Oh, one more thing." Liz swiveled around to face Mika once more. "Ketch is going to call his daughter tonight from the restaurant. He's really jazzed about it."

"So you know about Annabelle?"

"Of course I know. Why would he tell you about her, but not me?"

Mika didn't know why she'd assumed Ketch hadn't told Liz. Perhaps she'd thought Liz was the kind of person who, if she had found out he had a daughter, would consider it a deal breaker. After all, "maternal" wasn't exactly an adjective that described Eliza Drabek. "I don't know," she replied, lamely.

"Like I said, Meeks, I'm open to change. That includes liking someone who has a kid."

As Liz trotted off to help a customer, Mika found herself wondering just how flexible Liz really was. It was one thing to say you're open to change. It was another to endure, let alone embrace, it. And while she wasn't really surprised Ketch and Liz were embarking on a relationship, being as their rough, independent edges probably did complement each other somehow, she couldn't see Liz's toleration of Ketch's more redneck habits stretching too far into the future.

Then she heard a reproving voice—whether it was her own or God's, she couldn't say—ask, "*And just how open to change are you, Mika Larson?*"

AFTER MIKA WAVED a limp good-bye to Sid and hurried out of the store, Lenny pulled him aside, motioning for another volunteer to take over at the register.

"Hey, was that the chick from Iowa who lives on your farm?"

"It was."

"Why didn't she buy anything?"

"I wouldn't know." Sid shrugged. "Looks like she just stopped in to talk to Liz."

"I tried to get her attention."

"I noticed." *No doubt everyone in the store saw you checking her out, Lenny. Maybe you should try being less obvious next time.*

"I'm sure she saw me."

Sid glanced at the clock. Removing his volunteer employee badge from the lapel of his shirt, he tucked it into his pocket and made a move to go. "Yeah, I don't know how she could have missed you, Len. I've got to head back to the farm."

Lenny followed Sid into the employees' break room. "But I don't get it. Why didn't she come over to talk to me before she left? Doesn't she know who I am?"

"Should she?" It was a rhetorical question, laced with sarcasm. Sid, taken aback by Lenny's self-importance, simply couldn't help himself.

"Well, if she doesn't know who I am yet," retorted Lenny, "I intend to see that she does."

Sid retrieved his jacket and keys from a cubicle bearing his name. He wasn't about to rebuke Lenny's presumption. He'd known enough men like him —charismatic in small doses but obnoxious and downright narcissistic in larger servings—to know they loathed any correction. He just wished he knew why Lenny was so hyper-focused on Mika. It made absolutely no sense to him. So, with nothing but a grunt for a good-bye, he opened the side door and stepped out into the parking lot.

With a forced laugh, as though he wanted Sid to believe

he was only being facetious, his boss called out after him. "Just remember this, my friend. What Lenny Tobin wants, Lenny Tobin gets."

Sid jingled his keys in the air as a sign he'd heard him, but to himself he grunted, "You'll never get Mika Larson, Lenny. I'll make sure you don't."

LATER THAT EVENING, Sid came home to an empty farmhouse. Apparently, everyone had Valentine's Day plans but him. Even Woolf had been invited to a dinner event at the American Legion Hall in Weaverville, where vets could meet and mingle with the opposite sex. At this moment, he was probably rubbing elbows with some girl and having a good time. Or, for Woolf's sake, he hoped he was.

Yet here I am, with no one.

Then again, he reasoned it had been a day of bombshell revelations, so maybe it was best he was alone. Considering everything Kate had told him, he had a lot of things he needed to process. And once he started going down that road . . .

I don't want to go down that road. Not yet.

Desperate for a diversion, he traipsed into the mudroom and readied to do his chores, but in his current state of mind, everything seemed riddled with hidden meanings. The act of pulling on his boots reminded him of all the sludge and slime he'd have to wade through if he were to do as Kate had suggested and dig into his past. And when he threw on his rain slicker, he found himself wishing there were some sort of invisible vinyl he could wear to protect himself from the despair he felt pouring down on him. Then, as he made his way from the mudroom out onto the porch, the ultimate spoiler, self-pity, slithered into his consciousness.

For years, he'd refused to address the wounds festering inside him. Even his first visit to Calvary after Halloween had been just an introduction of sorts, a recognition that he needed to face his past. But now his afflictions roared to life afresh; raw, legitimate, unresolved. It felt as if they were all coalescing into one giant seething tumor inside his head. His scalp began to tingle. The sensation was so real, he raked his hand through his hair to make sure he still had some. Had it been any other time or place, he'd swear he was tripping on acid. *Psychosomatic—that's what this is. This aching, this pain, this lonely abyss.*

Outside the barn, unable to continue walking, he buckled against the wall, his mind racing out of control. Squatting down, he lowered his head and tried to breathe evenly, deeply, to avoid hyperventilating.

Get a hold of yourself, Sid.

But this barn, the farm, the house. Everywhere I turn, I see them. I hear them. I remember them. I can't get them out of my head.

They're gone. You have to deal with it.

But I want them. I need them. It's not fair.

Life's not fair. Do you think you're the only one who's ever lost their parents? Sooner, or later, it happens to everyone.

I was too young. They were too young. They weren't ready. I wasn't ready.

No one's ever ready.

But . . .

And then, through the back-and-forth internal dialogue, it hit him. What tormented him most—more than being orphaned at such a young age, even more than his father's death—was the loss of his mother; of being deprived of her maternal, unconditional love all those times he'd needed it.

Like now.

To his astonishment, out of nowhere, a desperate urge to connect with a woman seized him. Not in the typical "let's hang out together and see what happens" type of hookup he'd pursued in Berkeley, but a literal partnering with a special woman on a deeply human level. Someone like his mother—strong, thick-skinned, and assertive, yet also warm and playful. Patient, and kind. He was overwhelmed with the want of it. With the need of "her." His breathing slowed. He raised his head. He felt hung over, completely drained by grief.

Well, great Valentine's Day this turned out to be, he muttered, as he rose and went inside the barn to feed Hester. *Not that I was expecting anything to begin with, but it would be nice to have someone tell me they love me . . . besides my grandmother. Fat chance of that happening while I'm on probation, though. I mean, who'd want a relationship with a guy who could very well end up in prison?*

Rubbing the cow's moist muzzle with the heel of his hand, he said, "I guess you're my Valentine this year, Hester. If I pour out my miserable heart to you, do you promise you'll keep everything in strict confidence?"

Hester heaved a mournful *moo.*

"Thanks, girl. I know you will."

HOURS LATER, A freshly showered and scrubbed Sid entered The Pearl. If someone would have asked him why he was there, he couldn't have said, other than—still feeling lonely and restless—he was acting on an inexplicable impulse to see Pearlie. Appearing surprised, and enormously flattered by his appearance, she quickly seated Sid at the counter, insisting he let her treat him to a late dinner. When he was finished eating, she begged him to try a new dessert she had concocted that afternoon.

"I made it especially for Valentine's Day," she said, explaining that she'd named it the *Flying Dutchman* because once a customer tasted it, she hoped there would be no going back. Served warm in a stemmed bowl, it consisted of two large coconut macaroons smothered in a peach, raspberry, and cinnamon compote with a dollop of sweetened whipped cream and slivered almonds scattered on top. Finally—because she probably worried how her traditional cooking compared to Back to Eden's—she strategically anchored a sprig of fresh mint to the lip of the dish before setting it in front of him.

Sid dove in. Licking the last remaining crumbs from his spoon, he said, "Wow, that was great, Pearlie."

"You really think so?"

"Of course. Everything you make is great."

"Why, Sid, coming from you . . ."

"Coming from me, you know it's the truth." Sid grabbed his backpack, stood to his feet, and planted a kiss on Pearlie's forehead. "I've got to get going. Thanks, again, Pearlie. It was good catching up."

"It sure was." Pearlie rose from her stool to accompany Sid to the door. "Maybe now you won't be such a stranger?"

Convicted by her comment, Sid paused. The truth was, since being busted last summer, he'd been afraid to be seen socializing too often with the Skinners. Afraid people might accuse him of having benefitted from Otis's favoritism. But then, wasn't that exactly what had happened? Given the same circumstances, Otis would never have advocated for someone else—say Max Quinn—like he had for Sid. Now, he realized how much his public aloofness over the past few months may have hurt Otis and Pearlie. *Well, people around here are going to think what they want regardless of what I do, or don't do. So I might as well quit worrying about it and just be myself.*

Pearlie repeated herself. "Sid? Maybe now you won't be such a stranger?"

"It's taken me a while to get into a routine up here, but I'm back on my feet again, so yeah—you'll probably be seeing more of me from now on."

Blubbering, Pearlie lunged toward him.

Sid let his godmother envelope him in her arms, her unchecked emotions making it difficult for him to say good-bye. But with a promise to drop by again soon, he tore himself away from her and headed to his car. It was dark when he arrived back at the farm, feeling lighter than he had all day. Crazy, he thought, how far a little maternal kindness and attention could go in making a guy feel like a loved-up little kid.

Dare he say it?

Trinity Springs almost felt like home again.

The Chesterfield

THE PEARL SAT EMPTY, WHICH WAS TYPICAL for a late Monday afternoon in early April. With the lunch crowd gone and warm weather luring customers outdoors, Pearlie Skinner didn't expect business to pick up again until suppertime. She propped the main door of the café open, letting a pleasant spring breeze in. School kids milled about on the sidewalk out front, killing time before heading home. A few of the more trendy among them wheeled their skateboards up and down the street trying to perfect their moves.

Picking his way around the teens, Otis entered the diner and took a seat at the counter. "Got a minute, Babe?"

"Sure," said Pearlie. "Coffee?"

Otis looked over his wife's shoulder into the seemingly empty kitchen and nodded. "Anyone here?"

"Only me." Pearlie poured some fresh brew into a large mug and slid it toward him. "What brings you in here this time of day?"

"Sid found out about Norm Clausen."

Pearlie nearly dropped the carafe. "What!"

"I bumped into Katie Quinn today. She told me she let it slip back in February—said she told Sid it was Jake's dad driving the log truck that killed his folks."

Pearlie thumped the coffee pot on the counter and collapsed onto a stool next to her husband. "I suppose it was bound to happen sooner or later. I was just hoping it would be later. That we'd be the ones to talk to him about it. I mean, who knows what conclusions he's come to without knowing all the facts? Oh, he must be so upset." Picking up a menu, she began fanning herself with it. "Come to think of it, Mika told me that Sid hasn't been himself for a few weeks."

"Is that right?"

"Said he's been stewin' and gloomin' around the house. She thought maybe it was because Billie Ketchum is spending all his time now with that other girl out at the farm. What's her name?"

"Eliza Drabek."

"Yes, her. Anyway, Mika said he even bowed out of some St. Patrick's Day barn dance they were all invited to outside of town. Some Irish thing-a-ma-jiggy."

"That sure don't sound like Sid."

"Sure doesn't—especially since Digger's Saloon has been off-limits to him. You'd have thought he'd jump at a chance to go dancin' and all."

"Has Sid mentioned anything about the accident to you?"

"No, and I'm sure he won't, either. All he has to do is go to the library, and he'll find out everything there is to know."

"Not everything, Pearlie . . . although that's the other thing I was going to tell you. Sid's already been there. I stopped at the library before coming here, and in a round-a-bout way found out he was last there on March 17. Evidently, he spent several hours digging through the *Trinity Times* archives."

"Dear Lord, what a fool I was to think Sid would never care to know the truth!"

"It's water under the bridge now, Pearlie."

"But there's no way he'll understand! Not just by reading the newspapers. He'd have to check other sources to get the full picture—he'd have to read the medical reports and . . ."

"Yes, and the investigation that followed. Then again, maybe he already has. Maybe he's found out everything there is to know and has come to terms with it without us having to say a word."

"So what do we do, Otis?"

"Either wait for him to approach us, or point blank ask him about it."

Pearlie buried her face in her hands. "We should have told Sid everything up front when he first came back home. Now he probably thinks we're involved in some kind of cover up."

"Don't go jumping to conclusions."

"You've got to talk to him, Otis. Otherwise . . ."

"That's just what I intend to do, Pearlie. But when and how, I don't rightly know."

Pearlie snapped her head back, her eyes suddenly bright. "I have an idea."

WHEN SID FIRST heard someone knocking at the door, he was half asleep. Rolling over, he covered his ears and ignored it. But when the tentative tapping turned into insistent hammering, he rubbed his eyes and yelled, "What!"

"It's me—Mika. I need to talk to you."

Sid sat up. Having fallen asleep on the rug in front of the hearth in the library, his muscles responded about as readily as clumps of clay to a spade. Rising to his feet, he rubbed his shoulder, growling under his breath.

"Let me in. I'm worried about you, Sid."

"Leave me alone."

"If you don't open up, I'll have to call Otis. Is that what you want? Are you listening to me? Because if you are . . ."

Trudging up the short flight of steps to the landing, Sid flung the door open. Mika squeezed past him, scanning the library. He could only imagine what she thought of all the newspapers, magazines, and photo albums littering the room, not to mention the empty wine and beer bottles.

"What a disaster." Turning her attention back to Sid, she added, "You, too. You like you haven't slept in a week."

"Thanks. What do you want, Meeks? Why aren't you at the Ranch?"

"I took the day off because someone needs to find out what's going on with you. You do realize that you've been locked up in here for over two days."

"I'm fine."

"Really? Then what have you been eating these last two days? Mika bent down and picked up the current issue of *Rolling Stone* in one hand and the *National Lampoon* in the other. "Magazines? Newspapers? Because I don't see any food in here."

"I said, I'm fine." Circling around Mika, he made his way back to the fireplace.

"Well, I don't think you're fine, and neither do Pearlie and Otis. When you wouldn't return their phone calls, they asked me to check on you."

"You can tell Otis, I'll call him when I'm ready to talk to him."

"You'll have to tell him yourself. He said if he doesn't hear from you by noon he's coming over for a probation check."

Arms akimbo, Mika asked, "What's your beef with Otis anyway?"

"Norm Clausen."

"Who?"

"Jake's dad."

"What's Jake's dad got to do with Otis?"

Sid crumpled into his father's old wingback chair, hooding his blood-shot eyes with his hands so Mika couldn't see the tears pooling in them. He was suddenly so choked up, he couldn't speak.

Mika sat down on the leather stool at the foot of the chair, astonishment written on her face. "Talk to me."

Sid wavered. When he finally replied, his voice was singed with bitterness. "Norm Clausen was driving the log truck that killed my parents."

"I take it you . . . didn't know that before?"

"No. Yes. I mean, I blocked the memories of that day out of my mind so much that when someone . . . brought it up recently, I realized I didn't know anything for sure." Pointing to the papers strewn around the room, he added, "Ergo, I did some digging in the town library."

"And?"

"I discovered a lot of people have kept me in the dark about a lot of things." Before Mika could ask him any more questions, Sid hurried ahead with an abbreviated account of the day the accident happened, explaining that he and his parents had just set out on a camping trip. He was lying in the back of the station wagon when they were hit, he explained, which, according to one report, was the one and only spot in the car anyone could have survived the crash.

"I don't remember anything about the impact. People said

it was a miracle I walked away with just a few minor cuts and bruises." Sid stopped to chew his lip. "My mom was six months pregnant at the time. Like I said, it was all a blur. Then this morning, for some weird reason, it all started coming back to me. I recalled that when Otis showed up, he tried to keep me from seeing my parents, but I broke away from him. I saw my mom and dad laid out on the road next to the car. Dead. I mean, just . . . *dead*. One minute they were alive and talking and laughing. The sun was shining. I didn't have a care in the world. Life was perfect. And then the next . . ."

Mika placed her hands over Sid's.

"In hindsight," he added, "I realize I was probably in shock, but I felt like I had to touch my mother's stomach to see if the baby was alive. Somehow, I thought that if it moved, maybe my mom wouldn't really be dead."

"Oh, Sid. I'm so sorry."

"Yeah, everyone was." Sid stiffened. Withdrawing his hands from Mika's, he leaned his head back and closed his eyes.

"What else did you remember about that day?"

When he didn't respond, Mika did something so unexpected and out-of-character, it knocked the wind out of Sid's dark sails. She crawled into the Chesterfield alongside him. Wedging her body next to his, she rested her hand over the center of his chest as though checking for his heartbeat.

Certain that he must be dreaming, Sid slowly opened his eyes. There was Mika all right, glued to him like a Band-Aid—so close, her hair, cascading over the front of his shirt and brushing against his fingertips, billowed in waves with each breath he took. He was immediately and acutely aware of one thing: her empathy had utterly shattered his stereotype of her. With her nestled snugly against him—Trinity Spring's bad-boy—he realized this was a woman who was willing to care more for him than herself.

He felt her shift slightly. Fearing she might be second-guessing herself, he debated whether to assure her that there was nothing sexual in their closeness. Well, not *overtly* sexual. At least, not by his definition of the word, anyway. A voice in his head, however, cautioned him from saying anything. *Come on, Sid, who are you kidding? One thing leads to another. She knows it, and you know it. Don't blow it by stating the obvious.*

So Sid didn't pretend that their closeness was inconsequential, but neither did he warn Mika that she was a flame licking at the mountain of dry kindling he'd become. Instead, he continued smelling her perfumed hair, knowing, but not caring, that he was playing with fire. Truth be told, he was dying to be torched. He yearned to have every fear and rotten memory in his head go up in smoke, even if it meant allowing a bonfire to be ignited in his soul to achieve it. In fact, after years of tossing his pain, disappointments, and regrets onto the burn pile of his heart to be dealt with later, it now occurred to him that perhaps he'd been waiting for this very moment, for this very girl sitting next to him, to walk into his life and set him ablaze.

Mika's waiting for you to explain what's going on here. If you don't hurry up, she'll jump ship. Speak up! Say something! Tell her more about the accident. Be honest about how you feel.

Tell Mika the truth? That would consist of him begging her not to budge until all his self-pity, anger, and equivocation was reduced to ash. How extraordinary, he thought, to have a caring human being this near, as though they were sharing the same heart in the same moment. If only he could keep Mika this close indefinitely. But tell her all that? *No way. She'd freak out for sure.* Besides, how could he explain the depth of his feelings for her when they were so convoluted and brand new that he couldn't yet put them into words?

Just then, with her hand still firmly on his chest, Mika whispered, "Do you feel what your heart just did? It's slowed way down."

Sid was quite aware that his heart had stopped galloping. Not only that, the hangover he'd been nursing had lifted. The piercing headache behind his eyes was gone. Come to think of it, within the span of five minutes, he had gone from barely being able to hear himself think because of the pounding in his ears, to hearing nothing but the boughs softly swaying on the fir tree outside the lower library's half-open window.

"It's the peace that passes all understanding," explained Mika.

Peace?

"If peace feels like floating higher than a kite," he replied at last, "then I believe you might be right."

"I guess it does feel like that, doesn't it?" Mika sighed with satisfaction. "I've been worried about you, Sid."

"Worried? About what?"

"Well, that you might do something. You know . . . "

"You mean, something that would screw up my probation and put me in prison?"

"Exactly. Having peace in your life will help you get through to the end."

Little did she know how much he'd craved getting stoned the last few weeks. How staying straight was getting harder with each passing day—not easier. Just last night, he'd slipped up to Ketch's room to see if his roommate knew where he could score some weed. When he'd discovered Ketch wasn't home, he'd decided to drive into town to get some from Max.

It was only after going back into the library to get his keys, and downing a half-bottle of cheap wine and some Scotch, that he'd blacked out in front of the fireplace, never making it to his truck. Sid's stomach lurched at the dim memory of puking in the upstairs bathroom a few hours before Mika had woken him up. Sniffing his still damp, shampooed hair, he thanked God that he'd had the good sense to shower before returning to the library.

Mika lifted her head off his chest. "You don't have to tell me any more if you don't want to. Although, I wish you would."

Realizing she might stay right where she was if he continued his story, Sid picked up where he left off. "All right, back to Norm Clausen. He was—and still is—a drunk. I found out he'd already had his license revoked once before the accident."

"You mean he might have been drunk when he hit your parents' car?"

"None of the reports I read indicated alcohol played a role in the accident, and Otis never said anything about the driver of the truck being drunk, but that doesn't mean anything. You see, my dad was the judge who originally revoked Norm's driver's license. Norm appealed the decision and got it back shortly before my parents died. Someone testified in the investigation that there was bad blood between Norm and my dad because of it. Another claimed someone had been vandalizing the farm for weeks leading up to the accident."

"In other words, you think Norm might have deliberately killed your parents."

"That's what I've been spending the last two days trying to figure out."

Stroking Sid's hand, Mika seemed to consider what he was saying. "If what you suspect is true, are you saying Otis is guilty of some kind of cover-up? I'd never believe it of him."

"Otis was at the scene of the accident, so you'd think he would have known all the details of the investigation. Why, then, didn't he ever tell me? I don't get it."

"He probably thought you were too young to handle that kind of information. I mean, how old were you at the time?"

"Twelve. I suppose it makes sense that he could have been trying to protect me from something because of my age. But what?"

"Maybe he figured that if you ended up living in Trinity Springs the rest of your life, it would be best to let the past go. After all, sharing the same town with a person who could have been responsible for your parents' deaths, but was never brought to trial for it, could make for some pretty nasty scenarios."

"Such as?"

"Two words: Dodge City."

"Oh, so you think Otis was afraid I might take the law into my own hands someday?"

"Would you?"

Sid flashed a wry smile. "I have to admit, a showdown with Jake's dad at the O.K. Corral sounds pretty appealing to me at the moment."

"I bet." grinned Mika. "Did you find out anything else?"

"I haven't had access to all the records yet, but so far it appears Norm's brakes may have failed. At least that's what most of the reports said."

"And you don't believe it?"

"Given the circumstances, would you?"

"I'm not God, Sid. I don't have all the answers."

"But Norm Clausen does. If his brakes really did fail, or if it truly was a coincidence, that would be one thing. But, if his brakes *didn't* fail—if Norm had been stalking my parents and knew where they were going that day—then he's a murderer. Plain and simple."

They both turned pensive. Then, as if she'd been startled from a deep sleep and realized for the first time where she was, Mika bent forward to get out of the chair.

Sid pulled her gently back toward him. He couldn't let her leave; he hadn't told her how he felt about her. But words still failed him. Every phrase popping into his mind sounded stupid, or flat, or woefully insufficient. Then, an epiphany hit him.

He was in love.

The revelation stunned him. If someone would have told him last September—even last night—that he would fall head-over-heels in love with a Jesus Freak from Iowa, he would never have believed it. Yet here he was, immersed in the reality of it as he struggled to get the words "I love you" out of his mouth.

As he tried, and failed, the moment was lost.

Mika scurried out of the chair and stood in front of him, her eyes unblinking, her hands shoved into the pockets of her jeans. Clearly, she was already regretting what she'd done. "I don't know what came over me, Sid. I hope I didn't—you know—I hope you didn't think I was . . ."

Sid rose to face her. "Meeks, I . . ."

"It's just that, as you were pouring your heart out, I looked at you and I guess I was so moved by your loss and your pain and, well, your dilemma . . ."

"You don't have to apologize."

"But, I've never done anything like this before."

"Like what? Comfort someone who needed it?"

"Well, no. I mean I've never done anything so . . . impulsive before. That is, not with someone like you."

"Like me?"

"With someone who wasn't a boyfriend, is what I'm trying to say."

"If you're worried David will find out that you sat on my lap for twenty minutes in my library—"

"I didn't sit on your lap. I was just sitting . . . next to you." A furious blush shot up Mika's neck. "You're making fun of me. And, besides, I'm not afraid of what anyone thinks."

"You're not?"

"I am *not*. And can you stop being so cynical?"

"I'm just trying to lighten things up between us, Mika."

"I don't think what happened between us is funny."

"Neither do I."

With a low growl, Mika turned. "That didn't come out right. What I meant was, there was *nothing* that happened between us, funny or otherwise."

"Answer me this then." Sid spun Mika around to face him. "If that's the case, why do you act as though it did? And where is this guilt suddenly coming from?"

"There's no guilt! You only say that because you think you

know me. The truth is, you hardly know me at all. Because if you did, you'd . . . " Mika's voice broke as she backed away from him.

Sid dropped his hands in defeat. But as he watched her make her way toward the door, he called out, "Meeks, wait." He approached her gingerly, as a horse trainer would approach a mustang, stopping far enough away so as not to make her feel threatened. "At least let me say this. You'll never know how grateful I am for the comfort you gave me this morning. I'm sure it was a stretch for you to get that close to me, but your closeness was exactly what I needed. In fact, it's what allowed me to open up to you the way I did."

Mika's blush returned.

"It's hard for me to admit it," he rushed to add, "and don't take this the wrong way, but for days I've been craving a human touch. Especially, a woman's touch. A woman who understands and cares. Mika, I haven't unburdened myself like this to anyone. Ever. As a matter of fact, you're the first person I've really talked to about the accident."

"You never talked to your grandparents about it?"

"How could I? They were grieving, too. I couldn't hurt them more than they were already hurt. They were the last people I felt I could talk to."

With Sid's affirmations, Mika's shoulders relaxed. "I guess I should feel privileged to have been with you today then, eh?

"Most definitely. No guilt—please."

"Imagine that." Mika's voice had a nervous pitch to it, betraying a lingering discomfort. "Me—the only creature on Earth who's wormed their way into Sid Jackson's inner sanctum. Besides your mom and dad, of course."

"Actually, not quite. Before you, there was Homer."

"A pet?"

"Yes, a dog. And there was Alexander the Salamander, too." Sid stepped around Mika to open the door for her, confident that he'd diffused her anxiety. "Maybe I'll tell you the story someday."

In the hallway, Mika wheeled around to appraise the unkempt library one last time. "So, you're sure you're okay?"

If you mean 'okay' as in 'I'm not bummed out anymore,' then, yes. I'm good. But if you mean 'okay' as in I can let things go back to the way they were between us? No. I can't promise that. You've got me wound up like a top. Why do you think I'm encouraging you to leave now, before this feeling I have for you takes over, and I lose control?

"Absolutely," he said out loud.

To make his statement appear genuine, he forced a yawn and stretched to his full height. "I'm going to clean up in here before I come downstairs. Oh, and if Otis calls again, don't worry. I'll talk to him."

I can't believe what just happened. I cozied up to my landlord as though he were my boyfriend! Sid Jackson? A law-breaking, agnostic pothead? How could I?

As she made her way downstairs, Mika berated herself for a dangerous lapse in judgment. Pausing in the foyer at the bottom of the steps, she lowered her nose to the neck of her blouse and sniffed. She was awash with Sid's presence. Nearly faint from it. Sprinting to her bedroom, she opened her dresser drawer, grabbed a new t-shirt, pulled off her old one, and tossed it into the laundry basket.

There. That'll do it. I don't care how hurt he looked, or how badly he seemed to need a hug. I shouldn't have crawled into that chair with him. Now I've gone and given him the wrong impression. He'll think there's something between us when there's not.

With a start, Mika noticed that Sid's woodsy, unmistakably masculine aroma lingered in her hair as well. No wonder she couldn't stop thinking about him. Quickly, she gathered her hair up in her hands, pulling it firmly away from her face, and began French braiding it. She should never have promised Pearlie she'd talk to Sid. From now on, she'd have to keep her distance from him. That's all there was to it.

Her jaws clenched, she finished plaiting her hair and looked in the mirror. Ridding herself of external reminders of Sid wasn't working. Somehow, he'd snuck through a crack in her fortressed heart, gaining access to places she hadn't allowed anyone to go to in years. Perhaps, instead of trying to deny her feelings for him, she could simply nip them in the bud by coming up with a solution that would prevent her from ever being in a compromised situation with him again.

Yes. That's it!

Then and there, she determined to curb her natural instinct to rescue, comfort, and restore Sid—something she tended to do with every creature she thought needed a healing or loving touch. But a moment later, as she caught yet another whiff of him on the palms of her hands, she wobbled again. How easy to make such resolutions in his absence. Sure, his last words to her as they had parted in the library, less than ten minutes ago, indicated he had regained control of his emotions. But what if he were to come downstairs right now, this very instant, and want to talk some more? What if they were to find themselves alone in the house later on, or . . . ?

In a panic, she found it impossible to even pray. The whole thing was simply ridiculous, she told herself. She wasn't Sid's type and, surely, she represented everything to him that he found inconsequential, if not downright offensive. Nor was he *her* type. Not by a long shot. Taking a deep breath, she began making a mental list of their many differences, before realizing that even her compulsion to do that was just another sign he'd succeeded in getting into her head.

I have to get out of here. Go into town. Go somewhere—any-where to get away from him. Snatching her purse off her bed, she tossed it over her shoulder and flew into the kitchen to grab a quick bite to eat before leaving. There, she bumped into Ketch and Liz.

"Well, don't you look like a country bride this morning," said Ketch, pointing to Mika's crimson cheeks. "That boy-friend of yours got y'all hot and bothered?"

"Boyfriend?"

Ketch snickered. "David Doodad. What's-His-Face."

Liz punched his shoulder. "Stop it, Ketch. Can't you see you're embarrassing her?" Turning to Mika, she added, "But Ketch is right. You do look . . . different. Why aren't you at the Ranch? Is something wrong?"

"I'm *fine*." Mika struggled with how best to avoid lying, before adding, in a less churlish tone, "I'm taking the day off today. I was just running around trying to get ready to go, that's all."

"Go where?" asked Liz.

"Umm . . . not sure yet. It's just too nice of a day to stay inside."

"Hey, I was only yanking your chain about David," said Ketch. "What say—unless you have other plans—you come with me and Lizzie?"

"We're going to Trinidad beach," explained Liz. "Taking my car."

Ketch winked. "My Harley doesn't have a trunk big enough for all the gear she wants to take."

"You sure you don't mind?" asked Mika.

"We wouldn't have asked if we minded." Liz shrugged. "Should we ask Sid to come with us? Ketch's been doing chores for him the last two days, you know, ever since he locked himself away in the Tower of London."

Ketch, drying his hands on a towel, said, "Yeah, I already fed Hester and the chickens, so he could come right now if he wanted."

Mika gulped. "I doubt he'd want to go."

"How do you know?" asked Liz.

"I just had a little talk with him."

"No way!" Surprise registered on Liz's face.

"Only long enough to find out he's fine." Mika hoped she sounded convincing. "He's not ready to go anywhere for a while, I think."

"Ah." Liz's eyebrows shot up knowingly as she brushed her hand along one cheek. "He must have looked pretty . . ."

"Scruffy? Yeah." A mental picture of Sid exploded in Mika's mind, causing her heart to thump so wildly in her chest, she thought if they didn't vacate the kitchen soon, Ketch and Liz would hear it pounding and know the truth.

"Okay, well, let's split then. Time's a-wasting." Grabbing Ketch by the elbow, Liz led him out the door, calling behind her. "We'll meet you outside as soon as you're ready, Meeks."

Mika took a deep breath and braced herself against the kitchen counter, trying to obliterate Sid's face from her memory.

Sid, with his ridiculously blue eyes and still-waters-run-deep soul.

Sid, an ellipsis at the end of an incomplete sentence.

Smart, strong, lighthearted, funny Sid—who could also be brooding, intimidating, and darkly mysterious especially when haunted by his past.

Too mysterious.

Sid, the kind of man no one would ever believe she could be attracted to.

Straightening, Mika curled her hands into a fist and vowed she wouldn't allow herself to be drawn into a relationship with him other than that of a roommate and casual friend. No matter how desperate or distressed he might seem.

Ever.

Just as she opened the mudroom door to go outside, the phone rang. Thinking it was Otis or Pearlie, she returned to the kitchen and picked up the receiver. "Jackson Farm."

"Who's this?"

"Mika. Who's this?"

"Kate Quinn. Is Sid there? I need to talk to him."

Mika's chest constricted. "He . . . can't come to the phone right now. Can I take a message?"

"No. I need to talk to him right away. Maybe I'll come out there and see if I can run him down in person."

"But he's . . ."

Click.

Outside, Liz honked her horn.

Mika hesitated, part of her wondering if she should give Sid a head's up, the other part convinced it was not only unnecessary, but it would make her appear overly concerned in his eyes. Turning, she headed back out the door.

He's a big boy. He can take care of himself. I'm washing my hands of Sid Jackson from now on.

AFTER MIKA VACATED the library, Sid squared his shoulders and picked up the mess he'd made. A half-hour later, he went downstairs to the kitchen and started a pot of coffee. *I wonder where she is.* He peeked down the hallway at Mika's open bedroom door. Strange that she would be gone already, so soon after their episode in the library. Stranger still that no one else seemed to be in the house. But then, it was a beautiful spring day, so maybe the boarders had gone out to enjoy the sunshine.

When the coffee was done, Sid poured himself a cup and sat down. He sniffed the air and then, drawing his nose down to his chest, he smelled Mika, an intoxicating blend of lemon blossoms and honey. The scent of her was so fresh, it made his head throb and ache—the kind of ache one feels in their face when they've smiled for too long. Lost in the memory of her, he spent the next ten minutes rehashing their conversation in the library, reliving their intimacy, and wondering if it had all been a dream.

Finally forcing himself back to reality, he got up to place his empty mug in the sink. The sound of tires crunching on gravel caused him to glance out the window. Seeing Kate

Quinn pulling up the driveway in Jake's pickup, he tore into the mudroom, bolted the backdoor, and then raced down the hallway to secure the front door. He hoped Woolf wasn't around somewhere to let her in.

Seconds later, Sid was back up in the library, headphones on, listening to his stereo in an attempt to drown out Kate's poundings and pleas. Any other day, he might have accommodated a visit from Kate, even though she typically only came around when she needed something from him. But not today. Not after two days of agonizing over Norm Clausen and his involvement in his parents' deaths. Not after the morning he'd had with Mika.

When he finally emerged from the library at least an hour later, Sid found a plain white, legal-sized envelope tucked into a crack in the sill of the back door, presumably from Kate. He was in no mood to open it, so he took it in the kitchen and tossed it on the counter atop a pile of mail he needed to sort through. But as he did, the memory of another envelope that had disrupted his family years earlier, stopped him dead in his tracks.

The Long-Ago Letter

T̲OM JACKSON PEELED INTO THE DRIVEWAY of his farm, his heart racing as fast as the engine in his new '60 Plymouth station wagon. He saw Sofia standing barefoot on the back porch of the farmhouse waiting for him, holding an envelope in one hand while her other hand rested on her protruding stomach. From his vantage point, his wife's face looked as if it were carved in marble. Sid, he noticed, was nowhere in sight. Most likely, the July heat had driven him down to the creek to play.

Turning off the ignition, he leaped out of the car, not bothering to close the door. As he bolted toward the house, everything around him turned surreal. He noticed a jet trail streaking across the cloudless sky above the house and heard the low hum of a wasp nest high in a nearby fir tree—as though those things, he chastised himself as he neared his wife, were of any importance whatsoever.

Finally reaching her, he scooped her into his arms. "Are you all right?"

She nodded. Pulling away slightly, she handed him the envelope. "It was on the ground, next to our mailbox."

"When did you find it?"

"I didn't go out to the road to check the mail until about

three o'clock. Someone had to have put it in there after the mail was delivered this morning."

Tom scanned the envelope. No name, no address, nothing. Opening it, he removed a sheet of paper, unfolded it, and read it. The warning, if it could be called that, was comprised of individual letters in all manner of shapes and colors from different magazines glued together to form a sentence:

THE SINS OF THE FATHER ARE VISITED UPON HIS CHILDREN.

While he studied the note, Sofia, her face drawn tight, whispered, "First there was the dead owl on our doorstep. Then someone breaking into the toolshed. Now this. Who's doing it, Tom? What does it mean?"

"It could be any number of people."

"Norm Clausen?"

"I have to admit, that was the first name that came to mind. But we can't jump to conclusions. It could just as easily be a hundred other people." Refolding the note, he slid it back into the envelope. "Could be one of our neighbors for all we know."

"Like who?"

"Hank Plummer."

Sofia looked surprised.

"You know how strange he is. He wanted to buy this place before we did. He could be harboring a grudge against us."

"Or, it could be someone trying to get back at Otis through us," suggested Sofia. "Sheriffs usually have a bull's-eye painted on their backs, right? Everybody knows we're friends with the Skinners."

"It's possible," agreed Tom. "But don't forget that me being a judge means I have plenty of enemies of my own." He handed the letter back to his wife and told her to keep it in a safe spot. Then he removed his suit coat and hung it on a hook near the door. "Otis will need it for evidence if it's determined to constitute a direct threat to us—which, honestly, I doubt that it does. Legally, anyway."

"Of course it does, Tom." Sofia held the letter out toward him. "Read it again."

"I did read it, Sofia. It quotes a scripture. That's all. You and I may infer a threat from it, but in a court of law, it's another thing. And it wasn't *in* our mailbox, so no law was broken there. This, the dead owl, someone messing around in my shed—they could all easily be interpreted as pranks. Some juvenile delinquent's idea of a joke."

"It's no joke, Tom. You and I both know it."

"Hey! Dad!"

He spun around. Sid had snuck up without them noticing. *How much had he seen? Heard?*

"Is something wrong?" asked Sid.

"No," said Sofia. "Everything's fine."

Sid pointed to his mother's clutched hand. "It sounds like you and Dad think there's something bad in that piece of mail."

Blanching, Sofia hurried into the kitchen and returned a moment later, minus the envelope.

Meanwhile, Tom explained that there was nothing for Sid to worry about. It was just a letter. That's all. Noting that his son was holding something behind his back, he said, "What have you got there?"

"Look what I found!" Sid held up a quart Mason jar covered with a thin square of muslin attached to the rim with a rubber band. Inside, reposing on tufts of moist shredded grass, was a salamander.

Tom dropped to one knee and inspected the blinking, bulging-eyed amphibian. "Why, that's a speckled black salamander, son. Where did you find him?"

"Under a log near the creek. Down by Cutthroat Falls."

"Siderno Porter Jackson!" Sofia's hand flew to her throat.

Even though he was nearly twelve years old, Sid had yet to cross-over into full-blown adolescence. Still a wide-eyed country boy at heart, he pulled his San Francisco Giant's baseball cap back on his head and asked, innocently, "Don't you want to touch him, Mom?"

"No!" shuddered Sofia.

"Sid, some salamanders secrete poison through their skin," cautioned Tom. "It could hurt your mom and the baby. I don't imagine you washed your hands after you touched him, did you?"

"No, but can I keep him, Dad? *Please?*"

"I'm afraid that salamander will die unless he's in his natural habitat. Look at him. See how tired he is already?"

Sid brought his face close to the glass, inspecting his prize carefully. "I could put water in the jar. Maybe that would help."

"It wouldn't be the same, Sid. He'd still be stuck in an environment that isn't natural or healthy for him." Hesitating, he added, "But, I suppose we could take a short walk and see if we can find a nice moist place where he might be happy . . . for a while, anyway. Let me just change my shoes first."

"That's a great idea!" Sid smiled. "I'll wait for you outside under the tree. By the way, I named him Alexander the Salamander."

"Good name, son. I'll be right there." Tom waited until Sid was out of earshot, then he turned and caressed his wife's cheek. "We can't let these threats affect how we live our lives, Sofia."

"But what if someone tries to hurt . . ." Sofia nodded in the direction Sid had gone. "You know."

"Trust me, I won't ever let that happen. Whoever's doing this is a coward—and a stupid, bungling one at that. Otis and I will get to the bottom of this thing. Don't worry."

Kissing her full on the lips, Tom then switched out his dress shoes for a pair of old sneakers and took his leave. Seconds later, he joined Sid beneath the shade of the magnolia tree.

"I have to tell you something, Dad."

"What's that?"

"Can we sit down?"

"Sure." He lowered himself to the ground next to his son.

Sid set the Mason jar between them and brought his knees up to his chest. "I changed my mind about where we should take Alexander."

"Why?"

"Well, I've been thinking about natural habitats. I probably couldn't find one close to the house as good as the one I found him in, could I?"

"Probably not."

"Then I might as well take him back to the creek and let him go."

"That's a great idea."

"Could we get another dog, Dad?"

The question, which seemed to come out of nowhere, caught Tom off guard. Homer, the chocolate Lab who had grown up with Sid, had been killed two months earlier—hit by a car at the crest of Prospect Hill as he chased a rabbit across the road. Not since they had buried him alongside the creek, where he loved to romp and tumble with Sid, had anyone mentioned replacing him.

He hesitated before answering. "I suppose it's time we started thinking about getting another pet. Homer was a good watchdog to have around." *Come to think of it, getting a guard dog might be just the ticket to allaying some of Sofia's fears.* "Maybe we can check out the ads in the paper and go look at some tomorrow. What do you say?"

Sid pulled the bill of his cap back down to shield his eyes, a broad smile pulling at his lips. "Gee, thanks, Dad."

Picking up the Mason jar, he studied the salamander, wondering what it would feel like to be trapped inside a glass cage; gawked at, poked and prodded, and at the mercy of a much larger life form. His stomach lurched at the realization that his family, now being victimized by an unknown foe, actually had more in common with Sid's salamander than he cared to admit.

Jumping to his feet, Sid reached for the jar. "Come on, Dad. Let's take Alexander back down to the creek where he belongs and set him free."

Tom heaved forward into a squatting position and then rose to his full height. "I'd like to go with you, son, but I have a feeling your mother needs me to stay close by. Women can be a little . . . skittish when they're pregnant. Have you noticed? Your mother being uneasy lately, I mean?"

"It seems like she worries more than usual."

"For example?"

"Well, like today, she told me I had to stay near the house. Said she had to be able to hear me if I called for her."

Tom raised an eyebrow. "In other words, when you went down to the creek today, you were deliberately disobeying your mother."

"I was still close enough to the house I could have heard Mom if she called me."

"That's not true, Sid. You said you were near Cutthroat Falls. You couldn't possibly have heard anything there but the rapids."

"But, Dad, I was only there for a few minutes. The water's not deep, and besides, Mom's never cared if I went down there before."

Tom pressed his hand against Sid's back, propelling him toward the barn. When they were well out of sight of the house, he thrust his finger into his son's face. "First of all, Siderno Porter Jackson, you must obey your mother in everything she tells you, even if it doesn't make sense to you. She's responsible for your welfare, and I expect you to obey her. *Always!* Do you understand?"

"Yes, Dad." Sid's voice shrunk beneath his father's reprimand.

Not wanting to overly scare him, Tom forced the muscles in his face to gentle and softened his voice. "You see, Sid, I need your help. Your mother is at that point in her pregnancy where . . . where I need you to keep an eye on her when I'm not here."

Sid's shoulders sagged. "But it sounds really . . ."

"Yes?"

"Really boring."

Tom bent down until they were eye-to-eye. "Yes, I realize it may be boring at times, but like I said, I need your help. When I'm at work, I want you to stay as close to the house as you can and be extra attentive to your mother's needs. If she's crying, or seems especially worried about something, I want you to call me at the office, regardless of how busy you think I might be. I'll give my secretary a head's up so that she knows to put you through to me no matter what I might be doing at the time. I know what I'm asking you to do isn't exciting, but believe me, it's very important. I couldn't go to work and do my job well if I didn't know I had you here to fill my shoes for me. Now, can I trust you to do what I ask?"

Sid's shoulders shot back to attention. "Sure, Dad. No problem."

"That's my boy." Tom beamed his approval. Resting his hand on the top of Sid's baseball cap, he added, "Now run down and find a spot for Alexander near the creek where he can be free to be a salamander. And tonight, after supper, I'll tell you the story of that creek. It's a good one."

When Sid finally disappeared from sight, he made his way back to the house, went into the kitchen, kissed his wife again, washed his hands, and called Otis.

THAT NIGHT, AS Sid lay in his bed waiting for sleep to overcome him, he heard a car pull into the driveway. Moments later, Otis's voice was booming in the kitchen below. Quickly, he turned on his bedside lamp, hoping the sheriff might see it shining beneath his door and come say goodnight to him before he left. Sure enough, within fifteen minutes, Otis was knocking on his door asking if he could come in. Sid was surprised to see him still in his uniform.

"How's my boy?" Otis pinched Sid's toes as he settled down at the foot of the bed.

"Pretty good."

"Only *pretty* good?" Despite his light-hearted tone, Otis looked tired. "You can do better than that. I heard you found yourself a speckled salamander today."

"I did!" Sid brightened. "But I had to take him back down to the creek where I found him and let him go. Otherwise, I'd show him to you."

"You did the right thing by putting him back where he belongs."

"I guess. Hey, how come you're here so late anyway? Is something wrong?"

"Nothing that the law and the good Lord can't take care of." Otis pulled a starched handkerchief out of his pocket and wiped his brow. "It sure is hot up here."

"Is something bad happening to my mom because she's pregnant?"

"Now what would make you think that?"

"Dad said Mom was acting funny because of the baby and asked me to keep a close eye on her when he's at work. Then tonight you come over. I don't know. Pretty suspicious."

"I'd say this little detective is letting suspicion get the best of him." Smiling, Otis leaned over and tweaked Sid's earlobe. "You've got nothing to worry about, son. Everything's right as rain with your folks."

Sid gave a sigh of relief. "I suppose."

"You just need to do whatever your pa asks of you, Sid.

Keep a close eye on your mother when he's not home. Pregnant women need lots of loving care. *Lots* of it. Now can you do that?"

"Yes, sir!"

Otis stood to his feet. "Me and Pearlie will always be here for you." Bending down, he ruffled his hair. "Just remember —no matter what happens, no matter where life takes you, Siddie boy, if you ever need anything, we'll be right here.

NEARLY A HALF hour later, when Tom Jackson finally tiptoed into Sid's room to tell him the story of Ransom Creek, he found him sound asleep. Tucking the blankets securely around his son, he kissed his forehead and whispered an apology.

"Tomorrow," he said. "I'll tell you tomorrow. I promise."

The Garden

APRIL BLED INTO MAY. FOR SID, THE DAYS since New Years 1973 sloshed into each other like dull waves lapping at a beach, as though September 1, the end of his probation, would never come. Compounding his lethargy, and making him even more vulnerable to the temptation to get high, was the fact that since the day they'd connected in the library, Mika had been avoiding him. The only time he saw her now was at mealtimes or when others were present in a room with them. So, in desperation, he decided to do what anyone raised in the country on a farm did in the springtime to channel their restless energy.

He planned a garden.

His roommates got on board with the project, excited at the prospect of having fresh vegetables at their fingertips throughout the summer. Mika and Liz immediately put their heads together and came up with a comprehensive list of herbs and vegetables to plant, as well as a plan for the layout of the garden. Ketch and Woolf were assigned the job of making sure they had all the right tools and soil amendments, while Sid took care of purchasing the seeds and plowing up his parents' old garden patch.

The day before Mother's Day, after weather forecasts assured them there would be no more danger of frost in their region, Sid set to work. The morning was exquisite—a warm, cloudless Saturday, drenched in promise. While he tilled the ground, he recalled the bounty from his mother's garden: her rich tomato sauces seasoned with fresh basil and garlic, her crackling-crisp dill pickles, and her Italian-flavored canned green beans. When he finished, he parked the tractor next to the barn, grabbed a hoe, and headed back. As he set to furrowing rows for seedlings, his mind still reminiscing, he could almost sense his mother's presence in the garden with him.

"Having fun?"

Startled, he turned to see Mika at his elbow—barefoot and puffy-eyed, looking as though she had just woken up. "I am," he replied. "I suppose the tractor woke everyone up. Sorry about that. I wanted to get a head start on the day."

Mika placed her palms over her lower spine and arched her back. "No problem. I heard the others moving around in the house. I'll go make some coffee and come back out to help you." With a quick glance around, she leaned forward and whispered, "By the way, I just want to say I'm sorry for avoiding you so much this last month. I was hoping it wouldn't be obvious, but I have a feeling it probably was—at least to you. Do you forgive me?"

Taken by surprise with her confession, Sid resumed hoeing and said nothing. He sensed Mika shadowing him—her mere presence making him break out in a sweat. *You're the calm in my storms, the light in my shadows, the fuel for my fire. You're my lodestar, and you don't even know it. You really don't have a clue . . .*

"Sid, what's wrong?"

"Why apologize now, after all this time?"

"Because ever since that day in the library, it's been so . . . uncomfortable between us. I'm worried I might have hurt your feelings."

"Well, don't."

"You know, I'm not imagining this awkwardness."

"Exactly what *did* happen in the library that day, Mika?"

"My perspective of that day isn't the point." Tensing, she added, "Besides, you're changing the subject. This all started with me simply wanting to apologize to you."

"Obviously, what happened in the library *is* the point of this conversation. Otherwise, you wouldn't have felt the need to say you're sorry for how you've avoided me since then."

Mika lifted her hands in surrender. "All right then, I said I'm sorry, so let's just leave it at that."

Sid tossed his hoe aside, seized her by the elbows and pulled her close. "Mika, that day in the library with you was life-changing for me."

"What do you . . . mean?"

"Somehow—don't ask me how—my head cleared. Years of anger and pain just disappeared. Not totally, of course. And not to say that I'm not still . . . " *I must sound like an idiot. Think Sid. Think hard. Find the right words.* "I don't know. It was so strange, I can't even really explain it."

Mika's answer came in small, measured bites. "That's wonderful, Sid. Really. But that was God. Not me."

"God or not, Mika, I fell in love with you that day." He watched the color drain from her face as he said it.

She pushed herself away from him, her lips parted in disbelief.

"Look . . . "

"You don't know what you're saying."

"Yes, I do. But the kind of love I'm talking about isn't what you're thinking, Meeks. At least, at first it wasn't." His smile, a droll stab at diffusing her shock, didn't help. He felt helpless as she took another step away from him. "What I mean is, it was the compassion you showed me that day that ruined me. That's how it started."

"I don't understand."

"How can I say this?" Sid plumbed his brain for the right words. "I never imagined love would look like you. I assumed it would have to look something like me, that it would involve someone who shared all my likes and dislikes, strengths and weaknesses, philosophies and worldviews. I've looked for love in school, in bars, nightclubs, concerts, football games— never thinking I'd find it right here on my parents' farm. Never thinking I'd find it with a girl who I assumed, when I first met her, hated me."

Nervously, Mika glanced over her shoulder at the house, as though debating making a run for it. "I've never hated you, Sid."

"How about disliking me then? You must have. I wasn't the easiest guy to get along with when you first came here."

Still poised to escape, she said, "Well, dislike is too strong a word, too. Maybe I was intimidated by you. You were pretty standoffish and . . . I don't know. You seemed kind of dangerous, being on probation and all."

In one stride, Sid eliminated the distance between them. Cupping his hand under her chin, he tipped her head back. "Do you still think I'm dangerous?"

For a moment, he thought he'd won her. The way she stared up at him, her eyes wide and limpid, as though she were finally willing to let him into her head.

"Well, Sid, you're . . . "

"Yes?" His nose touched hers. "I'm what?"

"You're a . . . you're a good friend. You've become a really *good* friend to me."

"A *friend?*" Now it was his turn to step back. "You're kidding."

"You have to realize that for me to count you as a friend is a big deal. There's no one in my life, other than my family, who means anything more to me than that."

"I suppose you expect me to be flattered."

"I expect you to understand."

"What I understand is that someday, someone will become more than a friend to you, Mika." He shook his head. "You assume it will never be me because I'm not good enough for you."

"That's not true."

"You're not afraid I would eventually drag you down to my level if you got too close to me?"

"How can you say that? If you really knew me, you'd see how unfair that is."

"All right then. Give me a chance to prove myself to you."

"Prove yourself?"

"Let me earn your trust and love."

"But it's irrelevant. And besides, you don't have to prove anything to me. I mean, I admit our differences might have set us off on the wrong foot with each other at first, but over the course of the last few months I've discovered you're a good guy. A *great* guy as a matter of fact. I already know you're a decent, hard-working, sensitive person. It's just that I have a calling on my life that can't be thrown away for . . . for . . . "

"For love?"

"For anything. For *anyone*. Honestly, Sid, I know what I'm supposed to do with my life, and right now, it doesn't include being involved in a serious relationship. I don't care who it's with."

"Not even David?"

"David? No, not even him. Although . . ." She took a deep breath. "Although, it's possible he and I may be connected in the future. But only because we share the same calling."

"What do you mean, 'calling'?"

"You know—from God. My destiny. My life's work. As in, I feel in my heart that I'm supposed to go to the mission field."

"Come on, Mika. For my sake, be more specific."

"Okay, I feel like I'm supposed to go to Southeast Asia with the goal of eventually doing missionary work in Vietnam when the war is over. Specifically, I want to work with orphans and refugees. David has the same vision."

Sid rubbed the back of his neck, his mind reeling, his heart stuck in his throat. How could he possibly compete with David or, for that matter, with Mika's God? Short of turning into a Jesus Freak himself, he didn't have a prayer. Yet he saw a hesitation in her—a hungry flicker in her eyes when she didn't think he was watching her, an inflection in her voice as though she didn't want their conversation to end.

"Wow. Vietnam. Orphans," he finally muttered. "Yeah, I can see you doing that. I'm impressed. And happy for you."

"I'm glad you understand, Sid. I was worried you wouldn't." Awkward pause. "What about you? Do you have any dreams for the future?"

"Of course I do."

"Really?"

"You seem surprised."

"I'm just curious. What are they?"

Sid lifted his eyes, taking in the scope of his parents' farm. "For one, I'm beginning to think there's a reason my parents left this farm to me, other than just financial."

"You're going to stay here then, after your probation?"

"This is confidential, just between you and me, but yes, I'm thinking seriously about it. I also need to take care of my grandmother, now that my grandfather's gone."

"That's . . . honorable."

"Honorable?" he laughed. "Interesting you'd choose that word in reference to me, considering I'm on probation."

"Sid . . ."

Then, not knowing why—except that maybe disclosure might force their conversation deeper—he blurted, "If you knew my past with women, you'd probably think I was anything but."

"Your past relationships are none of my business. Although I'm sure you're quite . . . experienced when it comes to women."

Again, that hesitation—that disconnect between Mika's words and her expression. Her eyes begged him to contradict her assumption, even as she prepared for the worst by squaring her shoulders.

"There've been a couple of women in my life," he admitted, "but none of them came close to making me feel the way I do when I'm around you."

"Please, Sid, I . . ."

"Let me finish. I'm not telling you how I feel about you in order to seduce you or sway you in any way. I just hoped that if I was honest with you, you'd be honest with me."

"Hey, you guys!" shouted Liz, waving her arms at them as

she descended the porch steps, Ketch at her heels. "What's with starting on the garden before we were up?"

Mika waved back. "Come on out! It's a great day for planting!" Then, turning to Sid, she said, "I'm going back in. I'm glad we had the opportunity to be honest with each other, but you have to realize that after what you've just told me, it's going to be harder than ever for me to act like nothing's happened between us. I'm sorry, but if I continue to avoid you, just know it's for our own good."

And with that, she was gone.

Freak Out

CHANGE WAS IN THE AIR, BUT NOT THE kind that mended fences, moved mountains, or swayed armies. No, the types of shifts happening on the farm were of the drudging, pragmatic sort. Hester the cow's pregnancy advanced, Sid's probation edged closer to completion—as did Mika's studies at the Ranch—and Ketch continued to pursue winning, at least partial, custody of his daughter.

If there was any hint that things weren't as they appeared to be on the surface, it was an anticipation of something unexpected about to happen, an undercurrent of suspense that tickled at the subconscious of the boarders whenever they ate or worked together, as though something yet to materialize was missing among them.

After the garden episode with Mika, Sid went to great pains to casually bring up things that the two of them might have in common. She, to the contrary, took every opportunity to highlight their differences. Typically, their conversations started with one of them making a benign comment, the other disagreeing, and then both of them walking away in a dead-lock.

"Hey, Mika. Have you been tracking Watergate?"

"Who hasn't?"

"It blows my mind that anyone would have voted for Nixon."

"My parents did."

"Your parents are Republicans?"

"Yeah, Sid, they are."

"You're not, are you?"

"It depends on the candidate."

"The candidate? What about a party's platform? Republicans don't care about the common man."

"So you're saying I can't be a Republican and be caring at the same time, but if I'm a Democrat I'm automatically compassionate? I've got to go, Sid. See you later."

Or . . .

"Hey Sid, can I ask a favor of you?"

"Sure."

"The Ranch is organizing an outreach to some vets in the area. Do you have any clothing or tools or extra camping gear you could donate? It's for a great cause."

"Uh . . . I might."

"Did I say something wrong? You look . . . conflicted."

"Not at all. I think it's great you're helping people. It's just, you know, the war . . . "

"Oh. You were an anti-war protestor at Berkeley, I suppose?"

"Well, yeah. Everyone was."

"My dad's a vet, Sid. It's not like I'm pro-war, but I love our country. I think our soldiers deserve to be treated with respect—not spit on and made to feel like criminals."

"For the record, I've never spat on anyone, and just because I believe in peace doesn't mean I don't love my country."

"All right, but please don't tell me you're one of those guys who calls soldiers murderers."

"Killing another person is murder, Mika."

"No, they're protecting the world—and us—from communism, so it's self-defense, not murder. Oh, forget it. I'll check with Ketch and Woolf to see if they have anything to donate."

Small wonder then that Sid began questioning his attraction to Mika. Maybe it *was* true that their differences were insurmountable. Or perhaps his feelings for her were purely physical. Worse, what if he was pursuing a dead-end relationship and everyone could see it but him? With no trusted female to confide in but Pearlie Skinner, he finally swallowed his pride and went to town to seek her counsel.

Pearlie's Take

S**ID'S SITTING IN FRONT OF ME, PICKING AT** a piece of rhubarb strawberry pie I've just served him fresh out of the oven. The diner's nearly empty.

"Go ahead," I say, encouraging him to eat. "Dig in!"

Ever since Valentine's Day, Sid's made it a habit to stop by the café and say "hi" to me at least once a week. Even during that rough patch in April, when he locked himself in his library, he swung by to see me. He wasn't exactly talkative then, of course, considering he was digging into the past in regards to the accident, but then me and Otis believe he'll bring it up when he's good and ready. It's hard to wait, but if I've learned one thing, it's that the Lord's timing is perfect.

"She hasn't said anything to you has she, Pearlie?"

Oh, dear, he caught me daydreaming again. "Who?"

"Mika. Has she talked to you about what she plans to do after August?"

"Well . . ." *Let's see. I know she's going on the mission field, but has she said anything else?*

Real innocent like, Sid looks over my shoulder. "I thought she might be working here this afternoon."

"Nope. She's not scheduled to come in for a while."

Twenty minutes later, Sid's still picking at his pie and I'm still listening to him. *What in the world happened to the Sid*

Jackson who showed up here last August? The young man sitting in front of me, the same book-smart hippie with the long hair Otis can't stand, actually looks and acts—well, vulnerable. Lost, even. But there's something else, too. As he keeps talking, I try to put my finger on it. Somehow, he eventually turns the conversation back to Mika, and after sharing some of his observations he finally asks, "So Pearlie, what's your take on it all?"

"Can you repeat the question?"

"What's *your* take on Mika and David and what she plans on doing after August?"

"Well, I think David's a nice boy, and I think it's a mighty noble thing for Mika to go on the foreign mission field. But Sid—can I be blunt with you?"

"Since when have you not been blunt with me?" he laughs.

"If you've got your sights set on Mika, you'd best beware."

"I never said . . ."

"You don't have to say anything, Sid. Lovesickness has its own language."

"But I'm not lovesick. I'm just curious about her. That's all. I'm curious about what all the boarders are going to do when their lease is up."

"Sure." It's my turn to chuckle. "If you say so."

"I'm serious, Pearlie."

"So am I. All I'm saying is, *if* you were to develop feelings for Mika, I'd be concerned because someone like her . . ."

"Would never want a relationship with someone like me?"

"Let me finish. Someone like Mika looks at men a whole different way than most other girls might. My guess is, she probably won't get serious about anyone for a long time."

"That's what she said."

I have to bite my tongue since Sid has just pretty much admitted he's talked to Mika about his feelings for her. I choose my next words carefully. "You know you're like a son to me, and it breaks my heart to think of you ever getting hurt. Now, I'm not saying I think anything's going on between you and Mika, but if there *was*, my advice would be to let it go. That is, unless you're willing to wait years for her to be ready to make a commitment, which I doubt you are. My daddy used to say, 'Pearlie, it never hurts to wait before letting go of your heart. It's when you let go of it at the wrong time, or for the wrong person, that it can get broken.' I'd say the same goes for you, Siddie."

Well, that ends our conversation. Sid thanks me, insisting on paying for his half-eaten piece of pie—even though I told him it was on the house—and leaves. As I watch him step outside onto the sidewalk, I suddenly realize what else it is about Sid that's changed. Even though he was clearly troubled about Mika's determination to go overseas, he was unusually calm and content.

I don't know what to make of it.

Especially when I look across the street and see who's hiding in the shadows watching him leave—waiting until he's completely out of sight before heading over to my diner.

In Mika's Own Words

I can't believe I just missed him. Stunned by the sight of Sid exiting The Pearl, I step out of the shadows. *Take a deep breath Mika,* I tell myself. *You can do this.*

Crossing the street, I step inside and see Pearlie staring at me as though she's seeing a ghost.

"Mika! I wasn't expecting you for another hour," she says. "Let me guess—you just stopped by for a visit?"

"As a matter of fact, yes." I sidle up to the counter. The stool I nestle myself onto still feels warm. The thought that it may have been the same stool Sid had been sitting on earlier fills me with a mixture of joy and discomposure, to the point I'm not sure I can speak.

Pearlie sweeps a plate with a piece of half-eaten pie off the counter and goes to the kitchen to get a fresh slice. "Here." She slides it in front of me. "Strawberry-rhubarb. Still warm. You'll never guess who was just here."

"Who?"

"Sid. He sat right where you're sitting now."

"Oh? What'd he have to say?"

Pearlie's eyes bore into me as I use my fork to toy with my pie, still savoring the warmth of Sid's body heat trapped in the leather cushion beneath me.

"We just had a nice little chat." Pearlie hedges, as though she might be holding something back. "He told me about the garden y'all planted up there. It does my heart good to hear the farm's coming alive in more ways than one these days."

"Oh, yeah. It was Sid's idea to have a garden this summer. We all help out when we can."

"He sure has changed the last few months, don't you think?"

"Sid?"

Pearlie nods.

"I'm not sure what you mean by 'change.'"

"For one, he seems much more—I don't know—at peace. More like the old Sid used to be before his parents died."

"*Hmm.*"

"Any idea what may have happened to bring about this change?"

The way Pearlie says it—the way she looks at me beneath her eyebrows—unsettles me. She's perceptive, far more intuitive than people, perhaps, give her credit for being. Is it possible she knows what's causing my heart to race? Casually, she mixes herself some iced tea.

"So then, Mika," she says, "what do you want to talk about?"

I'm so jittery, I blurt, "It's my birthday."

"You don't say! Happy Birthday, darlin'! How old are you?"

"Twenty-two."

"Are they having a party for you up at the farm?"

"I haven't told anyone."

"Why not?"

"I don't want the attention."

"Well, here." Reaching behind the counter, Pearlie pulls out a box filled with birthday candles and sticks one on top of the pie. Then, grabbing a lighter from her apron pocket, she lights it. "I'd sing, but you'd thank me not to. Make a wish!"

I close my eyes, make a wish, and blow out the candle.

Removing it, Pearlie says, "A penny for your thoughts."

Thinking she wants to know what my birthday wish was, I say, "I just wished that everything in my future would be in the Lord's hands."

"Amen to that. Speaking of the future, are you still going on the mission field after your lease is up at the farm?"

"That's the plan."

"No road bumps or obstacles in your way?"

Sid must have said something. "Why do you ask?"

"Just wondering. You're young, honey. Only twenty-two. You have your whole life ahead of you, so any road bumps that do come your way are bound to be minor—as long as you're sure of your calling and can keep your eyes trained straight ahead. For example, is going to Vietnam after the war still your goal in life right now?"

"Yes, it is."

"Is there anything that would prevent you from doing it?"

"No. Nothing."

"Not even love?"

"I'm not sure I'm following you." Another lie. I know exactly what Pearlie is getting at, and I'm terrified of going there.

"If you fell in love with someone stateside—someone who wasn't called to the mission field like you are—would you still go?"

"Yes. Besides, I would never let that happen in the first place." I fidget with the remnants of my pie and feel myself wilting beneath Pearlie's discerning eyes.

"Well, that's good to hear."

"Why do you say that?"

"Because it proves you understand how much sacrifice it takes sometimes to make your dreams come true. I only hope it doesn't prove something else as well."

"Like what?"

"That you're afraid of men."

I'm speechless. Blown away. It's ludicrous, really. I love men. I do. I have a great relationship with my dad and brother and uncles—all the men in my family. And I've had lots of guy friends over the years, so what would I possibly be afraid of? Finally, I find my voice. "Trust me, Pearlie. I'm not afraid of men."

"So, no man's ever hurt you?"

That does it. I choke on the piece of pie I've just put in my mouth. Gulping down some water, I buy myself time before answering. Well . . . yeah. A guy hurt me a long time ago. But it's no big deal. Everyone's had their heart broken at least once."

"I suppose a lot of girls get their hearts broken at some point in their lives, but not everyone. How old where you when it happened?"

"Eighteen."

Pearlie's eyes promise immunity if I explain, so I take a deep breath and gush ahead with my story about Glen Shaw—my first real boyfriend. About how we'd hooked up our junior year in high school. "He was smart, handsome, and popular, and I was in awe of him. One thing led to another, and soon after we graduated we started having— you know . . . "

"Sex."

"Yes." *Wow, she's more hip than I thought.* "Anyway, everything seemed great at first. I was sure he loved me as much as I loved him. I really believed he was the one for me and that ultimately we'd get married and settle down after getting our college degrees. Then, I missed a period. I was beside myself at first, but then I thought, 'Well, my parents got married when they were twenty, and it worked for them. They won't be happy that I'm pregnant, but they'll get over it and be cool with us getting married.'

"In hindsight, I probably should have waited to tell Glen until I'd seen a doctor and knew for sure, but by then I was too far down the road with my emotions. Besides, I was convinced he'd be thrilled, too. But when I told him what I suspected, he freaked out."

"What did he say?"

"He said if I was pregnant, he'd marry me, if that's what I wanted, but that he couldn't be a faithful husband because he'd never had the opportunity to 'sow his oats.' Then he said he'd look around for someone who would 'fix the problem' if I wanted to do that instead. It was up to me."

"Oh, darlin'." Pearlie, seeing me tear up, pats my arm. "Sounds like that boy had one thing on his mind, and it wasn't you."

"Exactly." I hate people feeling sorry for me, so I press ahead. "I started my period two weeks later. The following month, I broke it off with Glen. I just couldn't stand the sight of him any longer. Shortly after that is when I got saved. For a long time, I beat myself up for how gullible and blind I'd been, until God showed me it was all in the past and that I had a better future before me."

"Which means you're able to trust men again—right?"

"Well . . ." *No.*

"I didn't think so. Back to your dreams then, honey. Are you sure going halfway around the world to work with orphans has nothing to do with running away from a relationship with a man?"

I scrape the last few crumbs of pie onto my fork as I think about it. True, for me, lines in relationships continue to be blurred. For example, at what point can I trust that a guy genuinely likes me for who I am, versus being attracted to me only for what he can get from me? In the end, aren't all guys interested in only one thing? *I want more from life than just pleasing a man and having a man please me. So, do I really want to sacrifice all my freedoms, all my dreams, just to ensure I have a partner to grow old with?* "I suppose getting burned by Glen could be part of the reason I've chosen to go on the mission field," I say, at last. "But, I also feel like God's calling me, too."

"Calling or allowing? They're two different things."

"Whatever—it's my purpose in life. At least for now. I'm sure of it."

Pearlie sniffs, as though she's a bloodhound tracking a scent. "Knowing your purpose is all well and good, Mika, but it's the meaning behind your purpose that's most important. You can do all the right things—go through all the motions of being a mother or a doctor or a lawyer or, heck, the President of the United States—but if you don't know why you're really doing it, if it doesn't have any meaning, then . . ."

Suddenly, the air in the diner is stifling. "Sorry, Pearlie. I need to go." I slide off the stool and start digging in my purse for some money to pay for the pie.

"No, no. It's on me. It's your birthday."

"Well, thanks, Pearlie. I appreciate it."

She *tsks* as she follows me to the door. "You and Sid are sure alike. He bolted out of here, too, practically in the middle of our conversation. Maybe I'm being too honest with you kids. I sure hope I didn't say anything to offend you . . . or him."

"You haven't offended me at all. I appreciate your honesty, Pearlie. I really do. It's given me a lot to think about. But if I didn't pursue my dreams and do what I feel I'm supposed to do, regardless of my motive, I couldn't live with myself. I'd always wonder what could have been."

"Of course. You're absolutely right."

"But," I add, "it doesn't mean that it's forever. It doesn't mean I won't come back to the States someday. Maybe I will, and maybe I won't. Maybe I'll be single all my life, or maybe I'll get married. And if I do ever marry, it could be someone I'll meet or work with overseas, or someone who lives stateside and has nothing to do with missions. Really, how can I go wrong if I keep my options open?"

"Lots of things can go wrong with your options when you're pursuing your dreams," she says. "You can lose Plan A, and if you do, you might never get it back. You'll never know what could have been. Of course, Plan B can be a good close second, or it could end up being even better. You just never know."

I'd never given much thought to a Plan A or B. Was there such a thing as Plan C or D—or for that matter, X, Y, or Z? The thought made my head spin, but it was the possibility of missing the boat on Plan A that made me feel really queasy.

Pearlie must have sensed my bewilderment. "So," she says, "if you want my opinion, I think you're doing the right thing.

I don't doubt one bit God will bless you for what you feel called to do. Just be sure that when it comes to men, you don't let your past poison your future. And if you ever do find yourself getting serious about someone, make sure they have more backbone, more character, and more respect for you than that old boyfriend of yours."

Lunging toward her, I hug Pearlie so hard I feel the underside of her shoulder blades beneath my fingertips. "Thanks again," I gush, before turning and rushing out of the diner.

I should've told Pearlie just how thankful I am, how relieved I feel after talking to her. Odd that my own mother didn't know why I'd had broken up with Glen, or why I hadn't had a serious boyfriend since him, while Pearlie Skinner —a woman I've known for less than a year—understands the machinations of my leery, gun-shy heart. *It must have been a divine appointment.* I reach my car and settle into the driver's seat. How else to explain my impulsive confession, or Pearlie's timely advice? Yet, the question of Sid—the burning, unresolved secret of my attraction to him—remains.

Pulling away from the curb, I'm comforted by the fact that, since I have less than three months left on the farm, I can surely detach myself emotionally from him for that short amount of time. But before I go to bed that night, I found myself praying:

God, I am so freaked out.

I am this close to giving everything up for Sid Jackson.

Lord, I'm not kidding.

I know—it makes no sense.

Absolutely no sense at all.

We are so opposite each other, it's not even funny.

That's the thing—we would never work out. A relationship with him is hopeless.

And yet it's killing me. God, I don't know what to do.

And if You don't give me a sign soon, I'm afraid of what will happen.

I'm terrified by my own weakness . . . by the power he has over me when we're alone.

It's You I want to serve, Lord: You, who have been the sole recipient of my devotion.

Other than my family, since I've given my heart to You, there's never been another.

Until now.

Jesus!

Unexpected Guests

The second weekend in June, two female guests descended on the farm. The first was Woolf's sister Crystal-Jett from New Jersey, a sultry musician with the stage name of simply "Jett." The second, who arrived a day later, was Liz's Alaskan sister, Claire. Neither Woolf nor Liz knew beforehand of their siblings' surprise visits.

Jett had hitchhiked solo, cross-country, to get to Trinity Springs—guitar in hand, a sleeping bag and knapsack slung on her back, her fine exotic features and dark skin in stark contrast to Woolf's tawnier coloring and rougher lines. Personality-wise, the two were exact opposites. Whereas Woolf was a quiet introvert, Jett never stopped talking. Or schmoozing. Or flirting. Producing a bag of primo Meshmican within minutes of her arrival, she had informed Sid and the other boarders that LA was actually her final destination. But following a short stint at a commune in San Francisco first, she had decided to take a little detour north to "hang in nature for a while." After all, she added, "Everyone in the country is talking about what's happening up here in northern California. This is where it's at!" And since her brother was living in the heart of the so-called "Emerald Triangle"—well, it was a cosmic convergence too perfect for her to pass up.

Woolf, along with Ketch and Liz, wasted no time in introducing Jett to the glories of the Grotto, where they partook of her weed while spelling out for her the unfortunate restrictions they were under because of Sid's probation. Jett agreed the situation was a real downer, but as long as she had somewhere to party and get high, she'd survive.

Claire showed up the next day. On a whim, apparently.

After getting off a bus in Redding early that morning, she'd hired a taxi to take her to the farm. Upon her arrival, the driver helped her drag two huge Samsonite suitcases onto the front porch, along with a ridiculously heavy cosmetic container and a backpack stuffed with fashion and hair magazines.

"Oh, hello," she trilled when Sid opened the door. "I'm Liz's sister, Claire. She's not expecting me, but she said I could come and visit whenever I wanted." Shoving her way past him, she shouted, "There you are, Liz! Surprise!"

Later, she told Liz her real purpose in coming: she wanted to prove to her doubting parents that she really had been delivered from her fears once and for all.

"Who knows?" said Liz. "Maybe you are. I sure hope so."

WITHIN DAYS, BOTH guests had developed a crush on Sid, evidenced by Claire's hyper-fluttering lashes and dreamy stares in his direction, and Jett's exaggerated body language, probing personal questions, and inappropriate comments— not to mention her constant appeals for Sid to get high with her in the Grotto. Even though she wasn't his type emotionally or intellectually, she clearly had all the right physical equipment to seduce him—if he chose to take her bait.

And that, he worked hard to avoid.

When she confronted him with requests—like going on a secluded hike with her, going into town to get a drink, or to the Grotto to het high—he made excuses not to go. When she invaded his personal space, he averted direct eye contact with her. When he found himself in a room alone with her, he looked for an escape. When she probed into his personal life, he changed the topic.

Then Otis entered the picture. He hadn't discovered the girls were staying at the farmhouse the first week they were there, mostly because they were gone during his probation check, but also because Claire bunked with Liz in her room and Jett stashed all her belongings with Woolf. It wasn't until the following week that the girls blew their cover.

First, the sheriff walked around to the back of the house and discovered Jett stripped down to her underwear, playing her guitar. "You should be glad I'm not naked," she said, when he asked her where her clothes were. "What do you expect, anyway, in this heat?"

Going immediately into the house to find Sid and take him to task, Otis entered the kitchen. He found Claire in her pajamas doing up Ketch's hair in cornrows. "Oh, you must be that probation dude Sid talked about," she blurted. Lifting several of Ketch's braids toward him, she added, "Far out, huh?"

Instead of giving Claire his opinion, Otis huffed about until he finally found Sid. Cornering him in the barn, he yelled, "What's going on here anyway? Who are those girls? Where are they from? And don't pretend they're not staying here—any idiot could see they are."

"I wasn't going to pretend anything. They're related to Woolf and Liz," replied Sid. "They're not staying long."

"That's right, they're not. They're going to leave right now, and you're going to see to it that they do."

"Why? There's nothing in the leases the boarders signed about not having guests on the farm."

"Oh yeah?"

Leading Sid out to his patrol car, Otis retrieved a folder from the front seat. He pulled out a copy of the official lease attached to some probation papers and directed Sid to the second page of the document.

"Right there, in black-and-white," he said, pointing to a paragraph at the very bottom of the contract. "It says, '*No person, or persons, other than the individuals whose signatures appear on this lease shall, under any circumstance, inhabit said premises unless approved by the executor of the estate.*'" Tossing the file back into the car, he jabbed his chest with his thumb and added, "I'm the executor, and since I was never notified, and since these girls were never approved, your boarders are in violation of their lease."

"I'm sure they didn't notice the clause when they signed the lease, Otis."

"Guess it'll teach them to always read the fine print then. How long have these two visitors been here, anyway?"

Sid shrugged.

"And why is this the first I've heard about it?"

"I didn't think it was a big deal."

"Well, all right," sighed Otis. "It wasn't your fault, so I suppose I can overlook it this time—but just this one time. And on one condition. I don't care where they go, but those girls need to be out of here by sundown."

"But . . ."

Turning, he began walking back to the house, motioning

for Sid to follow him. "I realize it ain't easy to kick guests out of your abode, but trust me, eventually you need to learn how to do it. Come on. I'll get the ball rolling. You can make sure they leave in a timely fashion. I'll explain the situation to them right now and then come back after dinner to make sure they've cleared out."

THE NEXT NIGHT, it took forever for Sid to fall asleep. With Jett and Claire now gone—as disruptive as their visit had been—a return to normalcy was almost anti-climactic. He couldn't decide which was worse: the craziness of having the two living with them for two weeks or the slump that followed their departure. One thing was for sure—he didn't miss being on edge around Jett. And yet despite that relief, a sense of increasing loneliness nagged at him. A loneliness he knew came from being incomplete. From living an unresolved life—a life he couldn't embrace because it would mean coming to terms with his fears and failings.

All night, he tossed and turned until, finally, he threw his pillow on the floor and kicked back his sheets. Although his window was flung wide open and his fan set to high, the air in his bedroom was stifling. What he wouldn't give for air-conditioning! Forcing himself out of bed, he decided there was no point trying to sleep anymore. It was five o'clock in the morning.

A cup of joe. That's what he needed.

Rubbing his eyes, he went into the kitchen and made a pot of coffee. As it perked, he suddenly remembered that he had dreamt about Kate. He couldn't recall exactly what he'd dreamt, other than it was disturbing. Disturbing enough to have woken him up. Something about her and him and Jake fighting, yelling, and chasing one other . . .

When the coffee was done, he poured himself a cup and sat down at the table, unable to shake the thought of Kate from his mind. He recalled the note she had left tucked inside the porch door back in April: *I'm sorry I had to be the one to tell you about Norm's involvement with your parents' deaths. Please don't hate me for it. I'm worried that you do. Can't we just talk sometime?*

Since then, he'd seen Kate in town on two different occasions as he drove by: once as she was entering the Five-and-Dime, and once as she was checking her mail outside the post office. She'd been alone both times. Not surprising since Jake was always either in the woods logging with his dad, or working in his shop, or breeding dogs—or whatever it was he did with all the dogs the Clausens had at their place.

But the problem was, every time he saw Kate he experienced —not attraction or longing—but a nostalgic wistfulness of days spent with her long ago, before he'd become a man, when they were both young and still somewhat innocent. Well, thank God, he no longer entertained any illusions about their relationship. Those days were gone, and neither she, nor he, was the same. It was like looking at a photo of himself as a child and knowing he had to erase himself from it in order to move on.

The process hadn't been easy.

Only recently, Kate had showed up unannounced at the house, acting high-strung and desperate. Running late for a Farm Bureau meeting, he'd brushed her off—left her standing in his driveway as he sped away. He'd promised to call her when he returned, but he never did. What was the point?

Kate had always been unique, that was for sure. She had a quirky independence about her couched in a dark, quasi-charismatic personality. He certainly wasn't the only one who'd been drawn to her because of it. But somewhere along the line, she'd changed. He couldn't quite put his finger on it, but the Kate he knew now—confrontational, demanding, irrational—was not the Kate he'd known less than a decade ago in high school.

Back then, she was at least likeable and somewhat sensitive—still the Kate he couldn't have hated if he'd tried. But the new Kate was intolerable. The new Kate had finally forced him into telling her never to come by the farm again. And her response had been the last straw. She'd flown into an almost psychotic rage, accusing him of being in love with someone else. As though his life were any of her business. As though anything could ever develop between them again. As though he cared. As though . . .

Sid gulped down the rest of his coffee. *All I care about is Mika.*

At the very thought of her, every image of Kate dissipated. Incredibly, the peace he'd acquired with Mika two months ago in the library continued to sustain him, though it was more on the order of a starving man's last meal than daily manna from heaven. The problem was, there was still no breakthrough between them. No resolution. Not even an acknowledgement of anything more than a shared friendship.

Maybe that's why I can't sleep and feel so exhausted lately. Not because of Kate, or having had Jett and Claire stay here for two weeks. Not because I'm working my butt off on the farm, or because of all my commitments with the Farm Bureau, or trying to ace my probation. I'm lovesick. Worn out from wanting Mika and not having her.

Sid placed his mug in the sink, went into the mudroom and slipped on his sandals. The sun was already peering atop the horizon. He might as well get a head start on his chores and shake off his this love-deferred misery. Picking up a wheelbarrow in the backyard, he pushed it into the orchard. Then, after spending at least half an hour clearing debris from the ground, he rested a moment beneath the shade of one of the larger apple trees. He used the bottom of his t-shirt to swipe his face. *It must be eighty degrees already.*

He closed his eyes and watched as leaf shadows danced across his eyelids. Just like Mika—the elusive shadow in the background of everything he did, felt, and thought.

When he opened his eyes, he realized he was facing in the direction of the Grotto, and despite his soothing notion of Mika, or perhaps because of it, he found himself jonesing for a joint more than ever.

A Chilling Fourth

JULY 4, 1973, DAWNED CLEAR, HOT, AND AS still as the bottom of a well. In Trinity Springs, Main Street sizzled with anticipation of their annual Fourth of July Parade. The Pearl—decorated to the hilt with red-white-and-blue streamers, colorful balloons, banners, and little American flags—was already drawing hungry locals through its doors. No doubt the kitschy sign above the front window, advertising the café's famous $10 Patriot's Brunch, would bring in even more business after the parade ended. Down the street, meanwhile, a completely different kind of crowd gathered at Back to Eden. Decked out in blue jeans, sandals, tie-dye skirts and bandanas, Eden's patrons congregated to share the latest counter-culture news and watch the parade.

All told, by mid-morning, Trinity Springs was teeming with people from all over the county. While pamphleteers worked the sidewalks, the back end of Main Street bulged with floats, horses, marching bands, vintage cars, and logging trucks jockeying for their appointed place in the parade. Boy Scouts readied their pooper-scoopers. The sheriff's posse and local National Guard recruits showed off their new equipment and small-talked with each other as they waited for the starting signal. Red-fezzed Shriners prematurely blasted

away on their go-kart horns as flouncy-skirted square danc-
ers practiced twirling on the arms of their silver-spurred
partners. Beauty queens primped and practiced their waves.
The mayor and his council wrangled with sound technicians
at the flag-draped gazebo over glitches in the speaker system.
Dr. Simpson and his wife waved to pedestrians from their
front porch swing. Lynn Keating, Otis's secretary, and her
husband Paul hawked specials in their Chevrolet car lot to
disinterested passersby.

The clamor emanating from Trinity Springs peaked at
eleven o'clock when over a dozen eighteen-wheelers simultaneously blew their air horns, signaling the unofficial start
of the show. In response, Norm Clausen and his son Jake—
with Kate, nursing an ice-cold can of Coke, seated between
them—merged their logging rig into the convoy. As the
parade passed The Pearl, Mika, who had come in to help
Pearlie with the brunch, stood in the doorway and laughed
at the children darting into the street to retrieve assorted
candies tossed to them by floats promoting local businesses.

Twenty minutes later, the last semi on its trek through
town blared its horn, declaring the official end of the parade.
People—sunburned, soaked in sweat and hungry—dis-
persed languidly, each to their own home or campsite or
chosen place of intermission, until it was time for the fire-
work extravaganza at sunset in the town's rickety high school
football stadium, home of the Trinity Springs Tigers.

The thermometer on First National Bank read 101 degrees.

To HIS RELIEF, when Sid arrived back at the farm following the parade, the house was empty. Other than the

distant gurgling of Ransom Creek, a mid-summer calm had descended over the farm, insulating the air with a hush only the most remote corners of earth might produce. After inspecting the vegetable garden, he took off his shirt, climbed drowsily into the backyard hammock, and fell asleep.

A blood-curdling howl pierced the silence. Jolted awake, he shot up. Listening intently, he determined it must be coming from an animal in great pain. A dog? A coyote? He swung his legs out of the hammock and raced toward the creek. By the time he reached the bank, however, the baying had stopped.

He debated whether he should follow the creek down to Cutthroat Falls, or ford it where he now stood. Choosing the former, he lowered his body parallel with the ground and squeezed through the barbed wire fence dividing his property from Hank Plummer's. Soon, he was standing above a gushing cataract where it was impossible to hear anything but the roar of water. Retracing his steps away from the falls, he sat down at the edge of the river and pondered what to do next.

Five . . . ten . . . fifteen minutes passed. Like a massage, each moment that went by untangled the knots of Sid's tense subconscious. Cool jets of water licked at his feet. The weight of the moment pressed against him until he was lying flat on his back, spread eagle on the warm stone ledge beneath him. Hypnotized, he gazed at hawks soaring lazily above in a sky sheening with vibrant colors from the mist of the nearby waterfall.

Sensing a movement to his right, he swiveled his head and looked toward a damp crevice in the rock near his fingertips. Less than an inch from his thumb, a speckled black salamander stared back at him.

"Alexander," he whispered. "Is that you?"

The spotted creature blinked and flicked its tail.

Ever so slowly, he made a fist so that only his index finger was extended toward it. "It's okay, Xander. Come sit awhile with me."

The amphibian tilted its head and hesitated before raising a delicate foot. Cautiously, it placed it on Sid's proffered digit. Then, in a black-and-white flash, it was gone. The conciliatory gesture had lasted only a second, but the touch of the animal's foot on his finger transported him back to the last summer he had spent with his parents before they died.

The warmth of the sun, coupled with the heat of the boulder beneath him, penetrated clear through Sid's muscles into the very fibers of his being. Closing his eyes, he imagined melting into the rock, not caring if he were to be vaporized by unseen forces beyond his control. When the moment finally passed, and he realized he was still alive—a mortal in need of something to drink and eat—he opened his eyes.

"Sid?"

Startled, he shaded his eyes against the low sunlight. Squinting at the form speaking to him, he saw it was Mika. "What are you doing here?"

Mika sat down next to him, lowering her feet into the water alongside his. "I need to talk to you about something."

"Okay." Sid raised himself into a sitting position.

"I came home to change my clothes before going back into town to watch the fireworks," she explained. "But then, I heard weird noises coming from somewhere in this direction."

"Did it sound like a dog howling in pain?"

"Yes! How did you know?"

"I heard it, too. That's how I ended up here. I followed the sound until it stopped." Sid tipped his head and listened carefully again, but it was impossible to hear anything over the cataract's liquid thunder.

"What do you think it was?"

"A wild animal, maybe? A coyote? It sounded like it was coming from over there in the woods, but it was too hard to tell."

An unusual ease settled over the two for several moments. Leaning forward, Mika sighed. "This is an amazing place."

"Yes, it is. It's called Cutthroat Falls."

"Interesting name."

"My dad once told me the story behind it and Ransom Creek. Do you want to hear it?"

"I would."

"I thought you were heading back into town," he teased.

"I've got time."

Selecting a small river rock near his ankle, Sid aimed carefully and threw it at a gaping hole in a rotted out tree across the creek. "Back in the 1850s," he began, "Trinity County was flooded with gold prospectors. There were a couple thousand Chinese immigrants here, too, and the whites resented them. Local politicians put a four dollar 'head tax' on each of the Chinese prospectors, but whites could pan or dig gold for free. Not only was it not fair to the Chinese, but they also weren't allowed to be armed.

"It all came to a head one day in a field where they were working, when some white gold diggers attacked the Chinese prospectors. They called it the Tong War. It only lasted one day, but it left ten Chinamen dead, and I can't remember how many others wounded. Rumor had it," he explained, "that the white man who started the whole thing split and came up here, where he'd had a claim years earlier—not too far above my parents' farm.

The guy built a shack on a bend in the creek where he believed there were still large deposits of undiscovered gold. He lived there like a hermit for a couple of years, never coming down into town for anything. My dad said they called him Black Jack because his hair and eyes matched the color of his heart."

Sid picked up another stone and tossed it across the creek. "After a while, everyone forgot about Black Jack. Besides, no whites had been killed, so no one was willing to hunt him down and prosecute him for murdering the Chinamen. Then one day, a stupid young kid named Richard Clarke wandered up to Black Jack's claim looking for gold. I guess he was only about fifteen or sixteen. The old miner was paranoid and half-crazy by then and thought Clarke was trying to jump his claim. According to legend, the boy begged him to spare his life; said his folks in Trinity Springs would come looking for him if he didn't return soon. Figuring Clarke's parents might have money, Jack decided to hold him for ransom."

Mika's eyes lit up. "That's how Ransom Creek got its name."

Sid nodded. "Anyway, Black Jack strapped a piece of Clarke's clothing along with a ransom note to his dog, demanding one thousand dollars in forty-eight hours, and sent him to town."

"Wait. Is this really a true story?"

"At least parts of it, probably. Who knows? I'm just telling you what my dad told me."

Mika motioned for him to continue.

"Well, the dog made it to town. The sheriff's posse immediately headed up the creek with Jack's dog in tow. They assumed the mutt would lead them to Black Jack's claim. A thousand dollars then was like, I don't know, a million dollars or something today—which means the kid's parents, who were dirt poor, had no way of coming up with the ransom money. In fact, they were so afraid the posse would blow it and get their son killed, they organized their own search party. Apparently, their plan was to beg Jack to return their son in exchange for a worthless claim they had on Trinity River."

Sid slapped his hand on the rock beneath them. "Both the posse and the boy's parents' party got this far."

"Right here?"

"Pretty much. Yeah."

For a moment, Sid lost himself watching Mika's astonished reaction. "Where was I? Oh, yeah. The two search parties decided to stop here and rest their horses. When one of the men stooped down to get a drink, he saw Richard Clarke's body wedged between some rocks. They dragged him out of the water, assuming he had drowned, but quickly discovered that his throat had been slit."

Mika gasped. "Jack killed the boy and threw his body over the falls? That's terrible!"

"No one ever found out exactly what happened. Clarke's parents took his body back to town while the posse continued up to Black Jack's claim with his dog in the lead. When they got there, Jack was barricaded in the shack with several shotguns. A shoot-out followed, lasting several hours. When it finally grew quiet, the posse guessed the old renegade had run out of ammunition. Just as they were about to storm the cabin, it burst into flames.

"Yelling from the window that he'd die before giving himself up, and swearing he wasn't going to go alone, Jack took one last shot and killed his dog—still tethered by a leash to one of the deputies. A moment later, the reserves of dynamite he evidently had stored in his shack exploded into a huge fireball, and that was the end of Black Jack and his dog."

"And Richard Clarke."

"Him, too." Sid gazed in the direction of the falls, a dozen feet away, and pictured Richard Clarke's mangled, bloody body cradled among the wet boulders at its base. "You know what's weird? Clarke's buried up at Calvary Cemetery—the same place my parents are buried."

"Really?"

"I'll take you to see it sometime if you'd like."

"I'd like," said Mika.

"You'd never guess what they engraved on his headstone."

"What?"

"Below the dates of his birth and death, it reads, '*Damnation Awaits His Murderer.*'"

"No way!"

"I swear. Crazy, huh?"

"Well, it's a horrible story, but I have to admit it's fascinating." Mika, scrunching her eyes up at the sun, scrambled to her feet. "I'd better go back to the house and get ready." But turning to leave, she tripped. As she did, Sid leapt to his feet and broke her fall before she hit the ground.

"Are you all right?"

Checking the palms of her hands, she laughed. "Aside from being embarrassed, I'm fine."

As before, in the library, Sid wasn't prepared for this unscripted moment with Meeks. Staring at her self-deprecating smile, he was struck dumb. *God, could anyone be more beautiful? Why does she insist on letting our differences keep us apart?* Forcing himself to look away from her, he started walking quickly upstream toward the farm. Mika hurried to catch up with him. When they reached the fence, Sid held the barbed wire apart so she could slide through first.

"Do you mind if I stop a second? It's so hot." Kneeling down, Mika cupped her hands, dipped them into the stream, and splashed her face with water. "Are there still people around here who pan for gold in this creek?"

"All the time."

"Have you ever done it?"

"No."

"What about your parents? Did they?"

"Not that I know of."

"So who does, then?" Mika splashed her face once more. "You said people do it all the time."

"I've heard Hank Plummer pans. He's the neighbor who owns the property where we were just sitting. He's a weird guy."

"How is he weird?"

"Let's keep going," said Sid, continuing toward the farm. "Plummer's place was originally a claim his grandfather had back when they first found gold in Trinity County. He's always thought people were out to get his share. It's why he put up 'No Trespassing' signs all over the place."

"Signs? I didn't notice any signs." Mika eyed their surroundings. "I would never have crossed the fence if I had."

"I removed the sign between our properties when I first moved back—before I got busted for trying to grow pot here."

"Why would you do that?"

"What, plant weed?"

"No." Mika clucked her tongue. "Why did you take his 'No Trespassing' sign down?"

"Because I felt like it. Plummer caused my parents no end of grief when they were alive. He constantly harassed them about property lines and land use rights."

"Okay, but . . ." Mika stopped dead in her tracks, her mouth open.

Sid turned to see what she was staring at. Across the creek, loping along the edge of the forest, was Woolf, carrying what appeared to be a large dead animal in his arms. A cigarette dangled off his lower lip. Stopping directly opposite them, he hoisted the carcass over one shoulder and waded across, dropping the lifeless beast at their feet. Blood covered his shirt and hands. The handle of his hunting knife was coated in it, as was the leather sheath attached to his belt. Before them lay a handsome German shepherd, its throat slit from ear to ear.

Mika covered her mouth and gagged.

Though Woolf reeked of alcohol, he behaved as though he were perfectly sober. Panting heavily, he said, "I heard the poor guy in pain. Found him over there." He pulled the cigarette from his mouth and used it to point across the creek toward the Grotto.

"Woolf," said Sid. "Your knife is bloody."

"Yeah?" Absent-mindedly, Woolf said, "When I found the dog, he'd been stabbed. I tried to stop the bleeding, but it was too late. By the time I got him halfway here he was barely alive, so I put him out of his misery."

A cold shudder sped down Sid's spine. The dog was collarless. "No tags?"

"Nope."

"Who do you think did it?"

Woolf shrugged. "Someone rifled through the Grotto, but they didn't find our stash. My guess is that *Rin Tin Tin* here is a stray who was either onto whoever it was, so they killed him, or he turned on his owner for some reason."

Peering into the woods, Sid said, "I heard him howling not that long ago. If what you say is true, someone could still be out there."

"I doubt it. I'm sure they split after all the noise this guy made. I was going to bury him and go back to look for footprints. I just didn't want to dump him in the forest where some wild animal would feast on him. Help me, would you?"

"Sure," said Sid. "Meeks, are you all right?"

Despite a chartreuse pallor indicating otherwise, she assured him she was.

"Sorry you had to see this." Resting the palm of his hand on the crown of her head, he said, "It's going to take us a while. Can you make it to the house okay? I'll be back as soon as we're finished."

Feebly, she assured him she could. When she was gone, the two men picked up the dead dog.

"I thought Meeks was a farm girl," muttered Woolf. "I'm surprised she's taking it so hard."

"I doubt she's used to seeing domesticated animals killed like this. It's pretty brutal."

"Brutal is right. I want to find out who did it."

"You and me both."

"Think we should try to find the owner?"

"That could take a while." Sid paused to readjust the weight of the shepherd to his other shoulder. "I've never seen this dog around here before."

Woolf scoped out their position. "We should probably head away from the creek. Got an idea where we can bury him?"

"I do. Up there near the next bend, beneath that wild pear tree—straight back from the barn."

"Good spot, huh?"

Sid's voice caught. "My old dog is buried there."

"Lucky you. I always wanted a dog when I was a kid. My parents said, 'we'll move out of town one of these days, and then you can have one.' Never happened. What was his name?"

"Homer."

"Heavy, man. As in the poet?"

"No, Homer as in home run. He loved chasing balls."

"Only dog you ever had?"

"Yeah. We were going to get another, but . . . it never happened."

They continued in silence until they reached the pear tree, where they set the shepherd down. Woolf volunteered to retrieve two shovels from the barn. While he was gone, Sid brushed debris off the flat limestone rock that marked Homer's grave. He could almost hear his old pet's bark, feel his devoted drool on his hands, see the excitement in his trusting eyes.

When Woolf returned, he handed one shovel to Sid and began digging with the other. "My gun," he said, between grunts, "the one you took from me last winter after the storm. Where is it?"

"It's in a safe place. You'll get it back before you leave in September."

Pausing to lean on the handle of his shovel, Woolf said, "I need it."

"What for?"

"I've got my reasons."

Sid stopped digging to wipe sweat from his brow. "Sorry, but I can't take any chances with my probation and all. I mean, what if you got plastered, or had, you know . . . "

"Flashbacks?"

"Whatever. A gun in the house could be dangerous."

"It would have to be a pretty severe trigger—like a tree crashing through my ceiling—to set me off. Be honest. When else have you ever seen me like that?"

"Let's just get this dog buried, okay? We can talk about your gun later."

The two resumed shoveling. When the hole was deep enough, they lowered the shepherd into it and covered him with dirt. Assuming a military stance, Woolf placed his hand on his heart and mumbled something under his breath. Then, hoisting his shovel over his shoulder, he said, "Might as well head back to the barn."

Ten minutes later, their shovels cleaned and stored away, Woolf announced he was returning to the Grotto. "I'm going to see what I can find."

"Don't you think it's kind of late? It'll be getting dark in another hour."

"Tomorrow the trail could be cold."

"I suppose you're right."

Watching Woolf as he headed toward the creek, Sid felt more conflicted about the vet than ever. Was he telling the truth about the dog? How could he be so cut-and-dry one minute and then—as when he'd had the moment of silence at the grave—so sensitive the next? And what was the deal with him wanting his gun back?

His mind whirling, Sid made his way to the house. As he opened the back screen door, Woolf shouted across the field to him, "Just so you know, Jackson, I'm going to keep looking for my gun until I find it."

SID STOOD IN the shower a long time, scrubbing away the last traces of dirt and animal blood from his body. When he was finished, he toweled off and pulled on a pair of clean Levi's and a fresh t-shirt. Combing through his wet hair, he examined himself closely in the mirror to see if he needed a shave. *Nope.*

Unable to shake the afternoon's events, he decided he'd rather watch the evening's fireworks display from the front porch of his house than go into town and make small talk with the locals. Plucking a beer from the refrigerator, he tucked a bag of potato chips under his arm and ventured out onto the veranda. There, sitting on the porch swing, was Mika, looking green around the gills.

"Hey," he said, drawing close to her. "You okay?"

"I still feel kind of sick. I called David and told him not to expect me. We were going to watch the fireworks together, but . . ."

Figuring it might not be the best time to sit next to her,

Sid dragged a three-legged stool over from the wall and set it a few feet away from the swing. Opening his beer, he took a long swig. Scores of frogs in a nearby pond *ribbited* their pleasure at the slight drop in air temperature. Beyond the dusking valley below them, where Trinity Springs lay partially hidden from view, the Trinity Alps loomed wild and remote, their crowns berry-tinged by the last rays of sunlight.

"So, I take it you're not going into town to watch the fireworks either," said Mika.

Sid lowered his eyes. In the faint glow of the porch light, Mika's bare toes pressed white against the veranda's chicory-stained planks. Looking back up at her, he said, "I can see everything I want from right here."

Mika blushed. "Mind if I stay and watch the fireworks with you?"

"Of course not."

"Do you know where Woolf is?"

Sid nodded toward the creek. "Out playing Daniel Boone somewhere."

"Did you believe his story about finding the dog alive?"

"I don't know why he'd lie about it. What do you think?"

Shivering, she said, "I just can't get the picture of him taking his knife to that dog's throat out of my mind, whether he 'finished the job' someone else did or not."

"Well, he's a tough, crazy dude, I'll say that. He was in Nam—that probably explains it."

A boom echoed from the valley below, followed by streams of multi-colored lights shooting across the inky sky in all directions. Hester, penned up for the night in the barn, bellowed. Sid opened his bag of chips and ate a few. Another explosion dazzled the sky. The *rat-a-tat-tatting* of firecrackers from a neighbor's house down the road crescendoed, peaked, and died.

Seconds later, the sound of running water in the house indicated Woolf must have returned home to shower. Sure enough, he soon joined them, plopping down on the porch stoop, his shoulder-length hair slicked back behind his ears, a fresh cigarette dangling from his lips, and the smell of Irish Spring soap masking whatever residue of death might still cling to him.

Sid discreetly observed him for a few moments to see if the fireworks would set him off. Apparently, they were far enough away that the loudest explosions were rendered harmless. "So, Woolf." He offered the vet some chips. "Did you find anything?"

"Yeah—foot prints. Two sets of them." Woolf reached into the proffered bag and shoved some chips into his mouth. "One looked to be a man's boots," he garbled. "Size twelve maybe. The other set looked like a woman's sandals, guessing about a size eight. They entered the Grotto from the southwest and exited due north, parallel with the creek. I lost the trail down by the waterfalls. Whoever it was, the dog was with them on the way up. It was like they brought him to the Grotto just to kill him."

"Sounds satanic to me."

"What did you say?" Sid turned to stare at Mika.

"Satanists live around here. You know, devil worshipers. Pearlie told me. So did David."

Partly amused, partly incredulous, Sid said, "That's superstitious. I seriously doubt—"

"I wouldn't be so sure about that," said Woolf. "Pearlie's privy to everything the sheriff knows, and since they've been around here longer than you, I'd say she probably knows what she's talking about."

"See?" Mika looked paler than ever. "Maybe we should call Otis."

"This close to the end of my probation?" Sid shook his head. "Otis is the last person who needs to know about the Grotto. Anyway, we can't go jumping to crazy conclusions. There's got to be some kind of rational explanation for what happened." Glancing sideways at Woolf, he added, "It could have been . . ."

"Hey, man," said Woolf. "Whatever else you might think, I don't torture or kill animals. I love dogs. Like I said, I only killed that shepherd today to put him out of his pain."

"It could be drugs," said Mika. "A deal gone bad or something."

"Why would you think that?" asked Woolf and Sid in unison.

Mika rolled her eyes. "I wasn't born yesterday. It's obvious the Grotto is a place across the creek where everyone gets high. I mean, maybe a dealer's sending you guys a message."

"Is that possible, Woolf?" Sid was surprised he hadn't thought of that himself.

Woolf cleared his sinuses and spit. "No."

"What about Ketch and Liz?" he asked.

"The way I understand it, nobody owes anybody. Everything's straight up."

The fireworks ended with a huge finale. Far away, an owl's plaintive hoot reverberated through the woods. Mika stood up and started toward the door. Before Sid could follow suit, Woolf asked if he would stay out on the porch a bit longer.

When Mika was gone, he said, "There was something else

I found across the creek, Sid. It was hanging on a branch near where I found the dog. I thought it would be best if we were the only ones to know."

"Oh yeah?"

Pulling a hammered silver bracelet out of his pocket, Woolf handed it to Sid.

He noted the unique turquoise stones set into it and recognized it instantly. He had bought it at a fair several years ago as a birthday gift for one of his friends.

It was Kate's.

Baby

SID DIDN'T SPEND MUCH TIME PONDERING the implications of the bracelet Woolf had found in the Grotto. After all, there could be any number of explanations for how it had gotten there—not the least of which was the fact that, since they'd been children, Kate had been almost as familiar with the other side of the creek as he had been. And being as it was government property, nothing prevented her, or anyone else, from hiking in the area whenever they wanted. Or, perhaps, she hadn't liked the bracelet and passed it off to somebody. People did it all the time.

Whatever.

Putting aside any suspicions he might have had about Kate's connection to the Grotto, Sid turned his hand to keeping the farm productive. By now, record-breaking July temperatures were sucking moisture and energy from plants, animals, and humans alike. Ponds disappeared, springs dried up, and the bottoms of small stream beds were laid bare. If it hadn't been for the boarders' extra labor and Sid's care in particular, the vegetable garden would have languished and died.

One Sunday toward the end of the month, as he was up early watering the garden, Sid reached down, plucked a red-and-green marbled tomato from its vine and took a bite. Though it wasn't fully ripe yet, juice squirted out and ran down his chin. A hummingbird hovered over a nearby mound of bright orange nasturtiums, and honeybees buzzed his ankles. Teetering on top of the eight-foot deer fence he had erected around the garden, a turtledove cooed its soulful melodies. Heavily pregnant, Hester lowed for Sid from the other side of the barn, begging him to pay her some attention.

"Don't worry, Hester," Sid shouted. "When I'm finished watering, I'll find a nice cool place for you to rest."

Suddenly a car veered into the driveway. Moments later, Sheriff Skinner was lumbering toward him. "Mornin', Sid!" he called. "It's going to be a hot one."

"It already is." Sid shut off the nozzle on the garden hose and lifted his hand in greeting. "What's up?"

"Oh, just stopping by to see how y'all are doing." Planting his feet firmly next to Sid, Otis slapped him on the back. "What with this heat, I'd think you'd want to cut that hair of yours."

"Sorry, Otis. It's staying, along with the rest of everything else about me you'd like to change. So, what really brings you here? You just did your weekly check the other day."

"I hate to be a bearer of bad news, but Pearlie felt it would be best if you heard it from me first, rather than through some big mouth in town. Kate's pregnant."

"What! Kate Quinn?"

"One and the same."

Sid tensed. "Who's the father?"

"Jake Clausen, I'd imagine. Believe me, there's no end of speculation about what she's going to do. Some folks are saying she and Jake are going to get married soon."

Sucker-punched by the news, Sid stared into space.

"I know she used to babysit you once in a while when your folks were in a pinch, and what with you and Max being friends since kindergarten—well, you've known Kate an awfully long time. That's why Pearlie and I figured you should know." Otis shook his head. "Seems like only yesterday Katie was just a little girl. Sad how life can change people, isn't it?"

Still dazed, Sid muttered, "She's more than four years older than me. I don't remember her being a little girl. Not like you do."

"No, I guess you wouldn't. She sure was an engaging kid though. Resourceful, too. And sweet as Tupelo honey. Probably still would be if her dad hadn't stolen her childhood away from her. A mean and nasty son-of-a-gun if ever there was one—all those drunken binges he took out on their ma!"

"I never saw Eamon beat his wife, but—"

"You never noticed Mrs. Quinn's face? The bruises and all?"

"Well, yeah, but I was too young to—"

"You were in high school, Sid. You couldn't put two and two together?"

"It wasn't like Max and Kate advertised what went on in their house, and I never asked."

"Hey, what about the time your pa caught you and Kate smoking up in your library? How old were you then? Eleven? Twelve?"

"Eleven. Kate was fifteen."

"If you'll recall, Pearlie and I had come over that day to visit. We sure had us a chuckle when your dad came downstairs and told us what happened. Do you remember what your punishment was?"

"How could I forget? I had to smoke a cigar with him until I got sick."

"Yes sir, your pa felt he had to discipline you even though he knew darn well you were telling the truth when you said Kate was the instigator. You know, he was always looking for ways to teach you lessons in manhood. He never wanted you to be the one who finds excuses to blame others for your own behavior."

"If you say so."

"Anyway, just wanted to give you a heads-up about Kate." Otis tipped his cap to Sid and started toward his car. Turning, he added, "Oh, by the way, did I tell you Paul Keating gave her a job at his dealership?"

"No, you didn't." In fact, he couldn't remember the last time Kate Quinn had worked a nine-to-five job.

"I know you and Lynn didn't hit it off well in my office, that day of your sentencing, but she and Paul aren't all that bad. They've been known to help people out in a pinch. And one more thing. Just so you know, Pearlie's telling everyone she overhears yakking about Kate to zip their lips and pray instead. Heck, she's even got her and the baby on the prayer-chain at church now, so rest-assured it's all in God's hands." Tipping his hat one last time, the sheriff slung himself into his car and started the engine.

As Sid nodded a good-bye to Otis in his rearview mirror, he found himself unconvinced that Kate was in anyone's hands but Jake's. Suddenly, he felt a sharp pang of guilt for ditching her at the farm a few weeks ago. No wonder she'd been an emotional mess—she'd probably come to break the news to him. Even worse, what if she was in some kind of trouble and had come to him needing help?

With a heavy sigh, Sid returned to the garden, picked up the hose, and resumed watering. Otis's mention of why his father had punished him after he'd been caught smoking in the library with Kate popped into his mind. *He was always looking for ways to teach you lessons in manhood. He never wanted you to be one who finds excuses to blame others for your own behavior.*

Sid counted the many times in the last year—in the last decade—he'd secretly blamed others for his misfortunes: God, for robbing him of his parents; Kate, for talking him into growing pot; an unidentified neighbor, for ratting on him; the American legal system, for criminalizing the growing and possession of marijuana; and Otis, for enforcing his probation. Never had he flat out held himself fully responsible for all of his troubles.

Manhood. If that's what this is all about, I still have some growing up to do. And the first step is to make things right with Kate.

When sid entered Paul Keating's new car showroom, he saw Kate bent over her desk, sorting through some paperwork in her glass cubicle, her hair obscuring her face. Discreetly, he began nosing about the '73 Chevys on display. As he stared at her over the hood of a baby blue, half-ton pickup, Paul Keating himself appeared at his elbow.

"In the market for a new truck, Sid?"

"No, just browsing."

"That half-ton you're looking at is one heck of a workhorse." Paul pulled a comb out of his mustard-colored, polyester jacket and ran it through his thinning hair. Tugging on Sid's arm, he led him over to the next model and pointed at it with his comb. "This here Camaro Z28 is something else, eh? With a 305 V8 engine, it's a car with muscle."

Nodding toward Sid's biceps, Paul added, "You've already got the He-man thing going anyway. All that work you're doing on the farm must be paying off. But, hey, you could do better with your image. Get rid of that long hair, buy yourself this little Camaro, and you could have your pick of any chick in town."

Paul ended his sales pitch with a shimmy—his wrists resting against his hips, his index fingers pointed toward Sid like smoking guns—and then pounded Sid on the back, guffawing until his over-extended belly jiggled beneath his tie. When Sid didn't crack a smile, he snorted. "Just kidding, just kidding! At least you *have* hair, right?"

"Well, Paul, if you don't mind . . . " Sid glanced at Kate again. "I'm going to keep looking around. I'm really not in the market for a new rig quite yet."

"That's fine, Sid. Take your time. If you have any questions, my office is right around the corner. Just remember, when you're ready, I'll cut you a deal you can't refuse. What are friends for, right?"

Once Paul was out of sight, Sid sauntered toward Kate's office. Seeing him approach, she rose from her desk and met him halfway, near the water fountain. "What brings you here?" she asked.

As determined as he was not to stare at Kate's stomach, Sid couldn't help himself. She didn't *look* pregnant, he thought. *Her eyes look tired, and her coloring's a little off, but other than that . . .*

"Sid, did you hear me? Why are you here?"

"Is it true?"

"Ah, you've finally heard I'm knocked up. Well, congratulations. No doubt, you're the last person in town to find out."

"I know this isn't the best place to talk," whispered Sid, checking to make sure Paul was still nowhere in sight. "Is there somewhere else we can meet?"

Kate folded her arms over her chest and eyed Sid carefully. In a lower voice, she said, "I have to go to the bank soon and make a deposit. After that, I need to deliver a part to a customer outside town. We could meet at that old abandoned schoolhouse on Ford Mill Road, the Lewiston Gulch School. Do you know where it is?"

"I'll find it."

"Park at the back of the building so no one sees your truck. I'll be there at three o'clock."

The phone rang and Kate slipped back into her office to answer it. Sid lingered near the door, listening.

"Hey Jake!" he heard Kate say. "I was just thinking of you . . ."

SID SPOTTED THE ramshackle Lewiston Gulch School to his left and turned his blinker on. At one time, there were enough mining families in the area to support the school, but now, with the claims abandoned, the miner's adjacent homes were empty and overgrown with noxious weeds and vines. All the windows and doors on the dilapidated school were boarded shut. The cement steps leading up to the front of the building were cracked, as though someone had taken a sledgehammer to them. The shingle roof was a velvety jumble of lime-green moss; the cedar siding, rotting and gray.

Making a sharp turn into the gravel turnaround in front of the school, Sid noticed two parallel rows of freshly-flattened, dead grass that continued on to the back of the building. Following them, he pulled up next to a white Chevy Caprice with *Keating Chevrolet* emblazoned on the doors. By the time he turned the key in his ignition off, he'd already noticed three things.

Kate's engine was still running.

All of her windows were rolled up.

She was slumped over the steering wheel of the car.

Like a crazed man, he bolted out of his truck and grabbed the door handle of the Caprice. Finding it locked, he pounded on her window. "Kate! *Kate!*"

She lifted her head slowly, a disoriented look on her face. Turning off the engine, she unlocked the door and opened it. "Sorry. I got here early. I was so tired and hot . . ."

Sid didn't wait for her to finish. Pulling her out of the car, he swallowed her in a hug. Only when a cement truck shifted gears on the road in front of the schoolhouse a few moments later, did they finally let go of each other. Kate smoothed her hair and rearranged her blouse. He let his hands drop to his side. "Sorry," he said. "When I saw you in the car like that, I thought you had . . . you know."

It seemed to take Kate a moment to catch his meaning—and his motive for embracing her. "Oh, I see. You thought I'd killed myself. Sorry, Sid, but I'm not that desperate. At least, not yet."

"No, you're taking it the wrong way. I just meant—"

"Clearly, pity is the only way to get your attention these days. I have to get back to work. What did you want to talk about?" Before he could answer, she snapped, "Wait. Let me guess. You want to know who the dad is."

"It's pretty obvious who it is."

"Really? I'm glad it's obvious to you, because I honestly don't know." Rolling her eyes, she sighed, "Oh, don't look so shocked."

"I'm not shocked."

"Liar. You forget I can see right through you."

"Don't flatter yourself, Kate. You don't know me as well as you think you do."

"Oh, I think I probably know you better than you know yourself. You might look and act all hip and cool, but on the inside you're about as straight as they come. There's a sexual revolution going on, or didn't you know?" With a toss of her head, she added, "Did they teach you nothing at Berkeley?"

"Just tell me who the father is."

"It could be a hundred different guys. I wouldn't know."

"Be serious, would you—for once in your life?"

Sid had gone into this rendezvous determined not to let Kate goad him. Provoking him, pushing his buttons, was nothing but a game to her. What he didn't understand was why he'd always tolerated it before. Who knows? Maybe in the past he'd viewed it as part of her allure. But now, he despised her nastiness; resented her intrigues. Swallowing a caustic remark, he listened as she continued carping about how patriarchal he was. And uptight. And unadventurous with new drugs. And not as sexually liberated as she was.

"Of course," she sniped, "what else should I expect? Look how you were raised. Pampered. Privileged. Born to a rich lawyer and a mom so out of touch with the real world that

she raised you to be just as macho as all her dago male ances-
tors before her. Old World dinosaurs with their caveman
mentality and stupid double standards and . . ."

"Shut up, Kate!" Sid shoved his face close to hers. "At
least I have enough self-respect and, I might add, respect for
women in general, to keep my private affairs behind closed
doors, unlike—"

Before he could finish, Kate slapped him so hard, his head
snapped back.

Seizing her wrists, Sid hissed, "I was *going* to say . . .
unlike Jake and the other guys you've latched onto. If you
keep using people, Kate, they'll use you right back. Don't
you realize they'll throw you in the trash and forget about
you when they're done?"

"I didn't ask for your opinion, and I sure don't need your
pity. I can take care of myself."

"Pity? No, as a friend, I just want to help you through this
mess you've made of your life."

"So, you feel *obliged* . . ."

"If that's what you want to call it."

"Screw your obligation."

"You need help, Kate, and if you want mine, you're going to
have to quit playing these stupid head games and be honest
with me."

"Fine." In a burst of strength, Kate wrested free of his grip.
"If it's honesty you want, here it is: I really don't know who
the father is. It could be a couple different guys because . . .
well, whatever Jake didn't get for me, I got for myself. Using
my own personal currency, if you know what I mean."

Ah, drug dealers.

"And by the way," she added, "Jake has no clue he might not be the dad, so it's important you keep this between us."

"Because he'd hurt you if he knew the truth?"

"Jake might be a bully and a jerk, but he's never laid a hand on me."

"Then maybe he wouldn't care whether he's the dad or not. If that's the case, he might raise your kid as his own, regardless."

"Don't count on it. Just because Jake hasn't physically hurt me doesn't mean he's a knight in shining armor. He's got an ego as big as the Pacific."

"If Jake's such a sugar daddy and no threat to you, then why work at Keating's?"

"To get myself some financial independence in case he dumps me."

"What about the other guys who could be the father? Wouldn't one of them step up to the plate if Jake—"

"One's married. The snake is such a scumbag, I doubt he'll ever leave his wife. The other can barely take care of himself, let alone anyone else. He'd as soon kill us both as have anything to do with this baby."

"Seriously?"

"Seriously."

The way Kate flinched made Sid realize she wasn't joking. *Kill her?* Mulling over what she had just told him, he noticed she was examining his face as though he were some sort of oracle through which she could foretell her future.

"You're wondering if I'm going to get rid of it, aren't you?" she asked. "I thought about it at first, but I'm almost thirty years old, for God's sake. You don't have a clue what it's like to be a woman with her options in life narrowing before her eyes. I look in the mirror and wonder how much longer before I don't recognize myself anymore."

Absently, she raised a hand and traced the outline of her cheek with the tips of her fingers. "Girls," she continued, "are born as smooth as a satin sheet. But they die a patchwork quilt—shabby and used; just a bunch of discarded scraps slapped together out of desperation. I mean, how does that happen? Most of the chicks I see getting all the attention in bars these days are younger than me. What's it going to be like ten years from now when I've totally lost my looks? When all my leverage is gone?"

"What are you saying?"

"I'm saying, I need to have this baby to survive."

Leverage? Survive? Sid could hardly believe what she might be implying. Did she really think of her looks as barter? Her own flesh and blood as nothing but a bargaining chip—a hedge against an uncertain future with men? Before he knew it, Kate was leaning against him, her hands linked behind his waist.

"Come on, Sid. You know I don't love Jake. In fact, most of the time, I can barely stand him. I only hooked up with him in the first place because he had connections and was willing to waste his money on me. You wanted the truth? Well the truth is, I would have given anything to have this baby be ours. When I came to your house—that day you rushed off saying you had a meeting—I'd come to tell you that I was pregnant."

"Kate, about that. I'm sorry . . ."

"I came hoping you'd offer to say it was yours."

"Excuse me?"

"I hadn't told Jake I was pregnant yet. You would have been the first to know. I thought you might offer to be the dad." She pressed her body into his, her face upturned. "I know I've hurt you in the past, Sid. What can I say? Early on, I suppose I let the difference in our ages get in the way of what could have been. Then, when I came back to Trinity Springs, I figured you wouldn't want anything to do with me, after getting busted and all. That's why I took up with Jake in the first place. He really did go over the top offering me anything I wanted. How could I turn that down?"

The weight of her body against his pushed Sid back a step. He braced himself against the bed of his truck, his mind trying to keep up with Kate's reasoning.

"But now look at you," she purred. "Everyone in town talks about how hard you've been working and how, if you keep the farm and continue the way you're going, you'll be rich someday. Haven't people always said you have potential? You just needed a little motivation to make it happen. I mean, you have to agree, thanks to me, getting busted and put on probation was the perfect incentive. Am I right?"

In less than ten minutes, she had gone from branding him an uptight elitist to hailing him as her savior. Sid steeled himself against what he knew was coming next.

"You would have made a perfect dad," she continued, "and I would have given you everything you'd ever want or need, but you wouldn't give me the time of day."

There it is. The guilt trip. I already said I was sorry, Kate.

Coming in for the kill, she began unbuttoning his shirt. "It's not too late for us, Sid. I could move in with you. Today.

Tomorrow. Whenever. Jake would just have to deal with it. I could tell him the baby was yours. That you and I—"

"That's not going to happen." With a sudden push, he held her out at arms length and stepped away from the truck. Then, firmly, he removed her hands from his wrists.

"But—"

"Stop it, Kate. Stop lying to yourself and trying to manipulate me and everyone else into getting what you want. What you *need* is to get grounded in reality and realize not everything is about you. Do you really think I'd lie and say your baby's mine just because you'd get better 'leverage' with me than with someone else? How long would that last? How long would I be good enough for you? How long before you'd move on to someone else?"

Kate turned and stormed toward her car, flashing her middle finger at him as she went.

Although he didn't regret his bluntness, he reproached himself for not achieving what he'd initially set out to do. Hurrying to catch up with her, he said, "Look, I just wanted to meet with you to ask if there's anything I can do to help. You're an old friend. That counts for something. It counts for a lot, actually."

"Forget it. I told you what you could do to help. Obviously our friendship doesn't count for very much."

"Because I won't take you and the baby in as mine? You know that's not an option. I came to offer you what little money I have saved up right now and my support with whatever—"

"I'm tired of living hand to mouth, Sid. What I'm looking for is easy money and long-term financial security. I'm not ashamed to admit it. Why do you think I came back to Trinity Springs? The competition isn't as fierce as in the city. Men here are a lot more gullible. And if worse came to worst, and my own brother ended up turning against me for some reason, there'd be less of a chance of me ending up on the street." With a sneer, she added, "I mean, look at you, for example. You'd do anything to see that wouldn't happen to me, right?"

"I'd never let any friend of mine go homeless."

"Basically, you just did."

"No, I didn't . . ."

"Good-bye, Sid." Lowering herself into her car, Kate slid her key into the ignition.

"Kate, wait. What are you going to do?"

"My job at Keating's is just a stop gap measure until Jake makes a decision . . . or something better comes along." She paused to strap herself into her seatbelt. "But you know what? If Jake ends up dumping me, the hell with it. I'll just move back down to Frisco. I've still got connections there. I could do some deals and make good money while I figure out what to do next. You don't have to worry about me. I always land on my feet." Before Sid could say another word, she slammed the car door in his face. Seconds later, she sped out of the parking lot, leaving him coughing in a thick cloud of dust.

So much for manhood. In his entire life, even after getting busted last year, Sid couldn't remember feeling like such a failure. He'd come to the schoolhouse with every intention of giving an old friend comfort and aid—to let Kate know that he'd be there for her if there was anything she needed—and he was leaving having given her nothing but a piece of his mind and a reason to look elsewhere for support.

Glumly, he returned to his truck.

But then, what did I really expect? Kate Quinn has become someone I hardly know anymore.

Love Breaks the Rules

Sɪᴅ ᴊᴀᴄᴋꜱᴏɴ, ᴛʜᴇ ɢʀᴇɢᴀʀɪᴏᴜꜱ ʙʀᴏᴏᴅᴇʀ, the extraverted introvert, attracted to women but wary of commitment, had grown so alarmed by Kate's predicament, he did something he hadn't done since his return to Trinity Springs: he sought help from Otis and Pearlie. About eight o'clock in the evening, on the last day of July, he knocked on their door.

Pearlie greeted him with a hug. "Sid! What brings you here?"

"I need to talk to you and Otis—get your opinion on something."

"Well, come on in." Guiding him into the entry, she hollered, "Otis! Sid's here to see us!"

Otis appeared seconds later, still in his uniform. He led Sid into the living room and pointed to the couch. "Sit down, son. Nothing wrong, I hope."

"I'm here to talk about Kate Quinn."

Otis glanced at Pearlie, who rushed to nestle on the sofa next to Sid. "Shoot," he said.

"You know Kate's pregnant. Well, she's in trouble, but I can't say exactly what kind of trouble it is." He wished he could tell them that Jake might not be the father; that a dangerous drug dealer could be . . . someone who posed a threat to Kate and her baby.

Otis shifted uneasily in his seat. "Trouble of a criminal nature?"

"No—at least, not yet."

"You can't be more specific than that?"

"Sorry. Her situation is messy, and it could get a lot messier if Jake Clausen ends up not taking responsibility for the baby."

"But why wouldn't he take responsibility?" asked Pearlie.

Otis coughed, his eyebrows arched with understanding.

"Oh." Pearlie covered her mouth. "Oh, dear."

Pressing ahead, Sid said, "Do you know someone who could provide a safe place for Kate to stay if worse came to worst? That is, if things fell apart for her and she didn't leave Trinity Springs?"

"What about her brother, Max?" asked Otis. "Couldn't she live in their folks' house with him?"

Sid shook his head. "Probably not the greatest environment for a baby to be in." *Not to mention her drug dealer would have no problem finding her there.*

"You've got a point," said Otis. "Only time will tell what kind of uncle Max will be."

"So," said Sid. "Do you know of anyone?"

Pearlie locked her lips together and stared through Sid as though focused on some invisible being behind him. Then, snapping out of her trance, she blurted, "Kate and the baby will stay here with us if need be."

"Pearlie, no. I didn't come here expecting you and Otis to take her in. I just thought maybe you knew someone I could refer her to."

"She couldn't be in a safer place than right here with me and Otis."

"I'm sure that's true, but . . ."

"But what? You think Otis and I are too old to have a baby in our house?"

"Of course not. It's just that . . ."

"Why do you think I saved all them baby clothes over the years? Do you think me storing the empty crib up in the attic was for nothing?"

How could he explain the problems they'd be facing if they took on Kate? Things could get nasty fast. But if that were the case, maybe Otis and Pearlie's house *would* be the safest place for her and the baby.

"All right, I guess it's settled then." Standing up, Sid made a motion to leave. "Thanks, both of you. I appreciate your help. I didn't know who else to ask."

The Skinners trailed Sid into the hallway. "Are you sure you can't stay longer?" asked Pearlie. "I made some cookies today."

"Sorry, but I have to get back to the farm." Reaching the front door, Sid stopped and turned. An unexpected, overwhelming sense of gratitude compelled him to reach out and hug them both. As he embraced them, an entirely different emotion overtook him. It was such an impulsive, spontaneous desire to unburden his soul, he didn't even think before speaking.

"Actually, there is something else I want to talk to you two about," he said. "I've been researching the accident and, well, I'm pretty disturbed by some of the stuff I've found out about it. I have a lot of questions I'd like to ask you."

Pearlie's right hand flew to her cheek. Her other reached for Otis.

"I should have mentioned it sooner, but I don't know . . . I guess putting if off was easier."

"Well, now's as good a time as any," said Otis. "Fire away."

"Like I said, I have to be getting back to the farm, so not today. But soon. I promise."

"Whenever you're ready," said Otis. "We'll be here."

Pulling his keys out of his pocket, Sid thanked them again before stepping outside. Just before reaching his truck, he heard Otis call something out to him. Turning, he said, "What's that Otis?"

"Don't forget to watch your behind, son," yelled the sheriff. "You've only got one month left on your probation. Whatever you do, don't blow it."

Sid kept his concern for Kate at bay by staying busy: feeding and caring for Hester, watering and weeding the garden, and nicking away at repairs on the farm. He also immersed himself in designing and building a state-of-the-art compost bin.

Made out of chicken wire and pressure-treated redwood, the three-compartment box was attached to the back of a garden storage unit he'd constructed from recycled cedar. Atop that, he placed a recently-salvaged, rectangular, sixty-gallon, polyethylene tank to catch rainwater. On one side of the bin, Sid fastened a large outdoor thermometer, and for the final touch, he added a birdhouse to the opposite side. It was a straightforward affair, designed specifically for bluebirds. Bluebirds, he had discovered through months of poring through *Organic Farming and Gardening* magazines, were notorious insectivores and a must for any serious farmer.

Taking a step back, he brushed his hands on his overalls and admired the completion of his brainchild. He had to admit, the carpentry skills he'd picked up over the last year had proven to be a surprise bonus of his probation. In fact, he was so energized by his recent woodworking achievements, he found himself already planning his next project: a pinewood picnic table and some bent-willow outdoor furniture.

His growing expertise—the result of helping his father with repairs when he was a boy, gleaning what he could from books, and asking endless questions at the lumber and hardware stores—was giving him a sense of pride unlike he'd ever felt before.

WHILE SID INVESTED himself more and more into the farm, the boarders did the opposite. Indeed, facing the inevitable, they began disconnecting from their future there, counting the days until their lease expired.

One night in early August, while sitting at the dinner table over a salad of fresh picked greens and garden gazpacho with homemade bread, they began discussing what they would each do after September first.

"I'm going back to Jersey," said Woolf. "My old man found me a job at the shipyard he works at. Starts the middle of September. It's not much, but it beats being bored out of my mind and living hand to mouth on disability. Worth giving it a go, anyway." Shrugging, he opened a new pack of Camels and tapped out a cigarette. "Don't get me wrong. It's been great living out here in the sticks for a while, but I belong back east."

"Cool," said Liz, helping herself to a second slice of bread.

"Well, as for me, I came here hoping I'd figure out what to do with my degree, but time's gone by so fast, and so much has happened since Christmas, and—"

"And we don't know what's going to happen with me and Annabelle yet," chimed in Ketch. Since Sid, Mika, and Liz all knew about his custody battle, Ketch had finally told Woolf as well. Now he spoke openly about Annabelle nearly every day. "The latest news from my lawyer is that there's a ruling coming down after Labor Day. Maybe by then, me and Lizzers can come up with a plan for a party of three." Turning to Liz, he slid his arm over her shoulder and winked. "Right, baby?"

Liz reddened. Clearly taken off guard, her face reflected caution. "We'll see whether a party of three is possible or not. Besides, a party for one still sounds awfully appealing to me. In fact, I'm considering going back to Alaska for a while. I might take some classes in the fall, or—"

"Come on," teased Ketch, "you know what I meant."

"Do I?"

Ketch guffawed so loudly, the table shook. Leaning in for a kiss, he said, "You know you do. But I love your spunk, girl! I swear, you're a Texan at heart."

Sid turned from the lovebirds' display and leveled his attention across the table at Mika, who was casting sidelong glances at Ketch and Liz. "What are your plans?"

"The same as they've always been." Her reply was stoic. "I'll find out soon if I've been accepted into the ministry I've applied for. If so, I hope to be overseas by mid-October at the earliest, or by the latest, the end of November. That'll give me plenty of time to move my stuff back to Iowa and see my family before I go."

"And if you're not accepted?" asked Liz.

"I'll try again next year or apply with a different agency."

A hush fell over the boarders—perhaps because the finality of their sojourn in Trinity Springs had sunk in. Or maybe the implications of Mika's impending move sounded more serious or risky than they'd imagined. Regardless, after a moment of somber reflection, Liz, in an apparent attempt to change the subject, blurted, "By the way, guess what I heard today at Back to Eden?"

They all shrugged.

"Lenny's divorcing Charlotte."

"I thought they were just living together," said Sid.

"Everyone did." Liz's voice turned confidential. "Come to find out, they were married—an open one."

Sid glanced at Mika, who was gathering up dirty dishes. Something about Lenny's fascination with her stuck in his gut like gum on the sole of a shoe.

"And get this," added Liz. "Last month, Lenny bought two tickets to *The Dead's* gig in Watkin's Glen, New York, and the second ticket was *not* for Charlotte. He ended up selling them, apparently because whoever it was he was going to take with him decided they couldn't, or wouldn't, go. The tickets were only ten bucks each, but by the time he paid airfare for two people to fly back east, he would have spent plenty. That's when Charlotte saw the writing on the wall. She was pissed to say the least. Can you blame her? Lenny's an idiot. Let me tell you, with all they have riding on Eden . . ." Liz snapped her fingers. "She could break him like that."

With a grunt, Sid abruptly excused himself and headed out to the barn to clear his head. He couldn't quite put his finger on why the news about Lenny Tobin's open marriage and divorce bothered him. But it did. And when Mika had shared what her plans were after September, he'd nearly tipped over his wine glass, he was so agitated. He even found himself still troubled by the thought of Kate leaving Trinity Springs. What was that about? Where was all this frustration coming from?

Then, it came to him. Nearly everyone he'd grown accustomed to, or accepted into his inner circle within the last year, including Kate, was moving on without him. Of course, the sense of loss that loomed on his horizon was nothing compared to what he'd experienced following his parents' deaths, but still . . .

A hungry lowing from Hester's stall snapped Sid from his malaise. Grabbing a wheelbarrow, he hefted a bag of silage into it, pushed it over to the cow, and cut through the plastic with his pocketknife.

"Sorry, Hester," he said, dumping the aged meadow cuttings into her trough. A faint whiff of sweet tobacco permeated the air. "Wish I could put you out to pasture, but the grass has all dried up." As Sid rubbed the bridge of Hester's nose consolingly, the barn door creaked open.

"Got a minute?" Ketch approached Sid, his broad shoulders slumped, the corners of his mouth twisted with trouble.

"Sure." Sid stepped away from Hester. "What's up?"

"That whole thing back there at the dinner table with me and Liz?" Ketch jabbed his thumb in the direction of the house. "I was just trying to save face. You know, with my sarcasm and all. Don't tell her I said this, but the truth is, I'm as much afraid of losing her as I am of not getting custody of my Annabelle. Lord help me, but I'm in love with that rascal. Can you believe how much she's changed since she first showed up on your doorstep?"

"In more ways than one."

"Got that right. I mean, she came here plain on the outside and gnarly on the inside. Now she's all different and, well, even though some of the gnarls are still there, she's buttered and sugared them up so much, I don't even notice them anymore."

Wow. He'd never seen his roommate so dead serious.

Ketch dug a Marlboro out of his shirt pocket and lit it, tossing the burnt match into a nearby bucket. After taking a few drags, he said, "Not sure what possessed me to come out here and spill my guts. What with the year comin' to a close on the farm and Annabelle and all—I don't know—it's just burnin' a hole in my head so bad, I can't sleep at night."

"Yeah, well, life can do that, Ketch. Guess all you can do is tackle one thing at a time."

"True that. Thing is, breaking problems down into manageable portions was a piece of cake in my Harley business, but somehow when it comes to affairs of the heart, as they say . . . "

"Love breaks all the rules, eh?"

"Amen, brother." Ketch snorted. "Besides, since when, I'd like to know, did common sense apply to women anyway?"

"If Liz is the one for you, she'll wait 'til you sort everything out with Annabelle. If she doesn't, then I'd say you weren't meant to be together."

"I know that up here." Ketch poked at his forehead with his index finger. "I realize if Lizzie goes back up to Alaska like she's threatening to do, it won't mean she doesn't have feelings for me anymore. I just need to remember that while I deal with getting Annabelle back. I don't want to get distracted and blow it. I already lost my little girl once. I don't want to lose her again. But then, it's not every day I meet a gal my equal—like Eliza. I just don't want to lose either of them."

Thinking of his parents, Sid said, "Take it from me, Ketch, absence really does make the heart grow fonder. You'll miss Liz if she's the one."

Ketch kneaded his chin thoughtfully. "I'm banking on the judge reaching a decision by Labor Day. But if they continue to drag out my custody case, and it takes longer than that, I'll just have to find me some digs somewhere between here and Frisco until it's settled." Then, like quicksilver, he grinned, thanked Sid for his advice, turned and left.

Sid watched Ketch make his way back to the house. *Maybe I should have told him he can stay here with me after my probation's over.* But then, what if Liz or Woolf changed their minds and decided they wanted to stay, too? It wouldn't be fair to make an exception for Ketch and no one else. *Anyway, my probation's not over yet.* A lot could happen between now and then.

With September 1 now less than a month away, he'd noticed a growing complacency had settled over the boarders, as though averting a prison sentence was a done deal for him. It wasn't. At all. He broke out in a sweat just thinking of how tenuous, how treacherous, the next few weeks could be if he wasn't careful. He should, he realized, take his own advice and not stress out about it. Tackle one day at a time, like he'd told Ketch.

As he finished feeding Hester, he could hear someone in the distance—most likely Mika—humming a song. It sounded as though she was on the back porch or perhaps in the garden. Marishka Larson. The only girl he'd ever clicked with on an almost cellular level. And yet, she seemed as removed from him in body and soul as sunshine on a foggy day. It made him almost envy Ketch. At least he had Liz—and Annabelle. Whether Ketch would ever be allowed to help raise her or not, she would still always be his daughter.

Other than his Nonna, thought Sid, *I have no one.*

Suddenly, Greta—the stray cat Mika had rescued—materialized at his feet. Scooping her up in his arms, he settled down on a nearby bale of hay and stroked her fur. He didn't care that he was allergic to cats; he just wanted to feel close to Mika somehow. Sure enough, despite a few sneezes, the cool of the barn's interior, the warmth of Greta's nose nuzzling the palm of his hand and the peppered serenity of an approaching California mountain dusk had soon soothed him to his core. He was now so calm that, if he had believed in such a thing as a spirit world, he would have sworn he could feel his parents' presence close by. Watching him; cheering him on.

And then it hit him. Even if he never had anyone else to love, he'd still have this farm. This, he thought, he could control. This, he could build on and manage. And someday—if he made it through this probation—he'd reap the rewards. *You knew, didn't you, Mom and Dad? When you left this to me, you somehow knew I would come back and pick up where you left off. You guessed I would love this place like you did.*

And you were right.

I do.

The Last Hurrah

LTHOUGH SID'S PROBATION WAS ORIGINALLY scheduled to end on the first of September, because the first landed on a Saturday, and Monday was Labor Day, the oversight was corrected, and the official date extended to Tuesday, September 4. A small detail, explained Otis. Only three days. How it was overlooked in the first place, no one quite knew, but it had been verified, and there it was.

The boarders, using the extension as an opportunity to throw together a farewell bash, gathered together the afternoon of Saturday, August 25, to work out the details. Mika, who'd had a last minute request from Pearlie to fill in at The Pearl, was the only one absent. Over a lunch of cucumber sandwiches, potato salad, and fresh tomatoes from the garden, the roommates readied their plans.

When Ketch finished eating, he went over to a rusty Coleman cooler propped against the fence and grabbed an ice-cold Coors. Liz, meanwhile, stretched out on a chaise lounge a few feet away, played with her food. Reclining against the Magnolia tree, Woolf whittled away at a piece of wood with a Swiss Army knife. Sid sat quietly on a small folding chair nearby.

Setting her plate on the ground, Liz said, "Sid, you haven't said a word."

"There's nothing to say. This meeting was your idea, not mine." The inner transformation Sid had been experiencing the past few weeks and months was so private, he was convinced Liz wouldn't understand if he told her that his fear of hurting Otis and Pearlie, of blowing his chance to inherit the farm, now ranked up there with his fear of going to prison.

Ketch finished off his beer with a loud slurp. "Dude, it's time you painted your butt white and started running with the antelope."

"In other words," explained Liz, pointing her finger at Sid, "stop fighting our idea for a party and do as you're told."

"Couldn't have said it better, myself." Woolf yawned. "I vote we party at the Grotto."

"Agreed!" cried Liz.

All three looked at Sid expectantly, as though challenging him to throw caution to the wind and go out with them in a blaze of glory.

He was unmoved. "I'm not the one leaving Trinity Springs. You are. So do what you want and have a good time without me."

Liz studied him. "You don't even know where the Grotto is, do you?"

"The Grotto?" Sid laughed in disbelief. "Of course I do. I know exactly where it is. Did you forget I grew up here? I know the other side of the creek like the back of my hand. It's just that, as you'll recall, I'm still on probation."

"That's the point," argued Liz. "The Grotto is the perfect

place to have a blow out. If we party here at the house and it gets out of control, one of your neighbors could report us. But we can get totally wasted across the creek and no one will ever know. I mean, what's the point of even having a party if we can't really *party*?"

"Hey man, if it makes you feel better," said Ketch, "we can start out here at the house with a few drinks and then head over to the Grotto."

"And if you get paranoid once we're there," added Liz, "you could just come back to the house."

"What about Mika?" asked Sid.

Woolf glanced up from his whittling. "What about her?"

"Doesn't she have a say in this?"

Ketch fished around in the cooler for another beer. "Meeks definitely wouldn't dig the Grotto idea. But then, knowing her, she wouldn't stop us from going over there either—if that's what we all decide we want. Am I right, or am I right, Liz?"

"Mika's cool that way," agreed Liz. "I'm not saying she might not get weirded out about it, but she won't try to stop us. So let's set the date and worry about the rest later. How about the last day of the month? It's a Friday, I think."

"One day's as good as another as far as I'm concerned." Woolf thrust his knife deeper into the block of wood he was carving.

"Fine by me," drawled Ketch. "We'll swap spit in the Grotto, and then, come September fourth, hit the road."

Sid stood to his feet. "Who's going to tell Meeks?"

"Don't worry about it." Liz dismissed Sid's question with a wave of her hand. "We'll take care of her."

THE DAYS LEADING up to the party were chaotic and bittersweet with everyone trying to prepare for their impending life changes as best they could. It was still beastly hot. Temperatures soared into the triple digits each afternoon, followed by evenings so unbearable, some of the boarders took to sleeping outdoors—in the hammock, on sleeping bags flayed open on the ground, on makeshift beds on the porch—anywhere they could find relief from the heat.

Because it was so oppressive, Mika and her other roommates took advantage of the cooler mornings to start erasing traces of their life spent on the farm. She and Liz began cleaning out the pantry and refrigerator and freezer, serving up whatever remained so that Sid wouldn't be stuck with a bunch of spoiled food after they left.

Liz, who had accumulated scores of books and a few, small pieces of antique furniture during the year, checked into the cost of renting a small U-Haul to transport her belongings to Alaska. Apparently, she was still determined to leave Ketch to deal with the legal battle for his daughter alone.

Unlike the girls, Woolf and Ketch had accrued little during their sojourn. Woolf spent his final days exploring the woods across the creek while Ketch prepped and polished his Harley.

Then on Thursday, August 30, Otis stopped by for, *perhaps* he said, his last probation check. After making his rounds, he went into the kitchen and struck up a conversation with Mika and Liz. "Sure does seem empty around here with everyone packing their things up," he said.

Liz sniffed several times in succession without looking up from the onions she was dicing.

Mika asked the sheriff if he thought Pearlie might like

some tomatoes from the garden. "They're coming on like crazy now," she said. "With everybody leaving in a few days, we don't know what to do with them all."

"You bet. Whatever you don't want, Pearlie'll use them. By the way," he said, as she began layering several ripe beefsteak tomatoes into a grocery bag for him. "When will you find out if you got accepted to go on that mission trip of yours?"

"I found out today." She handed Otis the sack. "I didn't make it."

"I'm right sorry to hear that. You must be sorely disappointed."

Struggling to find her voice, she sputtered, "I'm applying with another agency. David got accepted, though. He's leaving for Calcutta in three weeks."

Liz excused herself. "I'll leave you guys to it and take some of these dishes out to the picnic table."

When she was gone, Otis asked, "You and him—that David—still like each other?"

"We're really good friends."

"Just friends, huh?"

"We both knew this could happen—that one of us might not get accepted, or that we'd each be sent somewhere different—so we never let our friendship get beyond that." Mika tossed the salad she had made with a mixture of oil and vinegar and picked up the large wooden bowl to take outside.

Otis followed her onto the back porch. "When do you leave?"

"Monday. I'm pretty much all packed and ready to go."

"It'll be one heck of a trip. Three days, I would imagine, to get to Iowa. Hate to think of you driving it alone."

"Oh, I won't be alone. David will drive out with me and then fly back here."

"I'm glad to hear it. He seems to be a good man, that David."

"Yes, he is." She placed the salad on the picnic table next to Liz's dishes and then accompanied the sheriff to his car, promising she would stop by to see him and Pearlie before she left.

Resting his elbow on the roof of his cruiser, Otis eyed her as if to say, *Something's not right with you, and I wish you'd tell me, but I respect your choice not to.* "Pearlie's grown awfully fond of you," he said. "Don't know what she's going to do without your help at the café anymore."

"She'll manage. Just like she did before I came."

"I suppose. *Whew*, it's hot!" He pushed his cap back and dragged his shirtsleeve across his brow. "Well, I sure hope you don't forget about us. I've told Sid this, and I'll tell you, too: When people walk into a life, it's always for a reason. We know the reason you were sent to us. Me and Pearlie both appreciate all the little things you did for us while you were here. You'll be sorely missed."

"I'll miss you and Pearlie, too. I promise, I'll keep in touch."

"I know you will." Giving her cheek a slight, gentle pinch, Otis settled into his car and started the engine. "Be sure to keep in touch with Sid, too, will you?"

And with Mika staring after him, curious as a cat, he was gone.

FOLLOWING A SWELTERING week of triple-digit temperatures, the last day of August proved to be the hottest day of the year. By dawn, it was already 93 degrees. The sun blanched the earth of color, bleaching the brownest soils, dulling the dark green conifers and oaks, and robbing summer flowerbeds of their vibrancy. Cracks appeared everywhere—in the ground, on sidewalks and cement foundations, even in some of the old, already checked timbers in the barn. There was no dew to soften the break of day, no cool breeze to greet early risers. Indeed, the heat that morning was so beastly that a semi-naked and perspiring Sid, splayed out on top of his sheets, cursed it before he even got out of bed.

Because his room had been so hot and stuffy, he'd scarcely slept. Instead, he'd brooded all night. So much, that his former optimism about the future of the farm was wavering like a mirage over hot asphalt. One of his most immediate problems, he'd concluded around three o'clock in the morning, had no solution. The boarders were too busy preparing to leave to help him anymore. Shouldering the entire responsibility for the garden, on top of everything else the last few days, had become overwhelming. How long would he be able to keep things operational after his roommates left?

He rubbed his eyes hard, as though in so doing, he could expunge all the negative thoughts invading his mind. Then he rose to face another impossibly long, torrid day. Grudgingly, he threw on some cutoff jeans and a sleeveless undershirt, shuffled into the kitchen, slugged down a glass of orange juice, and tucked an energy bar into his pocket. Then he slipped on his fine-tooled buffalo leather sandals and headed out to the garden. Uncoiling the hose from the side of the barn, he turned on the spigot and began the painstaking job of watering each individual plant. Twenty minutes later, the boarders began trickling out of the house.

Ketch was first, slinking down the back steps in his riding chaps and boots—bare chested. A cigarette stub languished between his alabaster lips. "It's a lost cause, partner," he muttered, as he passed Sid. "It's so dry, the trees are bribin' the dogs. Headin' into town to check my mail. See ya later."

While Ketch revved his Harley, Liz made her appearance. Comb in hand, she stood on the porch, several yards away, her head down as she intently attacked a stubborn knot in her hair. Giving it one last furious yank, she tossed the freed hairball over the railing into the flowerbed. "Oh, mornin', Sid," she said. "Bummer you have to water again today. I've got a ton to do, otherwise I'd help."

"Don't worry about it."

Mika stepped out next, holding what appeared to be a glass of iced tea. Standing alongside Liz, she waved at him. "Good morning! It's a hot one, isn't it?"

"Sure is."

"I'd help you in the garden," she said, "but I still have some things I need to do at the school today before I leave for Iowa."

"No problem," he lied, feeling for all the world like an old man looking through a chain-link fence at a playground of happy-go-lucky kids.

Liz turned to re-enter the house, but not before calling out, "Now don't forget about the party, Sid!"

"What party?" asked Mika.

Nobody told Mika about the party? Unable to conceal his curiosity, Sid adjusted his stance so he could more easily watch what happened next. Liz drew close to Mika, seemingly to answer her question. When she did, he noticed Mika's demeanor change from passive, to wounded, to shocked. Unfortunately, their voices were too low to hear what they were saying.

As both girls traipsed inside the house together, Woolf tore past them. Loping toward Sid, he said, "Hey man, I need my gun."

"Stick around 'til Tuesday," replied Sid. "Once I'm officially free, I'll make sure you get it." Woolf's quicksilver reaction was hard to read. At first, he wondered if the vet's threatening body language meant he was angry or if it was just a case of Woolf being Woolf.

"All right." Woolf's eyes sparked. "I'll come back to see you Tuesday, but I'll keep looking for it until then."

Sid nodded. He didn't need to be told that Woolf had been searching the grounds for his gun. It was apparent every time he went into the barn, or any storage room in the house, that someone had been poking around.

His eyes still boring into Sid's, Woolf said, "I'm heading over to the Grotto to check things out."

"Okay." *Whatever, Woolf. Why would I care where you're going?* "Later, man."

"Later." With a smirk, Woolf added, "And by the way, have fun watering."

WHEN HE WAS finally finished watering and weeding, Sid fed Hester. Half-heartedly, he cleaned her stall, as well as the chicken coop, and sharpened a few tools. Then, after doing all his other chores and puttering around some more, he strolled through the meadow leading to the apple orchard in search of some solitude. He had assumed it would be cooler there, given it was located near the creek, but it wasn't.

Meandering down an avenue of miserly semi-dwarf trees, he tried not to be disheartened. In less than two months, the orchard had gone from being a fresh green refuge to a graveyard of sickly fruit. He reached out and touched a diseased brown leaf curled back over a scaly, runted apple. It crumbled to dust in his fingers. Continuing on, he surveyed the other trees. Because they hadn't been pruned in years, many were mere specters of what they should be. *This is all from a lack of rain. Dryness has sucked the life out them. Is this what's happening to me?*

Overtired, he slumped down at the base of a particularly sickly looking tree. Plucking a long piece of grass from a nearby clump, he placed it between his lips and began chewing. A good two hours later, he was in the same spot, having done nothing but ponder to the trickling of the creek and the drone of bees and cicadas. When he finally decided to get up, the angle of the sun indicated it was early afternoon.

The temperature had risen at least another five degrees.

And adding insult to misery, he had a raging headache.

BACK AT THE house, Sid approached Liz as she stood over Ketch beneath the magnolia tree. She was scrutinizing the food and drinks he was packing into the metal cooler. "How do you expect to carry that huge thing all the way across the creek?" she asked him.

"That's what wheelbarrows were made for, darlin'."

"Did you remember the flashlights and batteries?"

"Yes, ma'am."

"Don't call me ma'am."

"Yes, sir."

Pointing to Woolf, she asked, "Have you got the matches?"

Woolf tapped his pocket. "Right here."

Sid had advanced so quietly, no one was aware he was standing there until he muttered, "What's going on?"

"Oh, there you are, Sid. We were looking for you. Are you coming with us or not?"

"To the Grotto?"

"Where else would we be going?"

"I thought you were going to start the party here first, so Meeks could . . ."

"We've been waiting forever for her." Her face flushed, Liz fanned herself. "She should have been back an hour ago. It's too hot to wait here much longer. The Grotto's calling our names."

"Well, then," he said, "Guess I'll go inside and clean up. Maybe she'll be here by the time I'm done."

"Okay," said Liz. "We'll wait for you, but don't take too long."

Ten minutes later, following a quick shower, Sid swallowed two aspirin, changed into a clean pair of jeans and a t-shirt, threw a sandwich together and headed outside. He found his roommates, lazing around, still waiting for Mika. A stereo plugged into an outlet on the porch blared the sultry melodies of Van Morrison's *Moonlight* album across the lawn. Selecting a cold beer from the cooler, he eased himself into the hammock as the boarders discussed how they were going to spend their evening in the Grotto.

"Hey guys, I just remembered," said Liz. "Look what I have!" Pulling a baggie out of her backpack, she held it up for everyone to see.

"Peyote!" Woolf pointed to the bluish-green cactus buttons visible through the plastic. "Far out. Where'd you get them?"

"Let's just say I know the right person and leave it at that." She waved the bag in Sid's direction. "Sid knows who it is. Want some?"

Whereas days ago he would have emphatically said "no," he now hesitated. Maybe the bad acid trip he'd had in Berkeley a few years ago was a fluke, he thought. *Sure, that was it.* He'd just been stupid. Inexperienced. He'd simply taken too much. What would a little peyote button hurt? He could take just enough to get a buzz. *But what if Otis were to drop by unannounced?* Well, he could tell him he'd had one too many beers . . . or plead a heatstroke. After all, there'd be no incriminating evidence to suggest otherwise, because Liz would be long gone with the evidence.

Just as Sid was about to tell Liz to throw him the bag, she stuffed it back in her pack.

"Maybe we'd better get all this stuff ferried across the creek first," she said. "I'd rather be totally kicked back when we start tripping. Besides, we've waited long enough for Meeks. I've had it. It's got to be cooler in the Grotto than it is here."

"Got that right." Ketch stretched into a standing position. "Bummer, but I don't think Meeks'll mind. Do you, Sid?"

He knew Mika would care, but she'd have to understand missing out was the price you paid for being late. "Nah," he said.

Ketch hesitated. "Sure you don't want to come with us, partner?"

Of course I do. "Maybe later. I still have a few things to do around here."

"Sure," snickered Liz. "I'll believe it when I see it."

Grabbing the wheelbarrow, Ketch began crossing the

yard. "All right then, adios!" he hollered. "You know where to find us."

Woolf, taking up the rear of the procession, stopped briefly to stroke Greta and ruffle her ears. When he caught up with the others, he turned and called, "Live a little, man. It'll be your last chance to party with us."

Sid watched the three boarders wind down the sawdust path toward the creek, the air fizzing with their chatter; with their uninhibited laughter. Everything in him screamed to join them. When they disappeared from sight, he settled back in the hammock, crossed his hands behind his head, and closed his eyes.

Should I? Shouldn't I?

Yes. No.

Yes . . .

At least ten unsettled minutes passed.

"Hey there."

Raising his head up, he saw Mika approaching him, taking in her surroundings as she came. "Where did everybody go?" she asked.

"Across the creek."

She scanned the distance where the forest stretched away from the creek. "I know I was late, but I didn't think they'd leave before I got here."

"They waited for you for a long time. They finally decided it was too hot to hang out at the house anymore."

"It is that." She pulled a lawn chair into the shade nearby and fell into it. "I can hardly bear it myself."

Silence. The never-ending whooshing of the creek. The *cak-cak-cak-ing* of a Cooper's hawk circling high above them. Then a faraway shout.

"I guess that's it for me, then," sighed Mika.

"What's it?"

"No farewell celebration."

Sid pitched her an unsympathetic look. "You're free to go over and join them, you know."

"I could say the same for you."

"True." *I'm just going to say it. Why not?* "It doesn't mean you and I can't have our own celebration, Meeks."

"Right," she laughed.

"I'm not kidding."

In a fluid motion, Mika swept her hair back into a loose knot and secured it with a band. Nodding across the river, she said, "That's where you really want to be. You can't fool me."

"I'm here, aren't I?"

"At least you're being smart. I'll give you that. If you go over there, you might as well kiss your farm good-bye."

"The thought never crossed my mind."

"I see."

"You see what?"

"The mood you're in." Several moments passed. A slight breeze, hot as the baked ground beneath them, soughed down through the Magnolia tree, rustling its waxy leaves in a chorus of whispers. "So then," continued Mika, "What are your plans for rest of the afternoon?"

Try as he might, Sid couldn't prevent a tone of derision from seeping into his voice. "I don't have any. What are your plans? Going to see David later?"

Mika leapt from her chair. Her arms akimbo, she stared down at him. "For your information, I turned down David's offer to go with him to Redding this afternoon because I thought we were having a farewell party here. What is going on with you?"

Rolling out of the hammock, he stood to face her. "Do you really want to know why I stayed here instead of going over to the Grotto with the others?"

"Why?"

"Because if I had to choose one boarder to spend my last day with, it would be you. And besides, there's no way I'd leave you here at the house by yourself. Not with everyone else over there."

"Well, that's . . . that's . . . thoughtful of you."

"So then, since it's just you and me, what say we go for a swim before it gets dark?"

"A swim?"

"Yeah, a swim. We'll have our own last hurrah."

Another silence—longer this time.

"Well?" he asked.

"Sure," she replied, as though accepting a dare. "I don't have anything else to do, and it's so . . . "

"Hot. Exactly." Trying not to look excited at the prospect, he added, "I'm ready whenever you are."

"I have to go inside and change."

"That's fine. I have to check on Hester, so just come out to the barn and get me when you're ready."

As Mika headed to the house, Hester moaned. Nearing the corral, Sid saw the pregnant cow rubbing her flanks against one of the wooden posts. *She's got to be miserable in this heat, especially this far into her pregnancy. It should be soon—any day now.*

Moments later, while filling her trough with water, an idea came to him. He went back into the barn and retrieved a ladder. Extending it as far as it would go, he positioned it against the wall and climbed to the apex, where an old deserted barn swallows' box hung beneath the eaves. He opened the lid, reached inside, and felt around.

Woolf's gun was gone.

Stunned, he shimmied back down the ladder, his mind racing. No one had been in the barn the night he had hidden it. No one could have seen him. He was sure of it. So where was the gun? Had Otis confiscated it during one of his probation checks? He couldn't have. *Otis would have told me.*

"There you are."

Sid wheeled around to face Mika. Noticing her baby-blue swimsuit top peeking out at him from beneath her bib overalls, his breath caught. In the close, earthy confines of the barn, it was all he could do to not pull her toward him.

"Before we head down to the creek," she said, "I need to ask your forgiveness for something."

"For what?"

"Well . . ."

Sid waited.

"Well, despite the fact that I hate it when people give me unsolicited advice, I realize that's what I've been doing with you. I'm sorry. What you do is none of my business."

"I don't get it."

"You know, before, when I warned you about what would happen if you went to the Grotto?"

Ah. Sid nodded.

"That's what I mean. I know it sounds weird, and I have no clue why, but I find myself feeling very . . ." She faltered. "Feeling kind of . . . protective of you."

He took a step toward her, his heart racing. "You can be protective of me all you want, Mika."

Just then, Hester bawled loudly. Startled, they both turned in her direction.

"Mind if I check her?" she asked. "I'm no expert, but we had cows on our farm in Iowa."

"Be my guest."

Wonder Woman

MEANWHILE, THE PARTY IN THE GROTTO was in full swing. The cooler had been unloaded, except for perishable food items, and the last of everyone's stash was placed on a makeshift table beneath the canvas awning they had rigged up earlier. All told, there were several bags of weed, some hashish, a bong, two hash pipes, rolling papers, a half-empty fifth of Jim Beam, and a case of Coors. Enough, they hoped, to keep them deliriously happy for at least twenty-four hours.

"Whoops, can't forget this!" Liz retrieved the peyote pouch from her backpack, helped herself, and passed it on to Woolf.

While Woolf measured out what he wanted, Ketch sprinkled a hearty dose of Oaxacan Gold down the center of a Zig-Zag. He rolled the paper carefully with a back-and-forth motion between his fingers until it was as thin as an asparagus tip. Running his tongue along the gummed edge, he sealed it, struck a match, lit it, and took a hit. Then, he passed it to Woolf who, having just swallowed some peyote, took a few tokes and passed it to Liz—who did the same before handing it back to Ketch again. The three continued their rounds until nothing was left of the joint but crumbling embers pinched between the blades of a beaded roach clip.

"Man, have I got the munchies," mumbled Woolf. "What's there to eat?"

Liz reached into the nearest grocery sack and tossed him a bag of chips. Missing her throw by a mile, Woolf staggered his way to where the bag lay on the ground. After several attempts to open it failed, he lobbed it back to Liz.

"You can't even open a freakin' bag of chips?" Ketch roared with laughter. "Dude, you are *ripped*."

Liz, however—to Ketch's further amusement—had no better luck. Giving up on opening the bag, she fell flat on her back, covered her belly with both hands, kicked her feet in the air, and joined in her boyfriend's side-splitting howls.

BACK AT THE farm, Sid and Mika leaned over the corral rail and studied Hester, who was anxiously pacing back and forth but no longer moaning.

"She's definitely in labor," said Mika. "See the way she's holding her tail up?"

"Yeah."

"And the fluid dripping from it?"

"Yeah."

"Those are sure signs. And see that yellowish bag protruding from under her tail?"

"It's her water bag, right?"

"Amniotic sac, but same thing, yes. Usually, cows will deliver within two hours after it appears. She might be more comfortable in the barn, but I don't know. I'll wait a bit and then go to her and check it out."

Impressed with her mettle, he said, "Are all Iowa girls as knowledgeable and gutsy as you?"

"I helped my dad deliver a calf once. I wouldn't call it gutsy."

"What would you call it then—intrepid?"

Smiling, she replied, "My, that's a fancy word."

He returned her smile. "Berkeley grad—gives me the right to use fancy words."

"Ouch. That puts undergrad Marishka Larson in her place." Mika's smile broadened. "Seriously though, when I was young, I was more impulsive than anything. In fact, my friends in junior high called me Lightning Larson."

"That's hard to believe. You seem so, I don't know, measured now."

"Measured—as in cautious, you mean? Make up your mind, Sid. Am I cautious or gutsy?"

"Both, apparently. Although . . . " He leaned closer to her. "I'm really liking the gutsy Meeks."

"I admit I do like to live my life with a certain abandon."

"You're splitting hairs, Larson." Sid grinned, relishing their sudden closeness. "Being gutsy and doing things with abandon—they're the same thing."

"*Au contraire.*"

"Speaking French now, are we?"

"I have to prove my intelligence to the Berkeley grad *somehow.*"

"Prove your original point, and I'll concede you're as smart as me."

"All right," she agreed, with forced gravity. "Being impulsive is not thinking or caring about consequences. When I was young, and impulsive, I made a lot of mistakes. Then, I did a complete 180 and turned . . . "

"Paranoid?"

"No, I turned cautious. Overly cautious."

"Uptight, you mean."

"No, I mean . . . cautious."

"It's semantics, but go on. I'm just messing with you, Meeks."

"Anyway, I soon discovered playing it safe had as many drawbacks as being impulsive."

Reaching out, he tucked a loose section of her hair behind her ear. "Such as?"

"For one, I stagnated. I was so afraid of making a wrong decision, I ended up not trusting myself to make any decision at all. It only lasted a few months—my sophomore year—but it was terrible. Debilitating."

"Fancy word. Debilitating."

Mika wrinkled her nose. "*Touché.*"

"How, then, did you become the brave Wonder Woman I see before me today—ready to leap into my corral to deliver a calf?"

"Stop it." She gave him a playful shove. "My parents noticed what was happening and intervened. Basically, they circled the wagons and walked me through it. I don't know how, but they helped me find a balance between impulse and caution."

A sudden sense of loss fleeted past Sid, like a bird startled from its nest. How different might his life have been if his parents had been alive to walk him through the vagaries of *his* youth?

"Somehow," she continued, "they made me realize that I need adventure in my life. It's part of who I am. Believe it or not, I actually thrive on it."

"Adventure, huh? I can see that, I guess. It would explain why you're going to . . . wherever it is you're going."

"That's not the main reason I'm going to the mission field, but yes, that's part of it. There's no adventure without risk, right?" She paused to study Hester as the cow continued to quietly pace back and forth in the corral. "By the way," she added, "once she starts moaning again, I'll go to her and see what I can do."

Sid winked. "As I said—Wonder Woman."

"Please." Mika rolled her eyes.

"Sorry, I didn't mean to interrupt. Go on."

"Where was I? Oh yes—over the last few years, I've learned to be more circumspect. I force myself to think things through before making important decisions."

"Always a good thing."

"I think so. And I allow myself plenty of time to make them, too. Then, in the end—if I want something bad enough, or I really know that I'm supposed to do it—I jump in head-first."

"Regardless of your emotions."

"Regardless of my emotions."

"Like I said, that's what I call gutsy."

"That's what I call abandon."

Enormously intrigued, Sid pressed ahead. "So, let me get this straight. You're saying the difference between gutsiness and abandon is caring about what the repercussions might be?"

"I care, but not as much as I care about doing what I know I'm supposed to do. Or what I *should* do. When it's all said and done, for me anyway, inspiration trumps reason." Her voice began to trail off. "I define abandon as taking a leap of faith, but . . . *ugh*, I'm talking too much and not explaining myself very well. It probably all sounds lame."

"Not at all. Very metaphysical. I like it."

"Of course you do," she teased. "You're a Berkeley grad."

"And you've proven you're intelligent. Congratulations."

"Thanks."

"You know," he said, in a more somber tone, "I have a feeling it took a lot of faith for my dad to move west and buy this place. I never really thought about it before. He was a city boy."

"What city?"

"Chicago."

"And your mom?"

"Born and raised in Sonoma. She wasn't really a country girl, but she wasn't a city girl either. Her parents were from Italy. In a lot of ways, she and my dad were opposites. I'm sure it took a leap of faith for her to marry my dad, considering their differences."

It had been an innocent enough statement in Sid's mind. He hadn't meant to draw any connections between his and Mika's relationship. But there it was, suddenly obvious to him . . . and probably her. He noticed an immediate change in Mika's demeanor. A slight stiffening. A shrinking of eagerness. A withdrawal of confidence. Before he could address it, she switched gears.

"What about you?" she asked.

He fumbled backward in their conversation. "You don't want to know what I was voted in high school."

"I wasn't talking about how people labeled you when you were young, but now you have to tell me. What?"

"Never mind."

"Not fair. You have to answer."

"I was voted most likely to break a girl's heart."

"Aha! A heartbreaker." Mika's jaw muscles tightened even more. "Yeah, I can see that."

"I'm not a heartbreaker. Trust me."

"It makes no difference to me whether you are or not. You don't have to prove anything to me."

"It's not about proving anything. I'm just saying, for the record, that even if I was a heartbreaker when I was younger, which I doubt I was, it's not who I am now."

Avoiding Sid's scrutiny, she turned her gaze to Hester.

He, however, wasn't about to let her off so easily. "So what did you mean, then, Meeks? What do I think of living a life of abandon?"

"No, I meant what do you know about calving?" She pointed at Hester, who was starting to moo loudly.

"Oh . . . that." Sid marveled at her ability to bring their discussion back to square one. "Everything I know—which isn't much, really—I picked up in books or rubbing elbows with some of the farmers in the Bureau. I figured when the time came, if there were any problems, I'd call the vet."

Just then, Hester gave a start, and the moment she did, liquid shot out from beneath her with the force of a guided missile.

"Her water just broke!" Mika hopped off the fence. "I'm going to make sure she's okay."

"Why wouldn't she be?" In the back of Sid's mind, he knew all the possible complications of birth, but now, in the moment, he found himself suddenly mystified.

"If the calf is breech—not head first—and gets stuck in the birth canal, we'll have to try to turn it around or pull it out."

"We?" Sid shook his head. "Look, Mika, I'm going inside to call the vet."

Pulling him back by the elbow as he turned to go, she said, "There's no time. The calf will likely come before he could get here."

Sid took a deep breath as he realized this is where his education and all the books he'd read would be rendered useless. Where every chore he'd done so far on the farm, every responsibility, would pale in comparison. Where he was thankful that someone like Mika was here to guide him through his first time helping a cow deliver its calf.

"Okay." Hurdling the fence, he sprang to Mika's side. "Show me what to do."

Up in Smoke

L ESS THAN FIVE MINUTES AFTER HESTER'S water broke, two hooves made an appearance out her backside. Unfortunately, the bottoms of them were pointing up.

"Oh no," groaned Mika. "The calf's breech. Can you get a rope for me?"

Sid hurried to the barn and grabbed a coil of nylon rope. As he handed it to Mika, a car pulled into the driveway.

"Who could that be?" she asked, madly unraveling the cord.

"No idea. I'll check it out and be right back."

When he rounded the corner of the barn, Sid saw Lenny retrieving a backpack from his VW van.

"Where's Mika," asked Lenny, "and why are you here, Sid?"

"Why wouldn't I be?"

Lenny nodded across the creek. "I thought you'd be partying with your boarders."

How does Lenny know about the Grotto, or for that matter, the party? And why would he assume I'd be with the boarders but Mika wouldn't? Ah—Liz. She was probably talking about it at Eden. "No, Mika and I are the only ones here." Jabbing his thumb in the direction of the corral, he added, "I have a cow giving birth. Meeks is out back with her."

"Damn. I hope she hurries up so you can go to the Grotto, and I can have her to myself."

"What are you talking about?"

"What do you think I'm talking about? I don't have much time left." Lenny pulled a flat Tupperware container out of his pack and waved it at him. "I came prepared. Grass brownies."

A dread suspicion wrenched through Sid's gut as he watched Lenny drop the brownies back in, replacing it seconds later with a quart-size Mason jar filled with a buttery-colored liquid. Holding it up to the sunlight, his boss studied it as though it were a magical brew.

"If she's still a holdout and doesn't go for the brownies," said Lenny, "I figure she'll drink the lemonade. It's spiked with acid. Far out, huh?" Tucking the jar away, he tossed his backpack over his shoulder and strode toward the corral.

Just as it had happened the day he met Kate behind the Lewiston Gulch School, three revelations converged in Sid's mind at once. This time they formed from three separate comments from three different people at three different times.

The first was something Lenny had said to him on Valentine's Day after Mika had come into Eden to apologize to Liz: *Just remember this, my friend—what Lenny Tobin wants, Lenny Tobin gets.* The second was Kate describing who the father of her baby could be: *One's married, but the snake is such a scumbag, I doubt he'll ever leave his wife.* And the third was Liz's reply just this afternoon to the question of where she had scored the peyote buttons: *"Sid knows who it is."*

Lenny's a dealer, thought Sid, as sure of it as he was of his own name. And not only could he easily be the father of

Kate's baby, he's hell bent on laying Mika. *Scumbag is right.* Outraged, Sid stormed after him. Tearing around the corner of the barn, he saw Mika frantically trying to fashion a lasso, oblivious to Lenny leering at her on the other side of the fence.

"Sid, I need a bucket of hot water!" she yelled.

But Sid, deaf to her pleas, charged Lenny. Ambushing him from behind, he slammed him to the ground.

"What the . . . ?" sputtered Lenny.

Yanking him back to his feet, Sid began battering his boss's head as though it were a tetherball. "You-no-good-son-of-a-bitch," he shouted, each word punctuated with a jab to his face.

Lenny—staggering backward, closer and closer toward the creek—was barely able to stay upright. Not only was he twenty pounds lighter and several inches shorter, but he was no match for Sid's rage and brute strength. Clearly, a year of intensive farm work had given Sid a muscular advantage.

So this is what retribution feels like, thought Sid, owning his fury; drunk on it, relishing it. He would use it to teach Lenny Tobin a lesson if it was the last thing he did.

They continued careening toward the creek, despite Mika's calls for them stop, until Sid noted that Lenny could barely raise his arms anymore. Then and there, teetering on a small embankment, he prepared to deliver his final blow. But as he took aim, a gunshot ricocheted through the trees. Panting for air, they both wheeled around in the direction of the Grotto.

"What . . . was . . . that?" gasped Lenny.

Sid shook his head. "I . . . don't . . . know."

Without warning, a deafening explosion shook the ground

beneath them, forcing them to duck and cover their heads. A moment later, they raised their eyes upward. In the distance, near what Sid deduced was the Grotto, a dark cloud materialized over the top of the trees. Within seconds, it morphed into a huge column of smoke chugging high into the sky. An enormous crackling sound erupted, like a million campfires set alight at once.

Sid leapt into the creek, motioning for Lenny to follow him. "Come on! We've got to get to the Grotto!"

"No way I'm risking my life to go over there."

Sid turned around in disbelief. "But that's where my boarders are."

"Forget it."

Disgusted, Sid lunged at his boss again. Seizing him by the arm, he dragged him back across the meadow, opened the gate of the corral and threw him in. "If you won't go with me, then you'll stay here and do whatever Mika tells you. No sandbagging it, Lenny. And I swear to God," he bellowed, "if you touch a hair on her head, you'll wish you never moved to Trinity Springs. You hear me?"

Lenny glowered at Sid, a dark ribbon of blood trailing down his chin.

Mika, meanwhile, had successfully tied the rope around the calf's protruding feet and was now straining to pull it out. Nodding toward the creek, she yelled, "What happened over there?"

"I don't know," said Sid, "but I'm going over to find out. Will you be okay?"

"We could lose the calf unless we pull it out. We could lose Hester, too. I can't do this myself, Sid. I'm not strong enough."

"You won't have to do it yourself." He pulled Mika up off the ground and ordered Lenny to take her place. "Start pulling!" Then, ushering her out of the pen, he told her to run to the house and call the fire department. "After that, come back and tell Lenny what else he needs to do."

"What if he's gone when I come back?"

"Don't worry, he'll be here. He knows what will happen if he cops out on you. But Mika, whatever you do, don't eat or drink anything he gives you."

Her face a mask of terror, Mika reached for his arm. "Please don't go over there, Sid. Stay here. Let someone else do it. If something happened to you, I'd . . ."

Remembering her fear of fire, Sid gently nudged her toward the house. "Where's that faith you were talking about before? Nothing will happen to me, Meeks. Now, go— before it's too late! And remember what I said about not taking anything Lenny tries to give you."

Snapping to attention, Mika turned and ran as though their lives depended on it.

While mika bolted into the house, Sid barked one last warning to Lenny before racing into the barn to retrieve a large metal pail and towel. Then, sprinting to the creek, he forded it, pausing to fill the bucket halfway with water. Dunking the towel in the stream until it was thoroughly saturated, he wrung it out and placed it over his nose and mouth before continuing. Minutes later, he was tearing through the unscathed forest floor leading up to the rear of the fire, cradling the sloshing pail tightly against his ribs. Soon, his gait quickened to a near gallop, adrenaline pumping through his veins like volcanic magma about to erupt. The effect was so intense, it was as though he could see his surroundings through a rifle scope: all grid, focus, and track precision. Tall stands of cedar, red fir, and ponderosa pine whizzed by—the undergrowth appearing as nothing but a mottled blur.

Still Sid chuffed along until, finally, he had to stop to catch his breath and confirm his bearings. The wind was coming from the north, parallel with the creek. He marked the untouched earth behind him and surmised that the charred ground he now stood on must be fairly close to ground zero. Once he was able to visually determine the fire's point of origin, he would be in the Grotto, so he set out again in a trot along the fire's smoldering flank.

Suddenly, surrounded by dense smoke, he stopped. Thinking he was lost, he started to panic. Then, a voice in his head, whether it was his own or not he couldn't tell, directed him to turn to his right a few steps and retreat. Moments later, the air around him cleared. Panting for breath, he heard the voice again. This time, it prompted him to call out for the boarders.

"Ketch! Liz! Woolf! Is anyone there?"

A slight noise to his left startled him. Spinning around, he surveyed the landscape but saw nothing. He listened, waiting for another sign, but other than the roar of the forest fire, he heard nothing. Gingerly picking his way over smoking debris, he scanned the area for any sign of life.

Wait! What was that? Directly ahead, halfway up a steep incline, he saw what appeared to be a hand waving weakly to him from behind a small boulder. "Hold on! I'm coming!" He set his bucket down and tore off his t-shirt. Ripping it into two pieces, he wet them, wrapped them around his hands, and scrabbled up the hill on all fours.

Midway, he noticed that the soil felt surprisingly damp, even spongy in parts—an indication he was on, or near, a spring. Almost involuntarily, he glanced down. There, to his left, a blackened human body lay entangled in a cluster of partially singed shrubs. It was a woman, stripped naked, her face unrecognizable. As Sid lifted her into his arms, she screamed in pain.

"It's all right, Liz," he said, fighting back tears. "Hang on. I'm taking you home."

Protecting her as best he could, Sid careened down the hillside, his heart pounding in his chest. When he reached its base, he retrieved the empty bucket, looping the handle over his wrist, and sped back toward the farm. Fifteen minutes later, he was sliding Liz's body gently into the shallows of the creek, supporting her so that her nose and mouth cleared the surface of the water.

Within seconds, Mika was kneeling next to him. "Oh, my God! Who is this?"

"It's got to be Liz."

"How do you know?"

"Who else would it be? I found her in the Grotto."

"Wait—it looks like she's trying to say something." Mika pressed her ear toward what looked like the woman's lips. Seconds later, she lifted her head and said, "It's Kate Quinn."

"No." Sid studied the woman he was holding and then looked at Mika in disbelief. "It can't be."

Mika cupped some water from the stream into her hands and began pouring it tenderly over Kate's burned face. "She said her name clearly, Sid."

As he tried to absorb the news, Mika asked, "What about the others? Did you . . . find . . . anyone else?"

"Not yet. What about you, Mika? Are you okay?" Although she appeared to be holding herself together, Sid could tell by the spark of fear in her eyes that she must be using every ounce of courage within her to stay calm. Not for the first time that day, he found himself grateful for her grit and stamina.

"I'm fine."

"Are you sure?"

"Positive."

"What about Lenny?"

"He left as soon as we got Hester's calf out. Mom and baby are fine. Otis came as soon as he got the call about the fire. Pearlie's here now, too. She's on the phone with Otis's office. She said fire crews are out battling the fire already."

"Good." Sid picked up the bucket he'd set down, filled it with water and stood up. No doubt, firefighters were focusing on the leading edge of the fire heading toward Trinity Springs, far from the farm. Unable to waste any more time, he said, "I'm going back for the others. Stay here with Kate and yell for Pearlie until she hears you. Have her call an ambulance and . . ."

"But Sid, there's something else you need to know."

"What?"

"Otis is in there, too." She pointed toward the Grotto. "I told him the boarders were in the woods when the fire broke out and that you had gone in to find them."

ON SID'S SECOND foray to the Grotto, near the same hillside where he'd found Kate, a blood-curdling shriek forced him to a dead halt. Looking around wildly, he saw nothing.

It had sounded as though it were coming through a funnel, and remembering that there were several caves in the area, he started up the incline in the direction he'd heard the scream. Climbing higher than before this time, he soon discovered what might be an opening to a cavern. Access to it was blocked by a still-smoldering sapling, roughly ten-feet tall, that had fallen across the entrance. "Anybody in there?" he yelled, peering through the lingering haze.

A high-pitched shriek replied, "Get us out of here!"

"I'm coming!" Sid set the bucket down and began rewetting his towel-bandaged hands. "I'm coming! Hold on."

"Oh God, *hurry!*"

As Sid shoved the downed tree away from the opening, Liz and Woolf, covered in soot and wheezing uncontrollably, tumbled out. Liz set to wailing so hard, snot began pouring in rivulets down her nose. Woolf, swatting crazily at his head and chest as though he were encased in a giant spider's web, gibbered about hordes of insects and demons that had attacked him while they were stuck in the cave.

"Where's Ketch?" sniveled Liz.

Sid leaned down and peered inside the den. It appeared to stretch back only eight feet or so and housed a high vaulted ceiling that seemed to be dripping with spring water. "He's not in here. Wasn't he with you guys?"

Struggling to her feet, Liz screamed, "Ketch! Where are you? Ketch!"

Grabbing hold of her arms, Sid said, "Look at me, Liz. Focus. Think! When was the last time you saw him?"

Instead of answering, she grew more hysterical.

With a commanding voice, he ordered her to pull herself together. When she didn't, he shook her. "Stop it, Liz! We won't find Ketch unless you answer me. Where was he the last time you saw him?"

Going limp, she said, "He *was* in the cave with us. We heard someone screaming close by. It sounded like a woman. He thought it might be Meeks, so he ran out to see . . . just before the tree fell and trapped us inside. But by then the air was so thick with smoke, I don't know how he could have . . ."

"That wasn't Mika. It was Kate Quinn."

"Kate Quinn? What was she doing here?"

"I don't know." Sid shuddered with foreboding at the news that Ketch had left the safety of the cave.

Then something switched in Liz. With a determined gleam, she looked directly into Sid's eyes. "What are we going to do?"

Nodding toward Woolf, still thrashing about as though he were being attacked by hornets, he said, "Help me get him back to the farm before the sun goes down."

"Maybe Ketch is already there." Liz watched as Sid hoisted the vet to his feet. "He probably is, you know. I'll bet you anything he is."

For her sake, Sid tried to sound reassuring. "Maybe, but if not, I'll come back and look for him."

It took a bit longer for him to calm Woolf into submission, but finally he and Liz were able to anchor him securely between them. Then, like characters in a post-apocalyptic saga, they toiled down the craggy ridge, skirting fallen timber and loose rocks. Cautiously, they dodged flare-ups and smoldering duff. They scrambled over hot rocks as best they could, stopping every now and then to rewet the cloth Sid had brought in the bucket and take turns holding it over their mouths and noses. All the while, they called out for

Ketch, peering through the tissuey haze as they searched for any sign of him.

Suddenly, Sid remembered Sheriff Skinner. "Otis!" he shouted. His echo reverberated back to him: *Otis, Otis, Otis, Otis . . .*

Woolf, though still unsteady on his feet, seemed to be increasingly aware of their predicament. "Skinner's out here somewhere, too?"

"Yeah. He came looking for you guys." *For me, too.* Sid's chest constricted at the thought of Otis risking his life for him. *What if he . . .* "Come on," he barked. "We've got to keep moving. It's getting dark."

Sɪᴅ ꜱᴀᴡ ᴍɪᴋᴀ waiting for them on the other side of the creek as they neared. At her side, Pearlie stood—motionless. Kate was nowhere in sight. Then, as though the mere smell of fresh water had revived them, Liz and Woolf broke away from him and set off running, stumbling headlong down the creek bank and into the stream. While they splashed and shouted in relief, he waded toward Mika. She met him midway.

Knee-deep in water, they stood staring at each other until Mika finally said, "The ambulance came and took Kate."

"Good." The word, he realized, sounded completely meaningless coming out of his mouth.

"Where's Ketch? She looked over his shoulder. "And Otis?"

He shook his head, incapable of responding.

Mika's face curdled.

Don't cry. Please Meeks, don't start. I need you to be strong for me now more than ever.

Blinking back her tears, she nodded toward Pearlie. "She's been waiting for you a long time. Go talk to her."

As though his shoes were filled with cement, Sid trundled heavily back to shore with Mika. Setting the bucket and towel down, he raised his hands in defeat. "I didn't find him, Pearlie. Ketch is still missing, too."

Pearlie doubled over, her hands clasped over her mouth. He reached out to her, thinking she might collapse, but she straightened at his touch. With an air of determination, she lowered her hands. "I'll be fine."

"Look, I'm going back to look for him again while there's still light in the sky."

"No you're not! I'm not going to risk losing you, too, Siddie."

Just then, the air around them changed. Slightly at first; then, drastically. An eerie stillness, distinct from all the distant crackings and crashings of the raging fire, permeated the atmosphere. With it came a strange sensation, as if their ears had suddenly been covered with headphones. Mika pointed to the sky. Directly above them, a towering thunderhead roiled and foamed.

The temperature dropped at least ten degrees.

The wind shifted to the west.

The heavens opened.

Woolf, still slopping about in the stream, leapt to his feet and started dancing in the rain. Liz looked skyward, her mouth wide open.

"It's a sign," wailed Pearlie, her eyes uplifted. "I know it is. Mika and I prayed for rain, and it's come. We prayed for you, too, Siddie—and here you are." Swiping her wet face with her equally wet apron, she turned her gaze fully upon Sid. "Otis is alive. I know he is."

Sid wished he had the faith to believe it. But he didn't. Instead, ignoring Pearlie's pleas to stay, he bent down to fill his bucket one last time. As he did, though he felt guilty for even thinking it, he found himself shoving aside a gnawing, underlying fear that his boarders would be found responsible for the fire. If they were, he could kiss his farm goodbye.

Then, with all the courage he could muster, he set out to find Otis and Ketch.

Death On Call

FIVE DAYS HAD PASSED SINCE THE FOREST fire, a disaster that had scarred the landscape for miles along the mountain ridges above Trinity Springs. The blaze had caused untold property damage, destroyed thousands of acres of timber, claimed the lives of two fire-fighters, and injured numerous others. As terrible as it was, many shell-shocked survivors reassured themselves it could have been worse. Had the winds not changed that night, and had it not rained, the flames would have eventually reached town—a small, though real, comfort for the scores of other Trinity County residents, ranchers, farmers, and outdoor enthusiasts who could have been displaced, wounded, or killed during the catastrophe.

Sid Jackson, however, was not counted among the reassured because one victim—Will Ketchum—was still missing. For Sid, there was no comfort; no silver lining to the fire. There was only anguish at the mysterious loss of a friend and the fear that he might lose another.

ON SEPTEMBER 4, the day after Labor Day, Sid trooped into Otis's room at Redding's Mercy Hospital to find himself, yet again, in another universe—a land of labored breathing, gurgles, hushed voices and whispers, and mechanical beeps. As usual, Pearlie sat next to her husband, stroking his unresponsive fingers.

A smile broke out on her face when she glanced up and saw Sid. "Look who's here to see you, Otis." Pointing to a chair near the door, she instructed Sid to pull it close to the bed, opposite her, and sit down.

Sid did as he was told. "How's he doing today?"

"Much better."

It was the same answer Pearlie had been giving him every day since he'd found Otis's limp body not far from the Grotto. *He doesn't look better. He looks terrible—as gray as the ash I found him lying in.*

"Just look how different his eyes are today," she added. "He's thinking. That's what he's doing."

Otis's eyes lurched and rolled beneath his eyelids like two Ping-Pong balls being whacked back and forth simultaneously. Sid fell to studying his godfather's face—his bristly graying moustache and bushy eyebrows, the vertical creases angling down each tanned cheek, his mandrill-like nose, long and curving in a broad-ended tip. On an impulse, he seized Otis's free hand and squeezed it in his.

"The doctor hasn't been in yet today," said Pearlie. "But I expect he'll note the improvement."

Sid faked his agreement with a nod. Just the other day, Doc Simpson, who was in constant contact with Redding's physicians and staff, had confided in him that the chances of Otis waking up were slim at best. He was in too deep of a coma. Too much smoke inhalation. Even if he were to somehow regain consciousness, Doc Simpson warned him the sheriff would probably never be the same.

Eager to change the subject, Sid took stock of the new flowers and cards displayed along the windowsill. "Looks like he's had more visitors since yesterday."

"Most everyone in Trinity County has come by to wish him well." Pearlie glowed with pride. "He's a well-loved man, Otis is."

"That he is. He risked his life looking for me and the boarders, Pearlie. That makes him a hero in my eyes. No wonder people love him. There's no greater love than that."

"You should talk, Sid. Otis might not be here right now if it wasn't for you. The firefighters had their hands full fighting the fire. I'd say you know all about love—and being a hero."

Sid flinched. Considering his boarders were also his friends, he was convinced he'd only done what most people in his situation would have done.

"Oh, I just remembered. Isn't this the day Otis would have signed off on your probation?"

"Guess it is."

"What a shame. You need to check with someone down at the courthouse right away and get that taken care of."

"There are more important things to tend to right now, Pearlie. I can wait."

"No, you can't. Don't you know that unfinished business leads to an unsettled mind? Which reminds me—does your Nonna know what happened?"

"Not yet. I don't want to worry her. Besides . . ."

"She probably wouldn't remember anyway?"

"Hard to say. Her memory seems to be really hit or miss. I arranged for another doctor to evaluate her. I should be hearing from him soon with the results. As for the fire, I called her yesterday to check up on her and let her know everything was fine, just in case she'd heard about it and made the connection with me. I plan on going down to see her as soon as my probation's settled."

"And our Bill? No news on him yet?"

Sid's stomach lurched. "Our Bill," as Pearlie called Ketch, was nowhere to be found. "They called the search off yesterday. Ketch is . . . gone."

"Now, now. He's missing, not *gone*, Sid. There's a big difference, and don't you forget it. But speaking of gone, I heard Katie Quinn's no longer with us. I'm afraid I've been so taken up with Otis, I don't know all the details. Do you?"

Hard as it was for him to believe that Kate was on the road to a full recovery, after seeing her disfiguring burns the day of the fire, that's exactly what her prognosis was. "The doctors said only a couple of her burns were third-degree. Mostly on her legs. They're not sure how she escaped being burned more severely than she was. She's been sent down to UC Davis Medical Center where she can get better treatment. I . . . didn't get a chance to see her before she left."

"That'll be spendy. She's going to need help with paying the bills, I would imagine."

"She's being well taken care of. Don't worry."

"You're sure?"

"One hundred percent." Sid knew with absolute surety because he had phoned Lenny the day after the fire, demanding he take full responsibility for Kate's medical care. He would never reveal to anyone the threat he'd used to force Lenny to comply, but suffice it to say, it had been effective.

Pearlie's hand fluttered to her throat. "What about her baby?"

"Last I heard, it's still alive. They're monitoring her closely."

"And that vet boarder of yours?"

"Pablo Woolf? Once he sobered up, the doctors gave him a clean bill of health. He flew out Sunday after talking to the Fire Marshal. He should be back in New Jersey now."

"And the other girl?"

"Liz is having a tough time. She liked Ketch, you know. A lot. So . . ."

Pearlie's head bobbed up and down. "I figured. Is she still here?"

"At first she was going to stick around until . . ." Sid fought down a bitter taste in his throat. "But after the search party . . ." He paused again, unable to fully explain the situation without losing his cool. Finally, he simply said, "She left this afternoon to go back to Alaska."

"Well . . ." sighed Pearlie, "at least Mika's still here. Thank God for that. I don't know what I'd do if she weren't helping out at the café while I'm here in the hospital with Otis. Not to mention, she's praying up a storm for him, you know."

"She's been a big help to me too—helping with the garden and the new calf."

"Named him yet?"

"The calf? Yeah, Mika and I spent an entire evening hashing out a name before finally settling on Blazer."

"That's a fitting name if I've ever heard one." Pearlie turned silent a moment. "I sure will miss that girl when she leaves."

Trust me, not as much as I will.

A knock on the door announced the arrival of Otis's deputy, Warren Murdoch. Ignoring Sid, the officer touched the bill of his hat when he saw Pearlie. "Afternoon, Mrs. Skinner."

"Same to you, Warren."

"I'm here in Redding on business and just thought you'd

like to know we've had a breakthrough in the case. The Fire Marshal's determined for a fact that the fire was started right about where Jackson here found Otis." Warren lowered his gaze in Sid's direction. "From the evidence they retrieved at the site, the Marshal judged it was arson all right. It started with an explosion."

"Do they know what caused the explosion?" asked Sid.

"Can't say. The department's still investigating some leads. But they hope to have it wrapped up today or tomorrow. In fact, they're questioning some more people as we speak. Who knows? They might even pay *you* a visit, Mr. Jackson."

"Oh for heaven's sake, Warren," snapped Pearlie. "Get off your high horse. Sid didn't have anything to do with it. Mika Larson was with him at the farm when the fire first broke out. I was there, too, right after, while Sid was out risking his life to save Otis. Or would you be calling my testimony into question?"

"You're putting words in my mouth, Pearlie. What I said was . . ."

Pearlie waved the deputy away as though he were a housefly. "Never mind what you said. Why don't you leave us alone now and get back to your business. I'm sure Otis would tell you the same thing if he could."

Warren cast a disparaging look at Sid. "Fine. I'll check in tonight before I head home to see how Otis is doing."

"He'll appreciate that, Warren. Thank you."

After the deputy left, Pearlie shook her head. "How Otis has put up with that petty man all these years, I'll never know. I hate to admit it, but at times my husband can be forgiving to a fault."

Sid bit his tongue. He'd never been a fan of Warren Murdoch either, probably because he recalled his father telling his mother he was convinced the deputy's secret desire in life was to one-up Otis someday. "Well," said Sid, "I suppose it's time I head home. I'll be back again tonight. Is there anything you need? Anything I can get you?"

"No, that's fine." She patted her husband's hand. As though speaking from a far-off place, she added, "I've got everything I need right here."

"Mika said she'd like to visit you both tonight when she's done at the café. Her car's in the shop getting a once-over before she heads back to Iowa, so I might bring her with me." Sid stood. Stepping around the end of Otis's bed, he leaned down and gave Pearlie a hug. "If you change your mind about needing anything, just give me a call."

Then, taking what he realized might be his last look at Otis alive, with a hoarse voice, he added, "I'll be back."

The Pickup

MIKA YAWNED AS SHE NOTED THE TIME on the dashboard of Sid's truck—almost eleven p.m. The drive to Redding had seemed so much faster than the ride back. Sweat pooled beneath her bra, between her toes, and along her hairline. Bending down, she took off her shoes and removed her socks, tucking them underneath her seat. Absently, she swiped her forehead with the back of her hand.

"The air conditioning's not working great." Sid glanced sideways at her. "Sorry. I need to get it looked at. If you're too warm, go ahead and roll your window down."

"I think I will." Turning, she caught her reflection in the window. Her hair, which she had spent so much time French braiding earlier in the day, had all but come loose. And those dark circles beneath her eyes! Well, after a long day of waitressing and going to see Otis at the hospital, what did she expect? With a tired sigh, she rolled down her window and snuck a peek at Sid. He had to be exhausted, too, but how was it that he, unlike her, didn't look like it?

Not fair.

She smoothed out the collar of her uniform. The wrinkled shirt-dress, made of 100-percent white cotton, was stained with spots of food splattered on it during her shift at

The Pearl. Not only was her dress soiled, but—with its fitted waist, short puffed sleeves, and mid-knee hemline—it was anything but fashionable. Embarrassed by how unkempt and outdated she must look, Mika had to remind herself that what was really important was the fact that Otis was still alive, and she'd been able to see him one more time.

Her musings on Otis and Pearlie, the fire, the end of her year at the Ranch, and her life in general, continued unabated until Sid banked right into the farm's driveway, the tires of his truck crunching slowly to a halt in the gravel. As he killed the engine, she automatically placed her hand on the door to open it.

"Do you mind waiting a few minutes before we go in?" Sid shifted his body around so that he faced her, his knee resting on the seat between them. "We need to talk."

"Can't we talk in the house?"

"Here in my pickup, you can't evade me so easily."

"Excuse me?"

"You've been avoiding me again. Like you did last spring—after that day we sat together in the library."

"I haven't been avoiding you, Sid. I've just been busy. That's all."

"I understand you have a lot on your plate, Meeks. Who doesn't? But you have to admit, other than the night we named the calf, you're spending a lot of time hiding out in your room. Or am I imagining it?"

Trying her best not to dwell on Sid's classic Italian features, silver-plated in the moonlight, she tried to concentrate on what he'd just said. Finding she couldn't argue with him, she said, "All right, go ahead. What did you want to talk about?"

"Basically, I'd like you to know how much the fire changed me. This whole last year has been a learning curve. You've been a big part of that for sure, don't get me wrong. But the fire is what's really, finally, brought my life into . . . perfect focus."

Transfixed, Mika spent the next ten minutes listening to Sid bare his soul, confess his weaknesses, list his milestones and describe his major epiphanies. He talked about how—in the instance of growing pot and getting busted, for example—he'd played the victim rather than accept full responsibility for his mistakes. And how he no longer thought of the farm so much as a duty or an impediment to his freedom, as much as an honor to his parents and a tangible sign of hope for his future.

His hand swept across the darkened farmhouse and surrounding fields. "Every time I look at it now, all I see is promise."

Then, he went on to explain that, at one point, when he found himself lost in the fire and thinking he might die, his life—and all the people in it—flashed before him. "It was a eureka moment. It really was. I don't know how else to describe it. I mean, everything that's truly important to me was condensed, solidified, within just a few seconds."

"You never told me you got lost in the fire."

"It only lasted a few minutes. Somehow, I was able to get my bearings and find my way back out. But the point is, Meeks, I realized I've been taking so much for granted. My friends, the Skinners, this farm . . . " Sid placed his elbow on the steering wheel. "From now on, I want my life to be relevant; each day, an opportunity for change. I want to make a difference in the world. I actually find myself weighing the consequences of my actions and how they affect others."

"As in . . . ?"

"As in, it's not just about 'me' anymore."

She was speechless. Not that Sid hadn't displayed admirable qualities in the past. Other than his trouble with the law, he was smart, hardworking and respectful. But a humble, transparent, and contrite Sid Jackson? She could scarcely believe it.

"More than anything though," he continued, in a now-for-the-bad-news tone of voice, "before you go back to Iowa, I need to tell you about Kate Quinn and me."

Taken aback by the mention of Kate, Mika started to argue that it wasn't necessary.

Sid, however, touched his lips with his index finger—a sign he wouldn't take 'no' for an answer. "I don't want you leaving here assuming things about me that may not be true," he said. "Not that the truth won't be worse than anything you might have already imagined."

"But . . ."

"Don't tell me you've never wondered about Kate and me."

Suddenly, Sid's pickup felt like a confessional with no veil separating her from him. With nothing to keep them safely apart, she turned her head, unwilling to meet his gaze. *Please don't, Sid. I can't bear hearing about you and someone else!*

She felt his fingertips brush her shoulder. "Can you honestly say you don't want an explanation?" he asked.

"Well . . . yes. There were times I wondered if there was something between you two."

Clearly taking her answer as permission to press ahead, Sid explained how Kate used to babysit him when he was a boy and how, in hindsight, he now understood that she had taken advantage of his immature attraction to her to eventually seduce him in college.

"Don't get me wrong," he cautioned. "I'm not laying blame for what happened between us entirely on Kate. I had a part in it, too. At the time, I thought I was in love with her, but now I realize I didn't know what real love was."

Mika swung around. "Of course you had a part in it, Sid. Obviously, you and Kate wouldn't have ended up together in Berkeley if you hadn't made a conscious decision to let it happen."

"Absolutely," he blurted. "I said as much, didn't I? Although, remember, I was totally out of it when it happened, so I don't know how 'conscious' the decision was."

"Easy excuse, Sid."

The fervor, which had up until now brightened his demeanor, cooled. "You're disgusted with me."

"I'm not disgusted." Strangely enough, though it made her feel sick to think of Sid and Kate together, she felt relieved at the same time. Unburdened. Was it because, despite everything, she was really jealous of Kate? Or was it because by him saying there was nothing between them anymore, it meant . . .

"If you're not disgusted, then why won't you look at me?"

She turned her head just slightly enough to prove him wrong. "What would have turned me off, is if you wouldn't have admitted to your role in the affair."

"We never really had an affair. It was more of . . ."

"Whatever, Sid. Don't worry about it. It's your life, and your life is none of my business. I'm just saying that you telling me about Kate confirms what you were saying earlier about taking responsibility for your actions."

Sid relaxed. Then, apparently emboldened by her encouragement, he launched into the details of Kate's pregnancy, expressing his concern for her welfare since the fire. He described it so passionately that doubt crept back into Mika's heart. Pivoting in her seat, she turned away from him again. From somewhere across the creek, a coyote howled, echoing the same territorial cry she felt tearing at her insides.

When Sid finished telling her about Kate's plight, he slid across the seat, placed the palm of his hand on the back of her head and let it glide slowly down her loosened braid. "Mika?"

She felt his breath on her ear and shivered from the joy of it. Terrified of her emotions, she refused to turn around.

"Maybe I've said too much."

No answer.

"I blew it, didn't I?"

From his tone, Mika could tell he was trying to sound facetious, but the underlying seriousness of his question pierced her to the core. She felt as though she were a wishbone being pulled apart by two opposing forces within her, love and reason, each fighting for the bigger piece. *Blown it? If you only knew, Sid. Please, please, don't say another word. Before this goes too far, move back to your side of the truck. Take your hand off my head—get out of my head, and end this pain for both our sakes.* "You didn't blow it," she finally muttered. "Anything but."

"Sorry—what did you say?"

Dare she repeat herself? If she let this moment pass, the opportunity to tell Sid how she really felt about him might never present itself again. By the same token, if she remained resolute, she'd spare herself a temptation that could well change the course of her entire future. She stalled, agonizing over the risks, waiting for the sound of Sid's door to open—waiting until the very last possible moment to decide what she would say, if she would say anything at all.

The clock on the dashboard clicked.

11:14 . . .

11:15 . . .

11:16 . . .

It was finally Sid who broke the silence. "Meeks, I can't let you go back to Iowa without knowing what you think of me. What you're feeling for me. Please . . . say something."

"I like you, Sid." Squeezing her eyes shut, she added, "A lot. More than I've cared to admit."

"How much more?" There was that maddening tease in his voice again.

She shrugged.

"If we never see each other again," he whispered, all traces of lightheartedness gone, "it would be nice to know how much you cared."

Stricken at the prospect, Mika swallowed down a little sob. Sid waited longer for her reply than she knew she would have if the shoe were on the other foot.

"All right," he sighed, at last. "I won't bother you anymore. But there's one more thing, and I don't know who else to talk to about it." Struggling to continue, his voice caught. "I miss Ketch. I never thought I could miss a friend so much. And Otis, well, since the fire, I realize he's the closest thing to a dad I'll ever have. If I lose him, too . . ."

Before he could finish his sentence, Mika turned and wrapped her arms around him. Then, laying her head on his chest, together, they wept.

Mika Undone

THE CLOCK ON THE TRUCK'S DASHBOARD clicks:

2:47 . . .

2:48 . . .

2:49 . . .

confirming that their weeping long ago turned to joy. Three hours after surrendering her heart to Sid, as they lay plastered against each other in the pickup like paint on primer, Mika is still voicing her shock at the sea-change in their relationship.

"Having a long-distance relationship is the only way we can be sure we're right for each other," she says, arching her neck back to kiss Sid for the hundredth time. "But are you sure you can wait that long?"

"Two years?" He groans, as though it's killing him. "No, I can't wait another day. But if that's the only way I can get you in the end, then it'll be worth the wait."

She brushes the tip of her nose along his jawline, the slightest touch of him sending shivers down her body.

Sid readjusts his position so he can remove his denim shirt. "Here," he says, draping it over her. "You must be cold."

"But now you'll be cold," she protests, patting the sleeveless t-shirt stretched across his chest.

"Not with you around, I won't be." His eyes bore into her, teasing, but also dead serious. "What if I were to say I *can't* wait two years for us to be together?"

She ponders the difference between living alone and living life with someone she loves. She had begun to think that, in her situation, independence was hard to beat. But now, buried in Sid's arms, wrapped in his shirt, warmed by his heat, she imagines a soul mate being like a second blanket on a cold night—the extra covering that makes all the difference in the world. The difference between being protected from the cold or being exposed to the elements, between getting a good night sleep or a restless one, or between waking up refreshed in the morning or facing each day haggard and wasted. Insulation, comfort, security. Right now, they all equal Sid. *But what if he can't wait two years?* The thought of returning from the mission field to find him no longer interested in her, or worse, with someone else, is just too unbearable.

"I love you," she whispers, ignoring his question.

"I love you more."

"That's not even remotely possible." She notices that his voice does what his eyes did earlier, conveying absolute conviction with a dose of comic relief.

How could something that had once seemed so wrong on every rational level, now feel so right in just a matter of hours? It's confounding, she concludes. And beyond wonderful. She's still Lightning Larson at heart, and the revelation gives her great satisfaction, as though she's been living an incomplete truth before tonight.

Sid is stroking her hair. Staring at her. Fiddling with his shirt to make sure she's covered sufficiently enough to be warm.

"I'm not sure I can wait two years, either," she finally confesses. "But I have to give it my best shot." Swallowing hard, she adds, "I have to, or I couldn't live with myself."

She reminds him of the agreement they came to less than an hour ago. She would go ahead with her plans for the mission field in Asia, while he worked to make his farm productive: a mutual understanding with no promises, no strings attached. Just a loose pact that would give their professed love for each other the time—two years to be exact—to be tried, tested and solidified.

"I know," he says, sounding like a disgruntled bear. "I know."

"It's only two years, Sid."

"It's a lifetime, Meeks."

"Remember why we agreed on that long of a time frame?"

He gives a cynical nod. "For 'destiny' to take its course."

Then he does an impersonation of her that makes her want to laugh, except that she can feel the desperation in his voice. "You're mad," she says. *Please, God, make him understand. Give him the strength to wait for me. If he can't, I don't know what I'll do.*

"Would you rather I pout? Go on a rampage? Lock you in my library and never let you go?"

"But two years will go by quickly."

"Not quickly enough."

"Someday, you might thank me for sticking to our agreement."

"What's that supposed to mean?" he asks.

"Well, if we don't work out—"

"We're going to work out, Meeks. There's no doubt in my mind."

He kisses her so hard she considers throwing in the towel. She wants to say she'll forget about Asia, that she'll never leave California, that she'll never leave his side.

I don't ever want to leave this truck, she thinks, molding herself to him. But she says nothing. She savors his kiss, pulls back, and leans in for another.

Only then does she reluctantly agree with him. "I trust we'll still love each other two years from now, too, Sid. Enough to make plans for the future and do all the things we've been talking about. All I'm saying is that we need the time to get ready."

"I *am* ready. I'm ready now," he says, covering her mouth with his so she can't say another word.

And in her head, as though she's drowning in surrender, she hears herself scream, *I'm ready, too, Sid. I'm so ready . . .* "

No Way, Sid

S ID WATCHES THE MINUTES ON HIS dashboard clock topple into each other like dominoes:

4:09 . . .

4:10 . . .

4:11 . . .

His back is beginning to hurt, but he doesn't move. He doesn't dare disrupt the perfect bubble he and Mika are in.

With her head tilted at an angle directly beneath his chin, he leans down and draws his lips slowly along the curve of her neck. Skin like warm silk. Rich. Creamy. The glorious softness of a woman. He just can't get enough of it. Can't get enough of her.

Why did I agree to wait two years? What was I thinking? He's been asking himself that question ever since Mika fell asleep. And every time he asked it, he knew the answer. *Because I'm hoping she'll change her mind. I'm planning on it. There's no way I can survive two years without her.*

Mika moans. Rolls over. Says his name in her sleep. Lifts her knees so that her bottom raises up slightly toward the roof of the truck.

No way can I wait.

4:18 . . .

Then again, I've been proven wrong before.

4:19 . . .

Maybe I'll see things differently tomorrow. Tomorrows do have a way of bringing reality back to the present.

4:20 . . .

Yes, I can definitely wait. Come hell or high water, I'm going to see to it that we're together in two years.

4:21 . . .

Mika stirs.

Sid, starting to nod off, opens his eyes to see her shift around and sleepily rearrange his shirt so that now only her legs are covered. He stares, fascinated, as her uniform rises and falls with the steady rhythm of her breath. He feels her fingers unconsciously reach for his. He smells her joy at being encased in his arms. She mutters his name again.

4:22 . . .

Ain't no way I can wait.

Sealing the Deal

A GENTLE, COOLING BREEZE FROM THE northwest wafted through the open windows of Sid's Chevy, carrying with it intoxicating smells: a spicy concoction of sea brine, smoked earth, a new day's dew, and hints of autumn. Sid sat with his back braced against the door, his blue-jeaned legs spread out across the front seat. Mika, lying against him in a sort of fetal position, bore the same stamp of sleepy bliss as him.

When the sunshine creeping into the cab grew too bright, she sat up. "Sid," she whispered, "are you awake?"

He opened one eye, groaned, and then closed it. "What time is it?"

"Six o'clock."

"No, then I'm not awake."

"Seriously, Sid, I have to get out of this truck. My legs are starting to cramp."

Kissing the top of her head, he said, "All right, if you insist." Then, sliding out from beneath her, he opened his door and waited as she retrieved her shoes and socks, stuffed them into her purse, and scooted across the seat. Despite her protests, he lifted her down to the ground.

Hurrying to remove the sleep from her eyes and tame her tousled hair, she said, "I must look terrible."

He tugged playfully at the sleeves of her uniform. "Actually, I've never seen you look more beautiful."

Avoiding his intense gaze, she dug around in her purse until she found a package of mints. After placing one on her tongue, she offered one to him.

"Do I need it?"

"No."

"Neither do you." Pressing her against the truck, he smothered her in kisses.

"How about I make us some coffee?" she asked, coming up for air.

"I just can't get enough of you . . ."

"Sid . . ."

"All right. But what say we spend some time together outside before we go into the house?"

Dreamily, she agreed. "You're right. It's too perfect a morning to waste it indoors."

Hand-in-hand, he led her through the garden gate and into the back yard. Stopping next to the hammock, he kicked off his sandals. Mika tossed her purse to the ground. Then, together, they counted to three and fell backward, their bare feet pushing against the ground, swinging the hammock into motion. A good five minutes passed, neither of them saying a word other than to sigh at the sweet *fee-bee* calls of mountain chickadees flitting back and forth in the trees, and the cedar waxwings' trilling *bzeees* as they swooped through the apple orchard and along the blackberry bushes near the creek.

After a while, Mika flipped onto her side. Tracing Sid's collarbone with the tip of her finger, she asked, "So, tell me, how do you feel today, compared to yesterday?"

"Is this a trick question?"

"Just curious."

"I feel like Lazarus raised from the dead." Caressing her face, he said, "How do *you* feel after last night?"

"Like Peter to your Lazarus. Like I'm walking on water. I mean, I still can't believe what happened. It doesn't seem real yet."

"This is as real as it gets, love." Rotating his body around to face her, he rested his head on his fist. With his free hand, he pulled a small leaf out of her hair. "Why wouldn't you believe it?"

"You'll laugh."

"Try me."

"Well, basically, I can't believe I was finally able to . . . overcome my fear of you."

"You mean you're not still terrified of me?" Pretending to take a bite out of her neck, he growled.

"See? You think it's funny!" She slapped his shoulder. "But I'm dead serious. We talked about it last night, remember?"

"Ah, yes." Impersonating her, he quipped, "Mika Larson was afraid she couldn't trust herself around me. She thought if we got too close, she'd lose control, or that I'd take advantage of her good character and be her ruination." Giving the edge of his mustache a dramatic twist, he winked. "Who knew I could be so irresistible? Quite flattering, now that I think of it."

"You keep joking, but it's true."

"I wasn't your ruination, though, was I? I was a perfect gentleman."

"Yes . . . you were that. Still, the question remains: will you *become* my ruination?"

Sid, who'd been enjoying their repartée until now, scowled. "I promise I won't, if you promise not to ruin this moment."

"I'm not trying to ruin anything. I'm just being honest, Sid. And I don't want to be your ruination either. We have to remember what we decided last night and stick with it if there's going to be any hope for us."

"I was hoping you'd change your mind." He kissed her hand before collapsing, discouraged, onto his back.

Twisting herself around so she hovered over him, Mika rested her forearms on his chest like a lioness extending mercy to her kill. "You said yourself, if it doesn't work out in two years' time, then we aren't meant to be together."

"No. You said that, and I *very* reluctantly agreed."

"Besides," she continued, "despite the fact that we're attracted to each other . . ."

"Correction. We love each other. I heard you say it with my own ears, Miss Larson. *Many, many* times."

"Oh, I do love you, Sid. So much, it's—it's scary." Beneath her smile, she paled.

"You're not doubting what happened between us last night, are you?"

"No, of course not! I love you—insanely, irrationally, I love you. But that's the problem. When I stop and think about it, it still doesn't make sense."

"Then don't think about it." He rolled Mika over onto her back. Burrowing down to nibble her earlobe, he groaned, "Where's the old Miss Lightning Larson when I need her?"

"I'm afraid she's still here."

"Aha." His lips traveled down her neck. "Just the way I like her."

"But what happens if this fire in our bones for each other fades?"

Pulling back, he stared at her. "Who says it'll fade?"

"But it *has* to."

"No, it doesn't. Love might morph into something that looks different than it once did, but a fire always leaves embers, and embers can come back to life. I don't see love dying unless it's smothered to death. Give it air, and it'll live."

"I'm scared, Sid."

"Don't be."

He noticed Mika running her tongue along the inside of her mouth—something she seemed to do whenever she was struggling inwardly.

"I hope you're right," she said.

"I am right."

"Maybe sometimes," she teased.

"Not sometimes. Always."

"That's up for debate."

"Let's do it."

Laughing, she extended her hand to him. "So, it's a deal, then?"

He hesitated. *Two years. A lot of water passes under a bridge of commitment that long.*

A second later, taking her proffered hand, he kissed it again. "Deal."

Suddenly, the telephone rang, echoing out onto the lawn. Their final words hung between them, as though there was nothing more to say; as though their future was sealed. Sid started for the house just as it stopped ringing.

"Do you think it was the hospital?" asked Mika, her eyes filled with dread.

"It could have been. Oh, wait . . ." He snapped his fingers. "My grandmother always calls on Wednesday mornings. I bet it was her."

"I'm surprised she remembers what day it is. I thought she had dementia."

"She's definitely forgetful, but I'm waiting on a prognosis from a doctor I wanted a second opinion from. Speaking of which . . . " He fell back into the hammock and took her hands in his. "You have no idea how much it means to me that you'd like to stay here awhile longer to help me get my grandmother moved up here."

"I couldn't believe it when you told me how long you've had plans for her and the farm. You never let on!"

"I wanted to wait until after my probation was behind me and, anyway," he shrugged, "it's going to take a long time to accomplish everything I want to do."

"Come on. Let's go in the house." Making a move to get up, Mika said, "I'll make some coffee, and you can call your grandmother back. And then, I want you to tell me all about your plans for the farm."

He tried to tug her back into the hammock with him. "Do we have to?"

But she was already gone, racing toward the back porch, calling over her shoulder, "Yes! Unless you can catch me first!"

AFTER SID CALLED his grandmother, he sat down to face Mika across the kitchen table. Scooting a cup of steaming black coffee toward him, she said, "Okay, I'm ready."

And so, for the next ten minutes, he laid out his long-term goals for the farm. In addition to continuing restorations, he told her he envisioned acquiring more beef and dairy cows. He also wanted to bring the orchard back into production, till up an acre close to the house to grow organic vegetables and, someday, maybe even breed a few racehorses. His father, he recalled, had seriously considered it. Most of all, he wanted to plant a vineyard on the back south-facing slope of the property.

"It must be in my blood," he said. "My grandmother missed having one in America, and my mother always talked about eventually planting one here. I think, in the back of her mind, she could see her parents living on the farm with us one day and knew my grandmother would love it. Trinity County isn't Napa or Sonoma, but if my Nonna has anything to do with it, she'll make sure it's a slice of paradise."

"When I come back to the states in two years," said Mika, "I expect to have a glass of your wine."

"Sorry, but it takes at least three years, maybe four, for plants to produce grapes. By then, my Marishka, you'll be helping me in the production." His voice faltered. "You know, Ketch planted some good business ideas in my head."

Mika stood and rounded the table. In anticipation, Sid scooted his chair back, giving her space to sit on his lap.

"Sometime today . . ." he said, pulling her close, "I need to go into Ketch's room and see if I can find something from his lawyer. Warren, Otis's deputy, called and asked if I could provide a contact number for Ketch's family, but I don't know who else to call or write. His daughter and his ex-wife need to know what's going on."

"I can help you, if you'd like."

"I would—thanks."

"Do the Skinners know about your plans for the farm? The vineyard and all the rest?"

"Not yet. I've been meaning to tell them, but . . ."

"But what?"

He flinched. "I had a dream last night when you and I were sleeping in my truck. Actually two. They were incredibly . . . realistic."

"Really." She inclined her head toward him. "What were they about?"

"The accident."

The Accident

IN THE FIRST DREAM, SID HAD SEEN HIMSELF reclining in the back of his parents' station wagon, sun-dappled light playing across the pages of a new Spider Man comic book he was reading. The car swayed as his father negotiated sharp curves in the road. Rolling back and forth with each turn, he was being lulled into a half-sleep by the rocking motion of the car. Above the hum of the engine and the drone of tires on pavement, he heard his parents discussing their camping trip.

His dad said, "Sofia, I'm going to slow down a minute. Can you stick your head out the window and make sure the straps are still tied on to the luggage rack on your side?"

He heard the window roll down. The wind whiffled the pages of his comic book. "Everything looks good," she said, rolling the window back up.

"Aren't you glad we have air-conditioning?" his father asked.

"Yes, especially now." Sid saw his mother look down at her pregnant belly.

Then, nodding off, his parents' voices receded. The next thing he knew, he was shivering cold, wrapped in a blanket, standing by the side of the road, surrounded by police cars and fire trucks. He wiped what he thought was sweat from the back of his neck and was shocked to see it was blood.

Reaching his hand up to his head, he felt his scalp. It was damp, matted with something sticky.

A log truck, he noticed, was stopped at the intersection on the opposite side of the county road. A policeman was interrogating one or two witnesses standing near the front of the truck, which was damaged. Another policeman was busy securing the highway with cones and flares. Above the commotion, Otis's voice—distinct and sharp—shouted commands. In his dream, Sid moved instinctively toward the sheriff. As he got close, he saw that Otis was standing over something, or some things, in the highway lying next to a demolished vehicle. Vaguely, Sid recognized it as their station wagon.

"Otis?" he asked.

Otis turned, his face at once both familiar and unrecognizable. The dark moustache was his. So were the gray eyes and high forehead. But his features were contorted into a mask of indescribable pain and shock. Frightened by his appearance, Sid lowered his eyes to the pavement near the sheriff's feet and saw two bodies—two beloved, blood-drenched bodies—exposed for all the world to see. His parents' eyes stared blankly upward, lifeless and void.

Bolting past Otis, he collapsed next to his father. In his dream, he could feel the sheriff straining to lift him up, could see himself kicking and screaming, adrenaline flipping a million switches in his head. His father's battered, broken face dominated his field of vision. It was magnified in perfect detail, down to the broken teeth dangling from his upper jaw and his partially severed right ear.

Before Sid could take in the condition of his mother's body, Otis hauled him away from the scene. Carrying all of Sid's eighty-five pounds in his powerful arms, the sheriff opened the back door of his cruiser, set him in it, and yelled at Deputy Warren to make sure he stayed there.

"He's in shock!" he heard Otis shout.

Then, in his dream, Otis paused. Leaning close to him, he whispered, "Remember them the way they were, Sid, not how you just saw them. Your folks were beautiful. I'll be right back to get you. Stay put."

Suddenly, the dream switched and he was running through the woods near the Grotto, flames lapping at his feet. Otis's words, "I'll be right back to get you," drowned out the roar of the fire. They played in his mind over-and-over like a stuck record: *I'll be right back to get you, I'll be right back to get you, I'll be right back to get you . . .*

He tripped over a smoldering log and fell. Pushing himself up on one elbow, he flipped around and came face-to-face with Otis, his limp, uniformed body draped over a log. His eyes were wide open, staring back at him; not lifeless like his parents' eyes in his first dream, but they didn't look fully alert either. Quickly, Sid placed two fingers on Otis's jugular vein and detected a faint pulse. "Otis!" he yelled. "Otis! Can you hear me?"

When there was no reply, he feared the worst. "Otis, can you move your arms? Your feet?" He waited several minutes and then, knowing it could be fatal to move him in his condition, he leaned down and whispered in his ear, "I'm going to get help. Stay put. I'll be right back to get you."

Like a man possessed, Sid began running, images of Otis's gaping, comatose face and his father's death mask flashing alternately in his mind. He ran in circles. He got lost. He shouted for help. Distant voices from the past replied—male and female—in strangely beautiful but discordant choruses. He strained to hear what they were saying.

When people walk into your life, it's for a reason.

Real friends inspire each other to be the best they can be.

I'll be right back to get you.

Then, to Sid's enormous relief, he woke up.

Woke up to his home on the farm.

Woke up to a beautiful day filled with hope, resolution, and change.

Woke up in his truck with Mika in his arms.

Sɪᴅ ᴀɴᴅ ᴍɪᴋᴀ had worked their way from the kitchen into the living room while Sid recounted his dreams to her. Now, they were squeezed together comfortably in the wing-back next to the fireplace.

"Both dreams were so real," he said. "I wonder if that's exactly how the accident was. Maybe I've just buried the memories all these years until now and . . ."

"And they surfaced in your subconscious."

"Right."

"I wouldn't be surprised."

"But why now—why last night?"

"Maybe they were waiting for you; waiting for you to be ready for them."

"If that's the case, you must have had something to do with timing." He curled his fingers around Mika's. "But there's something else. Just now, as I was telling you about the dreams, I remembered being at Otis and Pearlie's house after the accident when they contacted my grandparents."

Mika brushed her forehead against his. "I'm listening."

"As Otis was talking on the phone to my Grandpa Jackson in Illinois, he held the receiver out from his ear and said to Pearlie, 'Tom's dad just hung up on me.' And she replied, 'He's probably in shock, Otis. We all are.'"

"'No,' said Otis. 'That's not why. He wants Tom to be buried back in Illinois in the family plot.' Pearlie was furious. She said, "After disowning him just because Tom didn't go into the family business? Not a mention of Sofia? And not a care for Sid?'"

Sid shook his head. "I can recall their conversation now like it was yesterday. Otis lowered his voice so that I wouldn't hear him, but I did. He told Pearlie that my dad's parents would never accept my mom into their family because she was Italian. Not even in death. They just wanted my dad's body so they could have their own funeral service for him back east."

"That's terrible," gasped Mika. "You'd think, at the very least, they'd be concerned about your welfare."

"You'd think so," he agreed. "As it turned out, my parents had specified in their will that they wanted to be buried together at Calvary Cemetery and that my mom's parents would be my guardians."

Drawing his thumb and index finger up to the bridge of his nose, Sid scalloped his eyebrows together in thought. "Wow. So much is coming back to me. It's all beginning to make more sense. I just wish I could remember more about Jake's dad that day. Something's not adding up."

The Squeeze

THE FOLLOWING DAY, WHILE MIKA HELPED out at The Pearl again, Sid stayed home, — per strict orders from Pearlie—to get some work done around the farm. But the next day, he insisted on driving to Redding to visit Otis.

"Well, well," crooned Pearlie, when he stepped into the hospital room. "You look full of secrets today."

Coolly, he smiled.

"If I didn't know any better," she added, "I'd say there's a woman on your mind."

"There're several women on my mind and you're one of them." He gave her shoulder a playful pat before sitting down at Otis's bedside. "How's he doing?"

"Much better."

He looks exactly the same. "Has the doctor been in yet?"

"No, but Warren was by earlier."

"By the way, I called Warren yesterday with the contact information for Ketch's lawyer. Did he mention anything about it?"

"No, but he said they found out who started the fire."

His head shot up. "Who was it?"

"Maybe you should ask Warren."

"I'd rather hear it from you, Pearlie."

"All right then." Shifting uneasily in her seat, she said, "For starters, Hank Plummer testified he heard a gunshot right before the fire started. Not only that, but two days later, while he was out near the falls checking on his property, he found a gun and turned it over to the police."

"What kind of gun?"

"Can't rightly recall."

"A Colt .45?"

"Could be. Why?"

With a shrug, he asked, "What did Warren say about it?"

"He said it checked out as belonging to one of the boarders —the war vet."

"Pablo Woolf. The truth is, there was an episode at the house after the ice storm we had last winter. Woolf had a psychotic relapse. A tree limb crashed through the roof in his room and nearly crushed him, and I guess he had some sort of flash back. So I . . . "

"None of that matters, Sid. Warren had the fingerprints on the gun analyzed. Jake's were all over it."

"Wait—Jake Clausen!"

"One and the same." Pearlie rolled her eyes. "Everyone knows Warren has always liked the Clausens, though why, I'll never understand. So of course, at first he didn't want to believe that Jake had anything to do with the fire. But once the detective assigned to the case got involved, it didn't take long for Jake to sign a confession. It seems he was snooping around your farm after that ice storm you were talking about. Said he'd heard some of the boarders had left for the holidays and figured he could catch you alone at the house while the power was out and finish that fight you had with him at Digger's."

"And with the telephone lines down, I wouldn't have been able to call for help. I take it that was part of his plan?"

She nodded. "Anyway, Jake said he parked his car down the road, out of sight, and spied on your place through binoculars, waiting for you to come outside so he wouldn't have to break into the house to get at you. Then he saw you head out to the barn and followed you. Claimed he looked through a crack in the siding, and when he saw you with a gun, he decided it wasn't such a good time to pick a fight after all. He told the detective he watched you climb a ladder and slip the gun into a barn swallow box."

"And then he went into the barn after I left and stole the gun."

"That's the story. He told Warren and the detective that he was eaten up with jealousy leading up to the fire; said you'd been meeting with Kate on the sly."

"Are you kidding? I met with her secretly once, but that was just to talk to her in person about her pregnancy—to see if there was anything I could do to help."

"Well, Jake's always been a loose cannon. Just like his dad. Them and their drinking and fighting and dogs . . ."

"What about their dogs?"

Eyeing him curiously, she said, "Why do you ask?"

"We found a dog across the creek in July that had been killed. A German shepherd. We never found out who it belonged to, or how it happened."

"Across the creek *where*? You mean at that place you said your boarders went to party? What did they call it?"

"The Grotto. Yes, there."

"When in July was it?"

"The Fourth."

"Otis got a call on the Fourth about a dogfight going on in the hills not far from your place. They all skedaddled before he got there."

"Maybe that's how he ended up in the Grotto."

Pearlie shook her head. "Maybe that poor dog had been hurt in the fight and . . ."

"Who knows? Nothing would surprise me when it comes to the Clausens."

"Anyway," she continued, "as Warren tells it, on the day of the fire, Jake thought you were with your boarders across the river. He told Warren that he took a can of gasoline into the woods, set it near where your friends were, crawled behind a rock a safe distance away, and shot the can. He just wanted to scare you. His words; not mine. Then he said he ran back to his truck, tossing the gun as he went. But here's the most unbelievable part." Pearlie's lips quivered as though she might cry. "You know how you found Kate Quinn that day—burned so badly? And we've been wondering why in the world she was there right where the fire started?"

"Yeah."

Motioning over her husband's comatose body, she asked Sid to lean closer to her. "Well, let's just say because of her, your boarders were saved."

"Excuse me?"

Pearlie repeated herself, adding, "Jake insisted that Kate was his accomplice, so the detective spoke to her in person at the hospital. Come to find out what *really* happened is that she'd gotten wind of what Jake was planning that day as they were driving up toward Cutthroat Falls in his truck. As soon as he slowed down to park, she jumped out and took off running to the place where she said she knew your boarders would be.

"Apparently," continued Pearlie, "she hollered for them to run, warning them that Jake was coming with a gun. The story gets a bit muddy there, what with your boarders being so 'high'—or whatever-you-call-it—at the time, and Kate saying she had to help round them up and get them headed toward the cave. But in the end, Jake confessed Kate's testimony was true. At least, as far as her taking off running into the woods before he got out of his truck. He swears he didn't know Kate was at the scene of the explosion, but then . . ."

As she continued talking, a picture of Kate's disfigured body seared back into Sid's memory. To think that Jake Clausen was so consumed with jealousy and revenge that he'd drag an innocent person down with him—not to mention perhaps his own child . . .

"Did you hear what I just said, Sid?"

"Sorry. What?"

"Kate lost her baby yesterday. A little girl. It could have been from all the trauma of the fire. The doctors couldn't say for sure." Pearlie dabbed at her eyes with a tissue. "Anyway, I wanted to help somehow, so I called her this morning at the hospital. You see, someone a long time ago talked Otis and me into buying an extra burial plot next to ours up at Calvary Cemetery. We thought we'd have a family of our own someday, but 'course, we never did. Kate was real grateful. Said she'd be honored to have little Baby Angel buried next to us."

Sid winced, not sure how much more bad news he could take. "Baby Angel?"

"That's what Kate named her. It's the name we'll put on her headstone."

"And Kate? How is she taking all this?"

"Well, on top of everything else, she's devastated. Aren't we all? If you'll recall, I was ready to help her with that baby when she was born. It just breaks my heart to think of it— just breaks it clean in two. I swear, beneath all of Kate's knots and gnarls, I always knew she had it in her to do the right thing when push came to shove."

For the next few minutes, Sid and Pearlie sat across from each other, lost in thought. He'd seen Kate transitioning into a bitter, hardened woman over the last few years and had hoped her pregnancy wouldn't push her over the edge. Now that she'd lost her baby, in addition to the trauma of the fire, he feared it would.

Pearlie broke the silence. Leaning close to her husband, she said, "Babe, I know you overheard everything Sid and I were just saying. I sure wish you could tell us what you think of this mess." Several contemplative moments passed before she sat back up. "I've got myself a headache, Sid. Would you mind holding Otis's hand while I get some aspirin?"

"Sure." Sid slid his hand into Otis's while Pearlie rummaged through her purse.

"You can talk to him if you want to," she said, absently. "Don't be afraid. He likes it."

How can he like it? He doesn't even know we're here. But, if it makes Pearlie happy . . . "Otis? It's me—Sid. Like Pearlie said, it's pretty messed up around here right now. It's probably just as well you're sleeping through it, but your wife needs you. A lot."

Glancing over his shoulder, he saw that Pearlie had found her pills and was now standing at the sink filling a Dixie cup with water. There was no indication she was listening to what he was saying, so he pressed ahead, his voice low. "I guess you could say I need you, too. Never thought I'd say it, but I do. I could use a dad right now and, well, you're the only dad I have left."

Having swallowed her pills, Pearlie crushed the cup, threw it in the wastebasket and returned to the bed. She picked up her husband's other hand and began rubbing it.

Touching his lips to the sheriff's ear, Sid whispered, "I know I made your life miserable, Otis. I disappointed you big time. I see that now. I wish I could have told you before the fire how sorry I am about that. When I found out that you braved those flames—that you risked your life for me . . ."

"He squeezed my hand!" shouted Pearlie, nearly jumping out of her seat.

That's not possible. Sid raised his head. *She just wants it to be true so much, she's imagining it.*

"Otis! Baby! Can you hear me? Squeeze my hand again if you do."

This time, with his own eyes, Sid saw Otis's hand contract against Pearlie's.

And then, faintly but definitely, the sheriff squeezed Sid's.

Resurrection

For the next few days, Sid kept a vigil at Otis's bedside with Pearlie, witnessing the sheriff's slow but steady progress. Along with his physical restoration, Otis's memory returned—one day, one hour, one moment at a time—until a week later, his short and long term memory were nearly fully restored. The only afflictions he continued to retain from his injuries were a slight limp in his left leg and a persistent dry cough. With some intense physical therapy, however, it was believed nearly everything would eventually be restored to normal. The doctors were dumbfounded, chalking up Otis's comeback to a miracle.

One of the first items on Otis's agenda, when he finally resumed his official duties on September 24, was the signing-off of Sid's probation. The judge agreed that the drugs in the possession of Sid's boarders at the time of the fire could not be used against his probationary completion because they did not belong to Sid. Nor were they, de facto, on his property. In addition, Sid's willingness to endanger his life to rescue the boarders and Otis warranted his immediate release.

After the necessary legal documents had been drawn up, Otis summoned Sid to his Weaverville office for the final signing and notarization. Taking a seat in the same chair he had occupied a year earlier, following his court hearing, Sid faced him across his littered desk. The sheriff's secretary, Lynn Walker Keating, made a brief appearance to deliver a file. This time, unlike at his initial sentencing, she looked at Sid with empathy. Perhaps even pride.

Maybe she noticed that his face and arms were tanned from working long hours on the farm, his fingers calloused, his neck thicker and his shoulders stronger. Though his hair was longer, maybe she also saw that his eyes were sharp and clear, that his limbs moved with renewed confidence, and that his steps were lighter, infused with an air of accomplishment. What she couldn't see, however, was the sorrow over Ketch's disappearance that weighed on his soul like a lead blanket.

Otis placed his hands on the desk, palms down. "Me and Pearlie are sure happy to see your Nonna all settled in on the farm with you now."

"You and me both," said Sid. "Mika was a big help getting her moved in."

"I don't suppose our Mika'll be around much longer."

"She leaves Friday."

"We'll miss her—as I know you will."

He nodded. "Nonna really took a liking to her, too."

"Still noticing a difference in her? In your grandmother, I mean?"

"It's amazing—she's like a different person since she's moved up here. A couple of days in, and she's sparkling old Antonia again."

"Glad you got a second opinion, son. Who would ever have thought a vitamin deficiency could mimic dementia?"

"No kidding. Doc Simpson thinks that her depression after

my grandpa died just made it worse. I've got her appointments lined up with him to get her B-12 shots every two weeks."

Otis studied Sid a moment before switching gears. "I had a lot of time to think while I was in the hospital. Had myself some pretty interesting dreams when I was there, too. As a matter of fact, you were in some of them."

"Is that so?"

"Remember when you said you had some questions about the accident, and that you were going to ask us about it some day?

"Yeah."

"Well, now's as good a time as any. I realized I don't want to go into eternity without you having all your questions answered."

"Actually, Otis, I had some interesting dreams myself while you were in the hospital. They helped me remember what happened that day and, I think, helped me to understand why you wanted to shield me all these years from the details."

Otis cocked his head, waiting for him to continue.

"I remembered that after the accident, I broke through the barriers you'd set up and saw my mom and dad's bodies before the ambulance came. It was . . . pretty disturbing. I can see now why I blocked the images out for so long."

"Sometimes I wish I could block out the memories myself, Sid, but I'm afraid they haunt me nearly every day. I sure am sad you had to see them that way. It's better if you remember them as they looked, you know, before."

"So why weren't charges pressed against Jake's dad? I read reports that some people smelled alcohol on him at the scene of the accident."

"Ah, yes. That." Pensively, the sheriff brought his hands together. "I'm afraid I was so intent on making sure your folks and you were being seen to properly that I left Warren to deal with Norm. He swore Jake's dad was able to walk a straight line when asked. Then, Jake testified he'd been with Norm all day and that the most he'd had to drink was a beer about an hour before the crash. Warren might be a lot of things—gullible, boastful, grasping—but he's not a liar. He's a decent officer."

"Another report I read said Norm's license had already revoked once before the accident."

"That's true."

"It said there were rumors of bad blood between Norm and my dad."

"That's the problem, Sid. They were rumors. There were lots of them flying around after the accident, but getting down to the facts was a whole other story. I talked with your grandparents about pursuing an investigation, but they were still too broken up by the loss of your folks to do anything but take care of you and make a go of getting on with your lives."

"So you're saying, 'that's it'? Norm Clausen gets to live his life as though nothing happened when really he . . . ."

"When, really, he might have killed your parents intentionally? Is that what you think?"

"Yes. Don't you?"

Otis stood and walked around his desk, settling down on the corner nearest Sid. "I would hate to think of anyone deliberately plowing into your ma and pa's car. Still, I can't say the idea never crossed my mind. Pearlie and I spent many a sleepless night talking about it. But, like it or not, the fact remains that people are innocent until proven guilty. Other than gossip, there's absolutely nothing solid I know of that would link Norm to manslaughter in the case of your parents' accident. Did you notice in the reports you read that Norm claimed his brakes failed?"

"I did. And I also read that a mechanic said they checked out fine."

"As far as function, yes, but they were also dangerously low on brake fluid. An important distinction in a court of law." Bending down, Otis said, "The bottom line is, that day's over and long gone. Pearlie and I finally came to terms with it because we felt that's what your folks would want us to do. I think that's what they'd want for you, too, Sid. Don't you?"

"Yes," he nodded, after a short pause, "I do."

Otis heaved himself off the desk. "Just remember, what goes around comes around. It may be un-Christian for me to admit it, but Jake going to prison for setting that fire is going to hurt Norm as much, if not more, than if he were in prison himself for what happened to your folks. Justice may not be swift, but it always plays out in the end."

"You're probably right, Otis."

"I'm always right."

"Sure you are." Smiling, Sid checked his watch. "Are we finished up here, then?"

"Not quite. You're twenty-fifth birthday is coming up next month, but your parents' will states that you can legally take possession of the farm before that—if I'm willing to sign a statement saying you've demonstrated the ability and desire to take on the necessary requirements of ownership."

"Well, then, with only a month to go, if I didn't 'pass the test,' it's no big deal. I've waited this long. I can—"

"Oh, but you did pass the test. With flying colors, I might add, which means you can sign the papers now. Although, I need to remind you the will stipulates a three-year grace period from the time of activation in which you actually work the farm before signing off on the final transfer."

"What? And if I don't?"

"You'll have to sell it to someone who will."

"I don't remember there being a clause about that."

"I thought you might not. Here it is, right . . . " Otis shuffled through a stack of papers on his desk until he found what he was looking for. He pointed to a section of the will marked with a tag. "See?"

Sid read the section in question carefully and then shrugged. "I know, I know—it'll teach me to read the fine print. All right, Otis. No problem."

With a grin, the sheriff reached in his pocket and handed him a pen.

After he finished signing all of the necessary legal documents, Sid stood up. "Someone once told me that people are in each other's lives for a reason. I've finally figured out what that means, and I intend to spend the rest of my life appreciating the fact."

The two men faced each other, years of distance and misunderstanding between them dissolving like seltzer tablets in a glass of water. Suddenly, Otis burst out laughing. Throwing his arm around Sid, he said, "Am I ever glad I can be myself around you now, Siddo. No more having to keep up a professional front because I'm your probation officer. Yes sir, it sure feels good. What say, we head over to Trinity Springs and get us one of Pearlie's caramel rolls? She made them fresh this morning."

"I'll buy," said Sid. "I owe you."

"No," argued Otis. "I owe you."

As they walked shoulder-to-shoulder down the corridor, past the offices of Otis's secretary and Deputy Murdoch and a handful of miscreants awaiting trial, Otis said, "Pearlie told me that you shared some of your plans for the farm with her."

"Yeah, I've got several ideas. The one I'm most excited about, especially with Nonna now on the farm, is planting a vineyard."

"A vineyard, eh? Not many of them around here. Sounds kind of hoity-toity to me."

"Hoity-toity? I don't even know what that means. The wave of the future is what it is."

"Bah! Speaking of the future, when are you going to cut that hair of yours?"

"When you grow yours out."

"Never, then. Is that what you're saying?"

"That's right," laughed Sid. "Never."

Exiting the courthouse, they paused in front of their vehicles. "Well," said Otis, hooking his thumbs through his belt loops, "at least you're done smoking pot. I can rest assured on that count."

"Am I?"

"*Aren't* you?"

When Sid refused to answer, Otis followed him around to the driver's side of his truck. "Siderno Jackson! Tell me you didn't smoke pot during your probation."

"My lips are sealed." Sid held up his signed probation release form. "All that matters is, I'm finally free and clear. Right?"

"You're not serious."

Hoisting himself into the driver's seat, he told Otis not to worry. "As long as my Nonna's alive, I'm not going to do anything that would put me at risk of not being able to take care of her. If that means not smoking pot, then I won't. At least," he added, with a wicked smile, "I'll be sure I don't get caught this time. Come on. Let's get over to The Pearl. I'm hungry."

APPROXIMATELY TWO WEEKS later, on October 10, upon returning from Calvary Cemetery where he had visited not only the graves of his parents, but also Kate's baby, Sid opened his roadside mailbox to find his first letter from Mika. He held it for a moment, soaking up whatever essence of her might be lingering on the envelope's surface, before sliding it into the pocket of his denim shirt.

Ketch's Harley Springer gleamed in front of the barn where he'd left it that morning. He had brought it outside as a reminder that it was one of the last things he still needed to take care of for his friend. What he hadn't anticipated were the emotions that gutted him as he now stood looking at it. Almost involuntarily, he grabbed a chamois from his truck and began reverently rubbing the bike's chrome detail. *If only your daughter could have known you like I did, Ketch. She would have insisted you be in her life. Nothing would have kept her from you.*

"Siderno! Lunch is ready!"

He turned to see his grandmother waving to him from the back porch. "I'll be right there," he called out.

Giving the chopper a final swipe, Sid folded the cloth and

put it back in his pickup. A moment later, as he was washing his hands in the kitchen sink, the phone rang.

Antonia answered it. "*Prego.* I'm fine, Otis, and how are you? Yes, my Siderno is right here." Covering the mouth of the receiver with her hand, she held it out toward him. "If it was anyone else, I would have them call you back when you're finished with your lunch. But as you know, Otis is not just anyone, no? Anyway, he sounds *molto emozionante.*"

Taking the receiver from his grandmother, he held it to his ear. "Yeah, Otis, what's up?" Seconds later, he collapsed into a nearby chair. "I . . . I can't believe it. Are you absolutely sure?"

Antonia, wringing her hands with worry, didn't have time to ask Sid what the call was about, because no sooner did he hang up, but the phone rang again. This time, the voice on the other end was female. It was so shrill, Sid had to hold the receiver away from his ear. "I can hardly understand you," he said. "Is this Liz?"

"Who else would this be?" squealed the voice. A flood of gibberish followed, to which he replied, "I know, Liz. Otis just called me, too. But do you think it's true? I mean, how could . . ."

Antonia's fretting lips moved as if in prayer.

"He *what?*" gasped Sid. "Ketch called you? When? But are you sure it was him? What did you say? He said he's going *where?* Liz?" Clicking the cradle of the phone several times with his fingers, he shouted, "Liz? Liz! Are you there?"

"We lost our connection." Staring blankly at his grandmother, he hung up the phone.

"Siderno—what is it?"

With painstaking care, so that she would understand, he explained who Ketch was. "He disappeared after the fire we had up here last month. And he was never found, so we thought he was dead. But now, Otis tells me that Warren, his deputy, got a call the other day from law enforcement somewhere over in Humboldt County that an unidentified man was admitted to a local hospital two weeks ago with untreated burns on his body.

"Apparently, he also had amnesia, so they were making calls to different state agencies to check missing person reports. Well, Otis got on the case right away, but the next day the hospital called and said the man had taken off. Just disappeared. The clincher is, they told Otis the man was an albino in his late twenties or early thirties who spoke with a Texas accent."

Her eyes widened. "Albino? You mean . . ." She pointed to her eyes and then stroked her hair.

"Yes, Nonna. The only thing I can figure is that Ketch must have escaped the fire and somehow found his way out to a highway where he hitched a ride to the next county and then just wandered around until he got help."

"The girl . . . on the phone. What did she want?"

"That was Ketch's girlfriend. His *amica*. She's in Alaska right now. She wanted me to know that Ketch called her. We got disconnected before she could tell me when he called, or where he made the call from."

"*Capisco*. I understand." Scuttling over to the cupboard, his grandmother grabbed two glasses and began searching for a bottle of wine. "Your friend was lost, but now he is found. It is time for celebration, no?"

Sid's fingers involuntarily reached for Mika's unopened

letter. He had to call her and let her know Ketch was alive. But just as he picked up the telephone receiver, he heard it.

A thunderous, reverberating roar coming from out near the barn.

The Harley coming to life.

He dropped the phone, leaving it dangling by its cord, and raced outside, his grandmother at his heels. There, straddling his bike—his head shaved and a patchwork of new pink skin splotched across one side of his face where his burns had yet to completely heal—was Will Ketchum in all his albino glory.

As Sid approached, he killed the engine. "Gave me up for dead, did you, Jackson?"

Sid threw his arm behind Ketch's neck and hugged him hard. "Only a cat from Texas with nine lives could survive a forest fire and end up in the next county not knowing his name from Adam."

"That's me all right. Still, leave it to a Yankee like you to lose faith so fast." Gripping the handlebars, he said, "Come on, let's ride."

Turning to his grandmother, Sid asked her if she'd mind. "I'll eat when I get back."

"Go, go, Siddo. I'm fine."

Ketch winked at Antonia as Sid climbed on to the seat behind him. "That your mee-maw?"

"The one and only."

Ketch jammed his heel down to start the engine again. "Living with you now, huh?"

"Yep."

"Pretty pathetic," he snickered, "but not as pathetic as it'll be when Annabelle and I move in with you."

"Annabelle? You mean . . . "

"Oh, *yeah*." Before tearing out of the driveway onto the open highway, he added, "I never did get around to getting a mural painted on your barn, but if things work out like my lawyer says they will, I've got a business proposition to make—one you won't refuse."

Sid glanced over his shoulder at his grandmother waving good-bye to them, her apron flapping in the breeze. He raised his eyes. Above the farm, in the distance, on a hill overlooking Trinity Springs, he caught the outline of Calvary Cemetery spread out like a welcome mat to eternity. Then, facing forward again, he checked his shirt pocket to make sure Mika's letter was still there.

It struck him how much he and Ketch, despite their core differences, had in common—at least, when it came to the arc of their lives in the moment. They both were once dead but now were alive—Ketch nearly literally, himself, metaphorically. Hope had definitely replaced despair. Confusion had given way to clarity. Loved ones were finally within their grasp. Sid shook his head at the amount of water that had gone underneath last year's bridge. If someone had told him in October that within twelve months he would be joined at the hip with a hard-core biker from Texas and in love with a Jesus Freak from Iowa, he would never have believed it. And yet . . .

"Let's burn us some daylight and melt this highway!" Ketch yahooed, kicking his Harley into fifth gear.

With a grin as wide as the horizon they raced toward, Sid pressed his spine firmly against the chrome backrest, breathed the mountain air, and let all his yesterdays fade into tomorrow.

Into the Future:
Five Years, To Be Precise

THE MANICURED GROUNDS SURROUNDING Bountiful Grace Chapel in Weaverville were dotted with wedding guests spilling out of the little church's arched doors. A lone woman, arriving so late she decided to stay outside rather than disrupt the ceremony, stood hesitantly on the sidewalk next to her silver Mercedes-Benz convertible. In a rare surge of insecurity, she fiddled with the buttons on her silk dress suit. Then she wiggled her toes in her Dior *peau de soie* sling-back heels. When those nervous tics failed to calm her, she repositioned her oversized, tortoise-framed Ray Bans in the hope no one would guess who she was. Peering through the tinted shades, she tried to take solace in the fact that she'd yet to see anyone she recognized.

But then, it had been years since she'd been back home, and people had no doubt changed—though unlike herself, perhaps not quite so drastically.

Change. So much of it in such a short amount of time. And yet somehow, despite all the positive transformations she had undergone, both on the outside and the inside, she all at once felt penitent. Stripped to her core. Naked, unsure, and vulnerable, as though the last five years had never happened.

The prospect of someone guessing her identity caused her to pull a section of her salon-dyed hair further down over her face. But then, lifting her chin slightly, she reminded herself that she had as much a right to be at this event as anyone else. Maybe more. She'd received an invitation after all. Nervously, she ran a manicured finger along the rim of her sunglasses, wondering if perhaps she'd only been invited out of a sense of duty. Or worse yet, as a mere afterthought.

Maybe I shouldn't have come today.

The growing throng of celebrants vacating the church pressed ever closer to her. To avoid detection, she stepped off the sidewalk so that now she stood in the narrow space between her car and the curb. She even debated fleeing the scene while she was yet still anonymous, but then she began catching snippets of nearby conversations.

"It's a wonder they finally got married," clucked one elderly woman to another. "Folks nowadays would just as soon shack up together as tie the knot."

"Isn't that the truth," replied her pruny, snow-headed friend. "What I want to know is, why doesn't she make him cut that dreadful hair of his?"

"I suppose because she's something of a hippie herself," said the clucker. "But it's that horrid beard and moustache I don't like. Such a pity he's hiding that handsome face of his behind all that stubble. Makes him look like some Italian Mafioso instead of a college graduate."

"Sad, indeed." The prune sighed, her fissured cheeks puffing on the exhale. "Oh well, at least he's made something of that farm of his."

"And he's taken such good care of his grandmother these last few years, too, I'll say that much for him. But still, what a travesty. Why, a stranger would never guess he has such a good heart by looking at him. He looks positively . . . dangerous."

The attractive woman, now leaning against her Mercedes for support, groaned. Why was it so hard for people to see beyond someone's looks? Of course, the old biddies were entitled to their opinions, however petty and superficial they might be, but it was just plain wrong to write off a person's character, or underestimate their future, because of how they dressed or the length of their hair.

Now me, I was a different story. I deserved to be stigmatized. I asked for it. I enjoyed it. I hurt everyone I possibly could, so what else could I expect in return? But Sid Jackson? He deserved nothing but respect and admiration.

Blocking out her neighbors' continuing gossip, the woman toyed with her wedding ring—a three-carat, brilliant cut diamond. Was there going to be a reception following the wedding? It looked like there would be, but she couldn't recall. Her decision to drive up from San Francisco had all been so last minute, and she'd been in such a mad rush to get there, she'd forgotten to bring the invitation with her. All she could remember of the rather complicated announcement was that it would be held at this chapel, in this town, on this day, at noon. Well, she'd thought it was noon. Clearly, it must have been eleven. Nor had she bothered looking at the full names on the wedding card, other than the one she knew and cared about. *So, if there is a reception, do I dare stay for it?*

"Did you hear how she and Sid broke up and got back together again?" twittered a red-headed teen to her brunette companion, standing in the shade of big leaf maple a few feet away from the Mercedes.

The woman, still fingering her wedding ring, perked up.

"I know!" sighed the brunette. "I heard she gave him an ultimatum, but he turned it down. Then, when she came crawling back a year or two later, he gave *her* an ultimatum, and she said 'yes' in a heartbeat."

"That's not how it was at all." The red-haired girl shook her head with disdain. "They both agreed to break it off and move on—something about them being too different from each other for it to ever work out between them. They even dated other people. But then the next year, when she came back to help Pearlie Skinner out after that big surgery she had, Sid apparently overheard her singing a love song—"

"Where?"

"In the kitchen at The Pearl."

"When?"

"One night when she thought no one was around to hear her. And then . . ."

"What song?"

"Roberta Flack, I think. 'The Closer I Get to You.'"

"Wow. Too cool."

"Yeah—and I guess she has a great voice, too. Anyway, from what I understand, Sid came around the corner of the kitchen and surprised her. Said something like, 'Singing to me, Mika?' She admitted she was and that was it. I guess they realized they couldn't fight destiny anymore. Now, here they are getting married. Amazing, huh?"

The brunette feigned a swoon in agreement.

Suddenly a communal "*ohhh*" erupted as the first bride and groom stepped out of the church. Descending the stairs, they ducked their heads beneath a raining canopy of rice.

"He'll never get that stuff out of his hair," tittered a woman's voice, nearby. "Not in a million years, considering it's the exact same color as the rice."

"Yeah, must be a real bummer being albino," a masculine voice chortled in reply. "All the same, I hear tell he's a pretty savvy businessman, what with that chain of motorcycle repair stores he's started. And successful, to boot. But his wife is such a freak . . ."

The Mercedes-hugging woman turned. Lynn and Paul Keating. She should have known.

While Paul continued rambling about freaks and albinos, Lynn stared at a cluster of long-haired men and gypsy-looking women on the south-facing lawn, who appeared to be watching an acoustic trio tune up. Nudging her husband, she said, "Speaking of freaks, can you believe how many of them are here today? Where did they all come from?"

"Who knows? They're everywhere these days," he grunted. "I never thought I'd live to see hippies actually outnumbering us in Trinity County. What's the world coming to anyway?"

Mandolin, fiddle, and bass guitar harmonies began to float across the green. Several wedding-goers kicked off their shoes and danced to the music on the fresh-cut grass. Late-arriving caterers scurried to assemble appetizers, casseroles, and salads on a long linen-clad buffet table hastily set up alongside the church.

Lynn watched the goings-on a few more moments before pulling a compact case out of her purse and giving her nose a quick powder. "Well, I suppose all that matters is that Sid's finally got his act together. He's already one of the most successful farmers in Trinity County. Got to hand that to him."

"I guess." Her husband sighed, his voice tinged with envy.

"And thank *God* he doesn't do dope anymore either," she added, "although you wouldn't know it by the looks of him."

Paul snorted so loudly, several people turned to stare at him. "You can bet his wife'll keep him straight on that count," he said. "I heard she already has him going to church with her. And what with him adopting those two kids she brought back with her, well, it's bye-bye to good times and hello to the family chain-gang."

"Speaking of *chain gangs*," said Lynn, who was infamous in Trinity Springs for her dislike of children, "it's too bad Max Quinn didn't have a good woman to keep *him* out of prison."

"You can say that again." Paul thunked his forehead with his middle finger. "What idiot thinks they can sell cocaine around here and get away with it? Max could have been here today—could have been Sid's best man if he would've had half a brain in that burned-out head of his. Now he's serving time with the likes of Jake Clausen in Folsom Prison. The bank repossessed his house; his mom had to be moved down to a nursing home in Frisco . . . "

My brother *was* an idiot, thought the woman in the silk suit. *No doubt about it.*

"At least his sister was smart," continued Paul, "marrying that plastic surgeon who worked on her after the fire. I heard she's a real knockout now. I mean Kate always was a sight for sore eyes, but now she's got money *and* looks—everything a woman could want, right?"

Kate almost lowered her sunglasses to give Paul a death glare. Instead, she lifted her weight off the door of her Mercedes and raised her hand to her stomach. *No, Paul, I don't have everything I want. Not yet, I don't.*

Lynn, meanwhile, glowered at her husband. "If I didn't know better, I'd think you had a thing for Kate Quinn."

"Now, Lynn, I didn't mean it that way . . ."

Before Paul could finish, someone in the crowd hollered, "Look!"

The red-headed teen who'd dished to her friend about how Sid and Mika had gotten back together, scooted nearer to Kate. Craning her neck, she squealed, "There're the flower girls. And that sweet little ring bearer. Aren't they just the cutest things? Adorable!"

Kate stepped back up on the curb to get a better view. One flower girl—probably ten or twelve—looked like Ketch: tall and thin, but dark-complexioned. The other, like the ring-bearer at her side, was Asian. They both appeared to be about five years old. *Adorable is right. Just adorable. If I don't get pregnant soon, I may just look into adoption myself.*

Lynn Keating waved at the sheriff and his wife as they appeared, helping Antonia down the stairs. Addressing her husband, out the side of her mouth, she muttered, "Otis is sure proud Sid asked him to be his best man. You would have thought he was the bona fide father of the groom the way he carried on at the police station about it." Standing on her tiptoes, she added, "And that must be Mika's parents from Iowa, and her brother, behind them."

Kate held her breath, knowing Sid and Mika would be next. Seconds later, when they burst through the doors, she moved forward, discreetly blending into the flock of wedding guests until she could see the bride's and groom's faces clearly.

There it was. What she had come to see—the look in Sid's eyes as he gazed at his wife with raw joy and undying devotion. It was a look so intense, it was as if Mika was not only his bride, but the wedding cake, the honeymoon, the sun, the moon, and the stars all rolled into one. It was, she realized with a burning pang of regret, a look she'd once dared to think Sid might direct at her.

Even as she had driven up to Weaverville today, she'd worried that her dysfunctional attraction to Sid would be rekindled when she saw him. She hadn't been sure she could trust her emotions around his disarming charm; his irresistible smile. What a fool she'd been to use him the way she had when they were younger. She'd looked a gift horse in the mouth and paid the ultimate price by rejecting him.

Yet somehow, witnessing his obvious love for Mika, she received a confirmation she'd long sought: that she had chosen the right husband for herself and the right path in life. And in that unexpected eureka moment, she understood that, finally, all of her past mistakes—all of her mess-ups and melt-downs—were really, truly behind her, along with all the guilt and self-reproach that had come with them.

What her life might have been no longer mattered.

What mattered was tomorrow.

And the next day.

And the next.

She was only thirty-four, for heaven's sake. The best years were yet to come.

Turning, she retraced her steps back to her car, slid into the driver's seat, and started the engine. There was no way was she going to stay for the reception. Lord knew her presence there among the revelers wouldn't be missed anyway.

There was, however, still one person she had yet to pay a visit to while she was back home. Someone she'd been avoiding all these years, but who, suddenly, she longed to be near. Pulling away from the church, she drove through old town Weaverville, down Main Street, and then headed south on Highway 3, toward a hidden cemetery on a rugged hill overlooking Trinity Springs.

A cemetery rich with myths and legends.

Filled with the bones of a particular baby calling her name.

Pure bones.

Goodly bones.

Bones filled with love deferred.

The bones of an angel singing, "It's a brand new day."

Acknowledgments

A YEAR IN THE COMPANY OF FREAKS—based ever so loosely on a wide-variety of personal experiences and observations during a two-year stint in Northern California in the 1970's—was a work in progress for a very, very long time. As a result, it morphed into something much larger, nuanced and complex than originally planned. Without the help of my impeccable editor and mentor, Sandra Byrd, it would still be collecting dust on my unfinished manuscripts shelf. Sandra, I've said it before and I'll say it again: "You are worth your weight in gold, girl, and that is no exaggeration!" Thank you for your wisdom, expertise, unflagging support and friendship. A big thanks goes out also to my amazing book formatter and designer, Jennifer Omner of ALL Publications. Jennifer, you, also, are worth your weight in gold. I always know I can trust you with my "babies." Mega-kudos, too, to my incredibly talented filmmaker son and daughter-in-law, Luke and Marika Neumann of Neumann Films. What a blast from the past we had on that photo shoot, eh? And finally, to my family, friends, and all those who enjoy my books and support my writing: you make life more rewarding than I could ever have imagined. Here's to you!

Teresa

The author and her husband then . . .
and now.

About the Author

Teresa Neumann, the author of *Bianca's Vineyard*, *Domenico's Table*, and countless other works in the making, lives in Oregon's beautiful Willamette Valley with her musician husband. An enormously proud mother of three children, and Nana to two, when she is not delighting in family, she is writing, musing, writing, spinning yarns to her grandsons, travelling, writing, reading, and . . . writing.

Find out more about Teresa Neumann and her books at teresaneumann.com or check out her Facebook page at Always Summer Books.

9 780983 121046